CW00871817

Domokos György Varga (65), a Hungarian writer of books for children and teenagers. His stories are characterized by a masterful combination of reality and imagination. The novel *Cin-Cin* is about a mysterious friendship between a toddler and a mouse. The protagonist of *Fittyfirity* is a kindergarten boy who gives a dog to a homeless. In *Habocska*, filth dunces and foam dunces are fighting for their everyday justice. *Jimmy Jumper* was first published in 2016 in Hungarian (as Bilhebolha). In the author's newest fiction (*Abo and Robo*), a dad and his son make together the first really humanoid robot of the world.

JIMMY JUMPER

Domokos György Varga

JIMMY JUMPER

Vanguard Press

VANGUARD PAPERBACK

© Copyright 2018
Domokos György Varga

Author photograph by Julianna Molnár

A CIP catalogue record for this title is
available from the British Library.

ISBN 978 1 784654 03 0

*Vanguard Press is an imprint of
Pegasus Elliot MacKenzie Publishers Ltd.*
www.pegasuspublishers.com

First Published in 2018

**Vanguard Press
Sheraton House Castle Park
Cambridge England**

Printed & Bound in Great Britain

Preface

Danny Boy was just scootering toward the Foreign Trade Park. He had left the Poppy Estate and the stop at the Cracked Fence; the Briar Patch would have been next, when he felt something bite his leg. It couldn't have been nettles, not only because the Nettle Street stop was a couple of metres further on, but also because Danny Boy was wearing trousers that covered his legs. So, what the devil had bitten him?

I don't need to tell you, Danny Boy jumped off the scooter and pulled up his trouser leg. But he couldn't see anything. He did feel something, but it was higher, at thigh level. It was unpleasant, that's for sure. He couldn't resist suddenly pulling down his trousers. He stood there in his underpants, and listened carefully. What on earth was taking liberties with him?

He couldn't see anything or anyone, but he heard something. A mocking song. Not just anywhere. In his own ear.

A big-nosed flea
invited himself over
to our house forever
For lunch and for dinner.

Danny Boy quickly covered his ear with his hand.

"I've got you!" he shouted. He hadn't any idea what it was he'd got. From the bite on his leg, he immediately thought of a flea; he had always heard of such creatures but had never seen one, and he never had occasion to suffer from one. Anyway, he wouldn't have thought that fleas could sing. Now there was something in his ear and blowing its own tune.

But his eyes were so
dreadfully big,
When he opened them wide
The house was bright

No doubt about it, Danny Boy was overcome with doubt. Perhaps it wasn't an exaggeration to say it was fright. He took his hand from his ear and muttered:

"You're free. Be on your way."

And with some difficulty he pulled his trousers back on.

That thing in his ear did not trouble itself about him. It continued to sing.

But his nails
were so dreadfully huge
that he scratched
the plaster off the side of the house.

Danny Boy was shaking by then.

"Can't you hear? You're free to go. Please deign to climb out of my ear."

But his belly

was so dreadfully big
that the Danube
would have been caught in it.

That was all he needed: in his fright, Danny Boy's mouth trembled on the verge of crying.

"No, don't do that," the thing spoke up. "I hate it when they make an elephant out of a flea. Maybe my singing wasn't in tune?"

"But you bit me! Not once but twice! Or wasn't that you?"

"So, what? Did you die from it? I've been hanging about here for a quarter of an hour for a stray dog or cat to wander over here. All I could feel was a nice smell approaching. I jumped. You're out of luck, that it was you. I have to eat too, you know."

"Must you sing? I asked you to climb out of my ear."

"Asking a flea to climb is an insult like asking a sparrow take a step. You know the riddle, don't you? How many steps does a sparrow take in a year?"

"Not one. Because it jumps," Danny Boy replied.

"All right. You don't seem a lost child. If you really want me to, I'll jump out of here. Although you could take me at least to the Briar Patch stop. Dogs and cats are more frequent there. Hedgehogs too."

Danny Boy forgot to close his mouth in amazement.

"How did you know that the Briar Patch stop was the next one?"

"Don't I live here too? In this neighbourhood, you mug. There's a big briar patch immediately after the elderberry bush. No?"

"All right, all right, but how come you know the next scooter stop is called that. It isn't written anywhere. Only in my head." He tapped his noggin.

The flea said nothing.

"Well?" Danny Boy pressed him.

"The truth is," the flea came clean, "that I can see inside your head."

"You mean to say you can read my mind?"

"You could say that. I can read your mind. It surprises me too. I hope it's not a big problem."

"Well, what should I say?" Danny Boy shrugged. "It's not exactly good to think about. Anyone whose thoughts can be read is exposed. Do you have any enemies?"

"Of course! Everybody has. Mine are a dog's or cat's claws. And human nails. If I'm not careful, they can crush me in a moment. The golden rule is if I'm pursued on open territory I jump hither and yon. Unpredictably."

"All right, that's exactly what I'm talking about." Danny Boy jerked up his head. "If we could read your mind, we'd know where you're going to jump next and we could pounce on you. If I, for example, were playing football with Mark or Christopher, my two cousins... I'll feint here, I'll dodge there, but in vain, because they could read my mind and they would jump in front of me. Or if I were playing hide-and-seek with Hanka and Julka, my two girl cousins... I'd hide in their cabinet drawer, but in vain, because I'd just venture out and they'd know at once where I was headed. Do you see?"

"Of course, I see. My body may be small, but my brain isn't."

Danny Boy considered this.

"Actually, what are you doing here? If your brain is so damn big, how could you be without a host? If I were a flea, I'd burrow into the thick fur of some fat animal and I wouldn't move out of there. If it had the sudden urge to scratch, I'd jump elsewhere. I'd have my meals for life."

"How strange," observed the flea.

"What's strange?"

"You're still just a child and you hand out advice like an adult. They always know just what you must do, though they never do it themselves. What's that under your feet?"

"Scooter."

"You're travelling."

"That's right."

"Or you like to travel."

"Very much."

"Why do you think I don't? Hmm? Because I'm nothing but a pip-squeak flea?"

Danny Boy lowered his eyes.

"Yes," he muttered. "That's exactly why I thought. But I'm glad I was wrong. I'd be glad to take you to all my stops. Should I tell you which stop is next?"

"Not necessary. I can see everything very well from here." The flea listed them.

> *Maple Lane, Terminus*
> *Hazelnut Estate*
> *Denes Street*
> *Poppy Estate*
> *Cracked Fence*
> *Briar Patch (EUROHILL Residential Community)*

Nettle Street
Gaspoint-Junction
Sharp   Bend   (LINDEN   GROVE   Residential
Community)
Foreign Trade Park, Terminus

Danny Boy couldn't say anything from amazement, then suddenly he began to plead.

"I would like you to please leave my ear. It's dreadful that anything I say, you know right away. This is just plain robbery."

"Robbery?" asked the big-nosed flea in amazement. "I'm not stealing anything. I'm not taking anything from you. Everything stays just as it is. I just read it, that's all."

"That's not true!" cried Danny Boy hotly. "You are stealing. You're stealing my joy that I can tell you. Or if I don't want to, I don't. I feel like you've put my whole head on your neck. Dreadful. More than dreadful!"

"Too bad that you think that," observed the flea after a while. "We've started to become friends." He was silent for a while. Then he said, "We two, together, we could have gone far. In the wide world. But I can't force you."

He suddenly jumped out of Danny's ear.

***

The next day Danny was scootering down the same way. And what do you know? He felt something biting his leg again. Truth to tell, he had gone a good deal further than their meeting place the day before; after all, he was just going around the Sharp Bend.

"Not you again?" shouted Danny Boy after braking and quickly pulling up his trouser leg. Now there it was, what he was looking for. The little black point didn't even try to scuttle away, but turned in place, then leaped about a bit, but not like it was trying to escape, but as if it wanted to signal or say something.

Danny Boy put his index finger in front of the tiny big-nosed thing, perhaps it would jump away. Instead, it jumped on his nail, and sat there peacefully. Danny hadn't the slightest doubt that this was yesterday's flea. He seemed to want to say something.

But what?

There was no denying it, Danny Boy was overcome with an irresistible curiosity. After hesitating a bit, he raised the big-nosed flea into the air and raised it toward his right ear. It was just an inch away when suddenly the flea jumped straight into his auditory duct.

"Good day," the flea greeted him gaily. "Things have happened since yesterday. I thought I'd tell you. Of course, only if you're interested. If not, I'm away."

"I'm interested, if it's interesting."

"Why wouldn't it be interesting? I was off to read minds. I can tell you that things are different from what you think. Thanks to my skill I've made peace between eternal enemies. Shall I tell you?"

Danny Boy exclaimed:

"Tell me!"

From then on, not a day, not a week passed when Danny didn't expect his nosy friend's unpleasant bites. He jumped up on the flying scooter here and there with new tales.

I've gathered a bouquet of these stories.

First Tale
CAT AND MOUSE

After I said goodbye to you, I said to myself, ah, I can wait here till dusk. Not even thirty seconds had passed when I felt a heavenly aroma waft toward me. It was a cat. I had to be alert to jump at the right moment, not too soon and not too late. Then I hopped on and found the best place, on his back. I hung on to his thick, warm fur. I ate a little, sucked at him – I tell you, there's nothing better than the fizzy blood of a fiery cat – then suddenly I got bored. There was no denying it, I missed the edifying chats. I thought I'd have a look in the cat's head. I had a hard time getting there, for the cat's ear was quite hairy. When I reached it, I understood right away why my cat was hurrying so frantically. He was pursuing another cat. It was not entirely clear why he was chasing it, but what was sure was that the thoughts of my transportation continually turned around the other cat. He thought she was as gorgeous as the loveliest dream; he got so excited his whole body got hot. I began to feel uncomfortable.

"What's the hurry? Can't you see it doesn't care a whit for you?"

It was as if the fat cat had been knocked on his head. He stopped in his tracks, puffed and blew, snorted and squirmed; I almost flew out of his ear. Fortunately, I was able to hang on to his fur. In any case, he turned around and went straight home. On the way home, he said only,

"Thanks for sobering me up."

Then he continued silently. As I saw in his head, I noticed that the cat, which until then had been running, had visions of lively mice. The further we went, the more of them he saw. By the time we reached the little one-story house, I saw only mice, and a plump female with creamy skin. All right, I decided to pay her a visit; I even licked my lips. The cat, however, came to a stop beneath the window, and listened tensely. The image of singing mice glimmered in his head. And I could hear them as they were singing.

When the cat's away
the mice will play,
when the cat's away
the mice will play.

In the twinkle of an eye, my cat sprang up on the window sill, and would have jumped in on the stone floor of the kitchen, when I bit his ear.

"Hands off," I shouted. "I'll have a word with them."

"There's nothing you can say to them," the cat growled. "They're a ne'er do well good-for-nothing lot. And they're unspeakably cheeky," he yowled bitterly. "Nothing will be right here, until I strangle them all." He snorted loudly.

But he didn't jump.

I immediately understood that he was getting tired of the hopeless struggle with this incredibly prolific mice people.

And he would have been glad if somebody would teach them a lesson or at least moderate or tame them.

I hopped out of his ear, and landed on the kitchen floor. By then the mice had scattered. I saw a hole in the wall half the size of a cat's paw, and I hopped to it. Meanwhile the cat had plopped on the stone floor and was heading straight for me. That was no good. With one leap I was back in his ear.

"Hey, mate, I think it'd be better if you made yourself scarce for a while. Like disappear!"

He understood at once. With dignity, he marched off behind the open door. I returned to the hole and waited patiently.

After a long while, a furry head appeared. I hopped on him. If only I hadn't been hungry for such a long time. But I knew that if I began to feast, there went the trust, which I hadn't yet earned. I controlled myself and set to work. I nestled in his ear, and I looked into his head.

Well, I saw such an ugly cat, which was only remotely similar to my willing transporter. His eyes, teeth and claws were five times bigger than my cat's, his body almost nothing. Hardly anything could be seen from his great belly, and flanks. I said to the mouse:

"Good day."

He jerked his head up, as if he had never been there.

"Calm down," I said to him. "The moggy is lurking behind the door at the other end of the kitchen."

There was no denying it; I was a bit surprised at the answer. He wasn't surprised at who it was, what it was that was speaking in his head, but what outraged him was that I had spoken kindly about that beast.

"What! That moggy? That beast!"

"I must say you have completely misunderstood his nibs. I just had the privilege of conversing with him. He said that you were very lovely folks."

"Oh yeah, of course!" replied the mouse. "What did you say, where is he?"

"Behind the door."

The mouse shot off. It was really strange to see in his head where we were racing. Up to the table leg, and quickly he ran up. On the table on a plate there were appetising roasts, over there an enormous soup bowl, a ladle leaning against the soup bowl. It was as if my mouse hadn't run up to gorge himself, but to tease the cat. It was hardly by accident he rushed onto the ladle and made it clatter, so that the cat was there in an instant. There was no denying it, I was terrified, as I saw in the mouse's head the cat's dreadful mug. The mouse must have been a chief of the mice, an old warrior, because he played a clever game of hide-and-seek among the plates, glasses and bowls. One after the other, the cat knocked over the glasses, then finally jumped on a long, flat utensil, and a devilled egg flew through the air. To her great misfortune, at that moment a buxom woman with a peaches-and-cream complexion stepped through the kitchen door – my God, I was hungry – and the devilled egg hit her full in the face.

We ran in all directions.

I was little on the verge of feeling ashamed for all this was my fault. I didn't even know suddenly how to patch up things. It was mostly the lady's delicate complexion that attracted me; her enormous body was full of tiny veins. Nevertheless, she played the least important role in the whole story. I preferred to hop back onto the cat who was venturing forth.

I hadn't yet uttered a peep, when he growled at me angrily. He knew that I was fumbling about in his ear.

"Traitor!"

I could barely speak.

"I know appearances are against me. But as God is my witness, I didn't know what I was doing."

"Oh no? I told you in no uncertain terms that they are an impudent lot. There's no gilding the lily."

"The truth is, I didn't have the time to talk to him." Suddenly, I had an idea. "You know what, don't hide now. Sit down a jump away from the mouse hole. Don't turn your back or sit sideways. Sit facing it. Don't lie low, as if you're about to spring. Just sit there, majestically, like a king, awaiting veneration. The mouse chief spoke of you with great respect; he repeatedly called you your royal highness. Once he even called you a lion. I didn't have time to tell him that the kitchen is your realm, and they can't come here to feast. Only with your special permission."

I saw that I was on the right path. The cat melted at all those flattering words. A kind of rose-coloured vapour began to spread in his head; it even reached the chief of the mice. In the end, he nodded silently, signalling that he agreed with my noble mission. That was all I needed. I headed for the mouse chief.

Now, what came next, it wasn't such a big deal, except that it was very slow. The mouse chief peered out of the hole from time to time, but when he saw the cat a jump away, he didn't stick his head out, so I couldn't jump on the mouse. If the mountain won't come to Muhammed, then Muhammed must go to the mountain. I slipped into the tiny mouse hole. It was so narrow, that I didn't risk even one jump, so I wouldn't break my smart head. I tell you, point-blank, there isn't anything more disgusting for a flea than crawling about in such a dark, humid place. But after all, life isn't worth a bean without great determination and great deeds. So, I set off. I was going for a good while. Like a wretched crab louse, I crawled on, when at long last the mouse chief came running toward me. You have no idea how much harder it is to jump on a vehicle that is coming directly opposite to you than jumping sideways. But God helps those who help themselves. I made it. I immediately sat in his ear and told him:

"How long has that poor cat been waiting for you. He would like so much to wave at you, but you don't even stick your head out."

"I haven't gone mad. So, he should grab me? You have no idea of the claws on that cat!"

"I do have an idea, but as you can see, there's nothing wrong with me. I tell you, this cat is goodness itself. He wouldn't lift a paw against me. Or against you. But he thought, poor thing, until now that you are a despicable, bad lot. And that God had created you just to annoy him. I explained to him in detail, for a long time what a huge mistake that was. You are merely looking for food, so you don't starve to death. And if you ran into each other, you always misunderstood the other's intention. You thought it was an attack, whereas, poor cat, only wanted to make friends. He only wanted to play. Perhaps to chat."

As a matter of fact, now the rose-coloured mist began to gather in the mouse's head. The cat's eyes, teeth, and claws shrank suddenly, so that he seemed much friendlier, more tolerable. Suddenly the sitting cat appeared before my eyes. I saw him tense up, but he didn't lie low, he wasn't ready to pounce.

"Wave at him! Wave!"

The mouse lifted his right front paw hesitantly.

"Wave at him!" I yelled at him. "Wave!"

Timidly, he waved.

"With the other paw, too!"

"Should I stand on my hind legs?"

"Yes. Wave with both paws!"

"And if he catches me?"

"He won't. He'll wave back at you."

That is exactly what happened. My mouse cautiously stood up on his hind legs, and waved cleverly at the cat, who nodded at him, lifted his paw, and waved gracefully.

What happened next, I could put together only from the mosaic images that flashed by like lightning in the mouse's head. The mistress of the house appeared suddenly in the crack of the door. Her face froze at the sight of cat and mouse waving peacefully at each other. She grabbed a broom and flailed at the cat then at the mouse. I quickly jumped out of the mouse's ear, breathed in the air, and waited for the right time to jump. I tell you, the Lord God made the right decision, that human blood not be any worse than a cat's.

That's what happened.

It was a tale, it was true.

Where are we now? I talked it over with the cat that he should pick me up at Nettle Street. He knew a dog in the neighbourhood. Maybe he would need me again…

Second Tale
IT'S A DOG'S LIFE

Well, I was surveying the terrain from my cat's ear, but not only with my eyes, but my nose too, when the dreadful maw of an enormous hound loomed into view. Actually, it wasn't at all dreadful. It was only that cats paint the devil on the wall, as they say, when they catch sight of a dog. They take fright, their hair stands on end, their back arches, they hiss like maniacs; they think that if they're not frightened enough, it will be the end of them.

It was a rather elderly, sluggish old beast with red fur appeared at the bend, on a long leash. "I think my client has come," I observed. "Thanks for the ride." I jumped.

I know that you are surprised, but I don't always feel like having young meat, or rather, young blood. If a flea gets used to something and grows to like it, he doesn't always wish to replace it with another. They often say that variety is the spice of life, and this is true, but I like to imbibe from my cat's neck a little, then from its flank. Now, there's the rub. After all, my moggy did me a service, when it brought me for free, and I couldn't abuse my situation. But by then I was so hungry I was seeing stars, and when I jumped over to the Red Fur, I began to feast on him at once. But so greedily, that it was thanks to blind fate – if not Providence – that you can converse with me.

Namely, *claws* virtually grazed my head, I barely managed to jump away, to avoid it hitting a bull's eye in its next dash.

Hip-hop, I landed in his ear.

"Can't you be careful?" I shouted.

Since he didn't answer, I asked him again.

"Can't you be careful?" After a pause, I added, "Are you deaf?"

"Not at all. But I don't know who's speaking."

"I," I replied.

"From a cell phone?"

"No. What's a cell phone?"

"Well... how shall I put it?"

"As it is."

"Well, where should I start?"

"From the middle."

"It has a cord on it, but it's not like a shoe lace. Its end forks and ends in a plug. Young Master has put one plug into his ear, and the other into mine. And we listened together."

"The plug?"

"No. The song. What comes out of this gadget."

"From the plug?"

"From the cell phone."

"On the cord..."

"Aha."

"Obviously, it's got a hole inside."

"I don't know. *I want that doggy in the window,* came from it. I liked it at the time. And at that time Young Master loved me very much... But who are you?"

"A flea," I answered quickly.

"Stop joking," he barked. "A flea is smaller than the tip of my nail, and its brain is no bigger. I had dealings with them. It doesn't know about anything other than sponging. It jumps on me, bites me, then sucks out my blood. I snap at it, and it jumps away. I just chased one away."

"You'd have liked to. I'm sitting on you, if you'd like to know."

Red Fur suddenly went quiet. He turned his head this way and that, sniffed excitedly, trying to find me so he could smack me one. I said to him,

"Don't you…"

At this, he retorted:

"I didn't say anything."

"You didn't say it, but you thought it. It would be a good thing if you knew, sitting in your ear, I can see all your thoughts."

Red Fur stopped short, as if his legs had taken root. I now noticed his walker. A slim little woman, but fiery, you know the kind. Her blood is delicious, almost as good as that of a cat or a dog. OK, OK, how could you know? So, she started pulling on the leash, a dark cloud began to gather in my dog's head. It wasn't a healthy red, like anger, but dark green, like bitterness. And then, when the voice said,

"Let's go. You can sleep at home."

At this he became completely black.

I took pity on him. I told him,

"Go ahead. Bite her."

"I'll bite off my own paw first."

"If someone does this to me, I'd bite him without hesitation."

"Only with us it's an unwritten law, if a dog attacks its master, it must be destroyed. Anyway, I wouldn't do it. She's my mistress and I love her."

Look here, Danny, that was exactly what I was afraid of. Every kind of soundness of mind has died out in these creatures. The one jerks the other who adores him. The other tolerates the unjust jerking, whereas all he must do is snap at him, and the next time he'll think twice. I told Red Fur, goodbye, I'm off. Just bear it, if you want, you don't need me for that. And I would have leaped away, when I was very surprised, and I thought about it. Namely, the gentle beast barked at me:

"I'm sorry you're going. I haven't talked to anyone for ages."

"All right, flea," I said to myself. "You're really needed here."

***

This was well concocted, Danny. Don't you think? Compared to you I am as small as you are to that high-rise building where Red Fur took me. Anyway, I'm teeny-tiny – still, I was overcome with the irresistible urge to set Red Fur's life to right. I never experienced this sort of thing with other fleas, so I didn't know whether this was a blessing or a curse. I just felt that something immeasurably large was towering before me, which I had to jump over, and this was making my brain hammer, my heart beat, and my blood fizz.

As it turned out, Red Fur's family lived on the sixth story out of ten, and through a dog's eye or dog's ear, the view was quite interesting. I thought that perhaps as many as a million fleas were cavorting about down below; I couldn't see a single one from my height. Apparently, the apartment was rather small, I'm not an expert on this, but what was sure, Red Fur had the run of the house. He got his food and drink, however, in the kitchen. He liked to hang out best in the living room below the table, and on the balcony, when the shade was lowered.

Now that you should understand, Red Fur was called Toffee at home, but why, not even he could say. He had been Toffee from time immemorial. He was brought to the house when Young Master was four years old, and they had made the mistake of asking him, what would you like for your birthday? He replied:

"A puppy."

"Wouldn't you rather have a big car?"

"No."

"A train?"

"No."

"Lego?"

"No. A puppy."

"You will take it for walks?" his mother asked.

"Yes, I will."

"You will feed and water it?"

"I will."

So that's how Toffee came to them. And it turned out that every day they squabble over who was going to take Toffee for a walk.

Papa says, "It was your idea to ask the child what he wants. You take him down. I have a lot of work to do right now." Mama responds, "I have a lot of work, too. Anyway, we bought him together. You can't get out of the responsibility." At this, Young Master, if he happens to be at home, shouts from his room, "Stop arguing. Let me study." Thereupon, they both rush into his room, almost knocking each other over. "Don't you say a word, when you've promised a hundred times to feed him, water him and take him on walks." But Young Master retorted, "But when he was small and cute, he was good for you too."

So that's the way it is.

All right. At first you must think what a selfish, mean lot, why do they have a pet? When we went up in the lift – funny thing, a lift, we just stand there, meanwhile a motor or what is humming, you are about hundred jumps from the ground and about – the same amount nearer the sky. So, when we stepped into the flat – I of course didn't make a move, I lay low in Toffee's ear – I felt like we'd arrived at a transformer station. The air crackled. It didn't take long for me to realise where the great tension came from.

It was the jitters.

I tell you, Danny, these people aren't trashy, they're miserable. They're always afraid of something.

You're not going to believe it, but they're afraid even of a teeny-weeny flea.

***

I thought it was the end of me, they launched into hot pursuit of me. I got tired of the ruckus and climbed out of Red Fur's ear for a rest. From then on, I saw and heard very little; on the other hand, I felt a lot, mainly the wonderful fragrance of that full-blooded woman. I didn't beat about the bush, but headed for her. Hip-hop, there I was beneath her skirt and began feasting.

Only I hadn't reckoned on one thing. That is, a few months ago Red Fur had brought home not one but several members of my own species. The family had learned how to catch fleas and get rid of them. Suddenly the fancy and frilly dress flew up and I was exposed to the blinding light. A moment's hesitation was enough for the lady to nab me. I was feasting somewhere above her knee, on a soft meadow of blood. Irresponsible and heedless. A clever flea does not take such a risk, but seeks the hem of delicate cloth, and takes nourishment with more circumspection. So, they can't throw up anything, he remains hidden, and can cut and run.

The lady caught me between her two fingers and began to rub them together to break my legs.

Oh no!

I began to wriggle and twist. The force of it surprised even me. They say, *pepper is small, but strong,* but we could easily say, *fleas are small, but strong.* Did you know, Danny, that we can leap two hundred times the size of our bodies? Whereas you, you're lucky if you can jump twice as high as your height. Right?

In short, in all this mad wriggling I managed to escape. I followed my nose and jumped back on Red Fur and whizz-bang, I was in his ear.

"Don't betray me," I panted.

He lowered his head and said,

"I can't lie to my master."

"Did I ask you to?"

"To neither one,"

I repeated.

"Did I ask you to? Of course not. Until they ask you where did that louse go, don't volunteer, 'Hello! Here he is in my ear.' Get it?"

I clued him in time.

"It's got away. Come here at once and help me find it," screeched the lady.

Young Master's dad shambled in languidly.

I sensed that Red Fur was ill at ease, but valiantly he said nothing, he didn't bark, nor did he indicate his ear.

"What escaped?" asked her husband.

"Another flea, the hell with it."

Pardon the expression, but that is exactly what she said.

At this the other one said,

"Aren't you just imagining things? Nothing has bitten me."

These people are interesting, don't you think, Danny? Who knows how many million years we've lived together, and they still don't want to recognise that we have just as much taste as they do. How could I even think of eating from that shambles, when that full-blooded lady with her marvellous fragrance was at hand?

"I had it in my hand, when it scrammed. Close the door, quick. We have to catch it."

"Is it only one flea?"

"How should I know? Maybe there are more. An army. We have to buy Toffee another flea collar."

"It's not worth the money."

"Then we have to use drops on his neck. And we must spray pest control everywhere. We must wash all the clothes, sheets, towels. All the rugs, even."

Good God! Think of it, Danny, all that for one flea the size of a poppy seed. Don't you say, to shoot a sparrow with a cannon?

Fact is, even the shambler lost his calm.

"Where have you been?" he inquired.

"Nowhere. The usual route."

"Didn't he lie down somewhere?"

"I didn't let him."

"Then how did the flea get to him?"

"That's what I'd also like to know."

"Maybe it wasn't he who brought it home but you."

"Oh, come on. Why not you?"

"Definitely not. It was on you, wasn't it? Or no?

"Yes. Even the fleas hate you."

At this even Red Fur began to whine. "You!" he snapped at me. "They're going to have a row and there will be a great slamming of doors. If you're not going to help, at least don't do harm. Take yourself off, at once!"

"I should jump off the sixth floor?"

"Yes, nothing will happen to you."

"But I haven't completed my mission."

"Nothing will help here. Those few years that I have ahead of me, I'll manage to make it through somehow."

"Well, if that is what you think, then I'll go," I replied and bustled about as if I really were about to leave.

"Are you still here?" he asked after a while.

I didn't answer of course, but lay low like a hedgehog. By the way, I like their blood too. Now I kept a deep silence, as if I had gone mute. At least I could watch them shake their clothes and rugs on the balcony, but they even ordered Red Fur out from under the table and felt him thoroughly. Fortunately, they didn't think of looking in his ear.

Meanwhile I watched Red Fur intently. Was he rooting for them or for me? And as I watched the changes in his head, I felt even more that Toffee was a good sort. He was hoping that I should escape without great trouble, but that I should get out of their lives forever.

***

I woke up when Red Fur jerked up his head. It was growing dark outside and the noise of keys turning in the entrance door lock could be heard.

Young Master appeared in Red Fur's head, while a pink cloud whirled around with dark green shadings.

Then I almost jumped out of my comfortable nest from fright.

"Where were you so long?" snapped his mother.

"I was with my mates."

"You were partying…"

"Yes, we were. Maybe we shouldn't? You didn't party when you were my age?"

"Yes, but we did our homework first and fulfilled our other responsibilities. Don't forget to take Toffee for a walk tonight. And take out the rubbish."

"When I finish my homework, I'll be glad to take him down."

A peculiar storm seemed to be raging in Red Fur. Behind the dark green, baleful clouds a pale ray of light flashed through, but only for fleeting seconds.

"You should have done your homework already. In any case, you'll take him down."

At this Papa arrived.

"So long as you live with us, you have to take part in the chores. If you don't like it, you can move away."

"Oh yeah, I like it, I like it very much. I like it especially that I can't even come home, without being welcomed by a big row."

"Don't be cheeky, or you'll get your ears boxed."

"And I'll report you, for violence against a minor."

If you don't mind, Danny, I won't go on with this ridiculous family spat. After all, I didn't want to tell you all this. It was because of Red Fur.

Young Master threw open the door to the living room and went up to the wretched creature that was wagging his tail.

"Hello, Toffee."

He scratched his ear, patted his sides and said,

"Sorry, I have a lot of studying to do."

And he buzzed off.

Hesitantly Toffee padded after him, but stopped at the door that was closing. He stood about, then trudged back and lay down under the table. He fell into deep silence, I could say, into sadness.

I reached a big decision.

To find Young Master and talk to him. It wasn't the conversation that seemed risky; the problem was getting to him.

Red Fur shut his eyes, and for lack of anything better to do, fell asleep, and I couldn't see anything at all. How was I going to find him?

I tried to conjure up the last image I saw, based on which I would go forth.

I cautiously tried to wriggle out of my warm little nest, and jumped down. As I hoped I landed on the rug. It was getting dark, but it was clear where the outside light was coming from, and where the door to the entrance was. I made a few jumps, for fortunately I didn't get stuck on anything, but hit the door. Our armour really comes in handy at such times, Danny. It saves us not only from being crushed. I crawled through the door, and got to Young Master's door, at the price of a few knocks. From then on, my task was easy, for I could follow my nose. I made a few jumps toward the source of the fragrance. But when I got there, I didn't find anything. I realised that the fragrance was coming from somewhere up there. I buckled down, made a good jump, and landed on something soft. And there, Young Master's full-blooded transpiration almost swept me away.

You must know, Danny, I had to collect all my strength and determination to keep myself from feasting on him right away. Have you ever been in a situation where you were as hungry as a wolf and the food that was tickling your nostrils was before you, but you couldn't have any? If I yielded to temptation, that would be the end of Toffee. He would perish, poor thing, from grief.

I swallowed and cautiously sought out Young Master's ear. When with one swift movement, I leaped up onto his earlobe and slipped into his ear, he made a grab at me, scratched a bit and then stopped.

It was interesting to see what he was looking at.

It was as if, on a sheet of paper, a thousand poppy seeds or a thousand fleas were lined up, in addition around a hirsute figure. It appeared in Young Master's head that he was Lajos Kossuth, but I hadn't a clue who that was.

Anyway, it didn't matter a whit to the story.

***

"Young Master," I said very, very softly, so as not to alarm him. He glanced up, looked around, then turned to his poppy seeds.

"Young Master."

At that he sat up.

"It's me," I said quietly. "A little flea. In your ear."

He closed his eyes, then opened them. He took a couple of deep breaths, then shook his head. I could see that he thought he was imagining things…

"Here I am. Sitting in your ear. Don't be alarmed. I came from Toffee." I thought it would help if I referred to our common acquaintance.

Red Fur flashed into Young Master's head as he was scratching himself.

I hastened to reassure him.

"He hasn't got fleas."

"What about you?" thought Young Master.

"I don't have fleas, either. I'm only a flea."

"All right, all right, but didn't you say you came from him?"

"Yes."

"You didn't bite him?"

I saw him reddening. I quickly informed him.

"Just enough not to die of hunger. We had a good, long talk."

"Don't tell me. I still have a lot of homework. The next time."

"There will be no next time. If Toffee pops off, I won't stay either."

"That's nonsense."

This erupted from Young Master. He said it out loud.

"What's nonsense?" asked his mother who opened the door. "What is it that's bothering you again?"

"Nothing at all, Mama."

I saw how he was overcome by the dirty yellow malice.

"I'm talking with a flea."

"A flea?"

"With a flea."

"Did you catch a flea?"

"I didn't catch it. I'm talking to it."

"Are you messing with me?"

"Not at all. You don't believe me?"

"I believe that you are talking to a flea… These computer games are hacking you off." After a short pause, she added, "We've been overrun by fleas. One bit me this afternoon."

By this time, Papa stuck his head in.

"What did I hear, son? You've got fleas too?"

"Not really."

"What do you mean, not really? Have you or have you not got fleas?"

"I haven't been bitten by any."

"All right. I'll give you money tomorrow. You can get a flea spray. And some vinegar."

"Can't you buy them?"

"I have a thousand things to do."

"What about Mama?"

"I have a lot to do, too. I can't see the end of it," she said.

"I have a lot of studying to do," fulminated Young Master. "Get off my back."

"I tell you, you have a half hour altogether before the evening walk," Young Master's father said on his way out. "And I'm not interested if you've finished studying or not."

***

"Thanks for not saying anything about me," I told Young Master when the air had cleared.

"You get off my back too," he replied angrily.

I had to restrain myself to keep from biting him. And sending my mission to hell. But there are things in life, dear Danny, when it isn't a question of whether you let something go or not, but whether it lets you go.

"We were talking about Toffee. He's heart-sick. He's going to die!" I informed him in the driest way possible.

"I'm sorry."

I looked at Young Master's thought, and I was reassured to determine that among the many bitter green jitteriness, anxiety, feelings of impotence, there glimmered the lighter, blue-green shades of sympathy. Only it was all hemmed in. That was what I felt between the fingers of the full-blooded lady. It was a hellish feeling. You know what I'm talking about, Danny.

"Hellish feeling," I said to Young Master.

He jerked up his head.

"Really hellish. That's exactly what I feel."

"Call Toffee. Let him lie down at your feet. The bad feeling will go."

"I can barely make any progress as it is, damn it."

"If the hellish feeling goes away, everything will go more easily. You'll practically enjoy studying. You'll get to the end much faster."

"But he's going to pant here and smell."

"It doesn't matter if he pants, it doesn't matter if he smells."

"It does. It isn't that I don't love Toffee, but after a while his panting makes me hit the wall. And his snoring! The whole house rings with it. And he has fleas as well."

"Wait. What did you say?"

"That he has fleas as well."

"But you know very well that he doesn't have fleas. I'm his only flea, and I'm in your ear, not his."

I said nothing for a while, then I went on.

"Somewhere this could be the end of the thread. You know he doesn't have fleas, and yet you say he does. You're escaping into trouble. That's where you feel safe. But why?"

I watched quietly.

"You know that the NOs are just rushing at you? 'NO! NO! NO! I can't stand it! I can't stand it! I can't stand it!' Now too you reached for your ear to catch me. To crush me. To make me stop talking. Aren't I right?"

"Yes, you are."

He reached for his ear and pressed his palm against it. Until then not too much light had filtered in, but now it was completely dark. "OK, flea," I thought. "Now you're a prisoner. You can't get in or out."

Then I realised that my dark cell could not be in a better place.

"You close your ear in vain, after all I'm inside. You have to listen to me."

"I don't wish to listen to you."

"Why not? You can't ignore me."

"Yes, I can."

"Are you afraid?"

This made him think.

"No. I just don't have any time for you. I must study, nothing else matters. If I get bad grades, they nag at me. If I get good grades, they leave me alone. That's all I care about. That they leave me alone. That you leave me alone."

He took his hand away from his ear, hoping that, moved by his dramatic tone, I would clamber out... I hadn't the least intention of doing so.

"You know, what I noticed, old man? That you guys are always shit-scared. That you won't manage to learn something, that you won't get good grades, that you won't succeed in something, that you won't make yourself be loved, and so on and so forth. That is why you're always sitting backwards on the horse. You think you are galloping forwards, but in fact you are going backwards. You see nothing but obstacles around you, whereas all these helps you succeed. If Toffee pants, you should be glad he's alive. If he snores, you should be glad that he is having a good sleep. If he smells a bit, be thankful you had so many fine years with your old dog. You create trouble and strife where there is none, so you must prove to yourself that you are sitting well on the horse, only the world around you is hostile. Do you understand?"

I saw in his head, that something was dawning on him here and there. But the darkness of impotence was also dominant. What would happen if he went off the well-trod path? However shaky the ground, everybody was walking on this…

"Let Toffee lie at your feet," I said quietly.

"No," he retorted sharply.

"Too bad. And yet one day you will get it, Young Master: *We become poorer with every NO, and we grow bigger with every YES.* Farewell."

I sidled out of his ear, but glanced one more time at his heart.

I nodded. Inasmuch as my armour allowed me.

***

Now that I knew the way, I went back quickly to Red Fur.

"I hope you didn't hurt him," he growled suspiciously.

"No."

We said nothing for a while.

"Where did you get to?" he asked.

"Not very far, I'm afraid."

He was overcome with sorrow from the tip of his nails to the tip of his nose.

We said nothing.

Then suddenly he jerked up his head.

The door opened. It was Young Master.

"Come, Toffee. We'll study some more then we'll go for a walk. Let's not forget to take down the garbage."

Red Fur backed out from under the table, and clambered up heavily. He went over to Young Master panting. He butted him with his head and his flanks. Young Master scratched and patted him with both hands. He laughed.

"All right, Toffee. All right."

When we went over all three of us, Red Fur lay down at Young Master's feet. Young Master was still reading his poppy seeds, while he asked this and that out loud, "Do you know, Toffee, where Lajos Kossuth died?" Red Fur barked, as if he knew, and I laughed to myself, that yeah, I knew from Young Master's head that it was Rodosto, only I hadn't a clue what Rodosto was.

We got along fine.

I had a hard day behind me, so I tried to take a snooze.

Something occurred to Red Fur.

"Flea. Are you here?"

"Yes."

He was swimming in pink.

"Thanks," he barked.

"You're welcome."

I too was swimming in pink. After a little time, however, I could no longer restrain myself.

41

"Toffee, I'm in trouble. I'm starving. Can I have a bit of your blood?"

He didn't reply right away.

"As much as you like," he finally answered.

"I promise I'll jump off you while we're on the walk."

After a while, he replied,

"On the morning walk. You can eat and drink until then. It's probably harder to find new accommodations at night."

***

That's exactly what happened, Danny, my dear friend.

No denying it, I got hungry and thirsty after all this tale-telling. "Please take me to some stop near the high-rises. Perhaps I will be lucky again, and some wretched creature will venture there."

"You know what, you go ahead and take your fill of me."

Third Tale
ON THE BUS

Well, Danny, you know, my head is so chock-full of all sorts of wise things I can barely hold it up.

I don't understand human beings.

They have the divine gift of being able to talk to each other. What does one human being know about life? Nothing. Many human beings? Everything. So, what do they do?

I'm sitting in a bus, in a lapdog's ear, watching the world.

All right, but how did I get there?

Simple.

I was peacefully dining on a stray black cat, when suddenly he went mad and jumped, then just as suddenly stopped, gasped and struggled for breath; I went up and down with him. I climbed into his ear to see what the problem was. The dreadful noise of a motor, an enormous house with lots of windows and doors lumbered noisily away on the road, filled to the brim with flesh-and-blood human beings. Of course, this aroused my interest.

It had barely moved off when another rumbled by. The doors opened, a few choice morsels got off, and others got on. I said to the cat,

"Shouldn't we jump on?"

"On the bus?"

He hissed edgily.

"I wouldn't dream of it."

"Looks exciting," I observed.

We exchanged words; it turned out that he couldn't get on it by himself, only with an attendant and in a carrier, which he loathed. "What am I? A bird? Anyway, who would want to go with me?"

I said, I did.

At this red rage filled his head, that I shouldn't mock it, and he told me to get lost. He didn't have to say it twice. I jumped off.

You know, Danny, you get fed up with every bloody thing and you want to escape.

I waited leisurely for a fragrance.

I didn't have long to wait. It was a bit of a cheap scent, bath foam, but mellow. The only thing was that I had to climb up to it, because it was kept in a lap. That was OK with him. It seems, my little friend, you can get used to everything, no matter how bad.

So, I'm sitting in the lapdog's ear, and I'm observing the world.

Suddenly I catch sight of something.

"Hey," I ask him. "Is that a cell-phone?"

"What?"

"What you're looking at. It's attached to that cord."

"For sure!"

"Do you know, *I want that doggy in the window.*"

"No."

"Maybe it's in it."

"Maybe."

"Are you a doggy, a puppy?"

"No."

"What then?"

"I'm a grown dog. I'm seven years old."

"Toffee, there in that high-rise building, is bigger than you."

I figured I would shake him out of his cool calm. He would ask who Toffee was, and then I can tell him about him. But he didn't say anything."

"Maybe," he growled.

He looked impassive, yawning all the while. At least he didn't go to sleep. I was slowly getting the picture.

Imagine, Danny. People were all higgledy-piggledy: sitting and standing, little ones, big ones, elderly ones, young ones. But they didn't say a word to each other, as if they'd all gone mute. They didn't look into each other's eyes.

Suddenly I saw something that electrified me.

"You, bring your head back."

"Where to?"

"Where it was before. The one with rag-mop hair and another hirsute."

He scanned the field.

"Stop. They're the ones."

He stopped. His look, that is.

"Are you watching?" I say to him. "They also have one in their hands."

"What?"

"A cell-phone. They've got it pressed to their ear. Both the boy and the girl. They're talking to each other."

"Maybe," he allowed.

"No maybe. For sure. I'm not blind."

It occurred to me that I saw only what the dog saw.

"You see it too. Their mouths are gaping."

"I see it."

"Why are their mouths open when they're not conversing?"

"Maybe they're talking to themselves."

I thought about this.

Fact is, Young Master's mother and father didn't talk to him through these gadgets. The voice came and went on its own. Still they understood each other. These two... they seemed to talk past each other.

I thought I'd take a closer look at them. Only my lapdog fell into a snooze, and I felt as if I were enveloped in darkness; I got neither sound nor image. I was forced to clamber out and head off.

***

I don't have to say, my dear friend, that I immediately got lost. The smells got totally mixed up in the bus, which confused me totally. At such times I can't trust my otherwise excellent nose. I must find another observation point, leap up on his head, then into his ear, and find my bearings again.

Yes, but it is dangerous and wearisome to constantly be retelling the story of who you are, how you got there, and watching what they're thinking. For one takes it this way, another one another way, and finally the whole bus is abuzz like an *overturned* hive. There are those who, if they hear the word flea, start searching, itching, flapping, and thrashing about... Others soften at the word "human(e)", and though you've cleared out long ago, they think you're still sitting in their ear, so they talk to themselves out loud like Hirsute and Rag Mop. So, it's better not to say anything, and wait quietly until they look at something interesting. If only because you'll have some surprises.

Imagine, Danny.

I tried to avoid the older ones; I went for the fragrance of the young ones. I was disappointed at the first one, for a cord was hanging from both ears at the end of which was an enormous plug. I couldn't get to him.

It was the same case with the other one.

Finally, with the third one, it seemed that luck was with me. I was able to settle comfortably into an agreeable ear.

Yes, but now I had found an observation post where I couldn't see anything of the bus or the passengers, let alone the couple I had picked out. The lady who exuded the delicate vapour was staring at a flat thing, and not for anything would she get off it. I tried by biting her ear to remind her that, hello, she'd got stuck, but she just made a grab at me, and immediately turned her attention again to the flat thing.

Without a doubt, it was strange to see that whenever she moved her fingers, everything changed at once. Changed completely. As if by magic. Do you understand? It was as if you clicked, and instead of the Poppy Estate stop, we immediately landed at the Cracked Fence or Sharp Curve. Or on the Moon. In the blink of an eye. Always a different image, another sight.

There was no denying it, at first, I enjoyed it. Nothing to do, just settle into the narrow ear duct, you don't have to move, and the world passes before you.

Amazing!

I didn't understand it, but after a short while something began to trouble me.

It must be my fault, I thought.

I said to myself, calm down, flea! If it's good for a human being, then it must be good for you. You can wander all over the place, and yet you don't even have to move. Isn't it great? Could you ask for anything better? Could you ask for more?

I began to look more closely at the lady's head.

It was mostly phlegmatic, dull, but otherwise everything was OK.

Then what was bothering me?

Something flashed.

***

A terrible thing happened to me once, Danny. It was a mild, summer evening, and at such times the hedgehogs are more restless than usual. I chose, or more exactly, *I smelled* a nose-tickling specimen. But it was running about in every direction and several times I missed. Finally, I jumped on, but I could barely get to easing my hellish hunger, when a terrible rumbling noise sounded, a booming, an enormous blow, and that was the end of the hedgehog. It was flattened by something; it was a miracle I escaped intact.

An enormous, warm puddle of blood was before my nose. Don't grow pale, I will say no more. All I will say is that my favourite dish was there before me, but I couldn't bear to even look at it.

I'm a flea, Danny, a respectable blood-sucker, if you understand. I'm not a scavenger or drinker of blood. I'm a flea because I do it right: I get wind of something, I make a move on it, I attack until I succeed. If I succeed, then I throw out a feeler for the best place and, thank God, begin gorging myself. Meanwhile, I'm eternally ready to jump – and if I must, I leap. If I can. My God, how many of my companions in distress didn't manage to escape.

All right, it's true that if sometimes they offer something wholeheartedly, I accept. But to exchange my life for an easy meal, no, absolutely not.

***

I was just searching for the suitable words to explain this to my observation post, when she got up suddenly and headed for the door. Oh, she was getting ready to get off, I realised and got ready to jump off. Of course, as always, fortune smiled on me. Barely a jump away, the image of Hirsute and Rag Mop leaped into view. I jumped without hesitation and landed on the best place, on top of the boy's head.

I was tormented by curiosity, so this time I didn't beat about the bush. As soon as I reached his ear, I asked him:

"Do you really talk to yourself?"

You should have seen how his thoughts rushed in. A cavalcade of loud colours welled up in the pale grey void: *"Bee-drone! National security! Attack of the drones! iPhone shoots back! Bubi balled it up!"*

I didn't understand a single word. It was all Greek to me. I couldn't refrain from asking the last one at least.

"Who's this Bubi?"

He couldn't catch his breath. After a great while, he stammered:

"Who are *you*?"

I was afraid that if I told him he wouldn't reply.

"You tell me first."

"Bubi's the class' brain. He amuses himself in class by secretly readjusting the filched smart phones."

"Aha, and I'm an elephant."

Poor thing, I confused him totally. I quickly added,

"I was just joking. I'm actually a flea."

"Drone?"

"What's that?"

"A remote-control thing. You can direct it to any part of the world. It might be as big as a small plane, but I've seen bee-drones too. And mosquitoes. True, only on a video."

"Well, I'm just a completely ordinary flea," I replied. "And I came on my own, I think."

"But not to destroy?"

"I can say that for certain. I'd just like to know, when you were *mouthing* into your cell-phone, were you talking to yourself?"

"I don't usually talk to myself."

"Then were you talking to this girl? Next to you."

He turned his head, and finally I could take a good look at Rag Mop. You know, Danny, it's difficult for me to tell with your hearts, if something or someone is beautiful or ugly. I can tell you, however, that suddenly the boy's head turned pink, and his eyes anchored on the girl with the moonlight face and sky-blue eyes.

"Not with her," he said finally.

"But I saw her speaking too."

"But not to me. A telephone is not for talking with people next to you, but with those who are far away."

"So, you mean, the cell-phone is a drone?"

"Interesting idea, especially from a flea. Who the hell sent you?"

He became restless again, and he was filled with the bitter green of anxiety. I hastened to dispel it.

"No one. I'm sitting in your ear, and I can see your thoughts."

"That doesn't surprise me."

"You like this girl."

Unintentionally, he jerked his head to the right. The pink vapour immediately began to spread.

"I'm not interested."

"Your words and your heart aren't the same."

"Even so, I don't care."

Involuntarily, he looked at his flat thing, and began waving his fingers about. He jumped about between two worlds.

"Look," and the image of various girls appeared. "I can choose whoever I wish. Even fleas. I can download whatever you want."

"What are you afraid of?" I asked quietly.

He retorted, not with words, but colours.

"That she will reject me."

"So?"

"No so."

I saw that he closed off completely. He was like a chestnut inside its spiny husk.

***

I racked my brains, what should I do now? Then I had a brilliant idea. I wandered over to Moonlight Face. I wasn't going to blab to Hirsute. Anyway, he'd say, what for? I wanted to take a look into the girl's head. Hay or chaff?

I snuck out, and in a hop, I was on top of Moonlight Face's head.

She had just lifted her flat thing to her ear. I had to cut through the brush of her head to get to her free ear. I made myself comfortable and listened.

Now, dear Danny, if I had to tell you what she was chatting with her birds-of-a-kind girlfriend, I would be in trouble. I could make neither head nor tail of it. You know what I noticed? If there was a silence, the lapse of a breath, the colours of anxiety poured in. There was no denying it, I had to rack my brains for long-long seconds, by the time I grasped what the devil this could be.

She was holding fast.

To words.

"That's a good sign," I said to myself.

***

I just pecked at her finely meshed auditory duct.

"I'm sitting in your ear. Can you feel it?"

As I expected, she didn't speak up. She was thinking that she was imagining things. Then that she most certainly was dreaming. She took out a water bottle and pulled on it. This calmed her a bit.

"Can I ask you something?"

She looked sideways. Hirsute appeared for a moment, but he didn't look back, but pushed the plug of his flat thing into his ear. "It wasn't him," Moonlight Face replied. She pulled out her water bottle again and drank greedily.

"You're not thirsty, are you?"

"I don't know who you are, but I do know that you don't have the right to badger me with questions," she said. Decidedly but unobtrusively.

"I'm just a nothing little flea."

"I won't take this," she hissed.

"If you reply, I'll leave."

This made her think.

"What's it to you? Why is this important to you?"

This made me think too.

"You know," I answered finally. "I put myself down from any place even in total darkness."

"Why should I care?"

"Well, it doesn't bother me that there's nothing for me to hold on to. Even though I may be jumping into death's throat, I'll take the leap anyway."

"But what's it to me?"

"You weren't thirsty, were you?"

Her lips whispered, "Obviously, otherwise why would I have drunk?" but the colours said something else.

"That's it," I thought to myself.

"Would you ask the boy if he wanted some? The one sitting here next to you."

"You said you'd disappear," she answered, not even looking up. But then she turned her head toward the boy.

She didn't say anything.

I didn't need her to say anything. What I saw was enough.

"He likes you too," I observed.

It was odd to see her struggle. I'd say something else, Danny. Reading. If only human beings could read each other's mind. How much easier things would be, Danny. How much simpler life would be!"

Moonlight Face would have gladly asked Hirsute, what is it you like about me? And "which school are you going to?" And she would have gladly thrust the bottle in his hand, there, you must be thirsty. And she would have gladly taken some good photos to send to her girlfriend. "All right, what do you say to this? He's cool, isn't he?"

"But you don't even know him," I cut in.

"I don't want to know him," she answered and added quickly, "Keep your promise."

***

I jumped. I learned what I wanted to know. Hay. Or it wasn't a hopeless case. That was enough for me.

But the fact that both of Hirsute's ears were occupied, presented an obstacle to my plan. I didn't beat about the bush, I was hungry as a wolf. Anyway, I would pay the price later. I bit into his neck. I didn't care if he thought I was a mechanical bee or mosquito drone or whatever, what was important was that I get into his ear as soon as possible.

He slapped his neck. I barely escaped the blow. The next moment he did what I expected: he pulled the two plugs of his flat thing from his ear.

"It bit me."

I thought that was what he shouted, for as soon as I climbed into his ear, Moonlight Face turned our way and said,

"It's probably a flea."

"Wow!" I rubbed my legs together. If I had been in the girl's ear, I would have told her to add, "I hate them! They're a bloodthirsty lot." Or something like that. I had to face the fact that the pink vapour that had suddenly sprung up had turned to ashes. Hirsute nodded for a while, but the best words swirled around in him in vain; he couldn't stammer out a single one. I began to think that he was mute like those snails around the Cracked Fence, but it occurred to me that when he talked to me, the words did come out of his mouth after all. And now he was filled with the bitter green donkey-grey of anxiety.

I saw that he was about to stick the plug back into his ear. I shouted as loud as I could.

"Don't you put it back! I'm inside!"

His hand stopped in mid-air.

"Where were you?" he asked after a pause.

"Over there."

"With her?"

"With her."

"I saw her looking at me."

"Yes, at you."

"And?"

"Hay."

"What does that mean?"

"It all depends on you."

In the blink of an eye, fright and despair ran through him. He curled up like a frightened hedgehog. Again, I hit on an idea to salvage the situation. Had I wished to, I couldn't have come up with it on my own. Young Master and Red Fur appeared in my mind's eye, as well as the forked cell-phone.

I looked up at the sky, nodded gratefully, and only afterwards did I come up with,

"Do you have, *I want that doggy in the window?*"

"No."

"It doesn't matter. Do you have some other music?"

"How many gigabytes do you want?"

"What's that? Anyway, it doesn't matter. I don't want any. I want it for her."

"I saw her smartphone. She can't have much fewer on hers."

"It's all the same to me, do what I tell you."

It surprised even me when he willingly waited for my orders.

"Put your favourite song on it."

"I've got it," he replied after a while.

"I'm sitting here in your left ear. Put one of the plugs of your smart phones in your right ear, show the other to Sky-Blue Eyes. You don't have to say a single word."

That's what he did.

A groan wasn't much, but that was all that came from him.

I waited excitedly what the girl was going to do.

She turned toward Hirsute. She stared at the plug. Then she smiled. She lifted her eyes slowly to us, and thanks to Hirsute, I could feel the intensity of her sky-blue eyes. She took the plug between her delicate fingers and, pulling her thick hair away, stuck it into her ear.

Well, dear Danny, now all I had to do was find my way back to my lapdog. A flea is fallible, not only human beings. I settled in its ear, it bore it impassively. "You were right," I told it. "They weren't talking to each other."

But it didn't seem to be so important to tell it.

"Please, look up a bit and ahead."

It did so. I navigated until the new couple with the forked wire came into view. Now I could see both from the outside – there's no denying it, I was thrilled with delight – I finally thought of you, my dear friend. Only I didn't know how I was going to get back to you, so I could tell you all this.

"Don't worry," barked the lapdog. "I'll take you back."

"Good God! Can you read minds too?" I cried in amazement.

"Not at all," it replied. "You were talking to yourself."

Fourth Tale
THE EXCURSION

Danny, you won't believe where I was. I went on an excursion!

I was practically yawning from boredom, then I was hungry as a wolf. No one wanted to come close to the Nettle Stop; then, suddenly, an enormous crowd of fragrant smells came my way. It came walking slowly, idly, so I was free to choose among innumerable fragrant kids, a girl to tickle the nostrils, a man smelling of cheap cologne and, yes, a real full-blooded dog. Of course, I chose the latter. It seemed a rather excitable sort, but as I felt in the breeze that others were coming after it, I thought it was worth risking the leap. If I made it, I'd have a good day, but if not, I could make it better with the others coming after.

I don't have to tell you, I was successful. My lucky choice, a chestnut dachshund, had short legs and a long back, so I didn't have a hard time getting to my goal, although I didn't reckon on his ears hanging down, instead of sticking up. So, it was a bit complicated getting in. But it was worth it.

I found myself in the middle of the racket of a crowd of children. They were a lot like you, Danny. I thought of you that day. What would you have done in this terrifying situation?

It took me a while to find out where the group of holiday-makers that I had joined were headed. No wonder, since −

pardon me, Danny – nobody talks more than you people. You all talk at the same time, everybody says their piece, and not for all the world do they listen to the other person. Of course, this is a hundred times better than those two tongue-tied and colourless creatures on the blue bus. That is what made the kids' day, their ceaseless chirping. I could barely piece out the essence of their sparkling stories, no matter how much I wanted to.

In certain respects, a little kid is just like a flea. They can easily talk and tell stories above his head, and he acts as if he weren't even there. Then, at the first opportunity, he comes up with the worst horror stories to make himself the centre of attention, to make everyone look at him.

I have no idea why this is so important to them, but I can see that it is important.

They almost knocked over that fragrant girl. She must have been an attractive creature, for it wasn't only the kids who danced around her, but the dachshund too. All I can say is that she was wearing brogues, but her legs were bare, and a long pony tail swung on her head.

Oh yeah, and she was the dachshund's master. The dog's name was Dachsi.

So, a little boy with a bristly mop top, a Buck Teeth said,

"Ildiko, Ildiko! A child turned around a bit in Bible-class, the teacher went to him and told him to take off his glasses…"

A chubby little girl interjected enthusiastically:

"The math teacher at our school dangled a child outside the window."

Buck Teeth held his own.

"…and when the kid took off his glasses, he got such a slap in the face…"

But Chubby stood her ground too.

"…because he was playing with his telephone during class…"

Buck Teeth puffed out his cheeks and pointed at them with both hands.

"…his face swelled up *like this!*"

Ildiko listened patiently, nodded, then asked,

"At your school or in your class?"

She looked first at one, then at the other. Dachsi followed her eyes loyally.

"Does it matter?" I piped up. There was no denying it, I needed to say it. In my mind's eye I saw the little boy with the swollen face, then the one that had been dangled out of the window, as he struggled in fear. I was horrified: what inhumanity! Compared to these, we fleas with our nothing little bites were goodness itself.

Dachsi snapped at me at once. "Ildiko always knows what she's talking about."

"Well, at our school," began Buck Teeth. And Chubby joined him. "At our school."

"But not in your class," Ildiko pointed out.

"Not in our class," they both said at once.

"That is, neither of you saw it."

"I didn't see it, but I heard about it." Buck Teeth nodded.

"I didn't see it either, but heard about it too," Chubby insisted.

"I see." Ildiko smiled. "You know, children." She looked around kindly. "Horror stories quickly take wing and go around like lightning…"

At that moment a thunderous voice boomed out and hit Dachsi's ear; if I had had enough room, I would have jumped up in fright too.

"Don't stop! Don't stop! We have a long way to go to the lookout."

"Who's that?" I asked Dachsi.

"The squad leader."

"The one with the cheap cologne?"

"Yes."

"The husky one. Wearing a green tie."

"Yes, that one."

I could see immediately from the dark fragments that he didn't care for him.

"You aren't crazy about him, are you?"

"No, but don't tell anyone."

"He looks like a decent enough fellow."

"He is. He likes order."

"So?"

"I don't know."

"Is the lookout really that far?"

"Quite far."

"Then he's right, isn't he?"

"I don't like him anyway."

You know, Danny, I once heard an interesting saying, *"A dog is lost when he has a good thing going."* That is what occurred to me at Dachsi's growling. With us fleas, this is inconceivable. We've got no beef with someone who doesn't hurt us. If he does hurt us, we do have a beef.

We walked on toward the lookout.

Whether on one's own legs, or on others'…

These kids weren't schoolchildren to stand it for long without saying a word. A thin boy wearing glasses behind the girl with the pony tail, announced darkly:

"I almost died once."

The group stopped at once.

No wonder. Death, the destruction of another is shocking even to us fleas. At least, insofar as I am concerned. I was very curious as to what happened. I watched closely what came from Dachsi. I tried to gather the tiniest crumbs of sound and image. But I couldn't get anything sensible, for these kids – what a surprise! – weren't in the least interested in their mate "almost" dying. One of them pointed to his eye, which had almost been knocked out; another grabbed his hand, which had been broken in class last year; a third had a stone bigger than a football fall on his foot in summer camp. Their eyes blazed as if in a fever. The little kid with glasses became even gloomier. They didn't let him finish his story. He couldn't tell Ildiko; he couldn't share with the others how he had almost died.

Ildiko raised a finger to her mouth, put the other on Bespectacled's head, looked around and said,

"Let Balazs speak!"

At that moment, the one with the cheap cologne barked,

"Ildiko! Don't stop! Don't stop! It's a long way to the lookout."

"Just a moment. Let Balazs say what he'd like to so much."

"Not even for a minute! Everything in its own time. Time is short. We'll set up camp at the lookout. Discipline is important!" He shouted this behind him, setting an example of how they could talk even while walking.

"You see. This is why I don't like him," growled Dachsi.

"You're crazy about Ildiko," I observed.

He said nothing for a long time.

"That's one thing," he replied at last. "But he can't see outside his head."

"When there are so many little kids, there's always trouble with lack of discipline."

"As if he were talking."

"Isn't it true?"

He didn't reply.

I watched what he was thinking. A whirling gloom, with islands of light breaking through the gloom.

"Anyway," I added, "he's responsible for the kids. He'll be blamed if anything happened to them."

We walked on silently. He on his own legs, I sitting in his ear.

Barely a few steps further, Husky's voice hit us.

"Ildiko, shorten that leash a bit! Don't let that dog bite some careless child! You have to be especially careful with hunting dogs."

Without saying a word, Ildiko shortened the leash with the self-winding gadget, so Dachsi resented him even more. "I've never ever bitten a little kid in my life!" he whined, so that I took pity on him. Still, I had to say what I thought.

"You know that. But how should he know?"

"He could look into my eyes. Ildiko reads my mind by looking into my eyes."

"You don't say. Are there human beings who can read minds?"

"Ildiko can."

"Go tell it to the marines!" I snapped. I didn't believe it. How could she read minds from outside, when she wasn't sitting in his head? Totally absurd!

I could have easily looked into the matter, if I hadn't been so interested in Bespectacled's near-death. After turning it over in my mind, I said goodbye to Dachsi and went on my way.

I never arrived.

And yet when kids were in bunches, it wasn't a big deal to get to my chosen victim. Anyone can take a little bite, a little bit of feeding, I thought, and after a few pretty tasty stations, I thought I should be near Bespectacled. I clambered up my next lookout, then I popped into his ear to have a look around.

I became totally confused.

The racket the children made seemed to me twice as loud. A gang of kids was going up the mountain, another was descending it, and suddenly I no longer knew whether I had chosen a suitable carrier or whether I had accidentally jumped on one that was going back. When I saw Ildiko ahead of me, I calmed down.

Now I had only to aim at Bespectacled, I thought.

***

Did I ever tell you, my dear friend, how difficult it is to look in a chosen direction with someone else's head, and even more to look around. It isn't polite to lay into a carrier that is doing you a favour, to say to them, all right, I'm just a flea, please will you turn your head. I chose to take an opportune moment and leap onto Ildiko, and hop down her bare arms to the automatic gadget, and, like a spider – oh, how disgusting! – I inched all the way across the leash to Dachsi's neck. I manoeuvred myself into his ungainly ear.

"I'm back," I announced.

"I know."

"Will you find me the one with glasses?"

"There are several."

"Balazs." To make sure. "The one who almost died."

He swivelled his head. Twice he scanned those going uphill, but our kid wasn't there.

Dachsi stopped, raised his head and sniffed the air quickly here and there.

Ildiko pulled on him, gently urging him for a while, then she too stopped. That was all Husky needed.

"Don't stop! Don't stop! We're not at the lookout yet."

"Dachsi is trying to tell us something," Pony Tail shouted back, apprehensively, and pointed at us.

I don't need to tell you, the kids' inexhaustible imagination swung into action again. It was as if Dachsi had signalled to them that the way was clear for all who could come up with the biggest absurdity.

"The Turks are coming!"

"Wild boars!"

"Bandits!"

"They're going to rob us!"

"Let's run!"

And some frightened, others laughing, were about to run in all directions.

"Stop! Stop!" yelled Husky.

From then on, they came up with new ideas more quietly and with more restraint.

"He smelled a wolf den."

"He found a cave."

"A carcass."

"A corpse."

"Children." Ildiko spoke up, in a dull repressed voice. "Be quiet! Dachsi wants to say something."

I thought if I could I would see what he wanted to say.

But I wasn't any the wiser.

As he sniffed the air, the evanescent image of the rocky mountain path, and the figures of the man and children mixed with colourful and volatile patches reminiscent of wild animals. At first it was as if it were a wild boar looming into view, then deer, fox, even a skinny dog, and a thin cat. Where the wind came up, and the mysterious images changed even more quickly, they appeared and disappeared. One thing was sure: the figure of the kid with glasses didn't loom into view, and didn't show up at all.

"Something is troubling him," Ildiko observed.

"Tell him, we've lost all trace of Bespectacled," I urged Dachsi.

My dachshund suddenly whirled round and went back sniffing. He pulled on the leash determinedly, pulling his mistress with him.

"It looks like we've lost something," shouted Ildiko. "Everybody, see if you aren't missing something. If you haven't left your backpack when you were taking a piss."

"Maybe your pisser," said Chubby, making a noisy hit with the group.

At that moment, Husky had enough.

"If he's lost it, he's lost it. There's a crumb of comfort. Off to the lookout! And now we're not going to stop for any reason or any excuse. We'll get there in one impulse, we'll take the heights. Get going! Get a move on! Come on, Ildiko! Come on, Dachsi!"

I was about to think that there was nothing to do; we had to get moving to inform Ildiko somehow of the sad situation. Perhaps she saw it in Dachsi's eyes, or it simply struck her. In any event, she cried,

"Where's Balazs? I don't see Balazs."

From then on events whirled like the wind.

Husky lined up the kids and, without taking a breath, asked, "Who was the one who saw Balazs last? Where? When? How many minutes ago? Who was he walking with? Did he say something? Was he getting ready for something? Well?"

The kids raised their eyebrows and shrugged their shoulders; they probed each other, then Ildiko, finally Husky, and fell silent.

"Odd," I observed to Dachsi. "Nobody remembers anything. As if he hadn't been with them."

"Ildiko could say why this is."

"Oh yeah. Ildiko can't even say where he's got to. I think you overestimate her."

Dachsi didn't answer. He rubbed against Ildiko's legs, thus signalling that he would do what he could to help.

The blood left Ildiko's face, but she controlled herself. In a choked voice, she said only,

"I know he's all right."

"That's precious little right now, Ildiko. We must solve this. If I understood right, Balazs wanted to tell us that he almost died. It is dangerous and irresponsible to toy with a child's soul, to stir up the wounds of infancy. It may have been nothing, but he thought it important, dramatic and we were pouring oil on the fire, making things worse."

"Stand your ground, Ildiko," growled Dachsi, and nudged his mistress.

Husky immediately pointed at us; I had the feeling that he could see me and was talking to me.

"Finally, we can use Dachsi's hunting instincts. Go get him, Dachsi. You children shout, Balazs."

"Wait a moment," interjected Ildiko, it was obvious she wanted to say something, but Husky shouted her down.

"We can't wait, Ildiko. Every minute is a loss, every lost minute increases the danger that Balazs gets lost, climbs up the quarry, goes down into the cave, falls into a precipice, falls off the lookout. You've been here before, you know that every irresponsible act and time lost brings its own punishment.

Ildiko grew even paler if that was possible. There was no denying it, I liked the way Husky was so decisive and logical, even to my flea brain. Still, I began to feel sorry for Ildiko. She may not have been right, but I felt very strongly, perhaps thanks to Dachsi, that she was basically full of good intentions, and deserved my assistance. I told Dachsi to stay close to his mistress, for I didn't want to walk up the length of the leash again. I wanted to go to her.

But my curiosity didn't allow me to set off right away. Events were spinning on, and when I'm on my way, I can't hear or see anything. Husky wanted to take hold of Dachsi's automatic reel. The kids crowded around, shouting that they wanted to see the quarry, the cave, and the precipice, and demanding that they call the helicopters, so they could rescue the injured one. Ildiko shouted for the first time, forcing not only the kids but even Husky to stop.

"Stop! Stop! You must understand something. First, Dachsi can't help now, there's been such a commotion here, a cavalcade of scents, that it's impossible to filter out Balazs's. Not even if we had something of Balazs's for him to sniff. Secondly…"

"Secondly?"

"Secondly…"

"All right, Ildiko, you'll tell us later," Husky interrupted impatiently, and raised his arms like a conductor. "All right, children, I'll count to three and you shout as loud as you can, Balazs! One, two, three."

"Balaaaaaazs!" The pack of children filled the forest with their shouting.

"Here I am," answered a child's voice, as he appeared in the bend of the forest path.

It was Balazs. A young creature like Ildiko, wearing a green tie, held his hand, and with the other hand pushed the glasses up his nose.

"I've brought back the little lamb that strayed away." His escort smiled and added, "He joined us somehow when the two troops of children were walking next to each other. I would have brought him sooner, but he really wanted to tell us something. Please excuse me."

"It's all right," Ildiko replied at once. "We thank you for bringing him back." She went up to Bespectacled and embraced him gently. "We're glad our little stray lamb has returned."

"Long live Balazs! Long live Balazs!" Chubby shouted and the kids joined in.

"Come on," interrupted Husky, "let's not cheer the one who brought the trouble on us." He tried to catch his breath. "The next time any child can go wherever he pleases, and does what he thinks is right. It was purely by accident that we noticed Balazs's absence, we stopped, and didn't go in all directions. It was purely by chance that we didn't go off in one direction or other. And it was purely by chance that he didn't leave the other group, didn't go off into the woods by himself, didn't fall into a precipice, and something really bad, irreversible, and unpardonable happened. Balazs should be punished instead, so that he and you too must learn that you are responsible for each other."

Well, my dear friend, I have to say that I agreed with Husky again. His every word was right. Logic itself. At least so it seemed to me. To the others too. At first the children ran joyfully toward their lost comrade, now they sidled back to Husky. Only Balazs, Ildiko and Dachsi stayed in a bunch. I only because I was in Dachsi's ear. One more thing. To tell you the truth, I was dying to hear what the heck the little kid was so eager to tell us.

Husky ordered that each child take the hand of the one next to him or her and not let go until we reached the lookout. Ildiko should take Balazs's hand and not let it go. Then he ordered us to get going at once, so I couldn't hesitate for an instant; I had to jump immediately. Unless I wanted to inch along the leash like a spider.

In the blink of an eye, I was sitting on Ildiko's deliciously fragrant bare leg. I thought it would be easy to climb over from her bare arms to Bespectacled, but as I was climbing up, the "secondly" flashed into my mind. I wouldn't be a flea if I weren't so keen on hearing what Ildiko had to say. I didn't hesitate, I sat into her ear and said to her,

"Ildiko, my dear…"

Well, my dear friend, Danny, I must tell you, I had never encountered such a spirit, such a fine and pure soul as Ildiko's. Of course, yours can be like hers, but you need to grow a lot first.

You know, for me God exists inherently, we could say, self-evidently. Without him I could not, a nothing little flea could not possibly rummage through the minds and souls of human beings. I discovered such a deep faith in Ildiko, that it touched even my little flea soul.

Let us start with Ildiko replying thus,

"Yes, sir…"

It was not as if she were speaking to the Lord God, for no image referring to this appeared in her head. She said it, on the contrary, as someone who believed that one who speaks sweetly, speaks lovingly. And love was everything.

What should I say? I marvelled. That details the size of a flea didn't interest her; she had faith in the big whole…

I wasn't like that, and I couldn't stop myself from introducing myself and explaining the purpose of my presence.

"I am a tiny flea. I am sitting in your ear. I would like to know, what you meant by the 'secondly'? What would you like to have said? And why didn't you say it?"

She went right in without beating about the bush.

"I stopped, because I realised that there are truths that can be experienced, believed, but cannot be communicated. I can't communicate to them that life is an immense and marvellous trust. I could not tell them that if a child disappears, then perhaps... something wonderful might happen to him."

"You can't communicate this, of course," I cut in. "For the most terrible thing could have happened to him just as well."

"Theoretically, yes," she said gently.

"Theoretically?" I said dumbfounded. "Even I know with my tiny flea mind that it's true in practice too. In reality too. I was just dining on a hedgehog when some immense dreadful thing crushed it to death. I escaped intact. So, is it the theory? And I the practice?"

"Well, yes. You see, that's why I stopped. The good is silent. The bad pushes itself forward, it threatens and shouts. How could I outshout them with quiet words that twenty-four children out of the twenty-five had not disappeared? Nothing bad had happened to twenty-five out of the twenty-five. And the twenty-fifth wouldn't have left us, if we had listened to him. And the bad that had happened to him wouldn't have happened. Are you with me?"

"Of course, I'm just trying to understand."

"I think that it can only be sensed. Not even my parents and grandparents understand. I went on a boating trip of several days. They pleaded with me not to go, for the weatherman warned of storms and heavy rain throughout the country. They were very anxious, because there were indeed thunderstorms and a lot of rain."

"They went on the trip?"

"Of course not."

"So why were they wet and cold?"

"They weren't. They were afraid, and they feared for me. Every blessed day they followed the weather reports on the radio and television. These broadcast only news about storms and showers, but never about before and after what a splendid sunny summer we had."

"But Balazs's disappearing isn't a wonderful summer."

"But is it a fatal storm? Here I am holding his hand, and we are walking peacefully next to each other."

"It isn't your responsibility if something terrible happened to him."

"Whose is it then? Why do you suppose he wants something bad to happen?"

Honestly, dear Danny, I tell you, I was getting confused. Although I didn't understand it yet, I was beginning to grasp Ildiko's special attitude. My tiny flea brain kept on protesting. I insisted to her, my hedgehog perished. And to not reckon on possible trouble was like sticking our heads into sand. It's irresponsible!

"Imagine, Ildiko," I explained to her, "what if Balazs's mother had dropped in and she saw that you adults were expecting cheerfully, hugely confident that Balazs would come back by himself. Wouldn't she think that her son's life wasn't important to you? And if something bad had happened, wouldn't she think about reporting the squad leader for serious irresponsibility and negligence? Now, with the children shouting for Balazs as loud as they could, and they were ready to send a hunting dog after him, he must have proved to you and others what a responsible man he was."

"All right, little flea. Now you understand everything. That is exactly why I said no more."

I thought I had ruined Ildiko's good mood. But as I looked inside her head, it didn't seem like that at all. A wonderfully lovely colourful enchantment swam in her, the kind that was very difficult to escape. How did I finally bring myself to do it? This must be like when the man couldn't resist the forbidden fruit, when he plucked the fruit from the tree of knowledge. By hook or by crook I had to know how little Balazs almost died.

Fortunately, despite the "forced march", we had a little time before we got to the lookout. So, I was able to get from Ildiko to Bespectacled.

***

"Hmm." That was all I said to him. I wanted to map out the changes that appeared on his trace. Would he be frightened, or would he receive it with indifference? "Who was that, what was that?" Clearly, he was waiting for what happened next.

"Could you tell me how you almost died?"

"Do you really want to know?"

"Yes. Really."

Suddenly everything went dark in front of me.

A terrible screeching of brakes, sharp and painful screaming, a little coat stretched out like the wings of a butterfly.

"I was three years old."

"What happened?"

"A car came. I didn't see it and ran out on the street. My grandmother grabbed me by my coat. I pulled out of the coat. I felt the car. Its wind hit me. My grandmother could never get up again. And she kept saying that I almost died. And it was her fault. But it was my fault."

"Did you say something?" Ildiko asked, looking down on us.

"It was my fault."

"Are you talking to someone?"

"Yes, I am."

"I'm very glad."

"He says he understood something."

"What?"

"He says that it can't be an accident that if someone has a very difficult time, they say that he has undergone a lot of trials."

"For sure." Ildiko smiled.

"He says every difficulty in life is a trial. Only one who isn't overcome by the difficulty can reach the realm of basic trust."

"He said, '*basic trust*'?"

"He said, yes, that's what he said. And he said that it was not my fault that I almost died, for it was an important door to the realm of basic trust. Do you understand this?" Bespectacled looked at Ildiko.

"Yes, of course I understand," answered Pony Tail. "I'm sure you will understand it someday."

***

Well, my dear Danny, that is what happened on this strange excursion. I was so tired that I slept all the way back. When we arrived here, in your realm, I said to Balazs, I have to say goodbye. He asked me to stay with him. He would even feed me if I needed to eat. Just stay. "I would gladly stay," I answered him, "but my dear little friend is expecting me." And you should know, Danny, it's good to know that you are glad when I come, and you listen to my stories with pleasure. I'll disappear for now, to fetch the next one. We'll meet at the Cracked Fence.

Fifth Tale
THE CIRCUS

I was the one who regretted the most, dear Danny, that I couldn't come sooner, but I fell into the deepest rings of hell. Promise me that as long as you live, you will never set foot in a circus. Especially a flea circus!

No! You're not right. It wasn't curiosity that led me there. I was the victim of a real crime.

First of all, that ugly big man, the ring-master, uses his own dogs to entice fleas. Can you imagine what kind of animal abuse that is? Not only does he not put a flea collar on them, but he intentionally allows fleas to proliferate on them, because we are quicker to sniff out a dog that has wounds and scratches itself. What is this but a trap? What is this but pure inhumanity?

Then the way he caught me!

In the pitch dark he threw over us a densely woven white sheet…You know, the kind they put on a small child's wound. Yes, gauze. So, he let me flounder in it until it wound itself around me so that I couldn't even move. Then they flooded us with light. I couldn't see a thing. I thought to myself, flea, this is the end. Say goodbye to your life. How could I have known that the really hard part was yet to come?

He caught me by the scruff of my neck through the net. I felt that he had incredibly skilful, experienced fingers, because when he caught me, I could neither swallow nor spit. I could hear the ominous cracking of my armour, although I didn't know whether I was dead or alive, when in my dazed state I saw a pipe like a hedgehog's quills coming closer. I got a shot from this quill, some disgusting, wet material. It hissed, like that Ugly Diri's smelly underarm jell, so I didn't come to until I found myself in the first torture chamber.

Oh, you poor thing, I frightened you. I don't know if I should tell you this story?

All right, I'll go on.

If only to prevent you from ever getting into such a trap.

Anyway, aren't I here? Calm down. Here I am, fresh as a daisy. Of course, truth be told, I wasn't fresh at all. I staggered and reeled. And when I could finally have a look around, I didn't notice anything unusual at first. I was in a glass cage. Very long and very narrow. I thought I had been put in there by mistake. I would have understood if they killed me, out of revenge for the blood feast. But I had never heard of anyone dining on a flea. Then why? Why did he catch me? Why did he make me a prisoner?

It's logical, isn't it?

If I'm here by mistake, I thought to myself, then perhaps the long corridor was the way out. I took a few steps and listened carefully. Nothing. It didn't look like there was any obstacle or danger. I didn't even sense any human nearness. So then, let's go.

After the first jump, I realised what the inhuman torture consisted of. But then I hadn't the faintest idea what this was all about.

Have you ever fallen down the stairs? Have you ever fallen off the scooter on your face?

What am I saying?

That's why your front milk teeth are missing.

That's why you have a scar on your knee.

That's why you have the scar on your elbow.

So, I knew what it was to hit your head, so you see stars. The glass cage was as flat as it was long. If I tried to jump, ding-ding, ding-ding. I kept hitting my head. And if I tried to climb, I saw myself as disgusting and as small as the lowest crab-louse. If I wanted to escape, I had no choice but to swallow my pride – I had to crawl, slither, creep, inch forward with no end in sight.

The thing that I feared most came to pass.

After labouring bitterly, I hit a wall again. A glass plate sealed the end of the corridor. In front, behind, above, below, everywhere, there was a glass wall. You won't guess why.

To make me quit jumping.

To make me drag this deuce of a big gold rig.

So big, you can't even imagine how big. About twenty thousand times my size. It's as if they'd tied you to a ten-story high-rise building and they'd shouted at you, all right, let's go, pull it to the end of the garden. Or what they did to me, a knock on the table, a knock on my head. One on the table, one on the head. When Ugly Diri took me to the flea circus, and showed what I and the other unfortunates could do, he didn't beat us about the head, of course, as how would that look? It would be clear instantly what an abuser of animals that perfectly dressed ring-master with perfect manners was. All he had to do was to knock on the table and we immediately set to dragging our rolling torture chamber. If we had had a decent harness like what I once saw on a seeing-eye dog, it might have been tolerable. But they just looped a wire around us. As if they had wound a piece of wood as thick as these here, beside us, around you. How could anyone survive that?

I did, but just barely...

***

I would gladly boast about my sharp mind, because, you see, I finally did manage to escape. But I don't like to lie to anyone, much less myself. No matter how many people I bury myself into, I see what a big plan they had for their life. I only must burrow a little into their head, and it turns out at once that they had been shepherded into a bypass, as many times as their life slipped off the tracks. Or he had to get his life back on track. You have a good saying, man proposes, God disposes. But no matter how many wise sayings there are, humans again and again come to, and immediately set off in a sure direction. And then they're surprised they've fallen on their face yet again.

And if that can happen to a big person, then what can a wretched little tiny flea say?

Soon they put three more of my fellow sufferers in the cage. The same thing happened to these three fleas. As soon as they came to, they tried to jump quickly to the end of the corridor, but after hitting themselves a few times, they soon descended to crawling like lice. So, I didn't see when or how they got there, perhaps it could have helped me in my attempts to escape. Where there's an entrance, there's also an exit. I crawled through the cage three times, but I couldn't find any sign of an exit.

It was not only me, but also my fellows. I saw that they all gave up after a few tries. They just sat there along the glass wall, silent and motionless.

My next plan was to play dead when they came for me. They'll think, all right, this one's had it. He can't even move, they'll hit me, knock on me, and I'll play dead. And just when they least expect it, suddenly, I'll jump up. Only they picked me up with tweezers, and before I realised what was happening, I was a prisoner again. And I may have had the strongest and most elastic legs in the world, dear Danny; all I could do was wriggle helplessly in the air.

The worst of it was that I still had no idea who they were and what they wanted of me. This was a pressing and suffocating question under any circumstances, even if you aren't clamped in a vice or caught in a snare, but in this case, it was particularly difficult to keep my spirits up. I didn't even know who or what I had to fight against. Or for whom or for what. Our strength and resolve can be multiplied if we know clearly what is our task, not to mention the mission we must accomplish. Now, when they passed the noose over me, in vain the thought flashed that I should vamoose now. I should gather all my strength, I should slip out of this terrible yoke, but my body refused to obey me. I didn't grasp yet that they had tied me to an enormous rig, that I would be forced to drag a gold rig. Not to mention the other things. I felt the exhalation of a dozen small children and a few adults. I especially felt the overpowering scent of a rose that swirled around me constantly, but at that time I hadn't yet got the picture: that we were being shown off on a tiny circus ring before an amazed and delighted audience. Some of them watched our ungainly dancing, whirling around on a merry-go-round, not to mention our playing with that disgusting ball. A smelly ball was pushed under our noses. Caught in a noose, we kicked and flung ourselves about desperately, so we eventually hit the light, white ball, which then went through the gate that had been placed there to the audience's delighted cheering.

By the time I was aware of this, I was sitting in Ugly Diri's ear.

Until then I had to live through many very sad days.

To be more precise, they weren't so many.

***

You know, Danny, by the time I became a grown-up, I've become less prone to taking the liberty of thinking about what I've experienced already and what kind of good advice I can give you. For example, how you should navigate your way through life. Now I would tell you if you find yourself in a similar situation, don't think about escape, don't mind that you're a captive, or that you're being tortured, that you're in a wire harness and they've given you a hedgehog to feed on. You just eat what you can eat, sleep soundly when you can sleep, and do what they ask you to do when you step into the ring. I can only tell you what happened to me, but what concerns you is up to you or your God.

One thing is for sure: if through some miracle you could have stood there above me in those days, and watched what I did or didn't do, you would have decided that I had given up, that I had resigned myself to everything. I just sat there silent, bitter, inert, hollowed out in spirit, and waiting for my last hour. And you would not have noticed – for you couldn't have noticed – that although I had stopped my feverish planning, searching for the exit, something had changed radically in me. A calm came over me, that was inexplicable even to me. Let me not say, a quiet serenity. I would gladly tell you how to do it, but I haven't a clue. For it really did come by itself, without clear antecedents or signals. What I can tell you is that it was an awakening thought that came from afar, slowly, trickling into me slowly. Or it would be better to call it a feeling. I had not heard a kind of distant sound, but it wasn't even a kind of logic that led me to that realisation. It became embedded in me with a kind of serene dignity.

And it made it clear without any kind of reasoning or explanation: I must not try to escape my fate. Speaking metaphorically: I had to stay in my cage. But not in servitude. In dignity. In this way, you can create your own state of freedom.

Do you understand?

I experienced it, I am telling you, but even I barely understand it. On the one hand, it was wondrous, on the other, incredible and incomprehensible. To be completely at the mercy of the whims of a crackpot, closed off from the outside world, from the gorgeous realm of liberty, trapped in a narrow glass cage, to build and enjoy your own free world? Totally absurd.

And yet, I sensed that something had changed radically. I wasn't on my own anymore. Abandoned. Not because I would have liked to believe this, and not because I had seen some divine vision. No, it came naturally, self-evidently. Suddenly I became part of something, and existed as a part, that I had always been a part of, only it had been deeply hidden to me.

Since I have always experienced every blessed moment that I was not alone, that there was nothing to do but wait. For a sign, for something unexpected to happen, or for my final destruction.

Ugly Diri had a favourite number. He pretended that a flea had escaped, straight into the audience, and he threw himself after it. With a long pair of tweezers in his hand. Of course, the flea hadn't escaped, as I couldn't manage to escape either, when he did this number with me. I wiggled in the cruel grip of his tweezers, but nobody in the audience was aware of this. Children and adults, both backed up in alarm, or leaped up out of their chairs when Ugly Diri looked at them, flailing about holding his tweezers high. He chose a kid with mouth agape or a young mother easy on the eye, and suddenly touched their ear or neck with the tip of the tweezers, and shouted, "I've got it. I caught it." And he showed us as proof.

And it was then that the penny dropped, it had all been a joke. They laughed heartily. Nobody in the world gave a hoot that they had almost snuffed us out with those damn tweezers.

Now, on one such an occasion, something happened that I couldn't help in the least. For when they threw me into someone's ear, and I caught the delicate scent, without a moment's hesitation, I cried out, "The flea can speak." I haven't a clue why I said that. I knew only that I *had* to say it.

Namely, how in the world could I have known that my benefactor, as it turned out, was a little boy barely older than you? He then said out loud, almost shouting, repeating my words,

"The flea can speak."

That was how I escaped.

***

It took a few days, but things were back on track. I gathered together tiny memory crumbs, thought splinters of what happened at that decisive moment.

Every head turned toward the little boy, every eye looked at him.

Ugly Diri smiled graciously. "Of course, he speaks. All my fleas can talk. I'll ask him right away, how he is." And he held me in the sure grip of the tweezers and shouted, articulating slowly, "How are you, my dear flea?" Then, placing me next to his ear, he pretended to wait for my answer. No, if he was waiting for it, he got it. Namely, I felt from his odour, that he was my man, that he had held me captive and tortured me from time immemorial.

"Your mother!"

I was about to say something much fancier, but I didn't lower myself. Even so, his face turned an angry reddish green, and I felt that he would crush me with his metal teeth. Fortunately, his venal side intervened, after his first shock and anger, his face turned into a beaming smile. He quickly bid the audience farewell, and announced that he expected them gladly at the next performance, then with his talking flea.

***

This Ugly Diri had a training room. Just big enough to allow a flea a respectable jump in this direction, and that, so that if his concentration lapsed at any time during the training and one of us took advantage of it and escaped, he could catch it in the white-washed room.

The only piece of furniture (other than his armchair) covered in a white sheet, was a heavily laden work table. He just sat there as he lifted me by the metal tweezers to his ear and cautiously inserted me, and waited for something to happen.

"La-la-la." That was all I said, half singing.

He got excited as he listened.

But I kept silent to get his attention.

The picture of a microphone appeared in his head, and two enormous loudspeakers, then the flea held by the tweezers mouthing into the microphone.

Why, why not, I began to hum. My flea song, which you, my dear Danny, know very well.

A big-nosed flea
invited himself over
to our house forever
For lunch and for dinner.

If you could have seen what golden colours came to him. He stood there with the microphone, beaming with joy. He waved his arms, receiving the hurrahs, the cheering of an enormous, flamboyant crowd.

I said to him out loud,

"If you don't let me go, I'll never say another word."

If you could have seen the horror that came over him at once. He looked back, making sure the door was closed, then he took me out of his ear and put me down on the white tablecloth. After some hesitation, he released me from the tweezers.

I was free again.

At least I had made a great leap toward freedom.

I knew that if I behaved now like every normal flea, I would never escape from the training room alive. I did not engage in frantic scrambling, but I staggered here and there for a while, then suddenly I jumped. I landed on him in one great leap, and before his heart stopped beating from fright, I quickly sat in his ear and curtly informed him,

"Ready for training."

Within minutes, again golden colours whirled and rushed to him…

From then on, my sufferings were over. I could come and go as I pleased, though I considerately showed myself frequently to reassure him. I danced and whirled around on the sheet, there right under his nose. I often returned to his ear for a bit of singing and gabbing. Instead of a live hedgehog, he offered his own arm for me to dine on. I accepted though with a certain amount of repugnance. I didn't wish to arouse any suspicions.

I lulled any suspicion to the point that he took me with him away from the training room before going to bed at night. I kept talking nonstop, while staying alert. He walked around whistling and even took me into the bathroom, not only at night but unfortunately even in the morning. I thought I was going to die when he sprayed that dreadful rose scent on himself. I don't have to tell you I bore it all without a word.

The next day he spent in the training room, in front of a shiny screen. Out of curiosity I sat in his ear to see what he wanted. If he hadn't held me prisoner, I would have laughed. He was looking for tiny gadgets that would have amplified my speaking and singing for an audience.

As the hours passed, he began to wake up to the bitter reality: that this miracle, this genuine flea miracle could only be his, his own private entertainment and wasn't for anyone else. If he could have put me into the ear of each individual member of the audience at the flea circus, that would have worked. But it was entirely up to me whether I spoke or kept silent. And if I spoke up, what I would say. If he threatened me or tried to force me, I might blurt out the torments he put us through, and he wouldn't know anything about it.

His disappointment made me act quickly. I left his ear, showed myself on the tablecloth, then leaped off the table. I knew my way about enough to get behind him unawares and jump up cautiously on his trouser leg and overcoat and reach his ear. I slipped in noiselessly.

I reckoned right.

Or perhaps I should say that my intuition was right.

Or even better, if they want to rescue you, you will be saved. If you help yourself, you will be helped. But if they don't want you to be saved, you can be the smartest in the world and you won't succeed.

As you can see, here I am.

Though he searched for me everywhere from top to bottom.

He put a rolled-up rug before the closed door.

He pulled down the blinds, turned off the lights, and with a flashlight scanned the room, from floor to ceiling.

He gathered all his flea jars, training tools, and covered them carefully, then took out the damned hisser. Yes, that thing that had stupefied me on the first day. He pressed a dishcloth to his nose, then sprayed the room thoroughly. I got a hit, but only enough to make me dizzy for a moment.

Ugly Diri examined the room inch by inch. He lay on the floor, stood on the chair, looked into every hole, dug into every little crack and fissure.

Finally, he punched the table, making the little bottles clatter under the tablecloth. Deep in my soul I felt my wretched fellows' fright.

There was no denying it, I was sorry to leave them behind. Though I didn't feel it was my job to free them. Or save them. Surely a brave, self-sacrificing flea would come into the world one day, if it hadn't been born yet. But I'm not like that. It doesn't hurt for us to be aware of our limitations. And our tasks tailored to our limitations.

That is why I didn't think I had to save Ugly Diri's dog either. If it was shameful or not, I prayed only that Ugly Diri would resign himself to the fact that he had lost all trace of me for good. And that he would take his flea-collector dog for a walk.

***

The rest I think you've already guessed, my dear friend. Perhaps not what I feel inside, I will never again be the flea I was. Though not because I was a prisoner, and escaped only with great effort. This can happen to anyone, after all. The miracle was that I became free, though a prisoner. That was the most unforgettable miracle, my little friend.

Sixth Tale
THE PARTY

You won't guess who I met, dear Danny? I was getting acquainted with the fragrance of these wonderful red flowers at the Poppy Estate, and relaxed as I was, I played with the thought of how well I could hide among the stigmas and stamens if need be, when I caught a familiar odour. "What's this, what's this?" I searched feverishly in my memory, but as it didn't come to mind quickly, I let it go. I had already forgotten it, when the familiar odour hit my nose again.

I jumped toward it quickly, then took another leap. The face of a sad dog flashed in my mind.

Of course. It was Red Fur.

Wonder what he was up to?

I quickly jumped up on his back, fought my way through the clumped-up fur, and climbed into his ear, that cosy place.

"What's up, my old friend? Is everything OK?"

If you could have seen how happy he was.

You know, that's a good feeling. I would have gladly patted his back. But as I couldn't, I just bantered with him.

"Don't tell me, your blood pressure is too high? Should I tap it a bit?"

Gaily, he took off, and in no time, we were near Young Master. He leaped about him happily. Young Master didn't know what to make of it.

"Toffee. What's got into you?"

"Why don't you go over to him?" asked Red Fur. "He'd be glad of it."

I didn't need much urging. A few healthy jumps and I was sitting in his ear.

"What's up, Young Master?" I greeted him. "Everything OK?"

"Is it you, Jimmy Jumper?"

Did you hear, Danny?

Jimmy Jumper.

Just say it.

Can you feel how lovely it sounds? What an honour for a nothing little creature? A flea the size of dust? A born blood-sucker?

I answered, almost touched.

"Yes, it's me." After a pause, I added, "I see that you're in a good mood."

"No school tomorrow. Tonight, we're going to party. Hooray!"

"Party?" I asked, uncomprehending.

"Birthday party. We are celebrating a classmate. Lots to eat, lots of drink, lots of fun."

"Sounds good."

"And how! Hooray!"

Such gorgeous colours rushed forth in his head, that I went yellow from envy. Though, God can see my soul, it isn't my habit. Everyone, human being and flea have their own life tailored to them, their own path, a lot of trouble comes from not realising it. Anyway, if Young Master went, Toffee would be glad I stayed with him, and at least I could be sure of dinner that day. The desire to go to the party proved stronger.

"Young Master, can't I go with you?"

He couldn't catch his breath from surprise.

"What are you thinking? You'll sit down at the table with us? A slice of pizza, a piece of cake, a glass of cola? Or you'll dine on us?"

I raised one leg and vowed.

"I vow on my life that I won't bite anyone."

"But you'll meddle in our game."

"I promise I won't."

"Then why come?"

"I've never been to a party," I said dreamily. This didn't change his mind.

"What's fun for us, is deadly dull for you. What's fun for you, is deadly dull for us."

I was forced to beg.

"Oh, please, let me go with you. Nobody other than you will even know that I'm there. It doesn't matter to you, but it means a lot to me."

I could see that he was hesitating.

"All right. You can come," he said. "I hope I won't be sorry."

I didn't understand.

"About what?"

"I mean, you will keep your word, and there won't be any trouble. It would be naff if I weren't invited again because of you."

***

I felt the same thing, Danny. For that same reason I decided to try harder than ever to be a simple contemplative. An outsider. Or insider. If I were given the divine gift of sitting in a box seat in which I can share in others' joy, and there was no reason for me to launch into personal actions. I would share in their pleasures with them and through them. As if I were watching a film.

Nevertheless, why deny it, Young Master's alarm was flattering. I, a tiny insignificant little flea, how could I cause a disturbance among a gang of teenagers.

Absurd.

Thought I. Until that evening.

***

It was still light when we arrived. The trip took a long time; we snaked up the mountain on a blue bus and walked for about ten minutes until we reached a two-story house with a garden. It was odd, sitting in an ear and to see the poppies, plantains, wild rose bushes in their fullness: they were resplendent, though I missed the usual view of their magical tracery and masterly designs.

Young Master's eyes scanned the name board, until he stopped on one. He pressed a button next to it and a distant voice of a boy answered:

"Who are you?"

"Stan."

"Hello, Stan."

"Hello, Kenny, is Cartman there yet?"

"You should know that pedestrians have priority. Leave the gate open behind you? OK?"

"OK."

I decided way ahead of time that upon our arrival I would suspend my questions and pretend not to be there. I could not even watch a film, if the performers were constantly being disturbed. Although it's at least as bad, if we don't know who's who, who is saying what and why. I could not stop myself from asking Young Master as we went in.

"Don't be angry, but since when are you Stan? And who's this Kenny? And who's Cartman?"

"Of course," he neighed. "You don't know South Park. There aren't many other than you who can say that about themselves. It's a hit worldwide. He started to talk very fast as if he were being pursued. *"The performers of our film are invented characters. Profanity can be heard, we don't recommend it for any age."* I'm an imaginary character. One of the main characters of South Park. Kenny is the other one. Kyle is another. Cartman is the fourth. They're coming too."

"So, there are four of you."

"Oh no, another boy is coming and three girls, but they're not players. Just classmates."

It soon became clear why they were needed at all.

You could hear car doors slamming outside. Kenny and Stan (that is, Young Master) ran to the open windows and watched who was coming from their observation post on the third floor. First Kyle, then Cartman clambered out, they clapped and shouted down to them: *"Hello, Kyle. Hello, Cartman. It's going to be a big battle."* When the rest of the guests, three young girls, and a tall, thin little boy emerged, up

95

there four hands clapped, overjoyed that the enemy had arrived.

For a moment my heart stopped beating. I didn't say a word. It flashed in my mind, however, that after the three cars turned around, we were wholly without adult supervision, but I felt that was OK. Even though the thought occurred to me, where were Kenny's mother and father? Of course, I wasn't going to ask Young Master.

One thing was for sure, that a set table awaited us, laden with snacks and munchies, bottles of cola and cartons of fruit juice. How crazy is this flea? When Stan scanned the table, I saw that there was a chair at each end, there were three chairs on each side, and I quickly calculated that came to eight. And I was capable of taking offence that I didn't have one. I laughed inwardly and continued to observe. Kenny smiling broadly, accepted the mysterious gifts in paper bags of various sizes. He didn't take them out, but made a juicy comment about each one. "Wow! That's bitching." Thereupon he asked the guests to come to the table. I enjoyed the adult, skilful way he did it. The others complied.

"We'll fill ourselves up with energy, then the fun and games can begin."

"Will there be war?" A girl's eyes lit up, on the other side of the table. Her face was square, and even sitting, her movements were square. And if I can observe to clarify subsequent developments, she was developing a full bosom.

Kenny smiled.

"Let's just say we are accomplishing a mission. Dad got the weapons, everybody gets ten bullets, we too and you too."

"Will I be with the girls?" asked Marko.

The tall thin boy was called Marko. He was constantly smoothing his hair carefully, or at least while thinking.

Somebody guffawed.

"Don't you go wanking off."

I had to wait for Young Master to turn toward him, to determine that it was Cartman. Not a tall boy, but all the wider, with swelling arm and leg muscles, and short bristly hair. The four players neighed, the girls shrieked. Marko sniggered in embarrassment.

I understood the film less and less.

Nevertheless, I waited excitedly for the continuation.

"And what will our mission be?" asked another little girl, next to Pouter Pigeon. She acted as if she were showing that someone in the same class could be as graceful and refined as a ballet dancer. Young Master glanced over so that the third girl swam into the picture, finally I could take stock of her. With my flea brain I could not tell whether she was pretty or not, but I could tell that her eyes and her little mouth were made up; her cheeks were powdered a light red. I'll tell you something else, Danny Boy. But just between us. She had captivated Young Master. Though he wasn't in a hurry to betray it.

"We are the only ones on mission."

It was Kyle who declared that firmly. It was funny, because he was the smallest one of the entire company. He liked to chew gum, drink cola, and belch.

"Our mission is to clear the area of the ballsy."

"From whom?" shrieked the girls.

"The husky ones." He pointed at the other end of the table, then moved his finger all the way to Marko and stopped in mid-air. "You will be the husky ones."

Pouter Pigeon sprang up and protested.

"I don't wish to be husky!"

"Have you any idea what the huskies are?" asked Kyle.

"No. But even so I don't want to be one."

"They are the character assassins. They destroy our characters in the War of the Worlds. That's why we have to clear the field of them."

"Then most certainly I don't want to be husky."

Kyle frowned, then asked Pouter Pigeon the question,

"So, you'd rather play the Adventures of Hello Kitty?"

The poor girl's broad face showed that she hadn't the foggiest idea what Hello Kitty was, but before she lost her inclination, the four main players broke into guffaws.

Young Master cheerfully sang,

Buy the War of the Worlds today, install it and be on the online-meeting before we blow you out of the water.

Kyle replied in a fading voice,

Oh dear, all right, I'll install it.

I'll come clean, my dear friend. I'm greatly embarrassed that I must tell you all this. I'm not fond of gutter language, but would a story be to your liking or would it be authentic if the way the players speak were completely censored? No, don't you think? So sometimes I quote them accurately, sometimes I charitably omit the naughty words that were said so volubly and with such great gusto.

Kenny passed my test, for he staved off the conflict. He raised both hands high and said,

"Listen, fuck, it's just a game. We four were always on the same team. That's all. True, you guys are our enemies, but we will be your enemies. It's all a matter of point of view. You can have a mission, too, if you wish."

"OK by me," announced Red Powder.

"I'm in, too," said Ballet Fairy.

"Then so am I," Pouter Pigeon gave in.

Everybody looked at Marko.

"What about you?" urged Kyle.

"I'm thinking about our mission. I'm not going to risk my life without a mission."

"Isn't it mission enough to liquidate them?" asked Pouter Pigeon.

"Not for me."

"Then think of something."

The truth be told, everybody, except for Marko, was hungry for a little war. Maybe even including me. Young Master was feverishly racking his brains to make up a mission that might interest Marko. The others were visibly thinking about the same thing. Me too. That's when I realised that I couldn't choose my mission, but I got it. It just came. It came up in me, then didn't let me go. All right, I thought to myself, the game hasn't even started, and it's over already.

The battle was already underway in Young Master's head. Everybody fired away frantically; here and there, the warriors fell one after the other. Red Powder would have got a lethal shot, but Stan threw himself in front of Cartman's bullet.

"Ssss," I hissed to Young Master. "That's very good. Throw that in. They'll bite on that."

He pretended not to hear me.

Good God, I broke my vow. I was panic-stricken. What's going to become of me? He'll strike me dead. It wasn't the ivy-green of vexation but the red of shame came over him. "Of course, so that I give myself away?"

I got it. I went on.

"You'll save the girls' life at the cost of your life."

Young Master still didn't deign to answer, but he said out loud,

"I save the chicks' life at the cost of mine. Marko, what do you say to that?"

Marko's eyes lit up. But his words fell with a thump. I understood from Young Master why, so I smiled enigmatically to myself.

"If you really want it, so be it." He scrambled to his feet.

"To battle!" shouted Kenny.

"To battle!" roared Stan, Kyle and Cartman.

"Let's go." Marko motioned to the girls.

***

I will describe the field of battle, so you can imagine it, dear Danny. Imagine that you go through the front door. It leads to a corridor, and there is another corridor to the right. You can't guess how I remembered which one was to the right, which to the left. Even though you are the one I must thank. The cars run to our left, and we roll to their right, and I am sitting in your right ear, for I suffer less from the noise of the motors.

So then, you go straight from the entrance, and two good flea jumps there's another door, then two more then another, and then yet another. When you enter that, you get to a little square, and from there you can jump in two directions. In one direction, you'll find an open door. That was Kenny's room, we went there for weapons. In the other direction you'll hit a closed door, and if you do as I did, you can take this literally.

But if you don't jump into this little space, but go straight ahead you'll reach where we were staying, an enormous living room. You must picture this living room as including the dining room and kitchen. This opens onto the balcony. And by the time you reach the end of the living room, you're where you'd have been if you had gone directly right at the entrance.

Namely.

Did you get it?

A real ambulatory.

A super battle field.

It's no wonder that the whole company was full of high spirits and excitement. They didn't bother much about who gets which weapon. Even though with four cartridges you could shoot a round, with the other four you couldn't. You had to load it up after each shot, and you had to insert a new sponge cartridge, and only then could you fire.

Now too Kenny was clever, he didn't hand out all four of the cartridge guns, but gave two to Marko and company. Marko immediately handed it on to the Ballet Fairy, the other to Red Powder, that is, I later found out, to Greti. He kept the one that you had to load up for himself and gave one to Pouter Pigeon.

Kenny informed us of the rules.

Everyone has five lives.

If anyone gets shot anywhere, he's lost a life.

After the fifth hit, he's dead. He must leave his weapon on the spot, and he must march into the room for the dead with hands raised high.

You can't leave the apartment, but you can go anywhere inside it, you can hide anywhere, you can fight anywhere, fire and kill anywhere, except for one room opposite his room. Anyway, it will be locked.

On the other hand.

Kenny raised his forefinger in warning.

If anyone breaks anything, he'll have to pay for it. If you wreck anything, you'll have to pay for it. Do you agree?

"Yes," roared the pack.

"To battle," shouted Kenny.

"To battle," roared the pack.

And the warriors flew off in different directions.

***

I don't know whether it's my fault or not, dear Danny, or the world's. Fact is that Young Master's opinion proved to be correct, that what was entertaining for them was dead boring for me. It seemed that I was attuned to different signals. I love delicate vibrations of the soul, killing bores me, in fact disturbs me. Even if it is only a game.

True, the fact that Young Master was hit twice, one after the other, played a part in this. One of the sponge cartridges got just under his eyes, and while he closed his eyes willy-nilly, and while he was defenceless, wiping the tears from his eyes, the next shot came. Somehow this slammed near me, so that I too trembled together with him.

Afterwards the battle continued for minutes so that Young Master ran from cover and back, but didn't get shot. Despite this, my own combativity cooled off quickly. Somehow everything was hanging on the same peg: everybody tried to find cover, break out, pick the others off, back up, reload, break out again, bang, back again. If they hit someone, an infernal howl went up, but not from pain (for that, to put it delicately, *fuck* was the answer), but out of a feeling of triumph that overcame the one who extinguished a life. It didn't bring excitement, when somebody hit, two warriors should attack the one hiding, and flush them out. The result was that there was even more rushing about and the noise of battle was even greater. The ambulatory filled up, they ran in this direction and that away from each other, they hid, turned off the light, so they could wait for those trying to enter or break out.

And then something took my breath away. I could definitely hear someone weeping. Very restrained, with tiny sobs, but without a doubt weeping.

Young Master was just aiming his reloaded gun at the door of Kenny's room, thinking that Marko and Red Powder were there. He was paying such intense attention that he couldn't hear the sobs.

I couldn't keep myself from telling him.

"Someone's crying."

"Be quiet."

"No. Really."

He turned around angrily. He stepped up to the closed door, and yanked at the door.

"You see, it's locked. There's no one there."

At that moment the door opposite burst open, but I couldn't see who was breaking out nor who shot whom, if they shot them at all. By that time, I flung myself to the floor, and quickly jumped to the first collision, and crouched there at the wall, so that I wouldn't be stepped on in the struggle. So, I would be the first guest in the room of the dead.

***

The moment the floor stopped creaking, I set off. I had a hunch in which direction to go, and after a few jumps I hit a door. Without hesitation, I slipped in under it. I smelled the odour of an agitated woman.

I headed in her direction.

After a few moments, I was perched in the delicate ear of a sobbing woman. Her head bent forward, perhaps because she had hidden it in her hands. I couldn't see anything, but felt it even more.

"Does it really hurt?" I asked, shocked.

"Oh, my God!"

"I'm just a flea."

"Oh."

"And who are you?"

She didn't answer.

"What are you doing here? Why don't you come out and play?"

She didn't answer.

"Are you locked up here?"

She finally spoke. She had a definitely sweet, in fact, a warm voice. But she was still catching her breath and wiping her eyes.

"Yes."

"You can't get out?"

"I could."

"Then?"

Outside the battle noise grew louder; it was obvious that several warriors had clashed. From the rush of feet at least four of them were moving about, but only Cartman's and Kyle's voice could be heard. They were shouting fairly incoherently.

"Get out of here, shithead."

"It's on a much higher level, this isn't fair!"

"Don't you have anything better to do, you ass!"

"Who's this prick?"

"Whoever it is, he's a shit-kicker, that's for sure."

It was my feeling that this was the way they talk in South Park. But my poor mysterious lady began sobbing again, and, swaying back and forth, she kept saying, "Dear God, what did I do? What did I do? I gave him everything." And she shook so that I felt it inside her ear.

Then the realisation struck me.

"Are you Kenny's mother?"

"I hate that name!" she answered when she had caught her breath.

"It's just a game," I hastened to reassure her.

"Murderous game." She shook again. "I raised him to appreciate only the beautiful, the good, dear God!"

I tried to say honestly, so there shouldn't be any misunderstanding, as I've always said, I was only a flea, though I got it that at this moment, it didn't matter at all. She was desperate. And there was nothing to do, I had to save her.

But how?

I was very worried.

Finally, I announced.

"You have a talented son. He's such a skilful organiser; he leads like an adult."

"He's following in his father's footsteps."

"Why is that bad?"

She replied in a pained voice,

"We're divorced. He's the one who is leading him down the wrong path."

"I'm sorry. Truly sorry," I hurriedly announced, and added immediately. "That happens to a lot of people. The essential thing is that Kenny is a good lad."

"Of course. That's why I'm locked up in here."

I gasped.

We shook again.

"He locked you up?" I asked incredulously.

I had to wait until she calmed down.

"I locked myself up, but he asked me to. It was the only way I could stay."

Now, something happened that happens to me rarely. You're my main witness, dear Danny. I got angry.

"Oh, dear. Why didn't you go see a girl friend? Why didn't you take a walk?"

"They're so wild. You don't know them."

"I do know them," I answered firmly. This didn't stop her.

"They might hurt each other. They might damage each other. They might set fire to the apartment."

"And they can't now?"

She went quiet for a moment.

"At least I'm near at hand. If something terrible should happen."

And as if life wished to prove her right, a shout of triumph shook the door. "Bravo, Kenny, you hit it." I think it was Cartman shouting, but his voice was rather hoarse, so I couldn't be sure.

"Marko, you got the fifth one. Did you die? Raise your hands and go to the room of the dead."

We shook again.

"Oh, my God. What did I do wrong? What did I do wrong?"

You won't believe this, Danny, but I broke into laughter.

What a completely mad world! This marvellous world!

There you are perched in the ear of a mature, adult person, and you can't make her understand that the dead can't raise their hands, and march on their own legs. If Marko can do this, then the whole thing is nothing but a game. A GAME! GAME! GAME!

"It's a game," I shouted. "A game," I howled, beside myself. "GAME, GAME, GAME."

"But WHY? WHY? WHY?" she shouted back in a choked voice.

That was when it dawned on me. I don't even know why.

Why was it quite obvious that what was deadly boring for me was pure excitement for them? Why was it a good game to chase their own classmates around with guns, hoping that they'll leave some body part uncovered and then shoot them dead? Why was it good to swear, and use nasty words, if you can say good ones, WHY? WHY? WHY?

I was forced to confess to Kenny's mother.

"I don't know."

After a pause, I added,

"I'll find out soon."

"Just don't betray me to my son," she whispered, wringing her hands.

***

After slipping under the door, I tried to quickly catch the scent, but it wasn't at all easy. For the sweating bodies made the air muggy. In addition, there was the danger that they would step on me, so I decided to go on hugging the wall for the time being. If somebody happened to pass by, I'd take advantage of him to get a better view. If by chance it was Kenny, I could have a look round.

At first, I sensed the odour of those rushing by and the tramping of their feet, but either they were too fast or too far from me. I was forced to keep to the wall, cautiously moving forward on my own feet. After a while, I noticed that the footsteps and creaking of the floor grew rarer, and faded entirely. I could no longer feel the waves of the full-blooded bodies, though I didn't really mind that, for I began to be hungry. What happened? The war was over? Did Kenny manage to clear the field? Or did the enemy manage to triumph even without Marko?

It was all the same for me, actually. The important thing was to get to Kenny as soon as possible.

I tried to imagine the field, as I had described it to you. And feeling my way forward, I advanced blindly from door to door, until I reached the living room.

There a surprising calm greeted me. At least with my modest gifts, I didn't sense the noise of battle. I did catch strong, decisive human speech. What was missing was the intermediary station, and naturally, I didn't understand a thing.

I began to jump quickly toward the sound, to get to a place where I could have a look round. On my way, I got hung up on the leg of a chair, then on a boy's leg. All I could determine was that it didn't belong to Young Master. I soon leaped up on top of the individual's head, and then immediately into his ear.

I breathed a sigh of relief.

My lookout, to my good fortune, was observing closely the events taking place in the living room. So, I deduced by process of elimination that it was Marko.

And I realised something else from Marko's thoughts. I couldn't deny it, I was knocked over. Kenny was playing at summary justice.

He occupied the middle chair on the opposite end of the table. He pushed aside the snacks, cola bottles, soft drinks at arm's length. Kyle was sitting on his right, on his left was Ballet Fairy. On one end of the table Red Powder waited with visible excitement for developments, and we sat opposite her on the other end of the table.

Young Master stood on one leg then the other, just opposite Kenny and the others. He seemed pale, but held strong. He faced Kenny's disdainful look.

"I think everybody has said what they knew. We can summarise the facts, and bring sentence," Kenny said, looking around. Since no one said a word, he went on.

"It has been proved, and Stan himself confessed during these talks, that he threw himself in the path of Kyle's shot on purpose. Knowing that with this fifth hit, he would save Greti, save her from death, thus leaving the cartridge gun for us, and he would have to march to the room of the dead. Based on the confession, it became unequivocally certain that Kyle was so surprised by Stan's behaviour that he forgot to defend himself, and Greti immediately hit him with two shots and killed him dead. The other serious circumstance that must be taken into consideration is that Stan understood that his four lives were gone. If he got another hit, it would be fatal. And that was exactly what happened. So, everything turned on this serious treachery. If Greti had died then, we would have won, and our mission would have been accomplished. Now, you've won, and for us that sucks. And on my birthday."

Kenny pounded the table with his fist.

Everybody was frightened to death. Even Marko, who, insofar as I could pay attention to him, seemed a very calm, balanced chap.

Kenny smiled.

"Relax. This was just the hammer. Now comes the verdict. Let's hurry, because we must get to the next case, and there's pizza to come and especially the cake... So then." He raised his forefinger. "What does this traitor deserve?"

Marko's look jumped here and there. As if he were trying to figure out what the others were thinking. The others also looked right and left. Everybody was reluctant to be the first to speak.

"So," urged Kenny.

I observed Marko's head. I watched the thoughts and feelings whirling in his head, the quick change in colours. It was exactly like the dance of the clouds in the sky, the dark shadows and the blinding rays of the sun roiling around us.

Naturally I couldn't see into my own head, although I felt that in there light and order ruled. And pay attention to what I'm saying to you, Danny. In my modest opinion, Young Master did the most noble thing that any human being can do. If I don't say anything else, if this noble act had happened in a real conflict, if he had done this with real death-defying courage, even though I am only an insignificant little flea, I would have done everything in my power to get Young Master a statue. (What's wrong with this?) Make him an example for the next generation, indeed, the already grown-up generation.

But. Let's be fair, my dear friend, what Young Master did was also pure treachery. It is easy for me to say, as I – outside of my own conscience – I owe no one an explanation. But is this the case with Stan? And Marko? What about the others?

No. Right?

Marko was struggling with himself.

As a clever child, he saw the indisputable fact of the betrayal. But in his mind's eye he would have gladly put himself in Stan's place. He would gladly have imagined that he had saved the girl's life, if not Red Powder's, but Ballet Fairy's, and now he was the one standing before the judges. And I saw that the vapour of swelling pride beginning to glimmer inside him. How could he have judged Stan guilty?

111

And, who knows, perhaps such thoughts were roiling around in the others' head too? Although I had my doubts about Kenny. The fact was, however, that the long silence was becoming embarrassing.

Kenny solved the situation skilfully. I couldn't really appreciate his skill... He announced that without a recommendation, the judges would retire and bring their verdict. But first, he informed us, they'll deal with the other, much less serious and simpler case.

"I'll tell you the facts." He launched into his speech and, speaking very fast, continued:

"We caught Cartman and Annette in the bathroom. According to Cartman, it was totally dark when he entered the bathroom; he couldn't see Annette. Since he had gone in there to hide, to finish off those who went in unsuspecting, he quickly closed the door behind him. But he heard snuffling, in fact, he felt someone's breath. He reached toward them, and his hand, as he put it, encountered *"a warm, pliant body part."* He said, *"he totally froze at this."* Now let's hear Annette's side. She essentially confirmed Cartman in everything. She did not think that Cartman wanted to feel her up, let us add, instead of fighting honestly. At the same time, she did not draw close to Cartman to make something happen between them. Though she too said, that *"she froze."* That was why they were the way they were when I unexpectedly caught them.

Here Kenny grinned.

Smiles and sighs of relief went up all round.

"Do you have any questions, any comments?" Kenny looked around. His face lost its cheer and, frowning, he continued, "If no one has any, I have two. In the first place, there's a hitch here, don't you think? All right, let's picture this: I go into the bathroom, instead of Cartman. It's totally dark. I hear someone breathing. I feel their breath. So, what do I do? Well? I shoot. Why?

He looked around airily, was there anyone in the audience who could figure it out? As no one said anything, he continued well pleased with himself.

"Now, whoever was in the dark had to see who came in. If it was on the same team, she would have said, "Hello, Kenny." If it wasn't, then it could only be an enemy. Who had to be shot. But let's move on a tiny bit. Why didn't he shoot? As enemy, he damn well had to do it. But I tell you point-blank, he didn't, because he wasn't focused on his mission, either. But on something entirely different... And if this is true, we have to say the sorry truth, Cartman and Annette are both traitors.

Kenny added that if this were the War of Worlds, we could know what to do: Death to traitors.

I focused my attention on Marko's head, and the others' eyes. It was the same swirling light-dark ball as before. A voice thundered in Marko: Traitors! Tie them up! Beat them up! Then suddenly another interjected, grinning maliciously, "Poor Cartman, his hand got stuck on Annette's crop."

The malicious grin flashed intermittently on Kenny's face amid the weighty words. It wasn't easy to tell how seriously he took the whole thing, or to what extent it was a show, mere entertainment. In any event, the dark clouds were gathering in Marko, when Kenny turned to the other "very important" point of view. But as soon as he finished his brief explanation, Marko and the others burst out laughing. He said the following: that Annette didn't shoot Cartman and Cartman didn't shoot him, didn't essentially influence the outcome of the battle. He said the following: *"It would seem that they were making out, though this wasn't the most appropriate time, but to their health."*

"It's time for pizza!" shouted Kyle.

"And cake," sang Ballet Fairy.

"No way," roared Kenny. "Stan foiled our victory, made our mission fail. You could say he ruined our game. So, I think his punishment is legit. I ask the other two members of our judges to withdraw for sentencing."

"Are you serious?" Marko asked incredulously.

"Dead serious."

"You know." Marko shrugged his shoulders. Pensively, he grabbed a knife. It may have been put there for the pizza. He lifted the tablecloth and carefully placed it on a dark brown, shiny table. With one movement he spun it round. He watched in amazement as it whirled unstoppably.

"Marko," I whispered. As much as I could, in a veiled, ghostly voice. As if I were his conscience itself. "Go to Kenny and tell him you'd like to be Stan's defence attorney."

Marko stopped the knife, held his breath, and listened intently. Only I didn't say one more word. I even took care not to make an accidental move. Finally, Marko clambered up, caught up with the martial law court and went up to Kenny.

"I'd like to be Stan's defender. I hope it's not a problem."

Kenny grinned in his face.

"Not a problem, Marko. We're the ones doing the sentencing. Anyway, we're done. They've both accepted my advice."

"Well then…" Marko hesitantly shrugged his shoulders. He wrestled a bit with his conscience, then turned on his heels.

I leaped at that moment. I caught Kenny's bush.

***

By the time I found his ear, he was sitting at the table, opposite him Young Master stood on one foot then on the other. He was still pale, but continued to hold himself together. I tried to find out quickly what Kenny was thinking. I focused intently. Would I see binding or beating or anything like that? Thank God, nothing like that came up. Suddenly, however, I caught something that struck me hard, and I knew should never be said. Kenny wanted to throw Young Master out of South Park. He wanted to take away the name Stan and wanted to exclude him from their parties.

It seemed that neither Kyle nor Ballet Fairy grasped the seriousness of the sentence. But, how could they?

I had only just understood it all. Only because for long, long minutes I kept turning in my mind the question, WHY? WHY? WHY? Why did Kenny, Kyle, Cartman and Stan throw away their own honest names? Why was this mad South Park game so important for them? This ridiculous War of the Worlds? Why was Marko playing with the knife, why had this simple earthly game captivated him and why not Kenny, Kyle, Cartman or Stan? And why did Kenny think that the punishment of not being Stan anymore was worse than, let us say, being tied up and beaten?

The answer was astoundingly simple.

He who has no role, needs one.
He needs a theatre, who hasn't one.
He who hasn't got a role, does not exist.
He who hasn't got a theatre, doesn't exist.

I tell you, Danny Boy, a spider has it easier than these South Park kids. It was once by favour of a kitten that I could see one weaving its web. It lets down a thread and lets it wave in the wind. The wind blows it against a branch where it gets stuck. And it has a sure point. The South Park kids had none. They hang by thin threads, and sway this way and that, and the most amazing and wonderful havens offer themselves. Where? Why, on the screen? They reach into their pockets and there. They lean on the table and there. They battle and save worlds, without getting off their butts. And yet there is more reality in a whirling knife than in any of them. Of course, they seek ever more restlessly the real possibility of a harbour. The true role.

Their true selves.

But where is the ferryman? Where is the ferryman who can help them?

Who could say: "Go ahead, you'll find a harbour there." "Watch out, there's a reef there."

Who could rescue them from their own prison, from their own fantasy roles?

Now, my dear friend, all this hit me like being struck by lightning.

I had no more than an instant. I threw myself before Kenny's words, like Young Master before Kyle's bullet. He opened his mouth to speak, to announce Stan's punishment, when I said to him,

"Hello, Kenny. This is Mission Control."

Of course, the words froze.

"From the War of the Worlds," I added.

He couldn't utter a sound.

The others saw that something completely unusual must have happened to him, but how could they guess what it was. Not even Young Master suspected me, at least for the time being, as I hadn't spoken to him for a long time. He may even have forgotten about me. If a flea doesn't bite you, it's easy to forget about him.

It was funny to see inside Kenny as he searched feverishly for the possible explanation, and what a serious terminator image he constructed of me, this being the size of a poppy seed. I almost laughed out loud. His eyes scanned the others, trying to read their faces and looks. Nothing appeared in anybody. Then he remembered Marko's offer. He thought that he was just concealing it cleverly. He couldn't keep from asking,

"Are you playing games with me, Marko?"

Marko looked at him wide-eyed, uncomprehending. The others looked at each other.

Kyle asked quietly,

"Is something wrong, Kenny?"

"No, nothing. We have decided on the following punishment for Stan…"

I interjected.

"Listen here, Kenny. You will not throw him out of the game, you will not deprive him of his name, and you will not ban him from your parties. This is an order from Mission Control."

"Let's hear it, Kenny," urged Kyle.

"But he committed a seriously treasonous act," he burst out loud. "And he didn't even try to deny it."

"We know that already." Kyle waved his hand. "Let's get it over with. Let's have pizza and cake. I'm fed up with the whole thing." He punched the air.

Kenny reddened.

"I wasn't speaking to you, you ignoramus. It was Mission Control."

Alarm showed in their eyes. Except for Young Master. At that moment he clicked. I was the one who was moving the invisible thread. Kenny was debating me, battling me.

It would surprise you, dear Danny, what Young Master dared do then. I didn't know him enough, without being in his ear and reading his mind, to grasp his motives.

He didn't betray me to the others.

He went before Kenny and looked at the others and said,

"I want to atone. I want you to punish me appropriately."

I would have liked to leap into his ear and shout into his head, "Have you lost your mind? Do you know what awaits you? They'll ostracise you. That's what you're most afraid of. *He who has no role, doesn't exist. He who has no theatre, doesn't exist.*"

Unfortunately, I'm not a thought that can fly hither and thither. I was forced to battle both.

"I told you, Kenny. NO! This is a strict order from Mission Control. You will *not* exclude Stan from the game, you will *not* take away his name, and you will *not* exclude him from your parties."

"But he himself wants it."

"NO! NO! NO!"

I could see the huge struggle he was going through. "You snot-nose," his father shouted at him. "You worm, have you no toughness?" Fleetingly, his mother appeared, sobbing, wringing her hands, but then she flitted away.

With mouth trembling, shaking in his whole body, he said,

"YES, Stan will be punished. And if this doesn't please Mission Control, from now on all four of us will depart his game."

What I answered to this, surprised me the most. It was, so to speak, completely logical, indeed, it was effective and successful, but still I couldn't say – I didn't feel it – that it had popped out of my head. The most I can think of is that the world is swimming in an enormous Spirit, whence inspiration comes at the most opportune moments.

I replied with a completely calm voice.

"Only he who has committed no crime, can punish."

Kenny retorted,

"I am guiltless."

I had the next question ready.

"Can anyone who locks up his mother be guiltless?"

He fell on the table, sobbing.

The others looked at him in alarm.

I would have sobbed together with Kenny, if I could, with my little flea soul.

***

What happened then belongs to the realm of miracles, my dear friend. I gave thanks to the Most High that I could see with my own eyes, I could experience it with my own little soul; otherwise, I wouldn't have believed it from anyone.

Suddenly such fresh and sweet colours began to spread in Kenny, as if a field full of poppies or a cloudless sky had come to life in him. He broke out completely from the rolling captivity of the hurtful angry greens and alarming dark greys and loud neon colours. He raised his head, and I could see from inside that he was smiling through his tears.

He got up and started off.

He advanced slowly and with wobbly steps.

He stopped by the closed door and knocked.

"Mama, mama," he shouted. "Bring the pizza."

The door opened slowly. Mama obviously had to stop crying and pull herself together.

"Mama." Kenny smiled. "Could you help us? We're ravenously hungry. We're seeing stars."

That night I just smiled to myself like a flea. A completely different story began to unfold in the same place and with the same players. It might be more correct to say that the same players began to play an entirely different role. They abandoned South Park and returned to their own everyday reality; it turned out that they could have a good time. True, I helped them in this a bit. By then, I was lying low in Young Master's ear, thinking about going home. I couldn't be sure that he wasn't angry with me, for depriving him of the high-minded experience of self-sacrifice, so I wasn't in a hurry to speak up.

Kenny's mother lit the stove, saying, the pizza was better than heated in a microwave. The company approved loudly.

Kenny set the table, the others sat down on mattresses put in the corners of the room.

The usual entertainment, diversionary objects, flashy smart phones were pulled out by Kyle, Cartman and Pouter Pigeon, Young Master and Red Powder; a little further on Marko and Ballet Fairy, but they weren't holding anything, but were talking quietly to each other. I would have watched their charming duets longer, but Young Master's eyes kept returning to his telephone screen.

Then I noticed something odd. He was looking at the screen, but that wasn't what he saw, but Red Powder. She was the one who had occupied his thoughts; she was in his heart, but so much so that he was breathing harder.

At that moment I understood something: why was the fate so hard of these children hanging from spiders' webs. It was inconceivable for a flea to sit mute and motionless next to his beloved. He will jump on her or leave her. But what could a human child do while he can at most say it, but can't do it.

Nowadays he clings to the screen world and buries himself in it.

Though this isn't necessary.

Anyway, I was terribly hungry too.

I sucked on Young Master.

Then I jumped out of him.

I leaped onto Red Powder, and took a few bites of her. About the others, I don't know who they were, I had a bite of everyone who crossed my path. Then I took in the flashy screens, one after the other. I danced a little on one, then leaped onto the other. It wasn't difficult, they were brighter than fireflies.

The world around me came to life. The blows came faster and faster, I caught more and more of the shrieks and laughter. And the sweaty bodies that were jumbled together fell on me, it was lucky that my armour kept me from being crushed.

The pizza was ready. Everyone went quiet. There was no denying it, I was a bit anxious about how I was going to find my way back to Young Master. Suddenly, the familiar full-blooded smell hit my nose. I was touched. He was looking for me.

***

Since I've been coming this way, I was not only waiting for you, dear Danny, but I'm watching out for Red Fur too, and his young master. In this beautiful, muddled world, even an insignificant little flea can encounter a surprise. On the long way home, Young Master couldn't resist revealing to me, his closest confidant, that he saved Greti's life, thus taking on the ugly role of traitor (changed the words here), not because he was so attracted to her, but because the room of the dead wasn't empty. Marko was waiting there…

What I know about you, dear Danny, you're close to having such secret motives lead your eventful life. You can always count on me, if you need to.

Seventh Tale
AT SCHOOL

I tell you, Danny, God bless these scrawny, flea-bitten stray cats. My chief transportation took me to a place that was special.

The children just rushed in here! Little ones, big ones. Backpack on their backs and shoulders, they crowded into a wide grated iron gate. "They must be handing out gifts," I thought. Or maybe they were getting ready for a big party. The parents buzzed off after they unloaded their kids from their luxury cars.

My stray tabby was watching the world go by under the fence plank. I was gawking with him. I didn't know what he was expecting, but soon it became clear. A girl with pigtails put a package in front of our noses. Eyes and laughter bright, she watched how our cat slapped the paper with his sharp claws, how he pulled out a fat slice of bologna, and how he made it disappear, munching loudly. Naturally I took advantage of the opportunity.

By the time I had clambered into the delicate ear of my pigtailed one, we were about to hit a glass door. It opened by itself – how, I have no idea – and we were inside in a flash.

Halls and stairs ran in every direction, so long that I couldn't see their end. They distributed wisely those rushing in; every door right and left had an equal number.

Playground? Office for kids? I couldn't decide.

We entered a lovely room. Cheerful figures from fairy tales adorned the walls. Colourful flowery canopies everywhere. There were red, blue, and black dots and little lines on an enormous board. "What a lovely place!" I said to myself happily. True, there were too many benches and chairs for playing and too little open space. "How can these kids run about, play tag and hide-and-seek?" I wondered.

Then suddenly a terrible ringing cut the air.

At that moment, the racket the children made, so pleasant and exciting to my ear, stopped. We ran with the others to our benches and chairs. At first, I thought this was a game; anyone who didn't get to one was a paper tiger. He loses out in the game. But every child found their place. Only one person was left standing, but she wasn't a child.

You must know by now, my dear friend, who that could be, but I had no idea. Perhaps a mother was forgotten here, I opined. Or maybe she was the director of the playground. I believed this, for every eye was on her.

"Good morning," she said firmly. The kids took a deep breath and shouted in chorus,

"Good morning, Aunt Ibolya."

My little pigtailed girl also roared enthusiastically.

"Give me the monitor report," Aunt Ibolya said.

What does she want?

I watched curiously. A little girl in a short skirt stepped forward, drew herself up and solemnly announced,

"Aunt Ibolya, I report one person absent. Vera Vidor couldn't be here, because she is still sick."

"Thank you very much, Panka! We wish Vera Vidor a speedy recovery. You kids come here, and sit on the rug."

We sat down.

"Who did Hobo visit?" Aunt Ibolya asked.

"Me," said a little boy with glasses, who stretched and waved a bear cub with a thick plush coat.

"Good, Andris. Then let's hear what you have to say."

This pleased me more and more. Andris jerked Hobo this way and that, as if it could talk. I've noticed that children are born actors. Andris changed his voice and started to growl; for a moment, even I was convinced that it was coming from the cub.

"I waaas veerrry gooood. Everrryboody looooved meee. At niiight IIII waaaatched the stoorrry on TeeeeVeee. IIIII gottt suppper toooo, but IIII couldnnnt eeeeeat it."

The children tittered. Aunt Ibolya smiled contentedly.

"All right, Andris, go on."

"Theeeen weeee weeenttt to beddd togettther…"

"Oh, oh!"

My pigtailed one immediately looked at a lanky lad, but so did everybody else. He grinned, insinuating much. Aunt Ibolya's smile faded. An alarmed venomous green began to shimmer in Pigtails' head. Aunt Ibolya's look shot daggers at them, as if she wanted to spear somebody.

"Bence, why are you wailing?"

Lanky lowered his head, and stole glances around. He seemed to be peering out of slitted eyes to see whether others didn't get it either. Didn't others want to understand?

"I was just kidding," he stammered.

Aunt Ibolya nodded coldly.

"Andris, please go on."

Andris continued cheerfully.

Suddenly the dark mist evaporated from Pigtails' head. Andris growled, then everyone growled with him, that is with Hobo. Everyone's eyes were bright, even Aunt Ibolya's.

What can I say? I enjoyed the whole thing too. I thought it a great idea. I don't know who had the idea, but he certainly was a clever one. How many of you are there at home, Danny? Three? Altogether? Even I would get bored. It's no wonder you always end up in front of screens. And here? The kids blossomed. They pricked up their ears, they told stories, they laughed, and interrupted each other. I enjoyed it all.

I even liked it when Aunt Ibolya sent everyone to their seat, and the children waited in silence for what she would tell them to do. "Take this out, open that, say after me." And the kids took it out, opened it, said after her. Even Bence, though not as enthusiastically as the others. Such as my little Pigtails, for example. "Bea Barka was going to continue," Aunt Ibolya informed us. My little Pigtails pulled her finger down the page of the book, enunciating syllable by syllable, "Oh wow! Thir-ty-eight-six! You are se-ri-ous-ly ill. He un-dressed him quick-ly, put him to bed. Then went out to the kitch-en to make tea."

"You read well, Bea. You're a clever girl." Aunt Ibolya nodded, and I saw my little pigtailed one overcome with warmth, so that she practically rose in the air.

In a little while, she raised her hand.

"Let somebody else have a word." Aunt Ibolya smiled at her.

"I just wanted to say…" and here Bea Barka stopped.

"Say it then," urged Aunt Ibolya.

"So, I thought I would pay Vera a visit, and make her some tea."

You know, Danny, even compared with you, I haven't lived for very long. But I have already learned that the world isn't this way or that. And who knows why I'm so lucky? That I should happen upon such a good-natured one as Bea Barka. At such times, even my little flea soul begins to rise. Warmth comes over me. I began to dream a little, and get a little sleepy too. A waking dream is strange, isn't it? Have you experienced that, Danny? All kinds of image and sound fragments swim in your head, they appear, then disappear, and swirl about until... Until? Suddenly a clear picture comes together. Virtually out of nowhere. It becomes concrete and materializes before you in its total reality.

That is what happened to me with this playground.

"Children." Aunt Ibolya raised her voice. "Now everybody take out their notebook and write in their own words what it means to say, *"a chill comes over him. What is it that chills? How does it chill? Why does it chill?"*

Well, of course.

This wasn't a *playground,* but *a school.* School makes you smart. This is where adults make their kids smart. They herd them together and teach them to read, to tell stories, understand, perhaps to count and sing too. Great! I could already see myself collecting all the small-fry fleas of the neighbourhood and teaching them the knowledge that I picked up here. I decided to stay with Bea Barka for at least a few days. I would go home with her every day and come back here. I would soak up as much knowledge as could fit into my little flea noggin.

Life decided otherwise. But let's not get ahead of ourselves.

I tell you, I was dreaming, and, in a reverie, I yawned a lot. Suddenly the image of Hobo swam into view.

Who knew why?

All I know was that I pictured it for myself half asleep, that if I got tired of all the learning, I could hide in Hobo's fur. Even if I didn't get bored. Every night I would go to bed with someone else, and gorge myself. I would have my fill every day forever. After all, who would suspect such a toy? Search for a blood-sucker in the fake fur? There wouldn't be such a crazy person.

Immediately afterward, another thought swam in, "*I will leave out Bea Barka.*" Why? She is so good. I couldn't bring myself to do it. What about the others? They're not good? How could I know? Even Bence…What about me?

I'm bad because I was born a blood-sucker?

And if I don't suck, then I'm already a saint? Or an impractical idiot. Crazy.

I was thinking such thoughts when that horrible sound sliced the air again. It was the school bell.

***

Of course, if you think about it, it's a great invention. Hats off to it. I thought about it. I ring, and all the little fleas leap about. I ring again, and they're all sitting on their benches. I ring again… How I could play with them! It isn't the bell's fault that accidents can happen in all the rushing and leaping about.

My little pigtailed one was skipping down the hallway, when I suddenly felt the world whirl around me. It was as if everything had been turned out of its four corners. The troop of children, the hall, the wall, the ceiling swept by me, then a terrible bang, shaking, and everything went dark.

I was scared.

Not because of me, I was conscious, I could move everything. I was fine. But I was worried about my pigtailed one.

Why doesn't she open her eyes?

Shouldn't I call for help?

I can't hear anything. I can't see anything.

"Help, help!" I shouted, but my calls at most reached my own ears.

Then she seemed to be sobbing.

Silence, then a sob. Silence, then a sob. She was trying to catch her breath.

"Help!"

Silence, then a sob.

At that moment a sweet voice swam toward me from a great distance. It surged toward me like the warmth of the morning sun.

It was a boy's voice.

Not a silvery chirping, like the little ones, but not as strong as that of the adults.

"Don't be afraid," it said quietly, calmly. I could almost see his encouraging smile, of course without his face. This voice was not at all familiar; I couldn't attach it to anyone. It was a voice that smiled. I don't have to tell you, it piqued my curiosity even more. Who could this phenomenon be?

"It's OK." The voice smiled. "You'll be fine very soon."

Can you believe it?

You're not going to believe it, Danny.

Pigtails really did get better. It was as if this smiling voice had caressed her and aroused her to life with its delicate touch. The little girl hadn't yet opened her eyes, though I would have liked to see the other's look. Her breathing became less laboured, and lovely, light-blue colours appeared.

"I see that you're better," the boy's voice observed, but it seemed to be coming from somewhere else. Then it returned to us. "You're very clever. Open your eyes."

Then with great difficulty, at a snail's pace, Pigtails' eyes opened, so that I could see the owner of the voice.

First his neck, which his shirt collar covered, appeared, then his rather round chin, with soft down above his upper lip. Finally, his eyes.

You humans say that the eyes are the window to the soul. I think there is truth in this saying. As this focused, but serene, child's look enveloped us, I felt as if our souls had been touched.

I jumped on him, as if I were being pursued.

***

I wanted to start – after a decent explanation and asking for forgiveness – by tipping my hat to him. Of course, speaking metaphorically. I thought up the appropriate words. *"You behaved magnificently. It was worthy of an adult. I tip all my hats to you."* But when I took up my place in his ear and was ready to read his thoughts, the words got stuck.

"Forgive me, Lord, I didn't want to."

We walked along the hallway, hugging the wall, with hesitant steps. He turned around for a moment. I saw Pigtails being escorted away by two adults.

It was like a dream. Little Pigtails' somewhat formless and weightless body flew toward us. Her eyes, though, shined, and her smile beamed as if transfigured.

Suddenly a paralysing fear.

"I'm very sorry."

It was strange to see with another's eyes, as if from the outside, what had happened to us. My pigtailed one had suddenly lost her balance, fell and hit the stone floor of the hallway, hitting her head. I thought I heard that terrible noise, and I experienced again the terrible shaking. Ow!

"I'm very sorry. I didn't mean to."

I think you are beginning to guess, dear Danny. And you have the same thought as me. As shocking as it may be, Pigtails didn't fall on her own. In her skipping in wild abandon, she hadn't lost her balance on her own. Instead of the words about tipping my hat, I began to search quickly for others. I wanted to reassure the phenomenon who was growing down on his chin and upper lip. It could happen to anyone; in rushing like that he could accidentally knock the smaller one over.

Life, as so often, proved to be much fancier.

I have no idea why this is so; don't ask, my dear friend, for I don't know. It's like this. Period.

"I wanted to," muttered Phenomenon.

He didn't whimper, as someone pressed by conscience pangs, but he said it dreamily, pensively, as if he didn't know himself what had got into him. If he didn't understand, how could I understand? With my tiny flea brain.

I was about to politely ask for an explanation when we reached an open door. An ear-splitting racket, then we saw the spectacle before us.

Here too a single solitary plant sat on the high window-sill, and a few colourful drawings decorated a trellised board, but otherwise everything was plain and bleak. The cheerful story-book characters, lively flower colours, the warm rug were missing. The tables and chairs weren't in order either, but most probably this was due to the dismissal by the bell and the release of emotions. They seem to have herded the bigger children into this place. Moustaches were beginning to sprout on some of the boys, and most of the girls were growing breasts. Almost everything and everyone were in motion. Compasses flew toward the drawings, making good-sized holes in them. Every hit was greeted with enthusiastic whoops and hollers. A shoe flew through the window, then another. A tall, thin boy with extremely long legs snuck behind a girl with a bare neck. He had a pipe as thick as a finger in his mouth. The girl was mesmerised by her telephone. Long Legs took a big breath and – he hit Bare Neck's neck with who knows what kind of shot. The girl sprang up. Long Legs zig-zagged among the tables and chairs. Bare Neck after him.

Not even the terrible ringing could slow them down.

Phenomenon sat down by a table near a window. He followed the events around him impassively. The film rolled *inside*. He put one hand beneath Pigtails' head, and caressed her face with the other. I could hear the smiling voice again.

Outside a dishevelled fair-haired lad and his burly mate dragged a thin girl and carried her to the coat-rack. They lifted her up a bit, the girl shrieked and struggled wildly. They skilfully hung her up by her linen jacket. I watched Phenomenon watching tensely, but as the girl's feet could touch the floor, he returned to his film. Pigtails skipped toward us...

"Have you all gone mad?"

Everybody turned toward the door, that was where the desperate shouting came from. A lady with her hair in a bun stormed into the door, high heels clicking on the floor, she rushed to the coat-rack. The girl had just peeled herself out of her jacket. The lady held her anguished face, looked deep into her eyes, trying to ferret out whether she was OK.

"Are you alive?"

"Of course," she replied with an embarrassed smile.

The lady turned toward the boys. She was much shorter than Burly and didn't look much older.

"Have you really gone mad?"

She grabbed them by the arms and shook them irritably.

"Please don't do that," Burly entreated her.

"We were just joking," added Blondie.

"You're hanging her for a laugh?"

"Camilla was laughing too." Blondie nodded toward the girl.

"I heard her shrieking."

"But she laughed too."

"In her anguish."

"No, Aunt Csöpi, not at all," Burly answered calmly. "I think she enjoyed it."

133

"She had an orgasm!" whooped Long Legs.

A few kids guffawed, but then stopped, as if they had suddenly been cut off. Aunt Csöpi glared at them, shooting daggers with her eyes.

She was struggling visibly.

She was overcome by a desperate feeling of helplessness. Visibly not only on her face, but on her whole body. She seemed even shorter, smaller, even more vulnerable.

I felt sorry for her.

I could tell that Phenomenon also felt sorry for her.

"Who could she be? What was she doing here?" I wondered. "Was she the director of the school?"

Phenomenon leaned over and fished a book and notebook out of his bag. He put it on the table before him. "Li-te-ra-ture" I read. That is what was written on them; printed on one, handwritten on the other.

"Thanks," I thought.

The Lady with the Bun snaked through the crowd of kids, half of them standing, the other half sitting; she headed for the blackboard. She put her bag and a bundle of papers on the large table that stood in the corner, then straightened up before the class.

She peered through a large pair of round spectacles.

"Would you please sit down? I'll tell you a story."

For a while, the chair legs wriggled and slipped on the linoleum floor, then silence.

"Thank you. It would be good if you could be quiet so quickly again…"

"Well, if you tell us stories at other times too," Long Legs said affably.

"You're not in nursery school any more, Levi, but in school. In case you've forgotten. If I make an exception now, it is because something happened that gave me back my faith a little…"

She was on the verge of tears.

She swallowed, holding her breath. Then sighing, continued…

"… that you are worth bothering about."

"Of course, we're worth it," Long Legs shouted.

"That you don't have such an all-fired big brain, but you have souls too."

"Of course, we have!" shouted Long Legs. But the Lady didn't look at him but at us. Then she went on.

"I would like you to know that a bigger boy knocked over a second-grade girl. At the end of the teachers' hallway, just in front of the WC. Coming out, I saw only that the poor little girl flew into the air and when she landed on the stone floor, poor thing hit her head so that she lost consciousness.

"Ouch!" could be heard here and there.

A film rolled in Phenomenon's head.

"Now, one of your school mates gave a very good example of how to behave in such a tragic situation, demonstrating compassion and sense of responsibility."

"I saw it too," Long Legs interjected.

Long Legs and Phenomenon looked at each other.

As for me, my heart skipped a beat.

Perhaps we would have an explanation of Phenomenon's odd behaviour. The missing details of the film would be played out… "*I wanted it.*" Could he have done it? On purpose? "Impossible," I thought.

"Not impossible." Phenomenon spoke up.

***

I was totally confused. The problem, my dear friend, was that I was in pain. How can I tell you all this illusion sensibly, and make you believe it?

I tried to conjure up what I did.

Had I accidentally blurted it out loud?

Or, should I say, I had found my man? A nothing little flea can read a human being's mind; why shouldn't a human being read a flea's mind? Obviously, not every flea can do it, nor can every human being.

I can see you laughing.

Why should this be more absurd than that?

I immediately made an experiment.

I closed my mouth firmly and asked him the question in thought:

"Did you trip her up?"

"Yes," came the immediate reply.

My breath stopped.

***

Phenomenon turned toward the Lady with the Bun. She was heading toward us, her heels clicking, a transfigured look on her face. Then she turned toward the class, but inching toward us all the while.

"I must confess that I was totally paralysed with fright. The thought flashed that perhaps I should call an ambulance, but I couldn't remember the phone number. Or at least I should see whether she was bleeding or not. But I couldn't move. But there was someone, though just a child, who could move. Who calmly went to the little girl, cautiously lifted her head and slipped his hand under it. I wanted to shout that you shouldn't touch her, maybe she was bleeding. But he did it so confidently, so gently, with such compassion that I was reassured. He stroked her face, called her little Pigtails, but so naturally that I wasn't even amazed, but I was overjoyed when the deathly pale little girl came back to life."

She was so moved, tears came to her eyes. She stopped next to us. She put her hand on Phenomenon.

"So, Toma was this upstanding boy." She smiled into our eyes. Then, turning toward the table, she confirmed it. "It was Toma. I tip all my hats to him. I have decided to commend him to the director."

***

You know, my dear friend, life has given me enough confidence so that I don't get overly upset about strange contradictions. I can judge fairly quickly and easily. But now I really was confused. Apart from Toma, I was most probably the only one who knew what had happened in the moment before the accident. It didn't fit my sense of good and bad that Phenomenon could get a precious director's commendation, perhaps with a seal, when he was the one who had caused the accident. Imagine what would happen if pyromaniacs were to be decorated for skilfully putting out fires that they themselves had set, or kleptomaniacs because they gave back what they had stolen. Finally, murderers could be decorated because they said a nice prayer over their victims. Wouldn't it be absurd?

On the other hand, you do have to consider this experience: a kid who is just barely growing down on his chin breathes life with overflowing love into a little girl who has lost consciousness. For that was exactly what happened, any way you look at it. You'd think that there is no such miracle, if we hadn't experienced it ourselves. But to elaborate further, he had barely got the moving appreciation from the Lady with the Bun, when the disgust felt by his mates made itself felt. Why? Only slowly did it become clear…

The Lady with the Bun looked at her watch.

"Good God!"

She ran to the table and grabbed a pack of papers.

"Your papers were very uneven," she announced. "There are a couple of A-pluses, four Bs, many Cs, and one D. Toma had the best paper once again. I couldn't even find a spelling mistake in his paper."

Maybe it was odd, but I caught myself swelling with pride. We were connected in some way, after all. That was what fleas are like; they like to share in the appreciation given to others. Toma punched the air. "Yes!" I was even more surprised that his joy shrank, and the blossoming patches of colour were suddenly surrounded by venomous green bunches.

"Genius!" someone shouted.

"Wise guy!" shouted another.

"Scholar!"

I felt a tiny, but unpleasant blow strike the back of our neck. Toma grabbed his neck. He had barely taken away his hand when the next blow struck. I don't think it was any stronger than a flea bite. Still, Toma's spirit went dark, and he jumped up. He stared at Long Legs – he sat exactly two tables behind us – then sat back down.

He was still seething, but it was as if from high above, rescuers had arrived, cheerful, warm colours began to reassure him.

Aunt Csöpi stood frozen.

"Levi!" she pressed through her lips.

Then she slapped the papers onto the table and rushed to Long Legs. Suffering no opposition, she put her palm in front of the nervously twitching face, grinning in embarrassment. I didn't understand why. I was afraid that as impudent and arrogant as he was, he would spit into her hand. But he didn't. He pulled his arm from behind his back and put something into the Lady's hand. It was a blow-pipe.

"It seems to be that kind of day," said the Lady with the Bun out loud. "I'm going to submit a director's admonition, as well as a commendation."

After a short pause, she added,

"This is the end, when someone is punished for doing something good."

***

I confess, dear Danny, my little flea brain found the whole thing incomprehensible. What profits it anyone to hurt another, because he knows a lot? I will try to persuade every little flea in the flea school that the more any one of them knows, the better for us all. After all, whether we like it or not, we are not alone in this world. We are all in this together. The more we know together, the better it is for each one of us. No?

At the same time, it occurred to me that Long Legs punished Phenomenon, because he deserved it, because he had kept quiet that it was he who had tripped up Pigtails.

"That's not why!" protested Toma. "I don't think he knew about it."

The film rolled.

"I barely touched her," he muttered.

"Maybe, but you threw her a bit off balance. Isn't it a bummer that you get a commendation for it?"

"It is."

Unexpectedly, Toma pushed his chair back and stood up.

"Aunt Csöpi."

It wasn't only Aunt Csöpi, who turned toward him curiously, but everyone else too.

"Aunt Csöpi."

"Yes, Toma."

"I'd like to ask something."

"Go ahead. What is it?"

"I'd rather not have the commendation."

The Lady's mouth stood open.

The others' too.

"Why?"

Toma didn't reply.

"Come on, why? Because the others are hurting you?"

"No. That's not why."

"Then why?"

Toma said nothing.

"I'm not going to go back on it," said the Lady with the Bun. "Where would the world be if the good ones back off and the bad ones advance freely?"

"Aunt Csöpi, I'd like this to be that kind of day." Toma smiled enigmatically. "I won't get a commendation and Levi won't get an admonition. So, we'll be even."

The Lady with the Bun was so stupefied by this absurdity that she couldn't even say a word. The class burst out even more loudly. "Hoorah, Toma!" several shouted. Others applauded, and still others pounded the table.

Something seemed to have broken in the Lady with the Bun. Or on the contrary, something was conceived and crystallised. Often it is precisely the contradictory things that are the most difficult to distinguish. It was a fact that, for one thing, she gave herself up, and on the other, she was visibly seized by the exploding mood. She smiled.

"All right, Toma, have it your way."

Long Legs dragged himself to his feet and went up to the Lady with the Bun. He stretched out his hand. The Lady did the same, though her eyes looked confused. Long Legs leaned over and kissed her hand.

Cheering, applause and stamping of feet.

"Let's play a game," shouted Blondie and Burly.

"Let's play," Camilla joined in.

"Are you happy now?" asked Phenomenon, when he sat down.

***

The truth be told, my dear friend, I was not entirely satisfied and communicated this outright to Phenomenon. I saw that he was surprised, but didn't become nervous. It is very rare to encounter people who, if pressed, don't get angry, but watch for the next obstacle with interest. They're glad for the challenge to their brains. So, Phenomenon was this kind. He asked me what was it that I didn't like, and he waited for my answer with curiosity. I answered that I wouldn't expect the truth from anyone else, but from him I did expect it. For he was an exceptional child, a kind I had never met before. And if even he lay low, if he didn't think it important for the truth to come out, then who could I trust from then on? Nobody. I might as well go back to the fleas, for there was no reason to look up to human beings.

Of course, I didn't really believe this seriously, since fleas weren't interested in the truth, not even to this extent. But in the heat of the argument, it felt good to say such uplifting things and it was good to think that, well, I'd caught this smart kid.

But I didn't catch him at all.

"We'll continue this after the game," he said at once, for he was next.

***

You should know, Danny, that I could never leave you people if only because of these games. Not only are there no games as witty and fun in our world, but there are no games at all. I have no idea how we were able to vegetate for millions of years without such things.

Aunt Csöpi pulled a notebook from her bag. It was small, but thick. It was as if she had come forward with some secret craze, she flipped the pages with such excitement.

"All right, listen up. I will ask you a question, each one after the other, and I expect a prompt answer. It's not important for it to be true in content, but only that it should suit in terms of sound. If for example, I ask what does the *crow* do? I won't accept *cries*, but *croaks*. And for example, what kind of animal is an *owl*. It's a *fowl*. Do you understand?"

"Yes. Let's begin."

"Stop. One more thing. Anyone who can't answer fast enough, is out. Anyone who can, stays sitting. We go around until there is only one sitting. He or she will be the victor. All right?"

"All riiiight," they shouted in chorus.

The Lady with the Bun went from child to child tirelessly, her high heels clicking. They gave good answers, there were hardly any who were out, who had to stand up. But even they enjoyed the good answers of others, and the halloos and neighing that accompanied the right answers.

"What animal makes a loud sound?"

"Hound."

"Which animal is crazy?"

"Loon."

"Very good. And which one scrams?"

"The ram."

"Correct. Which animal jumps over a log in the fog?"

"Frog."

"What animal stunk?"

"Skunk."

"*Which one trots?*"

"Fox."

"*Which animal runs the course?*"

"The horse, of course."

"*Outstanding! Which one watches TV? Don't you know? How about you? And you? All right then, stand up.*"

"Well… the flea."

"*Bravo! You can keep on sitting. Which animal makes a nice dish?*"

"Fish."

"*Splendid! Which one rattles?*"

"Rattlesnake."

"*What animal likes to eat carrots?*"

"The parrot."

"*Wonderful! And which animal puts you to sleep?*"

"The sheep."

"*Tell me quickly, what does the lark do?*"

"It larks about."

"*What animal's funky and spunky?*"

"Donkey."

"*Which animal has a lot of pride?*"

"Lion, of course."

"*What animal dances to the didgeridoo?*"

"Kangaroo."

"*What creature is snug in the rug?*"

"Bug."

"*And which animal sat on the mat?*"

"Cat."

***

Half of the class was still in the game when the pitiless bell rang. This racket from hell didn't even care that I was getting into the swing of things, and the good ideas came to me ever more quickly. I was on the verge of asking Toma to let me take the next round instead of him. I wouldn't draw far-reaching conclusions from this, dear Danny, but the fact is that Long Legs, Blondie and Burly were still sitting when the bell rang. And their eyes were shining. Just like the Lady with the Bun's.

As for me, however, I was deflated, for two weighty reasons. I threw it to Phenomenon: *"All right, Toma, do you know what is my real fear?"* Of course, he knew. After all, he could see into me.

"You get hungry in my callow ear. But I wouldn't like you to make a meal of me."

My God, but I was surprised again. I would have understood and accepted from everyone else. But from Phenomenon?

"Why not? You don't want to keep it from me."

"No."

"Then?"

"I haven't answered your question. And I wouldn't like you to accept my answer, because I fed you full."

I couldn't tell whether he was joking or being serious.

He was very serious.

We stood up and walked out into the hallway. We walked cautiously, hugging the wall, amid the racket, rushing, skipping and sliding about. We conversed in silence. Meanwhile, the film rolled on.

"Do you see how obliviously she is skipping about?"

"Yes, I see."

Her two pigtails were dancing hither and thither. As incredible as it may be, it made my little heart beat.

"It made my heart beat too. Wouldn't you like to stop her?"

"Yes, but very carefully."

"Touch her?"

"Yes, but very carefully."

"I only put my foot out a little bit."

"Did you want to trip her up?"

"I tripped her, but not intentionally. I didn't want to trip her up. I put my foot out without intending to."

"But why did you do it, if you didn't wish to?"

"I wanted to touch her, to stop her. I wanted to catch her. That is what I wanted. But I didn't want to trip her. I didn't want to hurt her. Not the least little bit."

I thought about that.

Then I got it.

"If you did it without intending to, you're not guilty."

"No?"

"Yes." I nodded.

I was forced to acknowledge that he was right. When I unrolled the stills of this story, I couldn't find a single one in which there was an underhanded thought or evil instinct. In fact, it was more love that motivated him, the pure desire for sharing overflowing joie de vivre. And we had to acknowledge, if it was only owing to an accident, or indeed to Phenomenon's credit that this tiny, instinctive, involuntary movement didn't prove fatal.

And I had to agree with Phenomenon, make him right, what he was in no hurry to reveal, he played a key role not only in bringing on the accident, but also in solving it. We were on our way home when I asked him,

"Wouldn't it be better if everyone knew the truth?"

He responded,

"Which truth?"

After a pause, he added,

"Do you know what they would have done to me if I had told them?"

Actually, I could imagine. They would have parroted it far and wide. "Did you hear, he almost killed a second-grade little girl." That's exactly what they would have done. Nobody was interested in the tiresome details. That's what human beings are like, my dear friend. But human children too. They would have competed with who would spit on the back of his neck? Who would hit him from behind? Who would trip him up?

Not out of evil intention. Of course not.

From goodness.

They would be glad that they could feel that they too were good. "Beast! He'd deserve it! Why did he have to trip up that poor little innocent girl?"

In any event, dear Danny, I had to see, though truth was a good thing, if it came out this time, it would be unjust.

**

At the same time, I had to admit, my dear friend, that I wasn't going to open a flea school. I asked Toma to wait for my tabby together, let my loyal transportation carry me back to you. On the way, I talked my moggy into carrying me back to the school, so I could visit Pigtails and Phenomenon now and then. Otherwise, I could do very well without a school. I could play without it. By the way! Can you tell me, Danny, what the clever rook reads?

"Book?"

"Right. You got it. Now you ask me."

Eighth Tale
JIMMY JUMPER'S CHRISTMAS

Shall I tell you where I spent Christmas? Fate must have wanted Red Fur to come here before you, dear Danny, and that decided everything. Red Fur knew that beanpole with whom Young Master got so warmed up in talking to that he completely forgot about us. Not so, as Toffee and I would have spoken up that we were there too, but still!

Beanpole's phone kept ringing constantly, but while he was talking with someone, Young Master didn't pay any attention to us, but drank in his every word. He even took the leash off Red Fur to let him run around as he pleased.

I asked Red Fur after a while who was this chap? He replied, journalist. "What's that?" I asked. He: "He writes up the news."

I didn't understand at all.

"At every moment something new happens to everybody. No? How can you write all that up?"

"To tell the truth, I don't know. I don't know that much about it." Toffee shook his head. "He must write what happened to him."

"But why should he write about that? He knows it already."

"But other people don't know."

"Aha! Or what if I write about what we're talking about, then I would be a journalist too?"

"I don't think so. We're not that interesting. I most certainly am not."

My modesty prevented me from protesting out loud. I thought to myself, I, a flea, am as interesting as any mother's son. I immediately decided to jump onto this fellow and tell him he wouldn't get such a good subject any time soon. If he wished, I could tell him my life. He could make such a good story out of it that the whole world would snap it up like hotcakes.

I told Toffee to get a little closer to Beanpole, for I had a yen to jump on him. Toffee was sincerely sorry. It was gratifying. Even in this freezing cold, he liked to go out walking and conversing with me. So, Toffee was sorry that I was leaving him, but he knew that if I wanted to go, wild horses couldn't keep me back. It was best to let me go so that I would want to come back soon.

I took the opportunity to make the transfer. I settled in Beanpole's ear, and waited for the right moment to bring up my alluring proposal.

You can't imagine, Danny, how difficult it was to find the right moment.

It was so difficult that I decided then and there forever, that no matter how the world would develop, I wouldn't ever in my life have a telephone like that. Am I crazy? It was as if I were being jerked around by a wire. Did I need that? The hell I did.

An excitable man's voice called him. He asked him,

"How are you with the headquarters scandal? Do you know who was cheating whom? Who gained the most? Wait, I've got another call, I'll call you back right away."

We didn't take three steps, before the phone rang again. Now it was an animated woman's voice.

"Are you going to the office today? Look up the Women's Magazine. There's a coupon in it, twenty-five percent discount for any sports equipment. Cut it out."

Poor Beanpole. I could see all kinds of angry green colours vibrating in his head.

"All right, all right." He nodded. "I have to put the phone down. I'll call you back right away."

He poked the screen with his forefinger; the gadget was already ringing again.

"Who are you yacking with, when you know I'm calling you?"

"Sorry, with my wife. Christmas jobs."

Animated guffaws.

"The woman was pestering me too. Christmas has barely begun, and I can hardly wait for it to be over. So, what about headquarters? I left a whole page for it."

"Well, I found out a lot of things. Every clue leads to the Multralo company."

"Oh hell. That's what I was afraid of. They're our biggest advertiser."

"So, what do we do?"

"For the time being, I only know what not to do, don't do anything about the subject. Unfortunately, it's out of our hands. There's nothing we can do. I'll call you back right away."

Why should I deny it, my dear friend? My eyes brightened. I virtually saw a sign from heaven in the way things were developing. I hadn't a clue what this headquarters affair was all about, or what was this Multralo Company, or what an advertisement was, but even my tiny flea brain understood that there was a whole empty page to be filled out. And then why shouldn't my life of a flea be written up there? I was searching for the right words to persuade him when that crazy phone rang again. In addition, Beanpole's hand must have been cold, because he put the phone on the ear in which I was sitting.

"Sorry, it's me again. I thought that you should buy one more copy of Women's Magazine; we can cut out the coupon and we can run over to the Bedeklon, if that's OK with you. We'll get the hockey set for Marcel. That'll be his Christmas present. When are you free tonight? Can you go get Marcel?"

"I can't tell you yet. The office is going to call me at any moment. I'll call you."

"They could leave us in peace at least at such a time! Christmas is upon us and we're nowhere…"

"I have to take the call. It's my editor."

"No, you don't. Let him get used to it. You have a private life, after all."

"Is it your wife again?" asked the excited voice coldly.

"Yes, unfortunately."

"Tell her, it's working hours."

"OK. All right. Have you worked out something? I've put a lot of time and energy into this…"

"I'm sorry. That's the way it is sometimes. How many subjects I've had to leave half-finished! Anyway, it's

Christmas now. Readers are less interested in juicy stories at such times. You need something touching. Something compassionate. Uplifting."

I wanted to say that I would be just right for that. I even made peace between the cat and the mice. But Beanpole got in first again.

"I know someone, who washes the feet of the homeless."

"Homeless all right, but we're not having anything to do with the mentally ill," Animated rattled on. "Find a couple and find out where and how they're spending Christmas. And it can't be more than twelve thousand characters. Be sure to take a good photographer with you; a good picture is worth more than a thousand words. Get it in on deadline. I have to have a look at it."

He just went on and on, without even taking a breath. My head was swimming. It seemed that I was a bit aggrieved. That is why I suddenly got a yen for a little mischief-making. I couldn't stop myself from commenting to Beanpole.

"A talking flea has a bit more spirit than a homeless person. Don't you think?"

Beanpole stopped in his tracks. He looked around then stared at Young Master.

"Did you say something?"

"No. I'm listening."

"It seems this constant stress is getting on my nerves. Do you know any homeless people around here?"

"Yes. Several," Young Master replied readily. "What kind do you want?"

"One who can talk."

"That's the only kind we have around here. There are more dead drunks downtown."

"And, if possible, ones that aren't mangy, or full of lice and fleas."

"Why are you insulting me?" I asked.

Beanpole didn't stop; he just stole a look at Young Master. Then he looked around, then stopped.

"I'm not going anywhere," he answered. "I'm going to ask for sick-leave."

"Something wrong?" Young Master looked at him intently.

"It's as if something were talking in my head. I must be hallucinating."

Young Master looked at Toffee, who immediately lowered his head in a hang-dog look.

"Don't get excited. You're not imagining things. It's a talking flea in your ear. He can read your thoughts."

"My thoughts?"

"Exactly."

"Flea."

"Talking flea."

"Oh right."

"That can come in handy in this Multralo affair. If I were you, I'd send him to the heads of the suspects for some information-gathering."

"I'm of the opinion that you should go on sick-leave too. What a crazy world! Even hallucinations are contagious. But first let's see the bear."

"See what?" I asked, amazed.

"Well, the homeless," replied Beanpole. But not to me, to Young Master.

"I understood, but…" Young Master stopped and didn't go on. After a short pause, he pointed to the Janos Hill that loomed above us right in front of our noses.

"We managed to locate several homeless tents on this side of the hill recently with Toffee. About fifteen minutes from here on foot. Shall we go?"

"Let's go." Beanpole nodded. And we all set off.

***

We hadn't got up very far, but Beanpole was panting hard even from this. Among the bare trees we caught a glimpse of a makeshift shed. Empty plastic bottles, plastic bags, crushed beer cans and empty cans led us there. Among a few slender trees far and wide were thinner branches, and the whole was covered with a plastic foil – that was a homeless shelter. Beanpole's heart was beating fast, not just from the steep climb but also from fright. He imagined all kinds of wild men, who would leap out from the tents and attack intruders.

He wasn't far wrong.

The branches crackled and crunched under our feet, no matter how quietly we tried to sneak up. Every crackle and crunch stopped our breathing for a moment. You can imagine, dear Danny, the fright Beanpole had when a wild man did indeed poke his head out of the tent. He was wearing not just one, but two caps, both pulled over his head; his eyes were barely visible from the hair. He was covered in an enormous, ragged blanket, under which a weather-beaten winter coat peeped out.

"What are you doing here?" he snarled.

Toffee yelped.

"Quiet!" Young Master ordered and waved at him to come to him. Toffee sloped over to him.

Beanpole cleared his throat.

"Good day."

The wild man turned toward him.

"I asked, what are you doing here?"

Beanpole grew more and more tense.

"I would tell you, if you'd let me," he answered irritably.

"Don't tell me. Get the hell out of here."

Beanpole didn't really wish to leave. Here was the subject within arm's length; he just needed to have answers for a few questions, and he would make something of them.

"I'm a journalist and..."

"I don't give a shit about your newspapers!"

"I'd like to have an interview with you for the magazine, *Worlds Swept Away*."

"I don't give a shit about the world."

"An interview about Christmas. I just need a few words..."

"I don't have a few words. You're trespassing. Get the hell out, if you know what's good for you."

The wild man swung a club for emphasis. That was all the group needed. Even Toffee made himself small. We began to back off and slink away.

"I'd be glad to help you," I told him after a short pause.

I could see that Beanpole was struggling; what should he believe and what not? He couldn't even imagine a flea talking in a human voice, but he had to accept that someone was trying to converse with him. And this someone was certainly not the familiar fellow on his right, and certainly not the rather elderly dog that was running up and down. But someone or something in his head. Of course, it was possible that he really was imagining things. But then why shouldn't he go into this game of his own imagination?

"Are you really a flea?"

"Really."

"And you really can talk?"

"Well, can't I? As you can hear."

"Well, yes. And how do fleas spend Christmas? How do they celebrate? What customs do they keep?"

I thought about it. Not about how, or what customs we keep, but about why don't fleas celebrate Christmas, if it's such a big deal with human beings?

"Well?"

"We don't celebrate Christmas," I confessed.

"A pity," Beanpole said, and I saw that he really was sorry.

Young Master asked him,

"Is there something wrong?"

"Everything's wrong," Beanpole said indignantly. Then he heaved a great sigh. "Where are we going?"

"There's a cave about fifteen minutes from here. Two homeless people live there, a man and a woman."

"And they're wild too?"

"No, not at all. I spoke to them once. They were actually rather sweet."

"Actually?"

"I mean…"

"I understand." Beanpole waved sourly. While we plodded along, he remembered the Women's Magazine. And the coupon. And the hockey set. And the Christmas tree. And the Christmas candy that he had to get. And a present for the wife. For his mother and younger sister. And his editor. And, oh yes, a Christmas greeting to the subjects of his reports. And to the more important politicians. Should they have fish for Christmas Eve or stuffed cabbage? Should his mother make poppy seed and nut rolls, or should he buy them? He had to bring a photographer the next day, if he succeeded in getting a story. Yes, of course tomorrow would be Bedeklon. Then he could ask this gracious young man. How devoted teenagers could be. How they can fall for a journalist. If they only knew how fed up I was with the whole thing.

"Here we are."

Young Master pointed at a cliff wall, surrounded above and by its side by trees. You could say it blended into the environment.

"Thank God," Beanpole huffed.

"Halloo!" shouted Young Master.

A short man climbed out of the belly of the mountain, from an enormous mouth. He had to lean over. The woman who followed him had to lean even further, so as not to hit her head. Or not mess up her hair.

"Who are you looking for?" she asked, visibly alarmed.

"I kiss your hand," Young Master went up to her. "We've met before. I came by here with Toffee."

"Oh yes, I remember." The woman's face brightened. One of her front teeth was missing, but this did not bother me much. But what definitely pleased me was that she leaned over and scratched Toffee's head.

"The gentleman is a journalist." Young Master pointed at us. "We know each other. He lives in the same apartment block as I."

"We are very glad." Little Man spoke up. Beanpole looked at him, so I could finally see him too. He had a short beard and a small moustache, and his gapped teeth were quite yellow. His look, however, was bright and alert, even though suspicion glinted in it.

"Can I ask what you're about?" he asked.

"Christmas for the homeless is my subject. It would appear in the magazine, *World Swept Away*. Have you heard of it?"

"Of course." Little Man brightened. "I even listen to excerpts from it on the radio in the mornings."

He had a lopsided smile.

"Please come in," he said, pointing ahead of him.

You know, dear Danny, it is curious, but even though Beanpole and I were looking at the same thing, we saw something entirely different. On my side, my feet were, so to speak, rooted in the ear. An enormous bed was inside the depths of the cave; mattresses, duvets, pillows and colourful blankets were on top of each other. The tassels were straightened. Dresses, clothes, nicely folded, some were hanging on hangers or nails. Logs side by side with books, illustrated magazines, and a floating wick. There was a tiny iron stove in a recess surrounded by smoke-blackened pots and pans. The long pipe of the stove came toward us, but the end turned up to the sky and belched out smoke.

I was totally fascinated. Beanpole quickly stepped back, saying,

"Thanks. I think I'll stay outside."

"As you wish." Little Man shrugged.

"Would you care for a cup of tea?" asked the lady, smiling. "I can make it quick on the little stove."

"No, no. Duty calls." Beanpole declined firmly, and pulled out of his pocket a flat object that looked like a telephone. But he didn't put it to his ear, but to his mouth. "One, two, three, four. One, two, three, four. Homeless Christmas. Please, introduce yourselves."

He shoved the flat thing before the lady's mouth, and waited.

"I'm Irene Kovacs…"

"It's enough to say Irene," he interrupted and pushed the flat thing before Little Man's mouth. Little Man leaned over and said,

"I'm Istvan."

"What's going on?" I asked, dumbfounded. I didn't understand, so I asked Beanpole.

"What the hell are you doing? What's that flat thing?"

"I'm recording what they say."

"With that flat thing?"

"It records the voices. I don't have to take notes, it records for me. But don't bother me now."

"What I say, too?"

160

"Quiet! Don't bother me."

He asked me so firmly that I went quiet very quickly. He put the flat thing before his mouth, then put it back to the gap-toothed one.

"Where are you going to spend Christmas?"

"Well, here at home."

"Here in this cave?"

"Where else?"

"Aren't you going to be cold?"

"We'll light the stove and put on warm clothes."

Then it was Beanpole's turn again, then again gap-toothed. Having nothing better to do, I listened.

"Advent is upon us. At such times, everybody prepares in their own way. What do you do? With what?"

"We rummage through the waste bins. Thank God, there are a lot of rich people. At such times, they do a big cleaning and throw out what they don't need any more. And we can use them. We found these two jackets in a rubbish bin." He pointed at himself and the lady.

Even Beanpole was amazed at this. He pinched Irene's jacket and rubbed it between his fingers.

"Hmm, even I would gladly wear this."

"Take a look at this and that too. If we dress in layers, we can keep quite warm. Of course, we weren't always this lucky. A few years ago, when there was a very cold winter, we hadn't yet discovered this cave, we didn't have so much stuff, and we couldn't dress well enough and didn't have enough blankets. And we didn't have heating either. We slept in a trash shed, which we had to leave at dawn. We returned late at night, snow fell heavily, it was cold, and we almost froze. But at least we had each other. But they cut off two of his toes, for his feet froze. Then I was alone on the street... So, you see, we've been through a lot."

"Is Christmas a fete?"

"Not for us. It's a day like all the rest."

In the silence that followed, Little Man leaned over the flat thing, and said,

"It will be a symbol for us. We'll put up a pine branch, and two pieces of candy on it. We'll light a candle. Anyway, candles are our light. So, it's all the same. That's how we'll celebrate Christmas. The two of us."

"Well, we don't give presents," Irene said. "There is no gift giving."

Little Man didn't leave it at that.

"Yes, there is. We give gifts to each other," he announced firmly. Irene's eyes went round.

"With what?"

Little Man nodded then replied,

"With each other."

Irene broke out laughing.

We stood there moved. To be more precise, I sat there fighting tears.

Or it could be that Beanpole was fighting his tears, and I was empathising too much with his emotion. The fact is that Beanpole pressed something on the flat thing and stuck it in his pocket, then announced,

"That was nice. I hope my editor will like it."

Fact is, I decided I would spend Christmas with Little Man and Irene.

162

***

The next day the photographer arrived, carrying a good-size bag on his stout shoulder, accompanied by Red Fur and Young Master. While Little Man explained to me, the fat thing that he pulled out and aimed at us took photos, not like the flat thing the day before, that recorded sound. As it shot us, it occurred to me that I should make an appearance; I should be in the photo too. I climbed out and grabbed Little Man's ear lobe. Only it was cold; it began to snow, and I soon returned to my comfortable nest.

There was not much mention of Christmas in the following days. We went the rounds of the area's trash bins, taking care not to arrive too early, for they weren't out on the street yet; but not too late either, for others in the same boat would fish out the really valuable pieces.

Surprisingly good things could be found.

For example, a transistor radio. Little Man wanted to give it to me, saying that they already had one, but I said I hadn't a clue what to do with it anyway; if I wanted to listen to it, I could listen to it in their heads.

All kinds of clothes in all quantities. Most of them were torn and patched up, but some were washed and ironed even, in nylon bags. At such times, Irene's eyes shone, and Little Man's head signalled joy. Just as when they found a pair of brogues that were still wearable, and a blanket that was only slightly torn.

Food was found joyfully, but there was as much as maggots and they had to be more circumspect with them. They opened the paper bags full of flour and corn flour and

163

poured out half a handful to see whether moths hadn't got into it. Little Man noted, "Although my favourite food is meat with meat, I'm not crazy about moth meat." He laughed... The returnable bottles were put aside; if they still had some contents, they opened them and sniffed. "I think it's still good," Irene said, and Little Man agreed. "I think so too. They're better preserved in the cold. Let's put them away for Christmas Eve." After waiting a little, he added, "We know that you don't like bean soup, but don't worry, we'll find something for you."

I knew they wouldn't find anything.

By then I knew my way around rubbish bins.

Once we found a whole bag full of jars of baby food. None of them, an unimaginably large selection, had been opened. Some contained meat, and some didn't. The only problem was they were all past their sell-by date. Little Man jumped with joy. "You know, son," he explained to me, "it isn't so easy to starve to death in this crazy world. There's nothing wrong with these delicious purées. Since they're intended for babies, they write a very short expiration date on them. If it's just one day over the limit, the parents don't dare give it to their little ones. Thank God!"

People threw out cream too, if it was old, but it still would have been good sour cream. They threw out cheese too, if it was mouldy, whereas Irene could cut the spots out with a few snips of the knife. But no one threw full-blooded living meat into the bin. Not even by accident. It was not as if I were surprised at this, but every day I grew hungrier and hungrier. Although we fleas tolerate fasting rather well, I must confess to you, Danny, not eating was not my thing. At other times, I didn't hesitate too much, I usually feasted soon on my transportation vehicles, but here I was a guest after all. Also, I'd become friends with Little Man, and with his woman, and I couldn't bring myself to bite them.

Although I often saw stray cats slip away while we were rummaging in the bins, I hadn't a hope of catching them. Anyway, I wanted to spend Christmas with Little Man and Irene. Or, as Little Man described it, the festival of love.

On one of our return trips, we took a different route. A few flea jumps from the little mountain train track, there was a little hut hidden on the side of the embankment. We knocked on the door, and after a while a tall, skinny man poked his head out.

"Quickly, quickly, the heat will be lost." He herded us inside. "I haven't seen you in a long time."

"We're working a bit," answered Irene. "It gets light late and dark early."

The little room had a narrow bed and a little table. That was all. We had barely settled on the bed, when three cats ventured forth. Little Man fished out a piece of sausage from one of the countless bags and held it before him.

"Did you just find it?" asked our host.

"Now. Would you like a taste?"

"First give it to the cats."

One of them, a tabby who was not at all thin, ran to Little Man. It snapped up the piece of sausage that had been thrown on the ground, then rubbing itself against Little Man's leg, and purring loudly, it begged for more. The other two cats appeared suddenly too.

"I hope there's enough choice," muttered Little Man under his moustache.

Even during the abundant feast, I thought constantly of how grateful I was to him. And, actually, I was having a wonderful time.

***

The snow falling softly and peacefully had covered everything when we headed off to gather pine branches. There would have been some nearby, but Little Man didn't want to wound any tree in our vicinity. Even so we found some very soon. After coming back, we stumbled onto a leg bone. Little Man picked it up, inspected it, then said, it must have belonged to a deer. We took it home and put it on a blanket, on which they had been gathering all kinds of things for days. Among others, a board game that had parts missing but was still usable, a slightly scruffy stuffed rabbit, and a Swiss knife. "Thank God, its handle is damaged," determined Little Man. "That is why it was thrown out." A log stood in the middle of the blanket, with a fat vase on it. Little Man put the pine branch in the vase. Irene tied on two Christmas fondants, a red and a blue one.

"Aren't there any more?" asked Little Man.

"Yes, there are. We found an entire St. Nicholas bag full of them."

"Then put on another."

"Tomorrow evening we'll put on a picture of Jesus and a candle, and voilà our Christmas tree," muttered Little Man under his moustache.

Most of the day was taken up with cooking.

Before darkness fell Little Man announced that he would go on another round.

"Tomorrow they won't be bringing rubbish," Irene said, amazed.

"That's true," answered Little Man. "But at such times they put a lot of things next to the rubbish bins."

"Oh, leave it. We already have everything we need."

"Yes, we have, but you never can tell when there's some big catch."

"All right, whatever you wish," Irene allowed.

Little Man was dressed up to his neck, still we didn't start off. Unexpectedly, he asked me,

"How can I tell whether you're asleep or not?"

"You can't tell. Only if I get out."

"Hmm. And you don't want to get out? You could go over to Irene for a change."

"To help her?"

"Yes, maybe to help her."

"I can't help her. I've never cooked in my life. I'd rather stay with you, if possible."

"All right, then off we go," he said.

We ambled down to the bus stop, and waited patiently. I in my warm place, he in the cold. Both of us looked at the stars. The snow had stopped falling softly. The sky had cleared up here and there, and so many fleas glittered up there at a fathomless distance. Fairly soon a blue box rolled in. There weren't many people in it, and we found seats. "If you wish to know, I'm going to sleep now," I informed him sleepily. That was exactly what happened.

I woke up to an army of people trooping by us. They were carrying bags, but there were some who had whole pine trees under their arm. They thronged forth from the depths of the earth, and another bunch seemed to have been swallowed up by the ground.

"There must be an immense cave down there," I noted.

"Right you are," laughed Little Man. "That's the metro."

"Let's take the metro," I suggested.

"No. That costs a lot of money. At most they make you get off the bus if you don't have a ticket, and you can go with the next one. But they don't even let you in here."

"Not even me?"

He laughed.

"Yes, you can go in."

He darkened.

"But you'd have to go to another person with more money. There are lots to choose from." He shrugged.

Suddenly I thought of something.

"Didn't you say, that you're going on your rounds of rubbish bins?"

"Diversionary tactic. I have work to do here."

"Here?"

"Here."

"Then why don't you want to go down there?"

"That's not why I came here."

"Why then?"

"Something else."

I was a bit annoyed that he wanted to keep something from me.

"Should I look in your head?" I asked him. There was no denying it, there was a bit of threat in my voice.

"Don't. I'll tell you."

He pulled his hand out of his pocket, and reached out. He held a little radio.

"I want to sell this. For you don't need it."

"Aha! You need money for a metro ticket."

"Not for the metro."

"What else do you need it for?"

"It's a secret."

"Should I look into your head?"

"If you want to ruin my mood and your surprise, go ahead."

Of course, there was nothing I wanted less than to ruin his mood. Though it was true, it wasn't so easy not to see what we see. For however incredible it may seem, my dear friend, a flea sees not with his eyes, but with his heart, and although it is easy to shut our eyes, it is much harder to shut our heart. In brief, we sold the radio quickly, and I knew what the game was about. But I pretended to have no idea about anything. So Little Man turned on the radio which was quite loud. Several people stopped, held it to their ear, turned it this way and that, then gave it back. Until an elderly lady elaborately rummaged in her purse and fished out the money agreed upon.

I knew what was to come next, that was why I fibbed to Little Man that this terrible crowd had made me sleepy and I would have a little shut-eye.

Little Man waited a while. Then he cut across the throng and headed straight for a kiosk. He put the money down and took what he wanted, then quickly dropped it into the bag.

"Wake up, sleepy-head!" he shouted, on the bus, for I was pretending to be still over there. It was totally dark by the time we got off the bus; nevertheless, we got home rather quickly. It was only the hill up to the cave that was somewhat tiring, for there, he was missing his truncated toes, and he could just limp up. But not only for Little Man. For some strange reason, also for me, even though I was squatting inside.

***

Well, what we were waiting for so long finally arrived. The sky was studded with bright stars; it was cold, but we pulled on a lot of warm clothes, and we made a great fire in the little stove. Three Christmas fondants hung from the pine branch, the third was wrapped in golden paper. Their shadows wobbled on the wall of the cave. A little picture was leaning against the fat vase.

"Do you see?" explained Little Man. "Baby Jesus in the manger."

Lamb, cow, donkey, they all gathered around him, only I didn't see any fleas. Of course, they could have been there. I told Little Man that I was somewhat sorry that I hadn't been born larger, then I would have appeared there too. He replied,

"If you're sorry only once a year, that's not so bad."

Little Man brought out of the throat of the cave a larger log, put on it an old bread-board, which Irene covered with a white tablecloth. Then with a quick movement she lit a match and lit the largest candle. It was thicker than the tibia. She held it in her hand for a while, then leaned it over a plate, and finally placed it in the middle of the wax puddle that had formed in the middle of the plate. Soon it stood there as if rooted to the spot.

Two soup bowls were also put on the tablecloth, with two spoons, two metal mugs, a bread basket and a half-full – half-empty – bottle of wine. Little Man thrust his hands in the opening left by the blanket he had wrapped around himself, and pulled out from his coat pocket a tiny plate and tiny spoon. Irene's eyes grew round.

"What's that for?"

"Not what for, but who for? Where there are three, you have to lay the table for three."

He said it so nicely, that it didn't want to leave my head. Not even when we gathered around the fat vase, and Irene, and Little Man gave thanks to God that he had given them shelter and their daily bread for the whole year. Little Man finally added,

"And thank you for bringing us a guest here to our little stable."

They looked at each other, deeply. Then, without a word, they embraced each other. For a long time, strongly, without moving.

We were all crying.

For me it was for emotion, but underneath their tears wailed pain.

Little Man heaved a great sigh, and the darkness of pain quickly receded and light, bright colours came forward in their place.

"Irene," he shouted gaily. "Reach down into that bag."

He pointed to below the fat vase, the blanket with treasure.

Irene kneeled and with eyes closed began to feel the contents of the bag. Finally, she grabbed something and pulled it out, showing it.

"Surely not!" I was surprised out loud, as much as I was able.

Little Man laughed.

Irene laughed too, shaking her head incredulously.

"Now this is a surprise."

All three of us gathered around the largest candle; we looked in amazement at the thick Christmas issue of *World Swept Away*. Above all, of course, the illustrated report on the homeless. "This is where Irene and Istvan live," Little Man read aloud. Above the caption the wide mouth of our cave could be seen, in front of it were Irene and Little Man, oddly enough looking directly at us.

"Hello." I waved at them. "Too bad, I'm not there too. Even though I had climbed out on your ear lobe."

"Well, of course. You're there! There! There! Open your eyes. Can't you see?"

He got all excited.

Then he became pensive.

"My mother always showed us the angel on Christmas Eve, from the window of our big room. "There! He's flying! There! There! Can't you see him?"

"Did you see him?"

"I did see him. Afterwards he didn't show himself for a long time. But I can see him again. Come here, look there, at the sky. Can you see him flying by?"

"I see only golden fleas," I muttered, completely spellbound.

"It's the same." Little Man waved his hand. He laughed from the depths of his heart but so that Irene caught it too, and in the uproarious laughter she spilled the bean soup.

Then silence fell onto the land. The rustling forest soon sent us to sleep. Elsewhere perhaps they were just lighting the candles; we three were pondering our fate under three or four blankets and quilts. Or to be more precise, I had the ear of a woollen cap on me, but I wasn't cold. Before I dropped off to sleep, it occurred to me that I hadn't had a bite. In vain was the bean soup improved with sausage; I couldn't bear to have any. Finally, I reassured myself that tomorrow was another day and Little Man would surely take me to the three cats.

***

He would have taken me, dear Danny, if we hadn't woken up to a "halloo" and Red Fur hadn't somersaulted over us. Little Man grabbed the deer shank from him and held it tight. "You see, little Flea's Christmas present." He pulled up the flap of his cap with his free hand. "Don't begrudge him a meal."

I mumbled thanks to Little Man, and jumped.

On our way home, I asked Red Fur not to look back. I confess that I was afraid my heart would draw me back. But if I could not tell you any more tales, it would be the end of me.

Ninth Tale
JIMMY JUMPER INVESTIGATES

Imagine, Danny, what a character fate brought me. I was just contemplating the world from Red Fur's head, when I see my favourite transport vehicle meekly lower his head and even his legs gave way in his great respect. A stately black dog with sharp ears and a pointed nose was approaching us.

"It's a tracking dog," Toffee growled meaningfully, and drew aside.

A short, though well-muscled fellow in dark sunglasses and track suit followed him. I can't say I found him overly sympathetic, but neither did he repel me. But he was mysterious. And emotionless. Like someone who disciplines his feelings. At least, so it seemed to me, or to be more precise, to Toffee. After all, sitting in his head and ear, I contemplated this exciting world.

Here, however, our thoughts went their separate ways.

This was as far as it went, as far as Red Fur went, as if he were saying, it's not my bone, why should I chew it? As for me, the dog and Dark Glasses excited me greatly, although, for the moment I hadn't a clue what was special and mysterious about them.

At a suitable moment, I leaped off Toffee, hoping to land on the dog. I must tell you, my friend, these leaps aren't without danger. After all, if my target suddenly stops or changes direction, I'll pass right by him and find myself on the road. From then on, I must rely on my nose and good luck. Perhaps someone might chance to come by. Therefore, jumping always freaks me out. When I land, I'm always so glad that, well, this time, I got lucky. That was the way it was with this tracking dog too. I quickly settled into his pointed ears, which were easy to enter. I said to him,

"Greetings to you, great investigator."

He wasn't even surprised. He replied conscientiously.

"I'm not an investigator. That's my master. I'm a tracker."

"But Toffee said…"

"Who's this Toffee?"

"Red Fur. I jumped off him."

"Aha!"

Toffee lowering his head appeared suddenly in his head. But what surprised me even more was that the image of a flea appeared suddenly too. "Wow! What a clever dog!" I said to myself, and if I could I would have clicked my tongue in appreciation.

"What does a tracker do?" I asked.

"Not certain a flea could understand it," he snapped.

"Let's do an experiment. It doesn't cost anything."

"All right, let's do it," he allowed. "Let's say, someone breaks into a house…"

"Why?"

"That's not interesting. He leaves the odour of his feet in the house or garden. For he sweats. And sweat penetrates through the soles of his shoes. The smell is there on the floor, on the rug, in the garden, on the road, wherever he's been. Now, that's why I'm called a tracker. You understand?"

"Perfectly."

"That's surprising. Can you perhaps tell me why I can never find the tracks of cold-blooded killers?"

"Yes."

"Let's hear it."

"They don't sweat."

His jaw dropped.

"My name's Nike," he introduced himself. "I'm a German shepherd."

"I'm a flea. Mind reader."

"Splendid."

"It's not such a big deal. I could say, barely a flea's deal."

"Your ability, that's fantastic. You're the missing link."

He got all excited.

"Let's have an experiment," he offered. "It won't cost anything."

"Let's do it."

"What am I thinking now?"

Dark Glasses shouted at him.

"Nike, who gave you orders to stop."

Nike started off again, but an image took shape in his head."

"I see three men sitting around a table," I reported. "One is holding a leash. The others are asking questions."

"That's right," Nike barked. "They're questioning him. Only a cold-blooded killer can outfox his interrogators. He leaves no trace. They can't shake him out of his self-possession. No matter how much they suspect him, what really happened, only he knows. It's only in his head. And no one can find out his secret. Except for…"

"Except for me."

"That's right. Except for you. The only one in the whole world. Isn't that fantastic? If they trained you like me, you'd go much further. You wouldn't only be a tracker, but a real detective. You could solve all the crimes. All crime would come to an end in the whole world. Can you imagine anything more amazing, more fantastic…? All right, why don't you talk to my boss?"

"The detective?"

"Yes, the detective."

"I could talk it over with him."

***

There was no denying it, I had my doubts about his great idea. But what a tangle our souls are: we are excited by the excitement of another. Nothing had happened in the real world, not even a single flea bite, but you are so excited by the imaginary miraculous changes that you take flight. I will tell Dark Glasses when I clamber into his ear.

"Detective flea, at our service."

He stuck his finger into his ear, the one in which I was sitting. He shook it, as if it had got plugged up, and waited.

"Yes, here I am. According to Nike, I'm the missing link."

He looked down at Nike, then stuck his finger in his ear again.

"You can take me out only with tweezers," I informed him quickly. "Perhaps you didn't hear me: I'm at your service. According to Nike, I'm able to find even cold-blooded killers…"

I saw that he was a determined, tough man, the kind who can hardly bear anyone else to come close. After a short pause, he said,

"Get out of my ear, then we can talk."

"If I do that, we can't talk. Only if I stay in your ear."

He wrestled with himself for a long time. He was tempted, or rather he was curious. On the other hand, he would have gladly been rid of me. Finally, he agreed.

***

I told him everything, almost word for word, what the tracking dog had said so enthusiastically. Even what I answered. I can't say that he was as excited as Nike was, but the idea grabbed him visibly. What worried him most, was what his superiors would think of him if he brought this up. At best, they would just wave their hands – leave me alone with this flea horror – although at worst, they might send him to the psychiatrist to have his head examined. This of course could be avoided, if I visited each of them, one after the other, and I would convince each one, up to the national police chief. Only that could have incalculable consequences. For example, if it occurs to someone to make it all confidential; indeed, he decided that in such an important case, the national security apparatus would have to be involved. And then would begin the infinite distribution of authority, bureaucratic niggling. By then every trace of all the cold-blooded killers would be long gone, if I weren't gone by then too, as fleas don't live forever. On the contrary. I agreed with Dark Glasses. I understood that he had decided not to utter a peep about me to anyone. His own crime-solving statistics would improve little by little, and he would be entrusted with ever dicier jobs, and with time – if crime came to an end in the world – the number of the most serious crimes would be reduced more and more.

That night Dark Glasses questioned me thoroughly. He wanted to know my attitude to crime and criminals in general, and whether I would vow to pursue crime and criminals at the cost of my life if necessary, as befitted a respectable detective. Of course, I vowed. On the one hand, for I believed that there can be few more meaningful purposes in life than that we should all live honest lives, with pure souls, without committing any crime; on the other, because I saw nothing that would endanger my life. Then I read the minds quietly of the cold-blooded murderers and learning the key details, then vamoose with their secret. They would never learn of my existence.

***

It turned out that we had already leapt into action the next day. I know, my dear friend, that you are burning with curiosity, but I can't paint the ugly details of the incident. Let it be enough that the unfortunate individual in question had not left the land of the living on his own volition in a secluded house on a leafy suburban street.

But it wasn't at the hands of a cold-blooded one, either.

Nike caught the scent immediately. Nose to ground, he ran this way and that, until he stopped suddenly, rooted to the spot before the gate of a small ramshackle house. Dark Glasses held the leash. Two more uniformed persons were with us who followed us slowly in a police car, and when Nike stopped, they braked at once. Dark Glasses planned to ask for reinforcements, so they would catch the "perpetrator", as he called him, if he tried to escape through the fence in the back yard. But the gate of the house opened unexpectedly and a "poor blighter" went through it. Dark Glasses called him "poor". He explained to me at length – so I will explain to you – this does not mean that the young man has ever nicked anything in his life, it only means that his ass was showing through his trousers, that he was shabbily dressed, so we could suspect with reason that he lived from nicking things, that is, stealing, or perhaps improving his tight circumstances by burglary and robbery.

"Who are you looking for?" the young man asked. He was intimidated, but he wasn't scared. Dark Glasses examined his shoes. They were running shoes of the cheaper variety. As he came closer, Nike got more and more excited, and stuck his sharp nose into the gate grate, trying to catch the odours.

"Perhaps you," answered Dark Glasses.

I saw that the confusion in his head was great. Nike's behaviour showed that he had found what he was looking for. Despite this, the fellow's eyes weren't glancing right and left, as those do who are trying to gauge quick as lightning ways of escape.

"This fellow is either cold-blooded or he's innocent," observed Dark Glasses. I don't need to say that I too got excited, at the mere word "cold-blooded". "My God," I thought. "There's a job for me right here. Let's go."

"It's too far," I said. "I can't jump on him from here."

"You don't have to yet," responded Dark Glasses. "I'll tell you when."

After a long time, Blighter stammered out what he wanted to so badly.

"I haven't done anything."

"Well, of course not," responded Dark Glasses. "This is just a routine inspection."

He waved to his fellows in the car.

They all were standing in a semi-circle before the gate.

"Do you have a gun?"

Blighter raised both arms and answered.

"No. I don't even have a pen knife."

"Open the gate, then step back," ordered Dark Glasses.

"I'm afraid of the dog."

"Don't be afraid. I'm holding him fast with the leash. He's only interested in your shoes."

"Should I take them off?"

"Yes. But first open the gate. And step back."

Blighter obeyed Dark Glasses' orders. It was a lovely spring morning, with a gentle sunshine. He slipped off his sport shoes, then stood barefoot on the stone path that led to the house. We marched forth with Nike straight to the shoes. Nike snapped up one shoe and took it to Dark Glasses. He immediately got a sugar cube as a reward in his open jaws.

***

They took poor Blighter to the police station. Even though when we got in and Dark Glasses said, "Now!", we'd hardly passed two streets when everything became clear. I asked Dark

Glasses why they didn't let him go as he was completely innocent, but he replied that he had to record everything that he knew about the shoes.

Trouble was they didn't let him go even afterward. Even though he didn't leave out a single element nor did he add anything to the film that rolled in his head, there in the police car. About which I – also in the car heading for the station – reported exactly and carefully to Dark Glasses.

Blighter had found the shoes on top of a trash bin. The pair had been placed neatly next to each other. He couldn't sleep, so he may have been wandering the streets for a long time, perhaps until midnight. Thereabouts as people turned in early, he didn't meet a soul. He was on his way home when he found the shoes. At first, he didn't want to believe his eyes. He inspected their soles, neither one had holes in it. Not like his own running shoes, which filled with water when it rained. He immediately put them on. Although they were at least a size too big, he walked home in them.

"And what did you do with the old pair?" asked Dark Glasses.

"I took them home," he answered. "They're at home now."

Poor Blighter's face brightened, as one who gave thanks to fate that he had enough smarts to take them home and how he could prove what he had said.

"It's a great pity!" Dark Glasses shook his head.

***

I slowly grasped his peculiar logic. And, actually, the kind of trap he had fallen into with me.

If Blighter had left his shoes there, where he had found the other pair, the garbagemen would have taken them away. And then they could have found them on the garbage mound. That would have proved the truth of what Blighter had told them and that he was innocent. Here, however, Nike's outstanding tracking was up against the confession of a suspicious-looking down-at-the-heels character. Which no matter how consequent it was, it could have been the clever story of the real perpetrator.

That he wasn't such, nobody knew better than I. When Dark Glasses said, "It's a pity," I deduced that he believed me, that is, he too was convinced of Blighter's innocence. The fact that he didn't let him go, led me to believe, however, that he was full of doubts. I saw in his head that he was indeed full of doubts. Though they were different from what I thought.

He reasoned as follows:

If he raised Blighter's innocence with his chief, his fellows would ask him immediately, "How do you know? Everything is against him." Obviously, he could not say that a flea had told him. But from what then? Intuition? Feeling? Others have other feelings…

"It could very well be that it would be like that," I reinforced him. "But perhaps Nike could help. If we tell him that he very cleverly found the shoes, but the real owner had to be found, then he would be on his way to tracking the other person."

"That's what you think!" snapped Dark Glasses. "If he took a smell pattern from the shoes, he couldn't go to anyone other than this unfortunate wretch."

"Or back to the trash bin," I stated.

"Well, of course. And back to the crime site. And what was the use of that?"

"I haven't a clue."

"But I have. Nothing. There are no other clues. There are no eye or ear witnesses. There was a lot of money hidden in the bed. Anybody could have done it, someone who knew about it and loved money. A lot of people knew about it and a lot of people love money."

I thought that over. Then I said,

"Fortunately, we know he's innocent."

But I missed the point again.

"What's the good of that? Those who are going to decide his fate must know. That I know is neither here nor there. That you know means even less."

***

Suddenly I was overcome with a rare feeling: impotence. Essentially, I had nothing to do with Blighter, still it stuck in my craw that they had put an innocent man in jail, and they weren't in a hurry to let him go. At first it seemed obvious to me that, although it was difficult to find out the truth, it was easier to make it prevail later. Until he wasn't contradicting himself, anybody could say what he wanted. Anybody could tell the story he wanted. And we couldn't know whether he was telling the truth or not. But if I could see into his head…

Only in vain was I convinced that Blighter's tale and the images that rolled in his head were the same, if the interrogator didn't believe a word of what he said.

"Where did you find the shoes?" they asked him anew. "I already told you," he stammered, completely depressed and in torment.

"Tell us again."

"On top of a trash bin."

"Not inside the bin?"

"No. On top."

"Curious. And why did you put it there?"

"I didn't put it there."

"All right. But the person who put it there, why did he put it there?"

"I have no idea."

"Do you think that's lifelike?"

"Certainly," he whimpered. "If I found them there."

"No. Not at all. Someone wearing those shoes had killed someone only a few hours before. If, let us say, you did it, and you wanted to get rid of this unpleasant evidence…You exchanged shoes…Where would you put the old ones?"

"I haven't done anything."

"We're just asking because of realism. Where would you put them?"

"In the bin."

"So, you see. In the bin. And not on top of the bin. Based on that these shoes have never seen the bin. They went straight home with you on your feet."

"But we know that wasn't what happened," I said to Dark Glasses.

"We know."

"At least tell them that yes, it could be realistic that the perpetrator put it on top of the trash bin. How can you say something isn't realistic when it happened in fact?"

"Easily," answered Dark Glasses. "Nothing that we don't believe is realistic and everything that we believe is so."

"Only the thing is the truth can't depend on what others believe about it. We have to tell them."

"We've already been there," he snapped. "If you want to, tell them yourself. But leave me out of it."

***

Well, dear Danny, I didn't go on my way. The more determined I was in trying to find the right words and reasons that they could bring up, the more I saw that Dark Glasses was right. I imagined, for instance, that I said to the interrogators, "I saw the shoes on top of the bin with my own eyes." They'd ask me, "Where?" And I, "In the suspect's head." They would laugh me to scorn. "Well, of course. What we imagine appears in our heads." And I wouldn't have been able to answer. In fact! I would have to admit that in principle, that is, logically, they were right. It was conceivable after all: I only saw the events in Blighter's head which he had made up in his excuse...

Or I pondered that if I had been the murderer, excuse me, it slipped out of my mouth. So, if I had been the murderer, what would I have done with the shoes? Or to be more precise, what would have made me put the shoes on top of the bin, instead of throwing them inside? And I came up with a logical, therefore possible, thus undoubtedly, realistic answer. After all, the perpetrator could have thought he would cleverly throw the suspicion onto someone else? There was scant possibility that this was the case, but still, the yield was all the greater. After all, you could never know that an accidental eye witness or anyone else could lead the police to some other clue? Although if they had a suspect, they would focus all their attention and energy onto putting the prisoner's clothes on him.

Just like Blighter's interrogators.

I said to Dark Glasses,

"Don't you think that your colleagues really weren't doing their job?"

"Watch what you say!" he snapped.

"I can tell from looking at them. They don't really want to catch the real culprit. They want to put prison clothes on Blighter."

He said nothing.

"Well, no?" I insisted.

"No."

"But then?"

After a long pause, he answered.

"They have vowed to pursue crime. There are many ways to pursue crime."

"What do you mean?"

"You don't have to understand everything."

"Then I can't help you."

"You don't have to help me. My ears are open. You can leave anytime."

I paid close attention to his feelings as he said this. I wanted to know whether he really wanted to be rid of me or he wanted to discipline me. There were colours that signalled this or that, and I drew the conclusion that I could stretch the rubber band for a while, but not for long.

"I will let myself be convinced," I suggested.

He understood. After a while, he asked,

"Do you watch TV?"

"No."

"But people do. As if they've been glued to the screen. They don't even go out of the house, their gardens, what for? Whatever happens in life that is important, they'll find out there. What we don't know from the TV isn't important. Is that clear?"

"Not really. Who decides what's important and what isn't?"

"Not who, but what?"

"And what?"

"What people need. What they get. What they are willing to watch. What you can be afraid of, that's important. What you can be outraged about, that's important. What is terrible, moving, tragic, all that is important. Sometimes, the good, the beautiful, the touching are important, but that doesn't belong here. What belongs here is our case. The whole country knows about it. That day, they turned the keys in all the locks in the country. And every good man was outraged at the kind of world this is. They believe anything can happen here. Now this is the kind of world in which we must calm them and reassure them. That is what our politicians want and that is what our police chiefs want.

He seemed to have ended there.

"And?" I asked.

"We have to prove that we're on the right track. That it is just a matter of moments before we strike. And we'll deter every criminal from even harbouring the mere thought of doing such a thing again. That's it."

"That's not all."

"Yes, it is. Compared with this, whether your Blighter is innocent or not is a tenth-rate question." He was quiet for a while. He was thinking. "Since you don't watch TV, you may not know there was a man in history who took upon himself the sins of humanity as a whole. He was crucified. The situation of your Blighter is a hundred times easier."

***

The least I can say, dear Danny, is that I thought I hadn't heard him right. That I was misreading the thoughts that flashed through Dark Glasses' head. That I was misjudging his insensitivity and callousness. That perhaps it wasn't a matter of insensitivity after all, but rather self-discipline. Not callousness, but its opposite: conscientiousness. It is often said of stupid people that they can't see the forest from the trees. Dark Glasses and his colleagues weren't making this mistake; they just didn't want one man to draw attention from humanity as a whole. They were ready to sacrifice him...

I hastened to announce to Dark Glasses that now I understood everything.

If I look deeply into myself now, I can't think of anything other than that I wasn't entirely alone; I could feel my guardian's breath on the nape of my neck, or perhaps my spirit and my mind carried out their tasks automatically? But at that moment, two essential things were decided at once. From that moment on, Dark Glasses and I were enemies, although I didn't blurt it out.

If my soul and my mind hadn't decided arbitrarily, after a bit of thought, I could have chosen another possible way: convincing him. I could have said that truth gives rise to truth, lies to lies. Later these beautiful and round thoughts spread in me: *"The mildewing threads of lies and the distrust to which it leads sooner or later enmesh and rip apart the strong fabric of truth. That fabric which, miracle of miracles, holds human society together."*

It's beautiful, isn't it? Fortunately, my mind and soul were involuntarily wiser than to try to come up with such complex and impenetrable reasons. I could virtually hear Dark Glasses retorting to my carefully chosen words: *"Nonsense!"* It is one thing, my dear friend, to see and understand the truth, and something entirely different to make others believe it and accept it. Fortunately, I had to confess: I was not capable of such a thing.

Anyway, now that I understood everything, Dark Glasses answered curtly, "that's good". Nonetheless, I felt very uncomfortable in his ear. Insofar as I saw the noble task floating before me, I definitely enjoyed that I, a little nothing flea, could be of help to a great man. From now on I felt as if I was sitting in jail. In the deepest recesses of darkness. My spirit and happiness shrank to the size of my tiny body. I watched for the opportunity to leap finally.

Every day Dark Glasses took Nike for training. I thought I would jump on him at the right moment, then on to Red Fur, and perhaps we could see each other soon, my dear friend.

And this almost happened.

I was hanging onto Nike and would have leaped onto Red Fur when I was paralysed by a sudden realisation.

I was incapable of leaving Blighter to his fate.

Leaving him to be the prey of a dislocated and venal "truth".

I was incapable of taking an active part in sacrificing an innocent man.

I didn't care what others thought of this. Unfortunately, or perhaps not unfortunately, I just couldn't bring myself to do it. Though with low spirits but I took the path back. I cautiously resettled myself in Dark Glasses' other ear, and I lay doggo like a hedgehog in the grass.

I waited for the next interrogation.

***

As it turned out later, Dark Glasses took part only now and then in the questioning of Blighter. They mainly turned to him in training Nike and using him. So, the days and nights passed, but still I couldn't get close to my protégé. Sometimes I snacked off Nike, just enough to not make him scratch ostentatiously, then I snuck back into Dark Glasses' ear. He was convinced that I was long gone. Especially after one day he plugged his ear with a thick wad of cotton. The one in which I conversed with him. He kept the cotton there for a whole day, and since I had not given any sign of life, he slowly began to forget about me.

On one occasion when we had just returned from a training session, he was informed that he was expected in the interrogation room. When we entered, to my great joy I saw Blighter. My joy evaporated quickly when I saw his deathly pale face. On the other side of the table were two detectives, colleagues of Dark Glasses.

One of them leaped up and went to the door.

"He confessed everything," he whispered.

"What did you do to him?" asked Dark Glasses, also whispering.

The other man looked at him severely.

"Nothing. He wanted to confess, and he did."

"Did he have a lawyer present?"

"Yes."

"Assigned?"

"Assigned. If it's good enough for him, it's especially good enough for us."

"He is just a miserable kid."

"That's his problem."

"All right." Dark Glasses shrugged.

"Do you want to read the record?"

"What for?" He was on his way out the door when I would have quickly jumped out of his ear, when he asked, "It occurs to me, did he tell you exactly how it happened?"

"He did. Exactly."

"That's decisive."

"That's right." The other man nodded.

Then he said something which stuck in my mind, my dear friend, as I am sitting in your ear now. "We did help him a bit to remember," he said, and, insinuating a great deal, he smiled.

Something became clear, my dear Danny, during the long time that I was forced to spend in the company of the police. Although there were a few talented detectives, who sensed the connections, and the meaning and significance of a clue, and then there was Nike's extraordinarily sensitive and useful nose, the solution of most cases did not depend on the skill of the police. Oh no. In such a big city where there were so many people, where in addition nobody knows anybody, even if they've lived side by side for twenty or thirty years, it is harder to find trace of a perpetrator than to catch a flea in a pack of dogs. And if they caught a relatively large number, that was certainly due to human weakness. Most of them talked and let the cat out of the bag. They couldn't resist boasting. Even more, if their crime could be seen on TV. They confided in all the world, just so they could tell their tale.

To my great luck, detectives weren't any different from criminals. If Blighter's interrogator hadn't noted proudly that "they had helped him remember", my protégé would still be in prison. I would have felt so terrible that I wouldn't have felt like chatting with you.

But let's not get ahead of ourselves.

I leaped across to the detective, and aimed at Blighter from his ear, and in a short while I was settled in his ear.

I started in on him at once.

"I know for a fact that it wasn't you."

He didn't answer.

"Hello!"

He had shrunk completely into himself. He was deathly frightened. He couldn't think. He didn't wish to think.

"Is there something wrong?" they asked him.

"I'd like to go back," he whimpered.

***

You've most probably noticed, my dear friend, that I am sparse in my description of the police, the detectives, the police chiefs, the interrogation room, the jail. I must speak of them because they are part of the story, but I wouldn't like you to think that it was necessary for you to imagine yourself in that situation. The outside world is so beautiful, the trees in leaf, the colourful flowers, the cats rushing about, that we should not have to bathe in this sight, in the dark side of life, to sink into this depressing desolation. It's another question that if we don't feel right in our minds with the world, everything can turn green and bright around us in vain, still we feel as miserable as a worm stuck in a tree. Like poor Blighter.

I blessed my good fortune that I could at least look into him, and I could be clear with him at least. In the opposite case I would have to think that only those who are dangerous and low criminals could end up behind bars. I know that it seems surprising and even shocking, my dear friend, but it occurred to me, was it right for me to drink the blood of criminals? Wouldn't I become a criminal too, or at least be unclean? So, I took care, as with Nike, that I should not take too much from my jail companions, nor the guards, so they didn't think of taking to a flea fumigator.

As it was, nestled in Blighter's ear, even the jail seemed comfortable enough for me, and I had enough time to study the situation. Returning to the interrogation, I waited patiently, until Blighter calmed down somewhat, and only then did I announce,

"I know for a fact that it wasn't you who did it."

I described to the last detail the series of events that I had seen in his head. Beginning with his leaving home, until he put on the shoes he had found on top of the trash bin. I even related details that had appeared clearly in his head, but he didn't think them worth telling the detectives. For example, he turned up the soles to see whether they were cracked or not, the reason these sport shoes in good condition may have been thrown out. After that, he had to believe me. He was forced to see that at this moment there was one single earthly being in the world before whom he couldn't play a role, and that being was me.

"Leave me alone," he whimpered.

I thoroughly examined every nook and cranny of his head. Finally, I reached the sad conclusion that they hadn't hurt him. At least they didn't beat or torture him. Thus, he had made the decision on his own to take on the terrible deed. Can you imagine anything more terrible, Danny?

Well, I couldn't. I simply couldn't wrap my mind around it.

It is given to a human being, a million times more than to a flea, that he can live freely and in dignity, that he can accomplish only beautiful and noble things... And here is a healthy young man who, indigent as he may be, had resisted all kinds of temptations until now. He didn't go wrong, he didn't steal from anyone, he didn't rob anyone. Not to mention the worst crime that a human being could commit. And suddenly he takes on himself the crime of crimes that he hadn't committed, not at all! He's much too peaceful and humble, he couldn't hurt a fly. Nevertheless, he took it on himself.

And do you know why?

I have to say that I arrived at this realisation with great difficulty.

**

I'm not going to tell you Blighter's life story. For one thing, the human mind is astonishingly flexible, and it believes it can find the reason and cause for everything. My protégé's parents had surely died. He lived from unskilled labour. His latest job, before being arrested, was pushing lines of shopping cars in the parking lots of enormous shopping malls. And finally, one after the other, the most beautiful and desirable girls left him. He had somehow attracted them because of his – although slightly ramshackle – house, but he couldn't keep them. Ay, we could shout together, there's the rub!

But it wasn't. For other people's parents die too, others live from odd jobs, others are left by their beloved. But the mad idea doesn't occur to them to give up their freedom, and carry this terrible stain for the rest of their lives.

It was difficult to grasp such a thing with a flea's brain.

I tried to put myself in Blighter's place. What would have to happen to make me decide to take such a bitter step? Then suddenly I understood something. A flea such as I am, sees the smallest person as so huge, that I couldn't imagine this kind of defeatism. In more fortunate cases, one would try to overcome the world and the people in it. To get his reward. He'll consume forty plum dumplings. He'll be a boss. Or at least an employee. Or build up his muscles so that he gets some respect. In a less fortunate case, the miserable one will feel like my protégé. The greater the wealth around him, the dizzier the whirling of the world, the tinier he will be. And the greater the chasm between him and those around him.

It was terrible to see, but because I felt it in myself, I was forced to believe: Blighter waited for his interrogation impatiently. He waited for them to be concerned about him, to pay attention to him. He found it pleasant that they talked to him kindly, and they initiated him into details of the events, of which he was ignorant. And which I won't tell you, my dear friend, so that you should understand clearly: the only thing about this whole story is that which is the least interesting to us, is the most exciting to others.

Nonetheless, a fact is a fact: the detectives virtually literally recalled the entire contents of the procès-verbal, and they pushed a great number of photos under Blighter's nose. And Blighter, sitting in the jail, recalled them, and I sitting in his ear, could observe them image by image. And something else: Blighter's change of colours. At first, he was dominated by a curiosity mixed with dread. He looked at them from the outside, as an outsider. Then slowly he himself appeared on one or another of the photos he gazed at. As an ungainly stranger, but still he was here and there. And at the next interrogation he explained some of the photos. That he had done this and that. At times they corrected him that it couldn't have happened that way. But in another way. He nodded in agreement.

I didn't interfere, not even by accident.

***

And why I didn't, you'll certainly realise, my dear friend.

Well, of course, Blighter was in the hands of his interrogators. If he had really wanted to slip out, perhaps we two could have got somewhere. But because he didn't, I would only have managed with my fidgeting to turn my protégé against me as well as the police. It would have been only a matter of time before they would have caught me or chased me away.

I had no choice other than to be very careful not to fling myself at their heads. Blighter turned out to be a warm-hearted and honest soul, and lying was not his thing. From spying on his thoughts, I determined that in his mind, assuming the dreaded crime wasn't a lie or a fib, but the facing of reality.

If I didn't wish to interfere in the developing story, we could exist in a marvellous symbiosis. And if we didn't talk about the weather – after all, it hadn't the slightest meaning in the jail – we had a good chat. But already wishing each other a good morning or good evening, or asking about how the other was feeling, had a good effect on us. But when I tried now and then to bring up his mad confession, he became restless and wanted to get rid of me.

At such times I felt it best to leave him alone. Until he began to miss me again.

In my hominoid earthly existence, I grew into the habit of having a rest, even if I wasn't sleepy at all, when faced with a problem I could not solve. That's what I did now. I sat on

Blighter's blanket in a dreamy half-sleep. I knew that I could get back to him from here at any time. Then, a happy thought flashed into my mind – the only possible solution.

When I returned to my habitual nest, I articulated what I had recently heard from Dark Glasses:

"There was a man in history who took on the sins of mankind."

I did not add, however, that he was crucified. Let Blighter believe, or perhaps to find the right words, that I had made a volte-face: I looked up at him for what he had assumed. I considered him a person of historical importance.

I saw that I had knocked a nail in Blighter's head.

Now that I had his confidence, I brought up subjects that he hadn't shared with me in the least, although I could read them in his head. Although he was aware of my ability to read his thoughts, he thought that I saw everything. That was exactly my goal. Everything! Even the future.

"This is good this costume," I observed when he was thinking about the coming trial. "What do they call this?"

"Robe."

"Who's that?"

"Who?"

"The one wearing the gown in the middle."

"It's the judge."

"What does he do?"

"He brings a judgment."

"He says that he isn't guilty."

"Who isn't guilty?"

"It seems to me that you are standing there facing the judge, but I may be mistaken."

I quickly changed the subject.

On watching him closely, I saw what an old girlfriend of his looked like. He brought up her image often. It wasn't very clear; nevertheless, I could make out a few details. The long flowing hair, the fluttering red dress, and the flying red scarf.

Once, as he spooned his soup, he was concentrating on fishing out the fairly rare pieces of meat; I, of course, did not join him. I simply observed.

"On the day you are released, a girl will be waiting for you at the gate."

After a long pause he asked.

"In ten years?"

"Of course not. In two weeks. Immediately after the trial."

He said nothing for a long while.

"Red?" he asked.

"It seems so. She has long flowing hair, a light red dress flutters around her. Her scarf which is blowing in the wind is also red."

"That was what she was wearing then."

"Is the soup any good?" I asked, as if the girl had occurred to me merely by accident.

"What?"

"The soup."

"It's fairly good," he answered sadly. Meanwhile, he had caught the flying one in his imagination; let him stay with her for a while. "I loved her best," he muttered, after she had vanished. "And perhaps she loved me best too. Then she slammed the door on me; she said that I'm a dud."

"You were."

He listened curiously. He waited to see where I was heading.

"Your house is very nice. You did a good job with it."

"I?"

"Who else? It's you I see."

"I didn't touch it. I don't know how."

"I'm talking about the future, you numbskull. Even a bird can build its nest. Why is it you who can't do it?"

"A bird can, but I can't."

"I'll help you, you idiot. Who do you think I am? Barely a year and it will be done."

"You understand this too?" he said in amazement.

"What did you think? I see the future, but I can't see up to the walls of a house?"

"But you won't push the wheelbarrow."

"No. You will be the master of that. All right?"

"All right. Once I pushed fifty shopping cars at once."

"All right, numbskull! You're a tough guy."

"I don't think so."

"It's enough that I think so."

"You think so?"

"I think so."

He smiled.

***

Oh, Danny, if you knew how relieved I was. Now I had to be careful that I didn't ruin anything before the trial. Blighter's soul split completely, almost palpably. One half spent his days in a strict prison, under armed guards, in accordance with a

201

well-defined order and a daily schedule. The other half sparked around the girl in the red dress, or he was embellishing his house, at another time, he was puttering about in the garden, of course under my effective guidance.

And it was good.

Nonetheless, it occurred to me, this balance was too risky and delicate. I had to foretell a bunch of odious cockroaches and bed-bugs in prison. But they showed so many films on the TV of comfortable cells with TVs that my horror stories didn't make much of an impression on him. I didn't insist on the subject. I put all my eggs in one basket: the public trial.

By the time we got there, I had got all the essential information from my protégé. I found out who were sitting at such times in court, apart from the audience, and the job each one had to do. The prosecutor would bring up the charges against Blighter. "All right, he's my man," I thought. If I could make him understand that the whole thing was just a sham to Blighter, we could win our case. I struggled with myself, until I finally saw that the detectives had served the facts up to him in such a way that it shouldn't even occur to him to doubt. But if it should occur to him, there was the confession. The machinery of justice was launched. And it wasn't his job to stop it.

For that, if he wished, there was the assigned lawyer.

"Of course," I smacked my mental forehead. "He'll be my man!"

What spoke against him was that at one of the interrogations at which he assisted, even before Blighter confessed, Dark Glasses commented to Blighter. "Just so you know: for the majority of assigned lawyers, even the most serious case is just a job to be checked off. You'd be better off with your own lawyer. You should mobilise your relatives."

"I don't have any relatives," whimpered Blighter. Dark Glasses shrugged. And that was that. It was to the credit of the assigned lawyer that the nimble little man, who appeared with Blighter, didn't seem to be that irresponsible type. True, he wasn't willing to enter into anything that was in the domain of the detectives, and he took Blighter's confession at face value. Nevertheless, he racked his brains feverishly on how to lighten the heavy prison sentence. Several times he told my protégé how important it was that his neighbours considered him to be a peaceful, well-intentioned young man, someone who couldn't hurt a fly. Also, he had a clean slate; he had recently become an orphan, and it could be proved that he hadn't gone to the crime scene to hurt anyone, but only because he was frightened – and so on and so forth. It was a simple thought process but because of one thing, one element, it was unacceptable: he was trying to ease the prison sentence, not escape it.

After this, I was pondering whether to choose my protégé or the judge. I was afraid to leave Blighter. I was afraid that this delicate balance would immediately shift to admission and confession of the crime, toward the desire to escape from freedom. More than that, I was afraid that the prosecutor's and attorney's intentions working together could prevent the judge from weighing the situation. And something would take place that I could not even imagine could happen with human beings: that despite their conscience, their sense of responsibility and undeniable good intentions they could do in a wretched innocent.

**

So that left the judge. Or to be more precise: the lady judge. Dark Glasses told Blighter that it was usually men who tried such serious cases. I have to say that I was happy about this unexpected development. She didn't seem young, still she had a sparkle. Not her black robe, not even her small light eyeglasses, but rather her eyes.

"We've won!" I said enthusiastically to my protégé. He couldn't even groan, he was so nervous, when they led him into the courtroom on a leash, before the sparse audience, all the way down the corridor, into the courtroom, up to the defendant's bench. "I think this judge will want what is good for you."

"Have you spoken with her?"

"Of course not."

"Then how can you tell?"

"I can see it."

I didn't tell him that in this dubious, balancing situation what it could mean to want the best for Blighter; after all, it was only important that he not be so lost, or as they say, motherless. That he shouldn't think that because I was leaving him to himself, it was the end of the world. I was afraid that he would bend in the direction they were blowing. But I didn't dare leave quietly, because he would be like a small child who notices that his guardian has left, and pisses in his pants from fright… I took my leave, encouraging him that everything would be all right, and finally I explained that we were sitting too far from the judge. I didn't know when I would be able to reach her, but that he could be sure that I would. And, God willing, from then on, I would direct the trial.

I surprised myself at what had slipped out of my mouth, but not so much for my bumptiousness, but I lay it down to my infinite determination.

Determination, however, like anger, is not necessarily a good advisor. I got lost three times, three times I had to clamber up to another observation post, when I finally ended up at the suitable robe, and I nestled in the judge's delicate ear.

Fortunately, it was still formalities that were going on, the data reconciliation process, review of documents, and so on. I hadn't missed anything. Indeed, I could rest from my wanderings in the courtroom, and entertain myself with trying to find out who I had leapt onto and from there to get here. The prosecutor was building his case on the "facts" that he had got from the police, and he kept mentioning the confession as if it were incontrovertible evidence. The lawyer valiantly insisted on all the extenuating circumstances. Blighter perched on the defendant's bench like a heap of misery. And he waited, dreading the moment he would have to speak.

I knew – I didn't have to be a visionary, but I knew my protégé's soul – that when the judge finally asked him whether he upheld his confession, he would mutter "yes". As befitting an accommodating and honest man. A bit of pride flitted through me suddenly that my protégé was such a splendid chap, even though he was just a pusher of shopping carts.

I set to work at once.

"Please accept my deep respect and admiration, my dear judge."

I tried to speak in my gentlest voice, to lessen her disquiet.

"Please do not question me about who I am," I continued. "All I can say is that I'm not a human being. And, incidentally, I can read your mind."

She thought instinctively that she should immediately suspend the trial, in accordance with the law, as a disturbance had come up.

"Please do not." I stopped her in a calm, soothing voice. "Nobody can see me. Nobody other than you knows anything about me. At the next occasion, if I should come to you and you suspend the proceedings again, they'll send you for a mental examination."

"But I can't work this way," she whispered desperately to herself.

"Yes, you can. For I will not disturb you in any way. I will do one only thing: tell you the facts, that is to say, the truth."

She said nothing in fright. Then she brightened as if she had found the way out of the trap.

"I have to stick to the law and not the truth."

"As you wish," I replied in as mild a voice as I could muster. "I'll tell you and you will decide in accordance with your best understanding. I told you I wouldn't disturb you."

"Are you all right, Your Honour?" The side judge sitting next to her leaned toward her. "Shall I fetch you a glass of water?"

"No, thank you. I'm fine," said the judge firmly. Then she asked, "At least tell me who you represent. The prosecution? The defence? The Ministry? The media?"

"The facts. The defendant never killed anyone. He wasn't even at the scene of the crime."

"Well, we shall see about that," she whispered and looked at Blighter. "Defendant, stand up."

Blighter clambered up heavily.

"You have upheld your confession, you said that it fits reality and was not extracted through physical or psychological pressure. Is that true?"

"Yes," he replied and nodded assent.

"So, you maintain that you were at the scene at the designated time and you broke into the house, and when they surprised you…"

Excuse me, Danny, but I could not finish the judge's sentence. You are a big boy now, so you can imagine, but it was very difficult for me. The essential thing was that Blighter announced again that he upheld his confession. The judge said quietly to me, "See, there you are." I asked her to "Please ask the defendant whether he got any assistance to his confession." "From his lawyer?" she asked.

"No, from the detectives."

I wasn't disappointed. The judge asked in a loud voice, articulating clearly.

"Defendant. Please try to recall, did you get any help from the detectives with your confession?"

Blighter answered willingly.

"I got a lot of help. I am grateful to the detectives. They helped me remember what happened and how. They even showed me the photos."

"Photos of what?"

"Well, of the house. The room. The victim."

"What victim?"

"The one that was killed."

"What did you say?" asked the judge softly.

"The one who was killed."

"Who?"

"Sorry, the one I killed."

"Bravo, Your Honour," I whispered to her. I fell in love with her and with life as a whole, so that I almost burst. I would have started dancing, if I weren't afraid to disturb her. We were past the most difficult part, but as it turned out, there was still a lot left. The prosecutor wanted to speak.

"Your Honour, I would like to comment that criminology knows of cases in which the criminal cannot bear the burden of his crime, and in his imagination, he puts the responsibility onto others. I would like you to take this into account when you consider the apparent contradictions of the defendant's confession."

"What do you think?" the judge whispered to me.

"Ask the defendant if he could tell you how he managed to climb over the fence."

"Why couldn't he?"

"Don't let him tell you. Ask him immediately if he could tell you why."

"Why?"

"You'll see," I added helpfully. "He can't lie. He'll tell you what he believes himself. He'll tell you the truth."

"Thank you, for your observation," answered the Judge. Then she turned to Blighter and did as she was told. Blighter began telling her how he climbed over the fence, when she interrupted him and asked him to remember exactly why he climbed over it.

My protégé said nothing for a moment; he was searching visibly through his memories, then finally announced,

"I don't remember."

"Did you have a reason?"

"No."

"Then why did you climb over?"

"I can't remember."

"Perhaps you didn't climb over?"

"It's not possible. They showed me how I climbed over."

"Aha. And who showed you?"

"The detectives."

"Did they show you how you should climb over, or how the perpetrator climbed over?"

"How the perpetrator."

"Young man, listen here. The detectives told the truth."

"That's what I said." Blighter's eyes brightened.

"The perpetrator climbed there and how they showed you."

"That's what I say too."

"But it wasn't you who climbed over. For you had no reason to do so."

Blighter said nothing for long seconds. Finally, he said dreamily,

"That's what the flea kept saying."

Now it was the judge's turn. She was so taken aback she could say nothing. Was it possible that it was the same "flea" who was carrying on a conversation with her? What in thunder could this be? An intelligent chip? Who had sent it to her?

In her honour – and her razor-sharp mind – let it be said that she didn't try to pursue that line of inquiry.

"Can you quote it exactly?"

"'I know for a fact that you weren't even there.' That's what he said. Literally."

"So, this individual is well acquainted with the circumstances of the crime."

"He knows what I did. He can read minds."

A murmur ran through the small audience. The judge pretended not to hear it. As if nothing special had taken place.

"Aha. And did you mention this to your lawyer? Why didn't you ask it to be your witness?"

"A flea?"

Some in the audience laughed. Blighter too smiled.

The judge continued undeterred.

"Where's the flea now?"

"I believe it is in your ear."

Now even the lawyer smiled.

The prosecutor leaped up and rushed to the judge. He leaned close to her.

"According to the psychological tests, he is an unstable personality, but he can be punished," he whispered to her.

The judge replied out of thin air.

"Anyone who can be punished can be acquitted."

"You're not going to acquit him?" the prosecutor asked flabbergasted.

"I'm going to acquit," said the judge firmly. I was thinking of how I could kiss this wonderful human being.

***

Well, my dear friend, I can't say that the days that followed were easy. Blighter kept looking for the girl in red whether she would show up or not. Since I had no power to bring her there, I fibbed that she was waiting for the proof, to see whether he was a tough guy and not a dip, and could he put the house right. "So, let's do it," he urged me day after day. After roaming about one night, I finally caught a glimpse of a family house encased in scaffolding. "Tomorrow, come here for me at this time," I said to him and I jumped. Nobody learned within one day as much as I did from the stone masons. The buzzing of a bee hive was nothing compared to what I felt in my head. I noted to myself, "God is good, very good. But he doesn't give anything for free."

Instead of the girl in red, other girls wandered that way. They saw how nimbly Blighter was rushing about with the wheelbarrow, how skilfully he wielded the trowel. They didn't see me there, and didn't see how skilfully I managed my former protégé, but that was as it should be. They stopped for a chat, sometimes, they stayed for a longer conversation. Then one of them went inside.

One day we got a surprise visit. At the best moment, for I had been racking my brains for days how I could get to you. Blighter cheerily motioned to Nike, but he was glad to see Dark Glasses too. They didn't stay long. Dark Glasses looked around the house, nodding intensely. Then he just asked Blighter to give me a message: he was very grateful for what I had done.

"I've already relayed it," laughed Blighter. "He's sitting in my ear."

"God bless you." I bid him farewell. After swallowing hard.

We discussed with Nike how peculiar the world was. We couldn't put all the criminals behind bars, but we had rescued an innocent. Could we ask for more? No, we couldn't, could we, my dear friend.

Tenth Tale
ON THE UNINHABITED ISLAND

You know, Danny Boy, if someone had offered to take me to an uninhabited island, I would have protested with every ounce of my being. Now that the whim of destiny has whisked me to an uninhabited island, there would be nothing I would regret more than missing out on the experience.

It's interesting that almost everybody wonders what they would do if they ever found themselves in such a situation. We enjoy thinking about what are the three things we would take with us, if we really had to spend time there.

And yet how many people would accept being left in the middle of the ocean on an uninhabited island when they might be stuck there forever?

Looking back at the chain of events, however, I'd leave out the plane crash. Not just because it was indescribably awful, but what edifying thing could I tell you about it.

When we finally managed to reach the island, well, to be more precise, when Abo managed to reach it, since I survived the tragedy, hidden in his ear; we still had a lot to think about. What were our options in that situation, how could we help ourselves? I'm telling you all this because if, God forbid, you should find yourself in such a predicament, you might like to know what to do.

And what could we have done to avoid the long scary shaking of the plane before it broke in two in the air, and we were flung into the ocean? There was nothing we could do. Absolutely nothing. And it's not entirely out of the realm of possibility that we survived precisely because we didn't do anything. Abo hadn't fastened his seat belt and wasn't wearing a life vest. We soon found out: he didn't even know how to swim either.

There must have been plenty of people in the water, because we could hear the choking, gasping, sobbing, and desperate splashing in the thunder of the waves. No one else survived, only we two.

How, you may ask?

Don't you dare tell me that even the most brilliant of minds could have seen it coming!

We managed to stay afloat because we hit the water right next to the wing that Abo grabbed instinctively in the pitch dark, and which helped us stay afloat in the raging waters. He couldn't swim, and he didn't even bother to try, which is exactly what helped him save his energy. He even fell asleep after a while, and when he woke up at the break of dawn, he still had strength enough to hold onto the fragment of wing and wait for hours until the storm calmed down and the horizon cleared. Maybe it was the twisted wing with the sides standing up that caught the wind and carried us far from the site of the crash. We didn't see anyone from the plane full of passengers and nothing was visible of the debris. We couldn't even hear the noise of the helicopters coming to our rescue.

Only much later did I grasp why they didn't look for us much longer, as they flew in ever bigger circles above the site of the crash. Only much later after we escaped the uninhabited island, did we find out that we were the only ones to survive the catastrophe.

Well, the thing is, my dear Danny Boy, that it isn't customary for anyone to survive these crashes. The would-be rescuers were all too aware of this. They circle above the water – mostly to reassure the relatives – without ever wondering, whether, by good fortune, anyone had escaped death. And if so, where on earth could that one be?

And yet we must include as a fortunate circumstance the fact that, although we hadn't given a thought to the temperature of the water above which we were flying when we embarked on our journey, Abo's body did not go stiff and cold in the water even without moving or swimming. He didn't have to let go of the wing. He was holding on to it firmly, and, thank God, he was carrying me too.

Many hours passed since falling into the ocean, but we still hadn't said a word to each other. It made complete sense from Abo's point of view, as he wasn't even aware of my existence. I too kept silent, because I had promised Abo's father that, no matter what, I would say nothing about my secret mission.

He was the only one, who knew about it. He didn't even let his wife in on it, nor Young Master, even though we had met thanks to him. I mean, Abo's father and I met, thanks to him. Young Master and Abo were first cousins, and when they saw each other, they often spoke about me. Abo's father tried to dismiss the story, because he was more than surprised that the barely twelve-year-old cousin had managed to fool his son, who was already fourteen. But he stopped when Abo shared with them his plan of flying to Australia during the summer holidays to visit his best friend. Needless to say, dear Danny, he met this friend on the internet. Neither he nor his parents had ever met him. Moreover, his parents knew only that whenever they asked him to do chores, he'd reply that he had no time as he was chatting with Tom. This most frustrating situation led Abo's father to call Young Master on the phone.

"Is there any truth to the stories you tell Abo about the talking flea?"

"Oh yes," replied Young Master.

For a while you could only hear him breathing. Eventually the uncle spat it out,

"Could you bring me that damn flea?"

"It's not that easy. He's friends with Toffee, not me."

"Then bring the dog, too. It's an emergency!"

"I can try," said Young Master, and, indeed, he came for me.

He was already proud of taking such a specimen to his beloved uncle. That afternoon he took Red Fur for a walk three times, and he got lucky that late afternoon. I was relaxing on my favourite stray cat, when I saw the old dog doddering toward me. I had just finished a hearty meal, and, in the ears of my carrier, I was enjoying the shining glory of the splendid summer. My moggy was about to decamp when I shouted,

"Stop! It's a good friend."

Puffed up, back hunched, claws out, she waited for Red Fur to come closer. When the time was right, I jumped.

"How's it going, Toffee?" I asked eagerly. "Is your blood pressure too high? Do you want me to bleed you a bit?"

"I'd rather not," he barked. "By the way, I think Young Master is looking for you."

I was quite surprised. My curiosity made me jump on him. He quickly told me the purpose of his visit and added that it was an emergency. I replied,

"This is how humans are. Whenever they experience any difficulty, they begin to believe in miracles."

We were on our way to Abo's father. I was very curious: what kind of urgent help could a serious person expect from such a pipsqueak? And one so mysterious that the moment I settled in his shaggy ear, he said goodbye to Young Master and Toffee. He added that he'd need my help for a longer time, but promised that not a hair on my head would be harmed.

I soon had to acknowledge that he was secretive for a reason. Owing to his age and his being an only child, Abo had a nasty temper. I'm not a psychologist, so, I couldn't tell the extent this might be related to a further two important circumstances. On the one hand, Abo was amazingly talented and clever; on the other, he was the only one in his classroom – including the girls – who was still being escorted to and from school at the age of twelve.

Abo's father tried several times to protest against this, but the female members of the family (Abo's mother and grandmother) learnt from the neighbours or from the TV about a terrible street crime. So, he eventually stopped.

One fine day Abo threw his schoolbag to the ground, and announced that he was no longer willing to make himself a laughingstock in front of his classmates by allowing his parents to accompany him, as if he were an infant – the issue was solved instantly.

Truth be told, Abo had good grades at school. Not only in math, but also in English, German and music, and he not only aced the school-level competitions, but also the district-level ones. And thanks to his good results, he earned the right to surf the internet, no matter how disgusted his precious parents were. And as a consequence of his constant internet surfing, he came across Tom, another interesting character.

What brought them together?

He's very important to the story, so I must tell you about him. My dear friend, I know you are curious about what happened on the uninhabited island, but if I don't tell you what came before, you won't be able to make sense of it at all.

One of the reasons these two managed to find each other was Abo's name. Believe it or not, he made it up.

He wasn't even four years old when he announced that he was a special creature and his name was Little Abo. He went down on his hands and knees, blinked hither and yon, and made cute faces.

"Where do you come from?" they asked him.

"Australia."

"Austria?"

"No, Australia. I'm indigenous there."

From that moment, he became Little Abo, and the name stuck not only with his parents, but the nursery school kids and later the school kids and even his relatives. One day when Little Abo announced that henceforth nobody could call him Little Abo any longer, just Abo, it was a sign that he had reached the threshold of adulthood. As it is on earth, so it is on the world-wide web.

The other thing that helped the two of them to become friends, despite the distance and continents separating them, was a video game. I wouldn't be surprised at all, my dear Danny Boy, if you were able to tell me the name of the video game I'm talking about. So, Abo asked the following question at a world-wide web forum. *"Hello, I'm looking for the following PC game: uninhabited island, where I need to explore the area, I need to build a hut, make weapons, catch fish, hunt and gather all that is necessary to survive. I was thinking about a survival game, where I need to figure out everything from scratch. Any ideas?"*

He asked the question in Hungarian on a Hungarian site, and the replies came back in Hungarian. Even the one that came from Australia was written in Hungarian. *"Look for this: Castaway Stories. I guess you can find it in Hungarian. Tom from Australia."* *"Tom, how come you know Hungarian?"* Abo asked. Tom replied at once: *"I speak some. My ancestors were fighting in the streets in 1956. I dunno if you know: Abo means aboriginal here."*

You understand, Danny Boy?

Can you imagine such a coincidence? A four-year-old makes up a name, Little Abo, imagines that he is living in Australia where he's from, and where the indigenous people are called Abos. Ten years later a boy of the same age writes him from Australia in Hungarian… No, no, there's no such thing as these kinds of coincidences.

I'm not the only one who thinks so. Back when Abo's father told the nannies what his son had come up with, one of them informed him who the Abos were. At home he asked his wife at once.

"Have you heard about the Abos?"

"Of course."

"Where?"

"On TV."

Long silence.

"Even if you gawp at the TV, you shouldn't let the child get used to doing it."

"Isn't it odd that you're the only one who hasn't heard of the Abos?"

***

Abo's father was not completely honest with Abo's mum. They agreed from the outset that under no circumstances should their son go on a trip on his own. The father blamed it on the expensive plane tickets, and pointed out that there were a lot of fine places to visit in Hungary as well. His mother said she couldn't leave her son unattended for such a long journey and for such a long time. God knew what might happen. Who knew, they might encourage each other in bad ideas, too. Who knew what they might get up to, these two teenagers.

But when Abo showed them Tom's e-mail reply, the situation changed completely. The letter said that Tom's parents offered to pay his travel expenses and host him in their home for a whole month, hoping that the two boys would help each other improve their English and Hungarian. They hoped there would be no impediment to Abo visiting them. He'd be welcome in their house as Tom's best friend.

From that moment on, Abo's father was supportive of his son and of the trip. Suddenly, the arguments in favour of the necessity for this trip came up. *"We should take advantage of this once-in-a-lifetime opportunity to let him discover that unique, remote continent. Finally, he'll be able to do something other than just stare at the TV or his computer screen. He can finally free himself from the trap of the virtual world. He can finally be free from his mother's overprotectiveness. He can learn what it means to be independent and responsible. His happiness might depend on it."*

Abo's mother turned white at every argument and started to tremble.

"What are you afraid of?" asked Abo's father, visibly annoyed. "You know how many kids of his age fly on their own? Thousands."

"Maybe, but they're all used to it."

"There's always a first time."

"Next year, maybe."

"And next year you'll put it off to another year."

"I won't!"

"Yes, you will. I know you."

"Is it so hard to understand that a mother fears for her child?"

"Yes, if it's for no reason. Because then, she's only thinking of herself and doesn't care about the physical and mental development of her son."

"What can I do if I have a bad feeling about it?"

Well, they say that was when Abo's father came up with the idea of asking for my services. After we made our agreement, he said to his wife that he had managed to find someone who would watch over Abo during his trip and luckily, thanks to his special position, he could also travel free of charge. And, on top of that, he didn't need to spend money for food either.

"Who is that?" asked the mother curiously.

"Because of his special position, I can't tell you. But I hope you won't doubt me. I don't think I've ever lied to you."

And if I smile at you right now, it's just because I remember how close I was to perishing, and yet I'm still here, telling you my story.

What was my agreement with Abo's father?

After he told me about his plans in one breath, I asked him,

"What would my job be?"

"To sum up: to be there, while keeping it secret and keeping quiet about it. If Abo found out you were travelling with him, that I've put him under parental surveillance, he'd blow a fuse. He'd never forgive me. And you might not get away with it either."

"Well then, maybe going on such a long trip isn't such a good idea," I said.

"On the contrary! The flight attendants are also important. Without them, passengers wouldn't be able to fly."

"At least they can speak and, if need be, help."

"Now listen to me! Only one out of a million flights has an accident. When you step out onto the street, your risk is higher. I mean, I really doubt anything will happen. You don't need to fasten his seat belt, nor give him mouth to mouth; you won't need to save him from the flaming wreckage, nor from drowning by lifting him by the hair. There's only one thing you must do; you must stay with him and keep your mouth shut. Meanwhile, you can also enjoy the view. Not many fleas can say they saw their homes from the heavens above… Well, is it a deal? Don't forget, you can never ever talk about this and give away the secret. My wife thinks I found a secret escort for him, but she has no idea it's you. Well, what do you say?"

Well, Danny Boy, we shook hands, figuratively speaking. Looking back on it, I have to say, I had no idea what was going to happen to us. And not only to us. We were only fighting for our own lives, but Abo's parents were worried about their only child.

On hearing the news, they were frightened to death, then almost went into mourning, if in their despair, they hadn't been holding on to their faith. "No, this can't be! God cannot do this to us! He will be found!"

Later, Abo's dad confessed that his wife asked him again and again to call that special person; maybe he's still alive and knows something about Abo. He had to tell her over and over again that they never kept contact by phone; the special mission did not allow it, and besides, according to the news agency, no one had survived the emergency landing. How could he find him? But, despite it all, he kept up the hope that I had survived. It's the flea, with its tiny but strong armour that has the best chance of survival. And maybe I would have a brilliant idea, and maybe Abo and I were somewhere carried by the waves. He was hoping his son was not alone. Or maybe a ship had sailed our way and taken us in, or we managed to reach land and soon they'd get a phone call…

I must tell you, thank God, I knew nothing about his feeble hopes. I would have been crushed by the enormous burden of responsibility: that I, a teeny-weeny creature should save this big, soon-to-become, human adult. I considered it impossible. And so, I had nothing to do while being carried by the waves other than to hide in his ear, keep quiet, and wait and see how things would turn out. The thought came to me, what would happen to me if Abo gave up? To put a fine point on it, my days would be numbered too...

I must tell you, up to that point, I hadn't used Abo as a source of food, not even once. I didn't want to ruin our budding relationship by making him scratch himself from the outset. At the airport, I must confess, as payment or rather as an advance for my services, I did feed on his dad. So, when, taking advantage of their emotional farewell, I jumped on Abo, and we boarded the plane, I could refrain from taking any food. Once on the plane, I visited all the sleeping passengers in the seats next to ours. Thank goodness, I was already in Abo's ear when we started losing altitude, so I had a chance of accomplishing my mission. If not the one I had signed up for, then the one that was really important to me, of getting both of us home alive.

***

It is out of sheer curiosity that I ask you, my dear friend. Had you been there in Abo's ear in the endless waters, what would you have done? Would you have kept quiet the whole time? Would you have encouraged him?

What would you have said to him?

How would you have encouraged him?

Would you have said, *"Don't be afraid, I'm here, I'm with you?"*

In the end, he might have laughed so hard, he'd have drowned.

Was it better to do nothing? To watch idly how he was throwing his life away? Think about it. You are there, more precisely, inside him, in a protected place. You are safe from the unpredictability of nature. And you still won't help him? Not even as much as a flea could?

I'm not saying this, so you can feel sorry for me, but I swear, of the two of us I was in the worse position.

At least so long as the sun was shining high up in the sky. By that time the wind had stopped blowing. It seemed our "dinghy" was barely moving. Abo suffered from sunburn and was beginning to get thirsty. I sensed that he regretted not drinking more mineral water on the plane, even if it was expensive. He was suffering more and more. He thought more and more of giving up. What if he let go of that something? At one point he even loosened his grip, and began slipping down. Everything went dark in front of me. The salty seawater hit me; I had to hold on really hard to keep from being washed away. Abo kicked his legs instinctively and reached for the wing again. He grabbed it and clung onto it again. I couldn't tell whether we were being carried by the waves again, or we were standing still. Meanwhile, he steadfastly searched the horizon. His heart leapt several times when he saw a remote dot far away, and he thought he saw land. Then, like a mirage, it vanished.

I was staring into Abo's head. I decided I'd talk only if he was on the verge of giving up. With my tiny flea brain, I wasn't sure what words would help or, God forbid, harm him. In case of a possible final moment, if he decided that he'd had it, that he wanted to give up, no matter what I said, my presence would have raised the stakes, and maybe, made a difference.

That I might be of help, was not only my hope, thin as a spider's web, but after a while – believe it or not – it became my strongest belief. The more I scanned Abo's mind, the more I breathed together with him, the more I clung to the wing with him, and fought the ocean alongside him. And even more vividly did I feel the perfect hopelessness of our situation and the dead end we were heading towards. Compared to the ocean, a tiny human child is as insignificant as a flea; and for a flea, the ocean is as unimaginably vast, as it was for Abo. The one who tries to fight the endless waters, who wants to win, is destined to fail. This may surprise you, Danny Boy, that it came on me as divine inspiration. There is nothing you can do to defeat the ocean; on the contrary, you can only survive if you give yourself over to it. If you keep it out of your mind, and even more, out of your soul. Even if you are in its throat and it can swallow you up at any moment, you must pretend that it isn't there at all. Even if your body could take it, its unfathomable immensity scares you. It crushes your feeble soul. Instead, you must think of people who lift you up instead of pushing you down. And save you. Hug you. There was no help in trying to get a hold of the heartless waters. But you can hold on to your beloved ones.

I was following the images and thoughts in Abo's mind. I was concentrating on whether his hand was losing its grip, whether the waters and despair were swallowing him up. I must have been exhausted myself, because I woke up when I was on the verge of being flooded, and it was only thanks to Abo that I wasn't washed away. He used his last bit of strength to flounder up, and even if it took him some effort, he eventually managed to hold on to our rescuer, the wing. As strange as it might seem, at those moments my first thought was that we shouldn't have the gall to abandon the wing that had saved us in these deep waters. Not perishing was only my second thought.

"Abo!" I said firmly. And then, as if pouring drops of life again into his parched soul, I started listing between long pauses:

Mum.
Dad.
Tom.
They are waiting for you, Abo.

After that I kept silent for a good while. I waited until the beguiling words sank into his soul. Let him be energised by them. As the images appeared in front of his eyes, his heart began to beat faster, and he started breathing ever more deeply. And what was even more amazing: the heavy, dark clouds were dispersed slowly by light blue and gold lights.

I added more doses of life drops:

Abo!
The Abos as well...
they are waiting for you.
They are proud of you.
They will honour you with an award.
There are no kids who are excellent at all subjects.

Both math and Hungarian.
German.
Music.
Abo, Abo!
This beautiful gold medal will be yours.
You see?
It is written:
"To Abo,
the great descendant of the Abos,
the Apple of their Eye."

Meanwhile, I was spying. The light blue and gold managed to win back more territory from the black and grey patches, but this time they faced more difficulty and their advance slowed. The sun was not so high anymore. "The heat is more bearable," I said. I thought Abo's sunburns would heal with time, but I had to realise that, as time passed, his thirst would become ever more unbearable. He wouldn't be able to hold for much longer. It was something of a miracle that he was able to hold on for so long.

"It's just a matter of time," I allowed imperturbably. "Maybe I shouldn't encourage him." I became doubtful. "I shouldn't bother him. Not in his last hours. Even if those were my last hours, too…"

I was fighting against myself, when, my dear friend, something strange happened. So strange that it still makes me shiver. I'll tell you all about it.

I shouted at myself, and if it wasn't me, it was someone else. "Stop worrying about time." I started to listen carefully. "It's endless like the ocean." It was as if I'd merged wholly with these words. Where they came from, I don't know. Whether from my inner self or from somebody else's, I have no idea. They echoed inside me; I absorbed them. The many words flooded in and invaded me with their truth.

There is only the moment.
The stupor of the present.
The ocean is not yours.
The horizon is not yours.
The elusive earth does not belong to you either.
The soothing dusk is not owned by you either.
The lifesaving rain is beyond your power.
Only the moment is yours.
You just need to live in the moment.
One by one, as it unfolds.
Floating lightly.
Leave the rest to the one it concerns.

By the time I had absorbed these words, I started chirping them up, the way restless sparrows do at home. My God, how many times did we slink up from behind, together with my favourite kitty, until they saw us and flew away? Up to that point, they just went on chatting and chirping tirelessly. I did the same. I said whatever came to my mind, and, as I suspected, it caught Abo's barely flickering attention.

***

I remembered Abo's Swiss pocket knife.

We had it, because right before heading to the airport, there was a heated debate about whether he could take it with him or not. Abo's dad measured the longest blade with a tape measure right in front of his son. He said that because it was a lot longer than six centimetres, it was not worth the risk of trying to take it on the plane; it would be confiscated. Anyway, he added, it's silly to make this trip even more dangerous. I didn't know what Abo thought, because I wasn't in his ear then, but he made a long face. He started opening and closing the blades dreamily one by one. I recognised the big blade, the small blade, the scissors, the saw, but nothing else. This morning interlude in the middle of the ocean reminded me of Abo's favourite pocket knife. I was as yet unaware of how we would miss that knife of myriad uses left at home, and how often it come up in our conversation in the coming days and weeks.

"Hey, Abo! You have such an amazing pocket knife. It's amazing how much you can do with it. I wish I had one. Of course, a small one that would suit me. Hey, Abo! What's that sharp thing on it? It's like a thorn! And what about that one, like a tendril? And what about that flathead? And then there is that long blade, which is not sharp, nor shiny, but rough like bark. What's that for? You hear me, Abo?"

I knew he heard me, as I began seeing the images he remembered as they flashed in front of his eyes. He just didn't have the strength to say a word...

I wasn't willing to concern myself with how long he'd be able to hang on. I was just hanging on to the moment I had stolen from the endless ocean and from eternal time, and I wanted him to do the same. We shouldn't interfere with other people's business. With endless humility we should give back what belongs to the Almighty. We should take only tiny fragments, the ones that indisputably belonged only to us.

If the Almighty wanted us to destroy us, let it be his problem. If he wanted to call us to himself, let him do it. We cling to our moments: the only understandable and palpable reality of our existence. Only this belongs to us.

The wind began blowing lightly, but not even that could distract me from my realisation and what I was clinging to stubbornly. I didn't want to think about whether it was a new trap, a new challenge, a mirage or the sign of heavenly mercy, the escape route we weren't expecting any more.

It was pointless to make ourselves believe we were being carried towards land, because it might as well be that we were being carried away from it. "Abo," I started calling him, and I don't even remember what I was saying to him, but I chirped to him constantly. I was putting each moment one after the other, the same as you do with a rosary when you pray, until my eyes closed from exhaustion. The water that got in woke me up; but for Abo it took a bit longer until finally, after many attempts he managed to emerge from the waters.

The light blue and gold light disappeared.

"This is the end." I sighed.

Soon we heard the first heavenly sound.

The squawking of birds flying above our heads.

***

If you thought that since then we've looked up the tiny island on the internet a hundred times, a thousand times, you'd be right. If the wind had blown a fraction of a degree from another direction, our unsteerable dinghy would have passed it by, and I wouldn't be able to tell you this story. Was it Providence? Luck? Sheer coincidence? It doesn't really matter – we make a deep bow to this direct hit.

Abo and I suspected that it was Providence behind all this. But what am I saying? We didn't start convincing one another. If anyone went through an unbelievable experience similar to ours, he wouldn't feel the need to convince anyone at all about the existence of his God. Like true lovers, who are not in any hurry to tell the world. Instead, they prefer keeping it to themselves; they prefer to keep the magic. If somebody goes through such an unbelievable experience, nothing can take away this intimate and sublime feeling. Not even the fact that our companions on the same plane had all perished took this away from us. Why hadn't Providence saved them? And why were we the ones he had made an exception for?

My dear friend, it all makes sense if we want to understand the state Abo was in during the trials we had to endure in the coming weeks.

Once, after we had finished all our chores, as we sat next to the drying rock, staring at the smooth surface of the ocean, he said quietly, "A memorable christening."

Forgive me, I've got ahead of myself.

I haven't even told you about our landing.

Not that you couldn't picture it. Run ten kilometres, and when you're done and you're completely exhausted, run another ten without stopping, and if all your cells are trembling, and you're using your nails to crawl ahead, and you finally get to your destination, start all over again.

Now you might have a faint idea of the state Abo was in when he finally lay down on the dunes. I was even more shocked when, after taking a few breaths, he tried to rise and continue crawling forward, even though we were out of the water. It began to get dark, and the sun was not so strong anymore. There was nothing to explain this superhuman effort. And there weren't any trees nearby that could provide us shade. It was also true that Abo could barely open his eyes, and if he did, it was only for a few seconds.

"Abo, Abo!" I called his name. "We've survived! We're out of the water!"

He couldn't even make a sound.

Nevertheless, I saw what he was thinking.

The ocean started creeping closer. He lay on the dunes, and the immense water rose higher. At first it reached his leg and then it was almost on his face...

In the following days, we admired this useful phenomenon, I mean, high tide. I couldn't even imagine that there were such wonders. The sun and moon, in their wanderings, either attract or push away the huge mass of the ocean's water. It was as if I, a teeny flea, were playing around with a huge rock. The waters rise at high tide, the ocean overflows and offers its manifold treasures to the earth. And if the earth in turn skilfully captures its offerings in the cavities and cracks of the dunes, before the low tide withdraws, carrying them with it.

You should have seen how skilfully Abo managed to take advantage of the bounty that the high tide had brought. He searched both the friable and rocky side of the coast several times a day, and dug out the tiny crayfish, mussels, and snails even from the tiniest cracks. He lifted or rolled the rocks over and reached into the cavities to catch the creatures hiding there.

Soon, he wanted more than what the island had captured for itself. Every cloud has a silver lining. Ever since plastic bottles were invented, there was no corner in the whole world where this waste couldn't be found. There were plenty of them on our uninhabited island; well, three of them, to be precise, but Abo used them skilfully all the same. He used two of them for collecting and storing water, and even though we needed the third one as well for storing water, Abo put it to use for catching fish.

Of course, I couldn't have known what he was up to. At first, I only realised that he wanted to cut off the upper part of the bottle, and I immediately became restless.

"Hey, you won't have enough reservoirs for water in the dry season!" I pointed out to him. "But I'm not going to be the one to die of thirst here…"

"Me neither. I'll solve it another way. We never have enough fish."

And he loved fish. Not I. I would have given all the fish in the sea for one full-blooded stray cat…

But I'm straying from my story again. I swear, my friend, I'll get around to the fish trap, too, but for now, we're still at the moment of our escape.

And it wouldn't have happened, had it not been preceded by the following events:

So, Abo went on crawling with a superhuman effort, to escape being carried away by the tide. Until then, I had never heard of this natural phenomenon, and I couldn't understand how this man child who grew up in front of his computer might have such a deep knowledge of the sea. My fears were about something else.

I was afraid he might have lost his mind. He had struggled so much with the ocean that he couldn't even stop any more… Well, this is where ignorance leads. Had I understood what Abo was trying to do, but was afraid of doing, I would have realised that he was no ordinary child. He was indeed worthy of the Abos' respect.

I fell asleep worried and I woke up worried.

It was pitch dark. But only inside him, as Abo's eyes were still closed. There was light, however, coming into his ear. I thought I might as well use the time to wander around.

The air was full of the smell of the sea. I didn't as yet know that this wonderful smell was made up of the odour of many creatures, some of them quite unpleasant, not to say stinky. I felt that it lacked one smell, that of warm-blooded creatures. I started daydreaming how nice it would be if a full-blooded domestic cat came our way. Or a placid dog. A daring rabbit. Or even a hedgehog… I didn't know then what later became a certainty for both of us; we were on a tiny island, so tiny, that we could circumnavigate it in half a day. There was not even a single house, not even a pet there. We didn't see any trace of hedgehogs or rabbits. We could hear the screeching of small monkeys and the shrieking of colourful flocks of birds. These sounds came from the forest that covered most of the island with patches of groves.

We didn't find any man-made huts, but we did happen on traces of human activity. So far as we could tell, based on the sun's path, there was an iron pole in the dunes on the southern shore of the island, in a place where high tide never reached.

When Abo saw it, he couldn't believe his eyes. He ran up to it and examined the iron ring on top of it. "You see?" He pointed to a shinier, smoother area. "People come here!" At that point we had no idea how often they went there, or when was the last time they were there, or when they would come back again. Abo scanned the waters, but in vain; no stray ships were coming our way.

A few days later, the tiny coconut plantation we happened upon near the dock offered more clues. It was made up of no more than six trees, at a distance of twenty human steps. They were all quite tall; they were bent a bit just above the ground, but then reached straight and slim high toward the sky.

Wait a second, Danny Boy.

Look around. The way you did when we stopped here long ago for a breather. Slow down. Even more. Yes, that's it. Well, when I saw those beautiful trees inside Abo's head, these pines here came to my mind. They didn't have a single branch on their trunks, only higher up, where I could hardly see even when looking through your eyes.

The coconut palms have huge leaves; some are even five times bigger than you are. And they're so strong they could hold you if you climbed on them. But they grow up high, and if they get old, they fall.

Now, think about it. How could you climb up such a tree?

Why would you?

To save your life.

***

236

When we happened on the tiny plantation, Abo was at least as shocked as when he discovered the iron pole. He ran towards it again, to have a closer look.

He checked the base of the trees, but found nothing he was looking for.

Then he looked at the light-green fruit hiding high up above the leaves. They were attached to one another and seemed huge even from down below. This sight didn't excite him either. Not because they were too high to reach, but because he had in his mind the image of a fist-sized, brown, hairy fruit. That was what he was looking for. I had no idea what he was talking about, so I asked him:

"Abo, what are you looking for so desperately?"

"A coconut. This tree looks like a coconut palm from the *Castaway Stories*!"

"If it's a coconut, we're saved! We can't die of hunger, nor of thirst."

"What about that one?"

"I don't know. I couldn't find any coconuts down here, and they look like small watermelons hanging up there. They don't look like coconuts at all."

Up to that point we had died neither of hunger nor of thirst, but to tell the truth, we had spent all our efforts looking for and collecting potable water; and I still hadn't said a word about cleaning the dubious creatures he later put on the rocks to dry. Obviously, we didn't have matches. How could we have made fire?

Well, Abo did try to make fire by rubbing two dry rocks against each other, hoping to set fire to a pile of dry leaves, but he failed, despite several attempts. Eventually he threw the rocks into the ocean, then exclaimed bitterly:

"This was a lot easier in the *Castaway Stories*."

He kept thinking of the six tall palm trees. We went back the next day, and this time examined a larger area. He peered into the thicket next to the plantation and found a kind of fruit similar to those on the palms, but more yellow, with cracks on them. On carrying them out from the bushes, he was surprised how heavy they were. He was even more surprised that he couldn't open the cracks with his fingers. He didn't waste any time, but threw them against a tree trunk, then against a rock, but no matter what he did, the yellow fruit wouldn't give in.

I'm telling you, what I've learned by spending time with fellows like yourself, Danny Boy, is that there is no greater virtue than patience. I would stray too far from my story, if I told you how Abo, thanks to his persistence and obstinacy, advanced millimetre by millimetre until he finally managed to crack open the unbelievably thick and fibrous fruit. How he swore for not having his Swiss pocket knife! He gathered rocks from the rocky shore, some as big as the mysterious fruit itself and threw them at the fruit or threw the fruit against the rocks to crack them open. He threw them against the sharp rocks. Eventually he managed to break the fibrous husk; it turned out to be at least as thick as two human fingers.

The sun had set by the time he reached the core of the fruit.

He didn't know whether to laugh or cry.

He also realised that the mysterious palm tree planters had been here not long ago. They collected the fruit that had already turned yellow from the base of the trees or from the trees and took them away. Who knew when they'd be back? In a month's time? Or three months? Or more? Since Abo discovered the plantation, none of the fruit had turned yellow and none had fallen from the tree. Yet harvesting them from on high was far from an easy task. He didn't think they'd be back any time soon.

My dear Danny Boy, hard seeds fell out from the thick, fibrous husk. They were a lighter brown than what Abo was used to at home, but no doubt, it was a hairy and rough coconut. He identified three characteristic spots on the hard husk. "If only I had my Swiss pocket knife with me!" He sighed. At home, whenever he bought the husked coconut, he used to crack the soft opening with a knife and let the sweet water pour out. Then he held the coconut in his palm and hit it hard with a hammer. Usually the first blow was enough for it to surrender, to split into two and render the lovely white flesh visible.

He knew that if he hit it with a bigger rock, it would also give in. He was trying to save the small amount of liquid that was sloshing around inside. That's why, the Apple of the Abos' Eye inserted a tap into the coconut, using a fish trap tool, an instrument created by nature.

On the second day of our arrival, while looking for food, water or any trace of human presence, Abo discovered a curious tree.

The trunk was covered with irregular thorns, some as long as his little finger, branching from one another. When he realised he could make a fish trap out of a plastic bottle, he took a long rock that fit in his hand and went to the tree with thorns. When we got there, Abo looked at it, apologised to it, then started hitting it until he broke off a handful of thorns.

Using the thorns, he made holes into the bottle which had the widest mouth and was thus perfect for a fish trap. First, he punctured an area that was narrower, piercing tiny holes close to one another. Using a mussel's sharp shell, he made an incision into it, which made it easy to cut off the upper part of the bottle. Then, he turned the bottle upside down and pressed it into the lower half of the bottle. Then he made holes here and there in the lower part, so the sea water could flow in and out freely. When he was done with it all, he lifted his masterpiece to examine it.

"Do you see?"

"Yes, I do."

"You know what this is?"

"A fish trap." I could read his mind.

"Well done. You're so clever. Do you also know how it works?"

"If you're kind enough to tell me…"

"It works the same way as a fish pot. The only difference is that fishermen make a fish pot out of switches, or a net. With a mesh as big as they like. They could even catch a fish as big as I am."

"And with this one?"

"With this one? You could catch a fish somewhat bigger than my finger."

"Are there any switches here?"

"Maybe yes, maybe not."

Suddenly, he became very serious.

"I could make a simple fish pot. It's just a matter of time. But I wouldn't like to be here forever."

Luckily, he quickly went back to the subject we were talking about. In those first days, he handled amazingly well being far from everyone he loved and who loved him, and far from the comfort of home. Sometimes it made me think that it all had to do with his longing for adventure, which most certainly had led him to the *Castaway Stories* and then, to Tom. Abo said something at one point which proved me right; but for now, let's stick with the story about the plastic bottle.

As I was saying, Abo was still holding his masterpiece in both hands and went on talking about it.

"I'll put some shrimp at the bottom, together with aquatic beetles, and pebbles to weigh it down. Then, I'll tie it to a stick stuck deep into the ground, and then all we must do is wait for the high tide to come in. The fish will be guided by the funnel toward the bottom, but then, they'll be unable to find the opening as they'll be looking for it down here, in the wider area."

"Really?" I asked, surprised.

"Yes."

"How come?"

"I have no idea."

"Even if they don't find it down there?"

"Yes."

"Why don't they try somewhere else as well? I would definitely try."

"I would, too. But we're not fish."

We were silent for a while.

"Abo, maybe it isn't their job to try it. Because if they tried, you wouldn't be able to catch them. And there goes your food."

Abo started thinking seriously about what I told him. I couldn't decide whether it was because I had said something silly, or because I had hit the nail on the head. I suspected that it had to do with Providence. What we refer to as, "God helps those who help themselves". That meant that Abo should be making the trap, place it, and leave the rest to the gods.

But Abo was thinking about something else. It might have been thanks to one of my ideas. "Are we to this island what the fish are to the plastic bottle?" he wondered. "We can't see beyond our noses. Why are we waiting for someone to dock here? Why don't we try to get away somehow ourselves? Why don't we build a raft? Or a boat?"

***

My dear Danny Boy, I still haven't told you about what happened to us on the second day of our arrival, when Abo finally came to. How did he react when he realised that he had escaped from the vast ocean, but his ordeal was far from over?

Since no warm-blooded food source had deigned to come our way, I quickly returned to his ear. I was afraid he might wake up, walk away and I'd never find him again. The sun was high in the sky when he opened his eyes.

"Where are we?" he mumbled.

Needless to say, this "we" made me feel warm inside.

He was aware of my presence, that there were two of us, and he had heard and understood what I told him when we pitched and rolled on the "dinghy". Most importantly, with this plural, he put me at his level. Don't take it as cockiness, my dear friend, but I began to believe that our escape was more and more possible.

"I only see with and through you," I informed him.

Somehow, he managed to push himself up to a kneeling position. He looked around. I was also able to see where this mysterious heavenly power had taken us.

There was no one around: not a trace of humans.

At a distance of twenty to twenty-five human steps, the shore began going uphill, and the dunes, covered with tiny water creatures, merged with the dense forest. After finally eating and drinking our fill, Abo told me we couldn't be very far from the equator. We couldn't have been close either, because the weather wasn't humid enough nor the forest tropical enough. Not that he'd ever been to one, but he took geography at school and, of course, one of his favourite computer games, the *Castaway Stories,* was also set there.

The chalky marine debris grazed his knees, so after several failed attempts at standing up, he finally succeeded and tried to reach the forest. He barely had enough energy to walk, but was driven by tormenting thirst. When we finally reached the forest, he fell to his knees and said bluntly, "This can't be true."

Right before our eyes, water was slowly dripping from a low berm. Most probably it had been created by the storm that had brought our plane down. It was surrounded by dense underbrush, thanks to the sunlight that had penetrated. As it reached the ground, the little streamlet vanished. Had we gone deeper into the forest, we wouldn't have found it… Abo put his hand under the streamlet, and before water filled his palm, he lifted his hand to his mouth and drank greedily. He managed to fill his palm with more and more water, and he started drinking more calmly, and in the end, he washed his face with it.

He was now a different person.

"I'm glad you're feeling better!" I said.

"Thanks for staying with me," he replied.

"So, you figured it out?"

"It wasn't that hard. If my cousin hadn't told me about you, I would have thought I'd lost my mind." He seemed absorbed in his thoughts. "It's not every day that such things happen to us."

"Well, that's true," I agreed.

"Would you like some water?" He held his hand in front of his face.

"I never drink water."

"Well, never mind then. We'll find a warm-blooded animal for you. Can you stand the hunger? Apparently, fleas cope well with not eating."

"You're right. That's true for most fleas, but not for me."

"It's nice of you not to feed off me."

"I came incognito. It was a secret mission."

"My Mum?"

"No."

"My Dad?"

"Maybe."

"I'm surprised. I'd have thought it'd be the other way around."

"In a way it is, but I can't tell you more."

"Anyway, it doesn't matter. The point is that you're here. I might have given up without you."

He looked at himself.

"I look quite hopeless."

His white T-shirt was torn in front; there was a hole the size of a palm. But the shorts that reached below his knees seemed quite intact.

"Where are your sneakers?" I said as I saw his bare feet.

"Somewhere in the ocean. I got rid of them; they were too heavy…"

As he recalled it, I could see how he did it.

"I suggest," he said, "since we've managed to stay alive up to now, let's not die of hunger now either!"

He looked around cautiously.

"It's quite a promising place. Where there are a lot of plants, there are lots of animals, and that means there's plenty of food." Red berries on a fat thorny shrub were smiling at us. "Don't you know them?" he asked.

"No."

"Me neither. Want to taste them?"

"I'd rather not."

"Are you afraid they might be poisonous?"

"No, I just don't eat this stuff."

"As for me, I'm afraid of eating them."

He went on thinking about this for a while, then we left the forest and went back to the dunes, whose cracks were filled with all kinds of debris. It hurt the bottom of his feet, but he kept walking towards the shore.

"We have a better chance of meeting someone here," he explained. "Fishermen, locals. Swimmers."

"Dogs, cats."

"Them too. Also, a dock. A bar. Kayak vendors."

Suddenly, he stopped.

"We haven't a cent. No passport either." Then he added, "In the *Castaway Stories* the sea washes a trunk up to the shore as well. Funny, ha? My bag just didn't want to come with me… Oh well, never mind! We'll just say we haven't eaten in two days. If nothing else works, we'll offer to wash the dishes."

We walked along leisurely.

Not a single soul anywhere.

We kept on walking more slowly, listlessly. Whenever we could, we walked alongside the forest, in the shade of the trees. In a rockier area we found three plastic bottles next to one another. They had been carried by the waters into a smaller gulf surrounded by rocks. Abo went and pried them all out and brought them close to the forest.

"Gift from the sea. Might be of use. It's so lifeless here, it makes one suspicious."

Then we stopped.

"What now?" Abo asked. "Should we stop, take a rest or should we go on?"

"It's your feet, not mine."

"OK, let's carry on, then!"

I could see – actually see it from inside him – that he was more and more worried about this place on which we had been cast away.

"Hey, flea! Do you think there might be an island in this world that has not been discovered yet?"

"Hey, Abo. What would you say if I asked you that same question?"

"That it's impossible!"

"That's what I thought, too."

"The satellites have made pictures of the whole planet, square metre by square metre."

"What makes you think that?"

"As many as a billion people have access to Google Maps. It's more than certain that the wealthy have access to them as well. They love to hide away from the masses, think how many hours they spend in front of the computer staring at the map of the oceans, searching for uninhabited beaches and islands. They'd see at once there wasn't a house or a hut in an area, and with a click they'd buy the whole island for themselves. Don't you agree?"

"Yep, that sounds logical."

"Well then, we should find at least one living creature here. And a bite to eat! A piece of bread, *this* tiny! A berry *this* tiny. Something."

He started chewing and swallowing unconsciously.

"And something to suck blood from," I added.

"Of course, that too." He nodded.

Not much later we found the iron pole. Abo announced with relief, "People are visiting this place." We were re-energised.

We continued our journey along the shore. Looking at the shape of the beach, Abo thought that we were either on a very narrow piece of land, or on a tiny island, only a few square kilometres wide. It couldn't have been a panhandle, because we still hadn't met anyone, even though the vegetation was rich. There were places on the shore where the sea had left a wealth of offerings, fish and other tiny creatures.

Abo spent more and more time sitting next to the murmuring waters, and soaking his feet. The salty sea was hurting the thousand tiny wounds on the soles of his feet, but he managed to stagger on. Once he even fished out a smaller mussel out of the water, sat down on the dunes, and announced,

"We're not walking any more today. Luckily, it's warm enough; we won't feel cold. And if we survive our first night, we have a good chance of surviving another. And tomorrow, after we've regained our strength, we'll start building a hut."

"Out of what?"

"There's a big forest here. And we'll see about the rest later."

I didn't want to be a burden myself, but I couldn't stop myself from saying,

"I'm hungry."

"What can I do? I'm even hungrier."

He examined and sniffed at the black-crusted sea creature. It looked like two human ears glued together… "The thing is I could never stand seafood. I liked fish though. But not crabs, mussels or shrimp or the rest… But if a miracle doesn't happen by tomorrow, we'll have to see what it tastes like."

"I won't try it, you can bet on it," I protested. "My stomach won't stand for it."

I saw that he felt really sorry for me.

"Tomorrow we'll look for something for you too." He nodded.

We said nothing for a long time. Then he finally said,

"Needless to say, I'm as thirsty as hell."

"No doubt!" I replied dejectedly.

He clambered up and staggered to the edge of the forest. The sun was going down. In the area close to the shore the underbrush was magnificently rich under the foliage of the forest trees bearing lianas and other parasite plants. It took us a while to find a rockier area in the forest gloom, but here on the tiny stone berm, the life-giving nectar was dripping unbearably slowly.

Abo stuck his tongue out under it and, as it started dripping, withdrew it, then stuck it out again. He didn't do this for long, because something occurred to him.

"Maybe the other spring is starting to dry out as well."

He stumbled and limped as he set out for another mission. He took the plastic bottles as well. The ocean had almost swallowed the sun, by the time we finally got back to where we were washed ashore. Abo's crawling body had left traces on the dune, as well as his body lying on the beach, then as he got up on his knees and even when he stood up. Abo put on his trousers and following the footsteps, we stumbled into the forest.

The water dripped slowly.

Abo fell to his knees, and stuck his tongue out. He let each drop of water soak in, then swallowed it slowly, as if planning to store water like a camel.

I just watched and watched, swallowing nothing. The sun had set when Abo stood up and placed one of the bottles under the slowly dripping water. Then he said:

"If there's no horse, a donkey will do."

"What do you mean?"

"Come on, get out of there and have supper on me, then get back in there. I'll tell you why we ended up here."

The Apple of the Abos' Eye, this young boy already knew a lot about life. My curiosity was bigger than my hunger, so I barely fed myself off him.

"Well, say it already!" I shouted as I jumped back into his ear.

Well, my little friend, I might tell you about it some other time. We ran out of time.

Well, all right, all right now, if you really want it that much.

***

While I was out there, Abo gathered some enormous leaves. Some were even wider than his head and longer than his arm. He placed them on the dunes, then he stretched his limbs on the first couch on an uninhabited island.

"Well…?" I said impatiently.

He was silent for a while, then jumped right into the middle.

"We're here because of the *Castaway Stories.*"

"You mean the computer game?"

"Exactly."

"You can't be serious!"

"Of course, I am. There's no other logical explanation. 'If you want it that bad, here, you can have it!' And now, here I am."

This is when he told me from beginning to end about his curiosity and how he wrote to "Frequently Asked Questions";

how surprised he was by the reply sent in Hungarian by an Australian boy; how they started exchanging emails; and finally, how he received an invitation to Australia.

"And you know the rest," he ended.

"The only thing that isn't clear is why the *Castaway Stories* should be blamed for this."

"I didn't say it caused it, only that it triggered it all. If it weren't for the *Castaway Stories,* we wouldn't be here."

I didn't have to hear any more. "Look, Abo!" I went on without stopping. "If it weren't for the storm, we wouldn't be here either. If the plane hadn't crashed, we wouldn't be here either. And if a piece of it hadn't dropped precisely next to us, if it had been bent another way, and if the wind were blowing in a different direction, we wouldn't be here either. And we probably wouldn't be here if I hadn't finished eating when I had, and I hadn't jumped back in your ear. Then we wouldn't have fallen together into the ocean either. Without you I would be lost somewhere in the endless ocean."

"Doesn't it strike you that we're both saying the same thing?" he asked.

"No. I never mentioned the *Castaway Stories* at all."

"What you listed is all true. All these were a consequence of the *Castaway Stories!* That's the starting point. Everything had to happen this way, so that the video game would reach its goal."

To tell the truth, he hadn't succeeded in convincing me. So, my reply was,

"I'll believe it if I want to, if I don't, I won't."

"Damn it!" he said. He was becoming annoyed. "The point is it has nothing to do with faith. Given the huge number of coincidences, it is utterly inconceivable for this to be a coincidence as well."

"What else?"

"Take a guess."

"God?"

"Indeed." Abo nodded.

But my doubts didn't disappear.

"Wait a second! What if we find a port here? Or a pub?"

"Then I'd have to say that it was sheer luck or mere coincidence that brought us here."

I was genuinely surprised by what I heard.

"Could it really depend on only one thing? Whether we find a person here or not?"

"Indeed," he replied firmly.

"We still haven't covered it all yet. There might be someone living on the other side of the island."

"If someone does live there, it means I'm wrong. My theory only makes sense if the island is indeed uninhabited, and there really isn't anyone to help us, and we must solve everything on our own. That would really make us survivors, and it would mean we were on our own and must find a solution on our own. That's when it really becomes a matter of survival, which proves our hypothesis."

I could see that he was still thinking about something. A certain Darwin popped up in his mind.

"Have you heard about evolution?"

"No," I replied.

"It's about how the species evolved… Does it sound familiar now?"

"No. I'm not at all sure my abilities are up to this."

"Well, of course they are! Educated people still believe even today, that we living creatures arose totally by accident out of inorganic matter. And what's even more striking, we came about as a result of the endless varieties created by endless time. Somebody said that if we believed this, it meant that we believed that if we threw up handfuls of dust in the air, eventually a living being would be created."

"Just like that?"

"Just like that."

"And could even a flea come of it?"

"Sooner or later, yes, even a flea."

"Then, I have to say, that's really ridiculous."

"I agree completely. Isn't it the same with our story? Could sheer coincidence make all this happen?"

I can see, Danny Boy, that your grey cells too are working overtime. Think about how difficult it must have been for me to understand all this. I told Abo,

"I must say it's very difficult to believe all this, but it's even more difficult to accept that God could be this convoluted in managing the lives of each living creature."

It's hard for me to believe too; that's why I choose only to talk about my own experience. Yet I can find no other explanation.

***

Needless to say, my dear friend, that night I fell asleep with a deep sense of peace. Abo didn't say so, but I drew my own conclusion, that we were saved. A story in which someone, who really wanted to be part of a survival game, died after having gone through a series of adventures wouldn't have made any sense at all. Sure, we can all imagine that his guardian wanted only to teach him a lesson, that life is more than just playing a survival game on your laptop. It was also possible that he had a plan for him, especially knowing how much Abo really longed for such an experience. So, instead of wasting his time playing computer games, he should really try himself out and gain the experience of a lifetime.

And, these experiences should not only teach him, but should be a lesson for everyone… It was utterly inconceivable to me that so much ado was for nothing, and we would both perish in the end. It would have made all our theories pointless. After all, we could have ended our lives when we fell into the ocean without anyone noticing.

Abo fell asleep and woke up at dawn in a similarly hopeful mood. Escaping from this remote uninhabited piece of land was simply a matter of time. His stomach had other ideas; it had almost begun to digest itself. Luckily, we had water. The bottle we left under the drips had filled up by next morning.

There were no miracles concerning food, so Abo had to examine what the sea had to offer. He was looking for shrimp and mussels, because at that point we had no fish trap and no sharp spear either, which the protagonist of the *Castaway Stories* used to catch fish.

He managed to collect a small pile of mussels in a short time. He took most of them from a rock partly covered by water. He only succeeded in catching a single shrimp. He could have found more in the deeper water, but he didn't dare venture in. I must add that I wouldn't have followed him there myself. It seemed safer for me to stay ashore and find something else to kill my time with, than follow him into the sea.

Abo made piles according to the species of mussels. He chose the largest mussels from all three groups, examining them minutely and sniffing them. They varied in shape and colour, but they all smelled the same. He was surprised to realise that he was not disgusted at all; on the contrary, his stomach did not protest against the thought of eating them. In fact!

We hurried into the forest and picked the smaller leaves of one of the old trees with a dried-out crown. We used them to make a fire and added thicker branches as firewood.

As I already mentioned to you, Abo failed in making a fire simply by rubbing two rocks against one another.

He had the mussels in his hands, and he was thinking of eating them raw, as they were, chew them, then swallow. His starving stomach showed no sign of disgust or protest, so Abo tried to open them up.

How should he start?

By the way, Danny Boy.

How would *you* get started?

The mussels' shells were stuck so tightly together, as a sparrow held its beak. Even if Abo had had his Swiss pocket knife, he would have struggled as well. But now he had nothing to separate the two valves of the shell and overcome the amazing strength of the mussel.

Eventually he chose a rather barbarian method. He took it to the rocks and smashed it with a rock. Still, it didn't give in. Then he hit it even harder and only then did he manage to break it into pieces. We could see its amazing silvery colour.

Then, with another shell he scraped off the remains of the invertebrate and lifted them slowly to his mouth. Then he started chewing slowly, then suddenly, he swallowed.

Having survived the first one, he opened the rest of the mussels, too, one by one. After not having eaten anything at all for a long time, the Apple of the Abos' Eye knew about the dangers of eating too much raw mussel; it might have brought an end to his promising life. So, he chewed two more, thoroughly, and then went on to the shrimp.

He looked at them, trying to figure out how to deal with the brown, carapaced creature. It was no longer than his little finger and didn't seem dangerous at all. He tried twisting and turning it, out of sheer curiosity, and the shell broke and left its scissors in his hands. The long, slim body of the poor shrimp was visible, and Abo sniffed it. He wasn't thrilled about it, and thought he might leave the shrimp until they dried. He found a rock's plain surface and put them there for drying. It was surrounded by taller rocks, so they were protected from the wind. But not enough, for the next day the shrimp were gone. Abo took a huge leaf, put it on the rock, then put four heavy stones on it.

Then he pierced the flesh with a thorn after he had removed it from the carapace and attached it to the giant leaf, as if making a giant stitch. He did the same with the small, shrimp-like, possibly edible creatures that were left behind by the water in low tide. The wind constantly blew in from the sea and the hot sun shone all day, so Abo could eat them at once as they were dried out. After making the dryer, Abo thought about building a hut. As we were no longer in imminent danger of dying of starvation, Abo decided to venture out to discover the unknown shore of the island the next day.

The hut would be built close to the spring, which would soon disappear into the dunes. There was no point in kidding ourselves; we had never felt safe in the forest. Close to the trees, we were afraid of poisonous snakes, ants, and spiders, and God knows what other creatures. And until we knew for certain that we were indeed trapped on an island, we were afraid that a tiger or another large feline might be lurking behind the trees, ready to jump on us. Eventually, however, we let our guard down, as the Apple of the Abos' Eye told me, it was impossible for such a tiny island to maintain such large animals.

At a distance of ten human steps – where there was shade during late morning hours – Abo stuck two poles into the ground. Then two more a bit closer to the ocean.

"It won't be too spacious," I said.

"Indeed not! We just need it to protect us against the sun and rain. If we're stuck here, and we're bored, we can always build a bigger one. I hope it won't come to that."

"What do you mean?"

"I mean, building a proper house and getting old here are not on the list of things we should be facing here."

"And what now?" I asked.

"Well, that's my question too," said Abo, scratching his head. He was silent for a while, then suddenly began laughing. In a mocking way.

"Do you know how to build a hut in the *Castaway Stories*?"

"No. How?"

"Imagine I'm moving the mouse. I mean, the arrow on the screen."

"I see it."

"Wait, there's something. Look, an axe! How did it get there? The waves carried it to the shore."

"What kind of waves?"

"The ocean… I go closer and it's in my hand. And what is this here? Is it a bamboo tree? Indeed! I touch it with the axe and it's down already. Now, my dear flea, tell me, where do you see an axe or a bamboo tree here?"

"Nowhere. But I can see only with your eyes."

"Why don't you use your own eyes? We could really use them out here!"

"I am, but I can only see through your eyes."

"By the way, what's your name?" he asked me unexpectedly.

"I have no name," I replied. Then I remembered suddenly: "Someone called me Jimmy Jumper once. It made me feel jolly…"

"That's great, Jimmy Jumper! From now on you're my captain and I'm yours."

"Do you also have it in *Castaway Stories*, too?"

"No."

"Then, how come?"

He paused.

"I don't really know. It just came to mind. It would be nice."

"Do you miss your father? Or your mother?"

"Possibly."

He stared at the ground; we kept silent for a while.

I shouted at the top of my lungs,

"Private Abo! Heads up, we're heading for the forest. Beware of snakes, do not step on them. Pick a hundred giant leaves and collect a hundred young trees."

"Orders are orders," replied Abo, and off we went. Soon after, he said, "Ten trees will do."

***

Soon we had combed through the whole area. We found just a few young trees that were at most three fingers thick. You see, Danny Boy, our woods up here are full of saplings. But there, the tall evergreens kept the young trees in the shade. But only when the old trees were down or had fallen because of the prolific parasites that sucked the life out of them, did they make way for the younger ones. Abo and I noticed that the roots did not go deep into the ground, as they usually do in our parts, so we managed to take down even those that were twice as tall as he was. "How wonderful that Uncle David had taught us how to climb a pole!" said Abo and grabbing a tree, he wrapped his legs around its slim trunk and pulled himself up higher and higher. When he had climbed high enough, he began to swing to and fro until the tree gave in and went down suddenly. At this point he only focused on not letting go, because if he reached the ground without the tree, he might not be able to stand up again.

At other times it wasn't the roots that gave in, but the trunk, but we were happy all the same. It's true that the landing was a bit more intense, but nothing happened that could justify a complaint. So many times, had he wrapped his legs around the tree trunk that blood began dripping from his feet. "Does it hurt, Private Abo?" I asked in a worried tone.

"It's not that bad," he replied, while looking for the proper lianas. "It's worth it if we can build our own house. Don't you think, Captain?"

"Well, it's your leg, not mine."

The sun had set by the time we gathered those young trees, giant leaves, and the sufficiently thin and flexible lianas we could use in building. The Apple of the Abos' Eye had planned a simple and inventive structure. As we had neither axe nor saw, we had to use the young trees as they were: roots, leaves and all. Abo crossed two trees together beneath the crown, then bound them together with lianas. Facing them he laid down two more trees, and tied them too with lianas. Then, he stood them up, and leaned them against one another. It's almost harder for me to tell it than for Abo to do it.

When he got to this point, he leaned the remaining thinner trees against the ones on the bottom.

The tent-like structure seemed covered with the dense crown of a single huge tree. We only had to weave the giant leaves between the trunks and fix them in a rough way with lianas. "Someday we'll do it properly," said Abo.

By the time we finished, the sun had set.

"I won't have trouble going to sleep tonight," he said, as he crashed onto the couch made of huge leaves in our barely finished shanty.

"Nor will I."

And we were both right.

***

It was as Abo suspected. We hoofed it around the island along the shore and returned to where we had started. We hadn't met a single person, nor seen a single hut. The chances of meeting anyone approached zero. We knew for sure we were not on a panhandle, but on a real island.

This also meant that we had to settle in for a longer time. For how long, we didn't know. It seemed possible that by the time the coconuts had turned yellow or started falling, the mysterious plantation workers would have docked on the island again. We had no idea when this would happen. It was true that up to that point we hadn't seen a single ship come our way. This meant that we were at least twenty or thirty kilometres from the nearest settlement of some size. This might easily mean that, because of the distance, the plantation workers didn't sail this way very often. Once a year? Once every two years? Once every three years? Who knew?

To celebrate our settling in, Abo positioned his fish trap bottle. Few things made us as happy as the first tiny fish. The Apple of the Abos' Eye gave it a kiss, then hit it on the head with a rock, then slit its belly open. After gutting it, he laid it flat and pinned it to the dryer. The next day, whoosh, he ate it all. But before that, he solemnly promised to invent a mouse trap, too. If nothing else, we were sure there were mice on the island and thus, my feeding problem would also be solved.

We didn't catch any fish for a while. The Apple of the Abos' Eye repositioned the trap, put it in different places, but without any results.

Raw mussels and sometimes shrimp were all the food he could find. He tried to eat snails, but chewing them or swallowing their tough, springy bodies raw proved impossible. He preferred to use them as bait in the fish trap.

Abo cracked open the coconut after many hours of trying and found its meat truly heavenly. When we went back to the tiny plantation, we took several rocks the size of a fist with us, in case we wouldn't find any there. Abo threw them at the fruit, over and over again. Three times he almost managed to hit some plump, light-green fruit. But they were barely shaken.

Abo went to the tree and patted its long, elegant trunk. He looked for a place where he could grab it. He hugged it, wrapped his legs around it, and tried climbing up higher. To no avail. It was too thick.

"Private, don't you fall! It's not worth it."

"Certainly not for you," he replied angrily.

"Why are you upset?"

"You really want to know?"

"Wait, I know. It's because of the *Castaway Stories*."

"Exactly, Jimmy Jumper! Because of the *Castaway Stories*. Picking coconuts is so lame there, there are no words to describe it!"

"Listen to me, Private. Didn't you know right from the beginning that it was nothing but a game?"

"Listen to me, Captain. I knew. Still. Imagine this: you position your mouse on the coconut tree, you click, and you're already climbing like a monkey. And before you're on top up there, you already have your husked coconut in your hands. Do you understand? Husked! If I didn't struggle with it for more than half a day!"

"You enjoyed toying around with it. That's why you wanted it. If you had to spend half a day opening it, you wouldn't have started the game again. Aren't I right?"

"On the contrary! Now that they've flooded the whole world with their *Castaway Stories,* couldn't they have just given us a hint about how to harvest that stupid coconut?"

The Apple of the Abos' Eye stared at the tempting fruit, hanging from the unattainable heights, and he flew into a rage.

"There must be some solution to this!" he shouted.

"Do it like the monkeys."

"If you're so clever, try it yourself. Hold on with the soles of your feet, grab with your hands and climb."

"Have you tried it?"

"No. I know for certain I'm not a monkey."

"Maybe this is just another challenge," I said. "A test. There's no way we can learn about it ahead of time…"

"Well, Jimmy Jumper, I think, even if there's no way of knowing, we can still feel whether it's our path or not. Let's say I'm up there, at three, four, five metres high and there's nothing I can hold onto, so, of course, I'd think they'd set a trap for me. There's no way I can climb up or down. My hands and feet barely hold me, and I'm shitting in my pants. And that's not the worst part. The worst part is, I fall down and break my neck."

I thought about it a while, then said,

"According to your logic, you can't break your neck here on this island."

"That's right!" Abo's face lit up. "You're so smart! But I'd rather not try…"

In the end we agreed that in case nobody came to the island within a couple of days, we'd husk the coconut; that is, with the help of a sharp stone we'd start cutting down one of the coconut palm trees. If it took three days, then three days it would be, if a week, then a week. We'll plant two husked coconuts; in case the plantation people caught us, we could prove that we had nothing but good intentions.

We didn't lack food and we had enough water. We were looking for a good place to set our mouse trap, when Abo saw some interesting shrubs. It had heavy pink leaves. He unfolded one of them hastily. He caught his breath when he saw the crystal-clear water shining in it. This special plant was collecting and storing the life-giving sap. The Apple of the Abos' Eye bowed to thank it for saving our lives.

By the way, it started to rain the following day, and didn't stop for days. Our spring had plenty of water, and we managed to refill our bottles.

The rain was warm, so it didn't bother us in our everyday tasks. The Apple of the Abos' Eye made excellent head-gear from the veins of the giant leaves combined with the evergreen leaves; thus, we were basically able to walk around undisturbed. We gathered what we could eat that day. We attacked the coconut palms, stared at the horizon and waited in vain for a mouse to turn up in the mousetrap.

Suddenly Abo had a great idea. Since we had neither wires, nor springs, we tried digging a hole. If we made a trap like the ones for larger animals, but proportionately smaller, according to the laws of physics, it would work the same way as the bigger traps.

So, we searched for the nearest pit made by the roots of the trees we had felled. We swept the light, moist soil from the sides of the pit towards its centre, and on the heap, we put all kinds of crops, fruits and berries so that a mouse or its larger relative could pick what it preferred. We covered the pit with young bracken leaves, that wouldn't be able to hold even the tiniest tropical mouse. We had no idea whether it would hold it or not. Our trap remained untouched for days in a row, and on the fourth day, when we found its collapsed cover, we couldn't find anything inside other than the bait.

I couldn't resist teasing the Apple of the Abos' Eye.

"How did they feed the flea in the *Castaway Stories*?"

"There's no flea in the *Castaway Stories*, only larger animals," he replied.

Then he added,

"Besides, it's crazy for me to try to find food for you. Isn't it enough that I must get food for myself, but I also need to fix traps for you? Am I crazy? It's easy to play survivor's game while sitting comfortably in my ear and sometimes jumping out, like an aristocrat to suck on my blood!"

***

Well, my dear Danny Boy, few things hurt me like Abo's words. I decided that our collaboration was over; we would part ways. We'll see what the Apple of the Abos' Eye could do without me. Sooner or later I had always managed to find the necessary source of blood, so why couldn't I do it now, on this island so enormous compared to my own size. Besides, it was good for me to try myself out; now I could show that smartass Abo that I could succeed where he had failed. I didn't have to do anything other than what I used to do at home. I stuck my nose out into the breeze, sniffed around intensely, and if I sensed the approach of a warm-blooded animal, I jumped instantly.

After I imagined it all, I wilted a bit, because I asked myself what would happen after I finished gorging myself? Do I stay for another round? And then what? If we trapped my food source we could tie it up somewhere, and that would be that. But if I jumped on to something, God knows where it might run off with me? And last but not least, how would I get back to you, my dear Danny Boy?

Well, I had lived long enough with Abo to realise something: he wanted to be alone. Of course, not forever and not even for days, but only for a couple of hours. We are all happy if we have someone, but we're at least as happy that we don't have to live the other person's life all the time. Living on our own is hard enough. Besides, we don't always like to share our physical problems with others. So, I told him,

"I got you, Captain. I give you back the leadership. I'll disappear from here, but eventually I'll be back to our shared home." Needless to say, I became so emotional at my own words, I thought I might burst into tears. I went on hastily,

"If you still need me, we can continue where we left off. If not, God bless you, Abo!"

I was on the point of jumping, when Abo begged me to stay. He didn't mean it seriously, I shouldn't be mad at him, and so on. I regained my mental balance, but in vain. Despite taking back what he said, he was right.

It even occurred to me, why should the Master of All Games focus on a single child? Why couldn't I be the focus of attention too? Why wouldn't he want me to stand on my own feet? Why wouldn't he want to test me as well? Isn't it logical, my friend?

That night I was able to eat as much as I wanted. I went out in front of our hut and waited patiently. I thought that if any warm-blooded animal passed by, it would come back on the same path as well. Danny Boy, I'd love to tell you about the animals I encountered on my journey, but, unfortunately, there's not much to say, because it never looked at itself, only sniffed at things in front of it. What I know for sure, is that it wasn't a cat, nor a dog, nor a hedgehog, rabbit or mouse, because it was much bigger than that, and that's how I could land on it on my first try. To my great surprise its first journey was to a well-known destination. It went to the drying rock, ate a couple of desiccated sea creatures, then headed back into the woods.

As it passed in front of our hut the following night, I could smell Abo, and I jumped without hesitation. I ate so much from my involuntary benefactor, that I felt full for several days. The next morning, I was in my beloved lookout. "Good morning, Abo," I said and watched his reaction. He was so happy, that I was moved again.

He wanted to show me something. "We can go," I said and off we went toward the shore. "Where are we going?" I asked him after a while. "You'll see," he said.

We kept walking and walking.

I was very curious.

"Did you manage to cut out the coconut palm?"

"No way! I'm satisfied with having cut only a sixth of its perimeter."

"Did the plantation people get here?"

"I wish!"

"Have you figured out how we could get out of here…"

"You're getting warm…"

"You'll build a raft."

"I've thought about it. Even if the situation here is different than in the *Castaway Stories*. There, suddenly, there's a ton of bamboo. Needless to say, cut into all shapes and sizes. And, ta-da, they assemble themselves into a raft. Isn't that ridiculous? I have an even better reason for not building a raft. There are plenty of trees, we can take them down and cut them into pieces. Why does it matter that the raft looks as if it were made by clowns? The real problem is that we wouldn't be able to sail off with it."

"It would capsize?"

"Oh, no! Not the one we are building? No way!"

"Then, what?"

"I would give you the orders,

    'Private, take us to the nearest dry land!' What would you do?"

At that moment, I grasped the absurdity of our situation. We hadn't the faintest idea where we were. How could we know whether we were getting closer to land or moving away from it?

Seeing that I understood him, Abo said,

"Once was enough, being in the ocean's throat."

"I get that." I nodded.

We reached the place where we found our bottles. Further on, the bank broadened a bit, and from afar I spotted something made of slim trees and old lianas. At first, I saw the big "O" letter, then a "B", and at last, an "A".

Then I understood.

"ABO".

I looked for words feverishly to express my shock without ruining our joyful reunion. Did we have the energy to spend glorifying ourselves? Cutting the coconut palms would have made so much more sense. Or making a mouse trap or a monkey trap. And we hadn't even tried making a hook out of a thorn either. There were so many things to do, and instead we spend time praising ourselves?

"So, what do you think?" asked Abo.

"That's exactly what I'm thinking about," I said.

"You know what this is?"

"I do. Your name. But why? To improve your self-esteem?"

"Of course not! It's a distress signal."

"Ah!" I said, beginning to see the light. "For the planes, right? In case one flies this way…"

"If only it would! But passenger planes fly too high to see this. The ones that fly lower would do so for the same reason ours did. Small planes never come this way; it seems we're not in an area with a lot of traffic."

"Then I don't know. I give up."

"Think, Jimmy Jumper! You're not a fish, which can't see out of your plastic bottle. Can't you see something unusual about it?"

I racked my brains. I didn't want to humiliate myself, to be as stupid as a fish. Without having any idea, I asked,

"But why 'ABO'? Why not 'SOS' instead?"

"Well done, Jimmy Jumper! You're getting *closer and closer*. If I'd seen planes flying above us, I'd have written that. But I can't count on planes flying low above us. Who can I count on in this world?"

"On me."

"You're great, Jimmy Jumper! But you're here with me. How could you bring help from the outside world?"

"You can count on your parents."

"Unfortunately, there's nothing they can do. If the authorities said there were no survivors, there was nothing they could do. They would have to accept it. And they must, because they won't come across my name."

I almost said I give up, when suddenly, I remembered Google Maps. Of course!

If the satellites made photos of every inch of the earth, these huge letters wouldn't pass unnoticed.

I was ecstatic.

"I have it!" I said. "You hope that some rich person might spot it on a Google Map. While looking for an uninhabited island, they might see it and send for help."

"*Getting there! Getting there!*" Abo was thrilled and jumped for joy.

"I'm still not *there* yet?" I asked with some disappointment.

"Not yet," replied Abo. "There's nothing they care less about than saving others. Besides, 'ABO' means nothing to them."

"Then I have to say, I have no idea."

"Of course, you do, Jimmy Jumper! Who will never stop looking for me? Who surfs the world-wide web like a monkey on a palm tree? And who knows what 'ABO' stands for? Well? Well?"

"Tom."

"Exactly, Jimmy Jumper! *Touché! Touché!*"

***

After all that help, my friend, you could have figured it out yourself. I asked him, feeling the excitement that overcame me,

"Then, maybe, by tomorrow Tom will have come and saved us?"

"Unfortunately, there is little chance of that. I can easily imagine Tom scanning this area every day, hoping to find us, but Google refreshes the images only every three years. So, if by chance, they had taken a photo of the area after I wrote those letters, then we might hear Tom's voice here in a couple of days. But if they made the photos prior to that, then, unfortunately our escape might take a few years."

Suddenly, I wilted.

"What's wrong, Jimmy Jumper?"

"Three years is a horribly long time," I said.

Abo replied with resignation.

"Master. Have you forgotten what you taught me?"

You can only have the moment.
You just need to live in the moment.

One after the other, as it unfolds.
Floating lightly.
Leave the rest to the One in charge.

My dear Danny Boy, you know, I almost lost my breath. I felt honoured, because the Apple of the Abos' Eye hadn't forgotten my words when I tried to save him from the ocean's deadly embrace. Maybe he thought all my efforts weren't in vain. What really struck me was, although I felt my mouth move, I wasn't the one speaking.

I am no master!

I just sit and listen. That's all.

I listen to the advice I'm given.

If Abo says, Tom will come and get us, I know it's only a matter of time. I believe in the words of the Apple of the Abos' Eye. Without ever complaining, I spent my time with him. Each moment as it came one after the other.

***

I can't tell you, my dear Danny Boy, whether entrusting one's destiny to higher powers would work the same way for others, too. I can only tell you that no more than two weeks had passed, when suddenly, we heard the humming of engines. Next to our hut we were covering with giant leaves the unbelievable amount of fruit that had fallen from the trees. We instinctively turned our heads in the direction of the humming and saw a small motorboat coming our way.

You can imagine how we felt.

Abo fell to his knees and started crying.

The people in uniform repeated the name quite often: "Abo. Abo." Abo nodded. They stared at him perplexedly, as if we were savages. That's when I realised, that I hadn't seen Abo's face not even once since we crashed.

Well, he hadn't seen mine either.

Besides, they weren't even looking for me. They ignored me, I have to say.

But at least they weren't examining me.

Abo and Tom became friends for life. When I asked Abo at the airport whether we were going to Australia or Hungary, he said,

"We're going home. Next year, we're going to visit Tom."

"Aren't you afraid of flying?"

He shrugged.

"Our story has come full circle. There's no reason to crash again."

When we took our seats on the plane, Abo grabbed the armrest and didn't let go for the entire flight. We said nothing most of the time. We were both replaying our film, each one remembering his own version. When the pilot landed at Budapest airport, Abo marked his relief with a sigh.

"What'd I say, Captain?"

***

Well, Danny Boy, I've never told anyone such a long story before. It's late now. To bed, sailor, the fleas are starving!

Eleventh Tale
DR. FLEA'S HAPPINESS

Imagine, Danny, Young Master said to me the other day, *"I'm going to ask for a commission as mediator for you." "What do you mean?"* I ask him. It turns out that a psychologist is eager to meet me. I should say that she was offering me work. When I clambered out of him, I was laughing so hard I had to hold my stomach. You know who these psychologists are? Healers of the psyche. She wants to employ me, an insignificant little flea, for psychological reconnaissance. She says to me, *"Master Flea, you could more easily reach the patient's real thoughts and feelings without his or her even being aware of your existence."* Master Flea. You hear? She calls me master. I, a tiny flea. And she says, *"What interferes with my judgement is that they all try to please me. They don't tell me what they're really feeling, but what they think I wish to hear. You, Master Flea, could help me by revealing psychological problems and healing them."*

Of course, I accepted at once.

Can you imagine a more beautiful task?

I asked Young Master, *"How did she find out about me?"* It turned out that it was through his cousin. Abo was put through psychological tests to examine whether the airplane accident had caused him serious psychological harm. And the isolation on the uninhabited island. The loneliness. The shrink quizzed Abo until he disclosed that he hadn't been alone.

"No?" the kind and enthusiastic creature said, taken aback. "So, the island wasn't uninhabited after all?"

"Yes, it was. But there was a flea with me too."

The shrink immediately informed Abo's parents that in such extreme, dramatic situations, people defend themselves against psychological traumas, by imagining a helper with whom they can talk about what to do, with whom they can share their pains, solitude, and vulnerability. *"That is what happened with Abo,"* she explained. *"Thank Heaven that this unconscious psychological defence mechanism helped him to survive."*

Abo's dad finally got a word in.

"Except that this flea is not a figment of his imagination. It is very real."

The shrink got all excited.

"That's exactly what is so amazing, dear Abo's dad. Our imagination can experience its creation as completely real. It can experience as concrete what is only the plaything of our mind. This is our great good fortune. Thanks to this it could effect a healing in Abo's case."

"Dear Doctor, you misunderstand me," he tried again. "This flea is as real as I am as I stand before you. You can touch it. You can chase it. You can even converse with it. Just like we are doing right now."

Poor little shrink. You should have seen her pained look. According to Abo, she couldn't decide whether father and son were playing her for a fool, or the father had gone off the rails, together with the son. She decided to get to the bottom of this.

"And where is this flea now?"

"Impossible to know," replied Abo's dad. "He's wandering about the world."

"Aha. So, I can't meet him. That's all right, I'll imagine him." She smiled.

"We do have a fixed point, however. He's a good friend of Toffee, my nephew's dog."

"The flea is friends with a dog?"

"Yes, the flea is friends with a dog. Should I bring him here?"

The doctor was visibly struggling with herself. Finally, she decided.

"You know what, dear Abo's dad? Bring him here. But not here, in my office. I'd like to ask a few questions."

"Of whom?"

"We shall see. Of you or the flea."

***

So that is what happened, dear Danny. I met the Shrink, who was truly an enthusiastic, pleasant psychologist. Well, what shall I say? She did need a generous spirit, and great determination, for you people have so many psychological troubles, my dear friend, that you could dam ten Danubes with them. If not a hundred.

Day after day I still think about this. Why should this be? Essentially, we fleas don't do anything different on this earth than you human beings. We are born, we eat, we live here and there, we seek a mate, we multiply, we live our lives, then we die. Just like you. And yet psychological problems avoid us, while you are up to your necks in them.

It's no wonder that I couldn't say no to the Shrink's unexpected proposal.

Otherwise, it was a whole cohort that accompanied me to her office. Toffee had to bring me. Young Master accompanied Toffee. Abo and I hadn't seen each other in a long time. Abo's dad was ready to answer questions. These were not asked, as soon as the door opened, I leapt onto the Shrink. Taken aback, she stared at the horde, then she said,

"It's not a good idea to bring a dog into the office."

"But he's probably carrying the flea," said Abo's dad.

"You're mistaken," I interjected gleefully. "Here I am, fresh as a daisy."

The Shrink just stood there in amazement.

Finally, she said,

"Thank you all. Could you come back in a half hour?"

When the door closed, and we were left alone, the Shrink did not say a word for a long time. Think about it, Danny, how many years had she spent at school? How many years had she been practicing her profession? She was a well-known family psychologist, so she wasn't just anybody. But never, never, not even once had she met a talking flea. Not even close. Not even a hint or allusion. She had experienced many times how enormous and complex a brain needs to be for a creature to develop the ability to speak. To create concepts and use them. How many billions of nerve cells, how many convolutions of the brain, how many nerve centres are needed. How many hearing centres, centres that understand speech and create speech… And in all the world only human beings have this ability. And now a flea just comes up with a saying. So, can we wonder, my dear friend, that the Shrink couldn't say a single word? No, indeed.

Finally, she couldn't, poor thing, do anything other than what human beings do at such times: she didn't try to find an explanation for the mystery. She contented herself with gauging the possibilities that were hidden in this, the possible uses.

"Can I ask you a few questions?"

"Of course," I answered at once. I could barely wait for her to ask a question so that I could finally reply.

"Where are you now?"

"In your right ear."

"And what do you see?"

"A lot of things."

"For example?"

"I can see myself, as you imagine me in your ear. I must say that I'm not so alarmingly ugly, and I'm not so terribly big. I can see that you are anxious… As if you were worried that I will damage your eardrum. I can assure you I won't. Now I can see a slight smile. I'm glad that I've convinced you… I don't know who just swam into my sight. A little girl, around nine years old. A charming child, but something is really bothering her. She's in turmoil."

"Very good," nodded the Shrink. "That's enough. Now you can come out. I would like to make an agreement to work together with you."

"Oh, that sounds very good. But if I come out, we can't talk to each other."

She pondered this.

"Do you have a body?" she asked unexpectedly.

"Why do you ask?"

"Because that just complicates matters. It's absurd to think that the human brain's capacity can fit into a flea's brain. Not only is it absurd, it's also superfluous."

Now it was my turn to ponder this. But I didn't come to any philosophical conclusion. Actually, it was my stomach that said the essential thing.

"Look here, my dear Shrink. I don't know yet what kind of agreement you wish to reach with me. I can tell you for certain that we can have a lasting collaboration only if you are able to feed me regularly."

"Of course, that's the least I can do."

We left it at that.

And what I already told you, dear Danny, that I would be willing to help her heal souls.

***

How could I know that there wasn't a more difficult profession in the world? I tell you straight, dear Danny, that we fleas don't have an inner life, only as much as absolutely necessary. That is why this unexpected opportunity excited me so much, that I could now engage myself with the mysteries of the human soul. Except that! The Shrink said that before throwing me into deep water, that is, sending me into a patient, she asked me to sit in her ear while she took part in a group therapy session. She wanted me to observe four children heatedly playing a popular board game. We would discuss the rest afterwards.

Now, I had so many questions to ask and so many things that filled me with amazement that in the end I honestly had to ask the Shrink, wasn't I unsuited for such a noble task? Shouldn't she rather try this with a human being? The Shrink immediately replied that at our current technical level no human being could worm their way into the same place as me. Then she added, *"Anyway, if the Doctor lacked self-confidence, he should go on a training course to develop self-confidence."*

I was just about to ask what doctor she meant, when the penny dropped.

Did you click too, Danny?

What a sweet and clever turn. With this *Doctor,* she banished my lack of confidence and my every doubt in the blink of an eye. And she clearly noticed that, because from then on, she never addressed me as other than *Doctor.* After that I didn't need any kind of self-confidence training.

Anyway, I tend to believe that neither the human psyche nor the human mind is capable of such sweet consideration. Only the two together, if they should luckily come together.

The game did hold the children's attention. You know what, I don't wonder at this. The Shrink said that truly since human beings have existed they've played this game, only in another way. We meet a stranger, we glance at his or her face and immediately we say, *"Ugh, is he ever disgusting!" "She's nice." "He was born evil", "He's honest through and through", "He's an exciting fellow", "Totally boring", "As stupid as the earth", "He radiates intelligence."*

The Shrink put photos on the table of total strangers. The next player pulled out a card, and read the question on it. For example, *"Who is the dangerous criminal?"*, *"Who is the one who takes everything to heart?"* Or this, *"Who had a difficult childhood?"* But other questions turned up too, such as: *"Whose feet smell?"* Or, *"Who's the one who gets on everyone's nerves?"*

The children looked closely at the faces for a long time, then picked a man or woman whom they thought the question applied to. And I was struck by an embarrassing surprise that led me to think that I should stay far away from the human psyche, away from this impenetrable labyrinth.

So, what is not really interesting, my dear Danny, is that, let's say, I had a difficult childhood, and your feet smell. Or the other way around. The one this, the other that. Only the children got into a fight over who was right about something they could not know. *"Don't you have eyes to see?"* asked the one of the other, while nudging with his index finger a fairly expressionless face. *"Really, can't you see what an irritating fellow this is? All I must do is look at him and he gets on my nerves? How can he be a peaceful sort?"*

How can you possibly know your way around in such a world?

Can you say anything intelligent about such souls?

It's possible that he got up that morning on the wrong side of bed, and that's why he hates him. Perhaps tomorrow he will get up on the right side of bed and he'll like him.

Or maybe she was reminded of an old neighbour who had pulled her pigtails. And the other reminds her of someone who had brought her strawberry with cream. Whereas the most probable thing was that the owner of that face hadn't hurt anyone, and hadn't brought strawberries to anyone.

"I'm totally confused," I complained to the Shrink.

"No matter, Doctor." She smiled. "It'll all become clear. In the meantime, let's pay attention to Biborka."

***

Biborka was that charming little girl about nine years old I had seen in the Shrink's head. She was one of the four children. There were two more little girls and one little boy who were playing with the faces. All these were about the same age – ten-eleven years old – and had the same kind of fate. *"The parents had separated and divorced, with other partners on the horizon; on the other hand, you could see clearly with more or less all of them the effects of visiting rights and two-sided spoiling,"* the Shrink listed in one breath. *"Although they were shaken by the break-up of their family, their psyches didn't seem to be seriously harmed."*

I was surprised at this.

"They got over it so easily?"

"Not easily, but they've survived. They noticed that they are in the majority in the class. That is, the divorced were the normal ones, and those who've stayed together were the ones who stood out."

"But then, why aren't the ones who've stayed together here?"

The Shrink smiled.

"That's a good question, Doctor."

She frowned.

"Biborka's family has stayed together. And yet she is the one in the greatest trouble."

She did not try to hide now that she was expecting my help in this case: to find out what was eating Biborka. None of the other three children caused her such a headache as this one.

She made me agree to just observe. Let the insights emerge by themselves, not to try to interpret or explain them immediately, for it was easy in this profession to end up in a dead end. The rootlets of the psyche branch down unimaginably far. In space and time too. Physical problems can eat at our souls; psychic problems can eat at our bodies. It's possible that mysterious ailments have their source in current circumstances, but it is also possible that they stem from earlier ones. It can also be that they can be traced back to the time of pregnancy and birth, if we weren't exactly wanted. Not to mention that we are able to inherit the tragedies of previous generations from our parents. Then we carry on this unwanted heritage in our psyches.

I was so silent as if I had gone mute. The Shrink immediately sensed the reason. She began to laugh loudly.

"Don't be alarmed, Doctor. That's why our work is so beautifully exciting."

"Groping in the dark?"

The Shrink was lost in thought.

"Who knows why, but it's never totally dark. Some light is always glimmering somewhere."

"And if we're mistaken?"

"Then we start again. We explore some more."

"A needle in the haystack?"

"Rather the key."

Transfigured, she continued eagerly.

"It's a magic key. The moment we find it, the secret door opens. Light streams in and dissolves the pain."

"Killing the psychic worm," I added.

Dark spots appeared in the Shrink's head. They wriggled in the shaft of light, then – presto – they suddenly disappeared.

"Very astute, Doctor." The Shrink smiled. "Killing the psychic worm. Yes, indeed."

"Biborka's too?" I asked after a pause.

"Yes, Biborka's too."

"Then… I'll begin, my dear Shrink."

"Then… begin, dear Doctor."

***

Now, if I'm right, dear Danny, in barely a year you will be as old as Biborka is now. Listen here, for wise men learn from other men's mistakes, fools from their own. But it is not only for your little ears that I talk about such serious grown-up things. But because, it is wonderful to watch the smouldering psychic worm beat a retreat and the human soul burst into flower.

Though until then – as they say – a lot of water has flown down the Danube.

Above all, I had to decide on a few important questions. Though I could have asked the Shrink even before I leaped, the truth was that we were both impatient in a healthy way to get to work… I was unable to decide whether it was better to say nothing, just observe silently to find the key, or rather, converse amiably. Finally, I decided on the latter, though I accepted the Shrink's caution, that Biborka should not know that she was being observed. I must pretend to be unaware of who this Shrink was and what on earth psychology was.

So, I said nothing for quite a while. I lay low and stayed quiet for a long time.

And I established what could be established.

Biborka enjoyed playing with the other children. She looked thoughtfully at the photos of the faces. What did they reveal? To which one did the definition apply the best? However, several times, suddenly, without a word, she dropped out of the game. The others shouted in chorus, *"Wake up, Biborka, wake up!"* and only then did she come back to the present.

Of course, I was the only one who knew where her mind had wandered. Slowly I realised that the one *"who laughed constantly,"* and *"had supernatural abilities,"* in the images that swam here and there must have been Biborka's mother. The one who was *"going his own way,"* and who was hunched careworn, with his thick glasses, over a book or in front of the computer screen, could be none other than her father, whom she called *"Papapa"*.

It goes without saying that, when the caption of the card made Biborka think of her own life, I had no problem in identifying it. *"Life is hard"* someone read; I saw my little client weeping in a wardrobe.

"Wake up, Biborka, wake up!" I heard from here and there.

***

Soon after, a creature that delighted the eye and the heart popped into the office. I immediately recognised Biborka's mother. A light, airy, white dress fluttered around her. The white pearl necklace, the wide smile, and the pearly teeth were becoming to her.

"Mama!" shouted Biborka. We sprang up and ran to her. Mama leaned over and hugged Biborka's head, kissing her for a long time. Who knew why, but I even held my breath.

"Did my little girl behave?" said Mama, looking at the Shrink. "Was there any problem? Sorry for taking her away sooner, but I had time now…"

"Tush," replied the Shrink. "We were just about to finish."

She looked around. The children looked in undisguised amazement at the exciting newcomer.

"Excuse me, I would like to steal Biborka's mama for a moment." The Shrink smiled at them, gesturing at the adjacent room.

"Couldn't we talk it over by telephone?" asked Biborka's mama. Biborka was hanging on her with both hands.

"Yes, of course," replied the Shrink. We were at the door when she called to us. "Well then, have a nice trip!"

Biborka and her mother looked back in amazement.

"Thank you." They shrugged.

"Thank you, my dear Shrink," I said to myself, and a pleasant warmth ran through my little orphaned soul.

As we stepped out of the gate, Mama crouched down, rubbed her nose with Biborka's, and announced,

"Now we're going to sin a little!"

As it turned out, this meant that they didn't get on the tram, but headed for the boulevard on foot, and they went into the evermore alluring shops. They looked at handbags and dresses, sipped freshly squeezed fruit juices, and, to Biborka's great joy, ate a Turkish pastry saturated with honey. She had eaten half of her portion when she suddenly darkened.

"What's the matter?" asked Mama.

"Nothing."

Mama's face clouded over too.

"I can see it on you."

Biborka pointed at her plate.

"Can't I take it to Papapa?"

"It's not even enough for you." Mama smiled. She added after a short pause. "It's not so important for him, you know."

"I know." Biborka nodded.

They ate the pastry and we got on the tram.

Papapa was occupying Biborka's head. Meanwhile, her soul swung this way and that. Now it was bathed in pink, now dark green and dark grey, she seethed and was full of anxiety. As for me, I was thinking, heck, I forgot to ask the Shrink for my daily lunch. I was thinking that for the moment at least, I had no choice but to consider Papapa as my main meal, as the delicate and tender skin of these ladies was not suitable for undisturbed, or imperceptible, feeding. Well, of course, I almost gave myself away when I laughed out loud when on arriving home, the front door opened, and what did I see at the threshold, but two astonishingly fat cats. Biborka's pets. "I'm saved," I thought to myself. Then it occurred to me, I got the missing story on a plate, how did I get to Biborka? Well, from cats. Not to mention that my local transportation was solved in one go. When they weren't lolling about, Pepe and Pimpo gladly wandered about in the rambling three-room flat. They

287

were ready to rub themselves against anyone to get them to give them snacks or scratch their necks.

My only criticism of Pepe and Pimpo was that each one was exactly as fat and white as the other. Indeed, they were both delicious, so that at first, I couldn't tell which one was which. Even now I can't say which one was the first to make my long-awaited feast, nor did I know which one I was snacking on, when suddenly he leaped up and ran to a draughtier place. Suddenly we rose into the air. I got a whiff of Biborka's fragrance. I immediately leaped onto her and to my great joy, order was restored. Perched in her ear, I could observe this peculiar human world and concern myself with my important assignment.

From then on, I waited for a suitable occasion to speak up and introduce myself. Biborka was sitting on a rug, with Pepe in her lap (or was it Pimpo?). We were watching Mama's naked legs flash by, when two grey socks and a long thin pair of jeans walked up to her. Biborka looked up, and finally I could catch a glimpse of the live Papapa. At that moment I got the picture. He must have arrived just then and Biborka must have grabbed us at the front door.

For that matter, Papapa made a fairly sour face. Though he didn't wear the thick glasses that would deface him. Though I was ashamed to say, I was glad how lucky I was to enjoy the company of Biborka and her mama, instead of spending my precious time with this careworn character.

Papapa leaned down to us and kissed Biborka. As if frozen, she accepted it without moving a muscle. She even stopped petting Pepe (or was it Pimpo?).

"How do you feel, Biborka? How was it at the doctor's?" asked Papapa. He had a warm, very gentle voice.

"Nothing," retorted Biborka.

In the blink of an eye, she turned into someone who had grown thorns or claws.

"If she isn't any good, you don't have to go. Mama took you to her, because she thought it would be easier for you."

"It will be easier," repeated Biborka, without conviction.

"I saw you having a good time." Mama stepped up to her. "Isn't that right, Biborka?" She leaned over us.

"Yes, it's true."

"I'm glad, really glad," nodded Papapa. "You'll see, everything will be all right."

A weak little pink colour spot battled in Biborka's mind with dark green and dark grey clouds.

Silence.

"Imagine…" said Papapa excitedly.

I had the feeling that he wished to fill the unpleasantly loud silence. Mama and Biborka didn't seem *to want to* show any interest. As far as Mama and Biborka went, later I understood them. Papapa began to talk about "an interesting thing" so boring that, dear Danny, I'm not able to tell you with the requisite fidelity to the story. So, as it turned out, on the way home on the bus, the loudspeaker announced several times that because of construction work on the square, the passengers are advised to *"take the 91 and 102 bus on the extended route."*

"What's interesting about that?" Mama asked.

"I've told you a hundred times. It's a false adjective structure."

"Who cares, other than you linguists? Maybe not even the other linguists, only you."

"That's what you think," protested Papapa. "Everybody who has a feeling for the language and comes up from the countryside or from across the borders and wants to use those buses. They will think, with good reason, that there are *buses on not extended routes* too and that's what they will look for. Who's the crazy person who wants to be jolted along longer than is absolutely necessary? Until they are told that, sorry, we just made a mistake."

"All right, but then they will tell them and that's that. Why is it necessary to make such a big deal out of such an insignificant thing?" barked Mama.

"Because it isn't insignificant at all," retorted Papapa. "Our lives are full of things that look like nothing, but we grab our heads when it's too late. When our lives are in ruins."

Mama didn't say anything for a while. Then finally she announced,

"It may be that what I say isn't grammatically correct, but I hope that you will understand anyway. Out of tens of thousands, indeed many hundreds of thousands of passengers only one person will have trouble with this wording. And who's that one? All right, who? My unfortunate husband."

Papapa swallowed hard.

"Must you in front of the child?"

"Must you constantly bring up some idiocy?" hissed Mama.

"If you only had some consideration, at least for the child," whispered Papapa.

"It's you who should have consideration for her. She understands very well what is going on. You are always engaged in things that have nothing to do with our lives. Did you get a job? Do you have a job yet?"

"You know very well that I have a great deal of work."

"It's just that none of it makes any money."

"Not so far. But sooner or later it will pay for sure. A society that doesn't pay for its values is going to perish."

"Good heavens! Always the big words! I'm curious how much longer you could keep repeating that if I weren't supporting you."

Papapa gasped. Then he exploded. Biborka was overcome with terror. She began choking. Unfortunately, I couldn't pay attention to her, for I felt that from the standpoint of finding the key, you could say, *key* words and thoughts would be said. *"You're sitting backward on the horse again,"* shouted Papapa. *"What do you think whose fault is it that the society is like this? Not those who can't see further than their noses? Not those who are always looking out for themselves? You don't have a poppy seed worth of self-sacrifice."*

Biborka gasped for breath, then broke into loud sobs.

The words that Papapa and Mama wanted to say stuck in their throats.

Both kneeled down beside Biborka. *"Don't be angry with us, Biborka,"* begged Papapa. Mama hugged us tight, and leaned her head on us. Biborka blubbered for a while, then went quiet.

"Aren't you hungry?" asked Papapa. "Or did you have something to eat on your way home?"

Biborka looked inquiringly at Mama.

"You can tell me. Go ahead," urged Papapa.

"You see how agitated she is." Mama hugged us even tighter. "Let her rest a bit."

We waited for them to disperse, then we slipped into the wardrobe.

Biborka's eyes were open, but we didn't see anything. More exactly, I saw the turbulence and swirling of her soul. I was thinking of how to get back as soon as possible to the Shrink. I would have liked to tell her urgently that the formula was clear to me. If my mother and father had fought so heatedly and so constantly in front of me, I would have gone silent too, as a flea. I would have cried, I would have tossed and turned. Or I would have done something that only slowly became clear in Biborka's case. When I was sitting in Mama's ear or Papapa's, I would have seen that Biborka was seized often with what the Shrink called, *ticking.* She ticked, her eyes jerked, her head jerked this way and that. At other times, she was overcome with the compulsion to pull up her socks. She constantly stopped on her way to pull up and loosen her stockings, as if they had slipped down even to the extent of half a rabbit's tail. Of course not. There was no reason for it, but I was certain that I had discovered the secret: Biborka – or more precisely her body – obviously was releasing the tremendous tension generated by the family dust-up. At times the air itself vibrated so that I was amazed at myself, how I could stand it, how it didn't drive me crazy.

Well, dear Danny, it was a good thing that the Shrink wasn't there. For as we sat in the wardrobe without moving in the pitch-black, the Shrink's cautionary words occurred to me, not to rush to conclusions. In psychology it was all too easy to end up in a dead-end. Not to mention that if I had really and truly found the key, Biborka wouldn't have had to huddle in the wardrobe, but she would have danced gracefully before the two cats. When I later reported this to the Shrink, she smiled in satisfaction. Then she commented,

"You know, Doctor, if children were ruined by this, not one would be intact and healthy."

***

I was so lost in my own thoughts at the bottom of the wardrobe that I didn't even notice that I had begun to hum softly to myself. The song that I sang to you, my dear friend, when we first met:

A big-nosed flea
invited himself over
to our house forever
For lunch and for dinner.

Well, of course. How can you forget my flea song?
And suddenly, what do I hear?
Biborka was singing with me. Or rather, she was whimpering.

But his eyes were so
dreadfully big,
When he opened them wide
The house was bright

"Biborka, you know this?" I asked, dumbfounded.

"I know it," she muttered. "From Papapa."

I could see in her head that she didn't really know where to put me.

"Who are you?" she asked finally.

"Jimmy Jumper. A flea."

"Cat flea?"

"Cat flea."

"Aha." She hesitated for a moment, not knowing whether to say it, then she announced, "We don't usually like fleas here."

"If you wish, I will swear I will never hurt you."

"What about Pepe and Pimpo?"

"I have to eat something." I tried to say it like someone who is really sorry. We quickly got on with it.

"Do you have parents?" asked Biborka.

"I'm afraid I'm an orphan."

"Sometimes I'd like to be an orphan."

I was genuinely surprised at this.

"You can't mean that."

"I'm telling you."

"Don't you love Mama?"

"Yes, I do."

"What about Papapa?"

"He really loves me."

"Aha... Well then, why do you wish to be an orphan?"

"Because it hurts."

"What hurts?"

"I don't know, but it hurts bad."

And I could see that it really did hurt. It was as if a dark, dismal vice was tightening around her small, panting soul.

Again, I felt the same uncertainty and hopelessness I had felt at the Shrink's surgery. It didn't seem at all that all I had to do was sit comfortably in my client's ear, and observe her thoughts and feelings. And everything would become clear by itself. I felt like I was sitting smack in the middle of the branches of a rampant spirit tree. A million branches, and I had to find out where I should go, where could the destructive soul worm be hiding.

While I was puzzling over this, I suddenly heard a soft knocking. After a short pause, I could hear Papapa's voice.

"Biborka?"

Biborka didn't reply. Involuntarily, I wanted to speak up and say here we were, but I couldn't.

"Why don't you reply?" I asked her.

"Just because."

"Papapa loves you," I pointed out.

I saw her mind clouding over.

"Please don't interfere," she hissed. "You're too small for this."

"As you wish." I shrugged.

Manfully, I confess to you, Danny, that I was aggrieved. Papapa pulled the sliding door and crouched down next to Biborka.

"Darling, please come out. I beg you."

"Go away! Leave me alone."

"Let's play a game."

"I'm only coming out for Mama."

Mama already towered above us.

"So, this is where my little girl is hiding?"

"I'd gladly play with her," Papapa offered.

"We already decided that we were going to paint. She got some nice homework from drawing class, and I promised to help her. Right, Biborka?"

I saw on Papapa that he couldn't decide whether to say what was in his heart or not. Finally, he couldn't stop himself.

"Couldn't she do it by herself?"

"We'd rather do it together."

"Wouldn't they like to know what she can do on her own?"

"Maybe they would like to know it, but it's a lot more important that it be beautiful. Biborka's aesthetic sense is developing."

"But then you'll deceive the teacher." Papapa fretted. "And if she praises it, who is it for? Biborka or you?"

At this Mama puffed herself up like an angry tabby. Her eyes threw sparks, her fingers curled up, like one who's going to scratch right away.

"Why do you have to stick your nose into everything?" she shouted. "Why can't you just shut your…" She used a word, Danny, that I don't wish to repeat.

By this time, Papapa's eyes were flashing thunderbolts too. I thought that war was about to break out and human blood would flow, although – you can believe me or not – I wasn't at all happy about that. Rather, I was scared and in my fright, I was feverishly thinking where the devil was that miserable key. Papapa glared at Mama, then at Biborka, then turned on his heels and scrammed without a word, most probably to his computer. Mama and Biborka settled down to Mama's drawing table. They surrounded themselves with a troop of tubes and pots of paints of various colours, thin paintbrushes, short crayons, thinner and thicker pencils; finally, they lay down a blindingly white drawing paper. From then on, I gawped in amazement. If only because, I didn't know this at the time, my dear friend, that Mama was an interior decorator. Biborka told me that drawing and painting was to her what eating my fill was to me. They brought forth an enormous bird, and not just any bird. It was as if it had a hundred beautiful eyes. At first Mama painted an eye that was the colour of grass, then added a bit of golden yellow. Then an even smaller dollop of mauve. To this she added even less sky blue. Finally, she let fall the velvety dark blue of grape hyacinth.

"There's the finished peacock eye," she exulted, and they both stared transfigured.

Then Biborka was next. With a no less graceful motion she dropped a few dabs, ever smaller ones from the tubes of paint all lined up. Another peacock eye.

I couldn't stop admiring them. I was over the moon with delight.

By the time we had finished, it was dinner time and, indeed, before too long, bed-time.

When we went to the kitchen, we found cheese and ham, and ham and cheese sandwiches on two plates. Beside them sliced cucumber, peppers and tomatoes. I saw clearly at once that no place had been set for Papapa. True, I didn't have one, either. Although I was sorry for it, I wasn't surprised.

Biborka asked,

"Shouldn't we call Papapa?"

Mama thought a bit.

"What do you want?"

"I want what you want."

"I think it's better if we put ourselves away for tomorrow in peace. If he wishes to join us, he'll come on his own."

Biborka nodded, then she asked,

"Can I sleep with you again today?"

Mama closed her eyes and heaved a great sigh.

"With me. But I have to talk it over with your father."

They picked at their food lackadaisically. Meanwhile, I tried to finally read something from the dark colours whirling around in Biborka's head and the images that swam in and out, but I must confess I didn't get very far. Suddenly I got a peculiar feeling, in fact, the definite conviction that the Shrink was the victim of an enormous misconception.

Just because things may happen one after the other, it isn't at all certain that they arise from each other. When Mama and Biborka decorated the beautiful feathers of the enormous bird, they painted the peacock eyes one by one. Each one separately, each one was created independent of the other, and, yet, in the end how wonderfully the picture came together. Why wasn't it possible that the Creator simply found joy in this cavalcade? He creates every human being separately, every moment is filled with a different mood, and yet they are part of the same world; not one is the cause or consequence of the other. The only cause is that it is the Creator's inscrutable will. And it is vanity to bristle against or go to battle with it.

Well, what should I say, Danny? This insight threw cold water on my psychological enthusiasm. Looking for the key is exciting for human beings and for fleas. But what if there isn't a key? Or, if there is, it is with the Creator – and then neither human being nor flea can get at it.

Well, I was sitting impassively in Biborka's ear and, having nothing better to do, I was dreaming of the corpulent charms of the two white favourites, when Papapa stumbled in. Mama immediately mentioned to him that Biborka wished to sleep with her.

Papapa cut a pained expression.

Biborka stared ahead wanly.

"I think in her condition, it's better if we let her have her wish," Mama urged.

"Slowly, you two are crowding me out," Papapa said.

"You are crowding yourself out," Mama hissed. "I didn't offer it to Biborka."

Papapa stepped up to Biborka, took her chin in his hands and turned her head gently toward himself. Biborka cast down her eyes.

"No matter," Papapa said. "Sweet dreams."

At that moment I leaped.

***

If by chance you think, my dear Danny, that we fleas always know what we're doing and why, you would be sorely mistaken. In this regard, we are not a bit different from human beings. If we think about what happened, I can only relate that when I leaped, I had no idea why I did it, but when I arrived, I knew clearly what I wanted from Papapa. So clearly, that I spoke up at once.

"God bless you, sir."

Almost everyone, other than me, would think that he didn't reply immediately, for it wasn't a daily occurrence that an invisible somebody spoke to him. Papapa said nothing for an entirely different reason. It intrigued him that I had greeted him in an unusual way. At this he gave a worthy reply,

"God bless you too."

"You weren't even surprised," I commented.

"Of course, I was. That fine, old greeting is rarely heard these days."

"That isn't what I meant. You don't know who I am, what I am, where I am. And you aren't even surprised."

"The bigger oddity supersedes the smaller. By the way, who might you be and what might you be up to?"

"Jimmy Jumper. A flea. In your ear. Otherwise, at your service."

"You are very kind. But I think I can manage on my own."

"I believe you can't."

"What? How so?"

"A dark vice is crushing Biborka's soul. I saw it with my own two eyes." I pointed, though I knew he couldn't see it.

Papapa nodded.

"Maybe you have something to do with it," I went on.

"Maybe," he allowed.

"That's all?"

"You know something better?"

I thought for a while.

"Yes, I do," I replied. "Here's this bus and this fake something. It's possible that you're right…"

"It's not possible, it's certain."

"OK. Have it your way. But you'd still be right, if you didn't say it. No?"

"Of course. The truth doesn't depend on whether we say it or not."

"Then why do you have to say it? Why can't you keep it to yourself? You'd avoid the conflict."

"One of them."

"What do you mean?" I replied in amazement.

He thought about how to put it.

"Do you know what *disunion* is?" he asked finally.

"I knew once, but I forgot."

Papapa smiled.

"It's not something that one can forget. For if one is divided in himself, he has lost himself. He may well appear his old self, all is well on the surface, but in reality, the worst thing has happened to him: he has lost his psychic balance."

I scratched my head. I thought hard how can one imagine this loss of balance, but I wasn't able to reach any sensible conclusion.

"Hello, are you still there?" asked Papapa.

"I'm here. I just can't imagine it."

"Well, if not, then from now on you have to be at my service. I'll tell you what to do."

The mere thought gave me the creeps.

"Oh no, you won't. You can't just order me about."

"I can assure you a bright future. You'll find a top military secret, and we'll sell it for good money. Or, if you'd prefer, we'll play cards. You whisper to me what cards the others have and the bank is ours. We could win ourselves sick. OK. You're in, aren't you?"

I pondered that.

Believe it or not, my dear friend, at first sight this offer was very attractive. Even the part that didn't come up: to dine on the owners of top military secrets, that's not given to every flea. Or to nip poker-faced card players. But when I looked more closely at this, however, something was really wrong. I felt a terrible emptiness.

It was dreadfully depressing.

There goes my service. There goes my mission.

I said to Papapa,

"I'd rather not."

"Why not?"

"Because. It's not me."

"Who else then?"

"I don't know. But certainly not me."

"All right." He lifted his index finger. "That's being at odds with yourself. Did you feel the terrible emptiness?"

I nodded. I suddenly forgot that he didn't see it.

"I felt it," I announced.

"All right. Then you understand everything. He who doesn't say what he should say, who doesn't do what he should do, is lost in emptiness. In addition, you feel as if you're being suffocated. As if our self that wishes to conform wished to strangle our real self."

That's what Papapa said.

But I wasn't convinced at all. I observed that on that basis self-killers would teem among human beings. *"And they do teem,"* he replied. *"That is why there are so many unhappy people. Dissociated souls are like lost souls, they can find no peace."*

"But I don't see them," I announced emphatically. "And Mama doesn't see them either. And Biborka doesn't see them. Among several hundred thousand you are the only one…"

"Sorry. I can't help it," Papapa answered sadly and retired into his shell. I tried to entreat him, but he didn't answer any more. Even when – God forgive me but that is what happened – I cast it in his face: *You have to be pretty conceited to think that you are right in contrast with hundreds of thousands of people.*

Only then did he make a sound when somebody passed by our room and closed the door. I don't know who it could have been, for we were sitting with our backs to the door. Papapa shouted, *"Please leave it open!"* The individual opened it without a word and left silently.

We sat there in silence for a while. Finally, I asked Papapa, at least take me to Biborka. He got up quietly, he didn't ask anything, he didn't say anything. Cautiously, he opened the bedroom, and tiptoed to an enormous wide bed. I recognised Mama and Biborka, as they slept hugging each other. Lying at their feet, Pepe and Pimpo raised their heads, but curled up again immediately. I thought, honest to God, I should stay with Papapa. For he was in a very sour mood, but I was very hungry, so I jumped.

***

Maybe I had eaten too much, my dear friend, who knows why, but the fact is I couldn't get to sleep for a long time. What Papapa said whirled incessantly around in my head. I didn't wish to accept it, for such a dreadful thing would have followed that I would have been poleaxed. And then the Shrink could have come to me with any number of keys, never again would I have any desire to do any psychological healing.

Think about it, my dear friend.

Papapa says that the key to happiness is to be yourself. Cleave to your truth. Then the secret to not only Papapa's happiness, but also Mama's, is to be themselves. Not to mention Biborka. But how could they share a world, if everybody is attached to their own?

Don't you think?

Think about it.

As for me, what I brought from home was to cling to my full-blooded meal and suck. Since then I've clung to that. As for you, my dear friend, you've learned at home since you were no longer a small child, that it was proper to eat with a knife and fork. Now imagine, we should like to live the remainder of our lives together. And any time you took out a knife and fork, I would ask you irritably, *"Is this necessary? Can't you eat normally, like me?"* I would begin to feast. *"Dear, haven't you forgotten something? Knife and fork. It's time you learned to use them."*

You get it?

Isn't this the key? The real explanation for Biborka's problem? And essentially for everyone else's problem? The wonder isn't that people kill each other. The miracle is that they don't kill each other en masse.

That is, if Papapa were right.

Papapa lived in his own separate world and Mama had her own special world. And therefore, it followed naturally that both had ideas of what was normal. They each had their own version of the truth. Then Biborka was born – and she also had her own special world. If what Papapa said was true, then you couldn't imagine a better stage for unhappiness. After all, you can't cram three worlds into one. In principle, the one that can stuff the most from his own at the expense of the others would be the best off. Save that he is the one who makes the others unhappy.

I had to see regretfully that if I'd found the key, it was completely useless. This may have led me to this insight, but it couldn't lead me to the solution: healing Biborka. This key was like for a ruined, rusty lock: it may fit, but you couldn't turn it. And the door would stay locked forever.

"Where are you, my dear Shrink?" I groaned in despair. *"Where are you? I hand you back my assignment."*

I was completely done in.

I couldn't find fault with my reasoning, but I couldn't escape the logical chain. I could only hope that Papapa wasn't right. That it wasn't so important, after all, that everybody live the life that was laid out for them. That a person could be quite happy if he lived another's life. Everyone stopped halfway. Or a third way. And everyone was content with a third of happiness.

These two cats don't scratch each other's eyes out, after all.

They were living together in plump peace.

It was as if my agitated mind was waiting for this reassuring realisation. I fell into a deep sleep, my dear friend.

***

I awoke to Biborka's loud sobbing. I was sorry I had slept so soundly, for I could have uncovered what had caused her terrible pain in her sleep. I was too late. By the time I woke up, she was fast asleep again, in Mama's gentle embrace.

Well, what should I say, dear Danny. To my great surprise I was swept away with a marvellous flood. It was so gripping that my heart pained me. *"Poor Papapa, he couldn't feel this now."* Biborka's breath was delicious, but it was more like an angel's. I imagined Mama's to be like that of a goddess. Its enchantment went through me from top to toe. It was as if I were in heaven.

Finally, I understood how one world could irresistibly attract the other. Indeed, not only to itself but into itself. And not only does the other let it, but it tries to surrender itself to it. I tell you, my dear friend, that it occurred even to this little flea, how good it would be if Mama were mine.

In addition, when I woke up that morning, I had an experience I had never had before. I saw a human face as breathtakingly beautiful. As Biborka opened her eyes, I could observe up close the comely curves, the exhaling pores, the fuzz that played with the sunlight, and the long, golden tresses.

"It's like a dream," I whispered.

"There you are," exulted Biborka.

"Good morning, Biborka," I shouted in my way.

"Hi, Jimmy Jumper," she replied softly.

"Shouldn't you be at school? Slug-a-bed."

"I don't have to go to school today. It's Saturday."

"Saturday? That's wonderful!" I cried. "The whole day is ours."

"I don't like Saturdays. I don't like Sundays either."

"You're joking."

"I'm not joking."

Alarming dark greys attacked the frisky shining clouds. I would have liked to hit them, but I couldn't.

"Did they bother you?"

"War always breaks out in the weekends. We're together too much."

"Who?"

"Mama and Papapa."

"And you," I noted.

"I don't count."

"Didn't they fight over you?"

"Yes, over me, but not because of me."

"Aha! And what would happen if today and tomorrow you would be very kind to Papapa?"

Biborka didn't answer. I was thinking that I may have overshot the mark, and she would snap back that it wasn't any of my business. Fortunately, an angel was busying herself in Biborka, but it seemed that dark vice had gripped her too.

"I'd like to be kind," she said after a long pause. "But I can't."

"You don't say. And why not?"

I saw her thoughts running to and fro. She tried to grab them by the ear, but they eluded her. Finally, she caught one.

"Papapa is good as a father, but bad as a breadwinner," she said.

"Aha! Now I get it. You'd like him to be a worse father, and a better breadwinner."

"No!" she protested at once. "I'd like him to be a good father and a good breadwinner."

"Biborka, have you ever gone hungry in your life? Was there ever a time when you didn't have enough to eat?"

"No, there wasn't. But because of Mama, and not because of Papapa."

At that moment, my dear friend, I witnessed an illusion, which makes me shudder when I think of it. I was sitting in Biborka's ear, completely steeped in her soul, while she peered at Mama's beautiful face. And suddenly I had a strange, shocking feeling that my little Biborka had Mama's head. If I had had even the tiniest brain, I would have immediately caught on that the key was right under my nose, indeed, under the door mat, but I didn't click. So, I couldn't defend Papapa. Whereas I could have made Biborka understand that anyone who takes the head of another on his or her neck, takes on the soul of the other. But it is enough for a small child to keep her own world, how could she cope with two at once?

Perhaps I couldn't discover the key, because Biborka was watching Mama's eyelids, their peculiar quivering before waking up, and this gripped me too. As if she had sensed Biborka's longing, Mama opened her eyes slowly, and looked at us. Both Biborka and I were immersed happily in her look. And neither Biborka nor I became any the happier when we heard Papapa's voice.

"God bless you in this new year," he sang.

Mama closed her eyes.

"That's stupid," shouted Biborka. "Right, Mama? New Year has passed a long time ago."

"It is so wonderful we can wish it all year long," Papapa insisted.

Silence.

"What shall we do today?" asked Papapa. "Let's go on a trip. It's such great weather!"

"We're going to the organic market," Biborka said. "Right, Mama?"

Mama didn't reply. She hid behind her closed eyelids.

"Would you be so kind as to reply?" pressed Papapa.

"I'm asleep. Let me sleep my fill at least at the weekend."

"Go right ahead. Just tell me whether you are really going to the organic market."

At this Mama not only opened her eyes, but she sat up.

"Why? Do you have something against it?"

Her fingers curved like the claws of an angry cat.

"Since you asked me, I'll tell you," said Papapa calmly. "In our current situation, I'm not sure it is for our purse."

"You mean for my purse," Mama struck back.

"We are still living together for the time being. It's our purse."

"I hope it's not for long," Mama stabbed again.

Papapa froze. Then he looked at Biborka. His eyes were full of anxiety and sorrow. I saw that Biborka had noticed, though she tried to stave it off. She stuck her leg out of the quilt and she began to toy with the two fat cats with her toes. They stretched sensually, yawned, purred loudly, then as if on command, they leaped up at the same time and jumped off the bed.

"I'll give them their breakfast," Papapa said.

"And I'll massage your shoulders. OK, Mama?" shouted Biborka and kneeled behind Mama. Papapa disappeared with the two fat cats.

Mama burst out,

"I break out in a rash from poisoned vegetables, but that doesn't interest him."

"Because he doesn't think that's what you get it from."

"From what then?"

"From yourself. In his view, who is angry at others, poisons themselves."

"That's so idiotic, I'd rather not say anything about it," exploded Mama.

"Isn't it idiotic?" Biborka joined in. "That's what I said to him too."

"Your father is only trying to get out of his own responsibility." Mama shook her head. "I'm not angry because I want to entertain myself."

I must tell you, dear Danny, that I began to feel worse and worse. Mama's beauty and Biborka's charm could not hush the growing nightmarish feeling that I had got stuck between three grinding mill stones – three independent worlds – and there was no way out. I realised that I was too much the flea, and very simple-minded. For if I had my own human world, I would have had a much easier job, for I would have my own truth. That is, my own point of orientation.

All right. How should I explain?

Imagine a head of cabbage.

You've got it?

It's a bright green, fresh cabbage. We put it on the table. We gather around it; we look at it.

Nobody can see inside it.

Everybody thinks they can see inside it.

In Mama's world, it is poisonous, because it gives her a rash.

In Papapa's world, it's not poisonous because it doesn't give him a rash.

In Biborka's world, whatever Mama says is the truth.

That's all they need to get into a fight. Three worlds have a row. Otherwise, this is not such a big deal, if you know who is right. Then you root for them. And it can fire you up. And it makes you happy too. You can pat yourself on the shoulder. *"Good flea, you stood up for the truth!"*

Only, how on earth should I know where the truth lay? Was the cabbage poisonous or not? Was Mama right or was Papapa or Biborka? I was on the verge of deciding with my nothing little life that I would partake of the cabbage. And the rest we would see. Only I, a garden-variety bloodsucker, could not eat any kind of plant.

So, what was left was to use my noggin.

I came up with something.

The most logical thing was that all three of them were right. And every life was right at its origin. What need was there in the world for someone who could not be right from the outset? Anyone who existed was necessarily needed. Who was needed was necessarily right. No?

Oh, I wouldn't wish to herd you, my dear friend, into that mad maze. It was enough for me to get tangled in it. Not only had I not found a key, not even one, but not even a door. At most a few signs: *"Past. Future. Passage-way. Way out. Soul worm."* It had all got mixed up in my pea brain. Finally, I thought that once I get to the Shrink, I'll beg her to put aside her every patient and deal with me before I go completely nuts.

I longed so much for peace and quiet that I clambered into Pepe (or was it Pimpo?). But not into his ear but onto his peacefully pulsating neck. And I didn't even suck from it, for in my agitated state nothing would have gone down my throat. And I didn't want him to hit me with his claws as I lay there exhausted.

My absence was both useful and not.

When I jumped back onto Biborka in the early afternoon and nestled in her delicate ear, they were beyond the market and perhaps a lot of quarrelling. It was as if everyone had a muzzle on; they walked around in the flat so silently. In the front hall and on the doors at forced meetings, everyone drew aside demonstratively, in fact, pulled in their limbs and chest, lest they accidentally come into contact with the other person. Whether this was the result of the morning clash or some new thing, I couldn't know. But truth to tell, dear Danny, it didn't make any difference. Where self-propelled worlds don't give each other space, the slightest difference gives rise to conflict. *"Why are you cooling the place so? Why are you opening the window? Who asked you to close the window? Why do you come in wearing your shoes? Why don't you hang up your coat? Why don't you lower the toilet seat? Why did you leave the dirty dishes? Why do you keep the telephone here? Why are you shouting? I'm not shouting. Yes, you are shouting! You're shouting. Because you were shouting."*

Biborka endured the tightening of the vice.

But I could see that she was hurting.

We sat at the bottom of the wardrobe.

She asked me if I were in her ear.

I confessed that I was.

"Why don't we talk?"

I confessed that I was helpless. I would like to take the vice from her, but I couldn't.

She didn't ask which vice.

She knew.

We were silent.

"Shall I show you the splits?" she asked after a long while.

"Show me."

I couldn't even imagine what she was thinking of.

We clambered out of the wardrobe. Papapa was working in the little study, his back to the open door. Mama was working in the kitchen, her back to the open door. We slipped into the living room and stopped in the middle.

Suddenly we began sinking. Biborka slipped one leg forward, the other backward on the rug. Until we thumped down.

That was the splits.

"Aren't I good?"

"Yes, you are," I replied sincerely. "I couldn't do that." We sat down on the rug and said nothing.

"I can do a bridge too," she commented after a while. "But I won't."

We were silent. We admired the feathery design on the rug. We started off with our eyes on a winding line and meandered here and there.

"Biborka."

It was Papapa in his gentle voice, from somewhere above our heads. We didn't look up. We continued to meander.

"Biborka."

Now his voice was not so gentle.

"Why don't you answer? Let's go wander for a bit. While the sun shines."

Mama appeared at the door, even the two cats, but they just watched silently. Biborka hesitated.

"*Egyenlőre*[1] I am meandering."

She followed the rug's design with her finger.

Mama smiled.

Papapa smiled, too, but meanwhile it was as if he had bitten into a lemon.

"Biborka, I told you not *egyenlőre* but *egyelőre*[2]."

"These days almost everybody says it this way," interjected Mama.

"It's more important that at least my daughter uses the right word."

"What can she do if not even her teacher makes a distinction?"

"Very simple. Listen to her father."

Mama took a deep breath.

"I thought language was for communication. No? Biborka told you unmistakably that she would prefer to go on playing. You understood that exactly. Everything else is pedantry and argumentativeness."

"Now listen here, my dear, I will tell you something," Papapa snapped. "Nobody is going to accompany us throughout our lives, not our parents, not our children, only our mother tongue. If you impoverish it, you will become poorer. If you make it worse, you will make your life worse.

1   *into equal parts*
2   *for the time being*

Every single word is a whole history, a little world, and if an incorrect word expels it, it will vanish forever."

At first Mama gaped at him, mouth open. Then she grinned awkwardly.

"Tell me, you must be joking? My husband can't be such an idiot when his little girl is in such trouble, as to lecture us on the magnificent mother tongue. You're joking, aren't you? Tell me, you were joking?"

Papapa froze.

You could tell from his eyes that he was struggling with himself, but you could also tell that he couldn't stop himself from saying what was stirring in his head. The words came slowly, apologetically. But they came, marching as if driven to the field of battle.

"I'm not going to resign myself *egyhamar*[3] and *egykönnyen*[4] that *egynémely*[5] persons obliterate our word *egyelőre*[6] out of sheer laziness or ignorance, and replace them with words that have a certain similarity in form, but not in the least in meaning."

"I don't wish to listen to you anymore."

Papapa laughed sardonically.

"Egyelőre, egyenlőre, what a huge difference! *'We have one last loaf of bread left! Should I share it?'* an ancestor of ours must have asked. If the chief had answered, *'Egyelőre not at all,'* everybody thought how wise he is, how astute, how foreseeing. But if he had said, *'Egyenlőre not at all',* he would

3   *soon*
4   *easily*
5   *some*
6   *for the time being*

have been hanged for that one letter. *'What?! He wants more for himself?!' 'Definitely not!'* There would have been a rebellion. For words had weight and importance, and it wouldn't have been considered pedantic and argumentative, if somebody warned you about the incorrect use of the language."

"Enough. I can't stand listening to you."

"If you had let me tell her, Biborka would have understood me perfectly. And she would have been the richer for her whole life. You didn't have to come here immediately, you didn't have to interrupt at once, you didn't have to disparage me in front of her, for you hurt her not only me!"

Mama burst into tears.

"Stop! I can't stand you!" she shouted. Tears streamed down her pretty face. "You are driving me crazy! Why don't you let me live? Why don't you move out? Why don't you leave us alone?"

She sobbed, and tried to catch her breath, wiped her eyes and nose with her hands. Papapa pointed at her.

"You aren't the only one in the world," he said. "You can't make the world conform to your whims."

Mama's face turned into an alarmingly misshapen grin.

"Don't worry. We'll be fine with Biborka. Biborka would like you to go too. Ask her, if you don't believe me." Mama laughed and sobbed. She buried her face in her hands, then staggered out and slammed the door behind her.

Papapa and Biborka stood mutely reading each other's look. I was convinced that Biborka would collapse too and begin to blubber inconsolably. Instead, she waited without moving a muscle. It was incredible to see, my dear friend. I looked at the vice; wasn't it ready to crush her poor little soul? To my great surprise, however, I saw no vice. As if it had disappeared. Or perhaps something had hidden it.

Papapa lowered himself down to the rug, just opposite us. He looked straight at us.

"Biborka, do you want me to go, too?"

He looked at her so entreatingly, my dear friend, that my heart pained me. However, Biborka was inexorability incarnate, implacability itself. I couldn't have imagined that a little child could be so cruel.

"Yes, that's what I want, too," said Biborka firmly.

Papapa's face was so sad, that whether you believe it or not, my dear friend, a tear dropped from my flea eyes. Biborka didn't cry at all. Indeed, for the first time since I had moved into her head, I saw the dark patches dissolve. Of course, I didn't understand how this was possible. Poor Biborka, was always dejected, in the grip of the pitiless vice; nonetheless, her soul always radiated a childlike charm. Her cold cruelty did not fit in my pea flea brain; I could not comprehend how she could treat Papapa like that before my very eyes. I was about to cry, *"Biborka, what has got into you?"*, but Papapa stroked our heads and stumbled out the door.

***

The strange thing, my dear Danny, was that the key lay right in front of my nose, but I didn't notice it. Although the Shrink had foretold that this was a completely magic key, as soon as we find it the secret door would have to open. How did she put it? *"The light would shine in and dissolve the pain."* Although

I didn't find anything, but this secret door must have opened, because without the shadow of a doubt, the light flooded into Biborka's soul, and visibly dissolved her pain.

If I had been even slightly cleverer, I would surely have grasped what happened. As it was, it took a lot of time for the picture to take shape, thanks to the Shrink.

We sat on the rug for about another half hour, without saying a word. Papapa turned up often in her head, as did Mama, but it didn't hurt her. I was the one who needed consolation. If I could have I would have gone immediately to the Shrink for treatment. Fortunately, as the minutes passed, I felt Biborka's good mood filtering through to me.

Without a word, Biborka leaped up and went into the front hall. When she saw Papapa's door shut, she stopped in her tracks. Papapa never shut his door and he didn't allow anyone else to shut it. They told him in vain that they didn't wish to disturb him while he was working, even then. When I sat in his ear, I could see what was troubling him so: the feeling that he was being pushed out. That he was being shut out of the circulation of the family.

Biborka snuck up to the door, cautiously pushed down the door latch and peered in. Papapa was sitting in his armchair, hunched over, motionless, head down. Biborka stepped up behind his back and put her little hand on his shoulder. Papapa turned around. A tired smile appeared on his tear-stained face.

"Thank you, you angel."

I don't know exactly why, but I was overcome with such joy that I began to weep like a shower. Fortunately, no one saw me, so I could surrender to the peculiar feeling of weeping from joy.

Biborka didn't cry. She didn't smile and didn't even say a word. We turned on our heels and walked out of the room. We were markedly light-footed. To my surprise – and of course boundless joy – not only had the vice disappeared but from then on Biborka's tics and stocking-pulling stopped entirely. We didn't sit in the wardrobe any more either.

If I had a phone, I would have informed the Shrink immediately.

But I didn't have one.

We found Mama in the kitchen. She was leaning with both elbows on the table, holding her head in her hands. She was staring in front of her.

Biborka stopped behind her back and announced.

"I told him."

Mama nodded.

"I don't wish to sleep with your father tonight. We could sleep on the couch in the living room."

"You and me?"

"Not a good idea?"

"What would you like?"

"So, you and me."

"I think it would be better if I slept alone."

Do you understand, Danny?

I didn't understand at all. I understood it so little that I could not even speak, could not even ask a question. What could have happened to this little girl in one day? I had been sitting in her ear, closely following her every thought and hidden feeling, and I didn't see anything that could have explained this perfect turn of events. If it had happened differently, or if Biborka had collapsed completely, or if she had lost her bearings, there would have been a reasonable explanation for that. But for what happened, I had not a single sound idea. How in the world could she have suddenly shaken off all her anxiety and trouble at one go? As if a heavy armour had fallen from her, and like a spring butterfly, she flitted about in her joy.

It wasn't even dusk when she pulled the chair to the kitchen cabinet, took out three plates and set the table. She peered into the refrigerator for a long time, then took out some things from here and there, unpacked a part in the middle of the table, skilfully sliced some other part and divided it equally among the three dishes.

"Aren't I good?" she asked.

"Very good," I said enthusiastically.

Then she shouted, "Mama, Papapa, supper is ready."

Mama and Papapa clapped their hands. *"Beautiful!"* they both exclaimed, while smiling wanly.

That night Mama and Papapa slept in the same bed, true, one at one side, the other on the other, clinging to the side, so as not to fall off.

Biborka and I crept into our own bed. The two tabbies curled up at our feet. I was sorely tempted by some feasting, but I didn't feel like leaving Biborka. I can tell you, it was wonderful to splash about in the light after the painful darkness.

Though this day had proved to be too long too. Biborka wished me good night, and we soon fell asleep.

I woke up early the next morning; everybody was sound asleep, even the cats.

It was my own restless curiosity that woke me up. The mysteries of the key. How could I tell the Shrink, if I didn't even know what it was, where it was, and who had it? And how could I help other children, other parents, in short, other people?

As I lay there half-asleep, how I don't know, suddenly a familiar image swam into my sight. The one that had astounded me so much when I woke up the day before. I suddenly realised that this image certainly had something to do with the key. Otherwise, I couldn't imagine why it would just swim in and out of my head.

"Oh, if only my dear Shrink were here, she would solve the riddle," I moaned to myself. Then I thought that after we got up, I would ask Biborka to ask Mama to call the Shrink for me. Of course, I immediately realised that I could not make a bigger blunder. There would go the secret assignment. Poor Shrink would have had a wretched time explaining how she had set a bloodsucker onto poor Biborka.

For nothing better to do, I fell back asleep.

All of Sunday passed peacefully. True, I was out of it that morning for a while, for I was so hungry that I leaped onto Pepe (or was it Pimpo?) and by the time I had finished feasting, the family had left.

Biborka said that they always went to church on Sunday morning.

It was good to sit in her ear again. The sun shone bright inside and out. But after a while, my brain began clicking again. You see, Danny, how crazy a flea can be! Instead of enjoying the sunshine and endless peace, I was racking my brains over how and why everything had turned out as it had.

One moment Mama and Papapa could have throttled each other, the next they were puffing up their chests in the front hallway as they passed each other. How could the three worlds that had clashed make peace so suddenly? Who had given way? Who had given up their own laws? Who had absorbed whom? That is, if anyone had absorbed anyone else?

***

Late that afternoon a feverish excitement took hold of me. Mama's telephone rang. Mama spoke with someone for a long time, then Papapa spoke for a long time with that person, then Mama shouted for Biborka. We were in the middle of playing with building blocks that could be fitted into each other, when Mama appeared at the door and held her telephone before her.
"Biborka, the Doctor wants to talk to you."

I could feel my heart beating in my throat.

"Hello, Biborka. What's new!"

"Well, I'm in the middle of building…"

"How are you feeling?"

"Well… good, I think."

"And how are the cats?"

"I think they're good too."

"Don't they have fleas?"

Biborka was surprised.

"How did you know? I found just one that came to me. It can speak. Would you like to speak to it?"

"Is Mama nearby?"

"Yes, she's here. And so is Papapa."

"Please, tell them that I put a bug in your ear."

"What should I tell them?"

"That I've put a bug in your ear. And one more thing, dear Biborka, we can't meet tomorrow, after all, for Mama and Papapa said, that you seem to have changed so much, as if you're another person. I am happier than I can say. And your little flea should not be bothered; Mama is coming to see me tomorrow."

I was as happy as a lark.

Biborka stood there uncomprehending for a while, then handed the telephone to Mama.

Mama asked her, *"Who came to you? Who did you talk to?"* Biborka answered, *"The Doctor put a bug in my ear."* Papapa was smiling from ear to ear, and he observed that there was nothing more marvellous in the whole world than the Hungarian language, except for Mama and Biborka. They both took this as a compliment and laughed. As for me, I could barely wait for tomorrow to come, so I could ask the Shrink my proliferating questions.

I stayed with Biborka until the morning, so that my absence should not tilt her back into the darker side of the world. When she opened her eyes a little after sunrise, I informed her fearfully that I was very sorry, but I couldn't accompany her to school, for my best friend, Danny, was anxiously waiting for me. I told her a bit about you, after all, who knew if you wouldn't meet this delightful creature some time in your life. Biborka listened, mouth agape. Finally, she announced that she had a scooter too, and she would gladly visit all your stops. I was amused at the clever things I had come up with by mere accident, until she set off for school.

Biborka urged me incessantly to hurry up so that I could fix her rendezvous with you.

Well, we've talked it over, my dear friend.

Good or bad?

All right, think it over well. It's better not to rush things.

When Biborka and Papapa were ready to set off, and Mama leaned over to Biborka, I used the last opportunity and leaped onto her magnificent hair. It wasn't as good to be in it as it was to see with Biborka's eyes. I could barely extricate myself and reach her ear. By the time I had settled in it, we were sitting at the table where they painted that beautiful bird with Biborka. A huge white paper lay on the table in front of Mama, full of the most interesting zigzags, shapes, and colours. I thought that I would have a look at her inner world. Who knows, I might find what I was looking for so hard with her? But she had become one with her exciting creations so that I saw in her virtually the same mysterious shapes, enigmatic figures and clouds of colours. After a while, I was titillated by the desire to speak to her; after all, I had not exchanged a single word with her. At such times the little devil is always hiding in me to see whether my carrier won't fall over backwards from surprise? I must confess, my dear friend, I didn't dare experiment with Mama. I was afraid that I would say something wrong, and then how could I shut off the torrent of words?

So, I preferred to sit there quietly; I meditated, and mainly I waited to start off.

The sun had begun to sink and make its normal rounds when finally, we clambered up and set off. Not much time passed, and we were before the doctor's office, where we had arrived with Red Fur, Young Master, Abo, and his dad, and where it was only a few days ago that I had begun my career as a psychological healer which I hoped would be a bit more elevated. I was so eager to meet the Shrink again that I didn't even notice the sign on her door, just under her name, with the same letters of the same size. I just noticed Mama staring at it in amazement.

"Dr. Flea." That was what was written on it.

Of course, tears sprang to my eyes, my dear friend.

Not only human but a flea's eyes could not remain dry at this sweet and moving attention.

When the door opened, and the Shrink saw us – mainly at the stupefaction on Mama's face – she began to laugh loudly.

"A new colleague?" inquired Mama.

"Not only new, but the most brilliant. He has solved the most difficult case of my life," said the Shrink, extending her hand. I got the message and jumped over to her.

"God bless you, my dear Shrink," I greeted her joyfully.

"You too, Doctor. All my admiration. You've done a great job!"

"If it wasn't someone else who did it," I observed, but said no more. I waited patiently, while Biborka's Mama filled her in roughly about the extraordinary developments of the past few days. Biborka's astounding about-face. "Did you do something different?" asked the Shrink. Mama flung her hands apart. "I have no idea. Unfortunately, we've been quarrelling a lot lately. But perhaps it doesn't matter, dear Doctor. Don't you think? The main thing is that Biborka is well. And finally, perhaps our problems are blowing over."

"Yes, that's really the most important thing," the Shrink confirmed, and soon took her leave of Mama.

Biborka's mama had barely stepped out the door, when the Shrink set upon me with her question.

"Doctor. Tell me at once what you did. Curiosity is killing me."

"My dear Shrink," I replied contritely. "The truth be told, I have no idea. I would have liked to learn it from you."

"You didn't find the key?"

"No. Though I thought I had so many times."

I told her about my blunders, and how right she was, how easy it was to run into a dead-end. But I told her about my despair too, about how many times I wanted to escape and run to her, how many times I thought I would go mad with the ceaseless state of war. The Shrink nodded and smiling told me that fortunately children are better able to stand it. If they went under from this much, there wouldn't be a single intact and healthy one.

Then she asked me,

"But if you didn't find the key, what made you open the door? For you did open it and the soul worm vanished. That's a fact. The whole family is unanimous in asserting that it is as if Biborka were a new person.

"Sorry, but it wasn't my doing."

"Was there perhaps someone outside the family?"

"There was."

"Who?" The Shrink jerked up her head.

"The two cats."

The doctor mulled this over.

"Although it has happened several times in my life that an animal healed a person, I don't think this is the case here. The cats were there before. Don't you have any other ideas, Doctor?"

"I don't have any ideas. But I had an extraordinary experience that hasn't left me."

"Don't spare me."

"I saw Mama's head on Biborka's neck."

"From the outside."

"Of course not, from inside."

"Aha!"

The Shrink got so excited that her excitement spread to me. She put her hands together and lifted them to her mouth, thoughts raced feverishly in her mind.

"You know, Doctor. At this age it's normal for a child to imitate one of her parents. I noticed this in Biborka. But that she aped her mother to that extent? I confess, this did not strike me."

She said nothing for a while.

"I can surmise what led me astray. Mama is a very exciting and attractive creature. I saw nothing strange about her prepubescent daughter adoring her so. But that she was carrying her mother's head on her neck? Unbelievable!"

"If you allow me, my dear Shrink, the incredible thing is something else. That she suddenly removed it. How? Why? One moment it was on her, in the second, it was no longer there. Who helped? What helped her? It must have happened right under my nose, but I didn't notice."

"Listen, Doctor. Where are you now?"

"In your right ear."

"Are you comfortable?"

"Most comfortable."

"Lean back a bit and let yourself go. OK?"

"All right."

"You're sitting in Biborka's head."

"No, I'm not. I told you I'm sitting in your right ear."

"Imagine yourself sitting in Biborka's ear. All right?"

"I'm sitting in Biborka's ear."

"OK. Mama's head is on Biborka's neck. Can you see it?"

"I see it."

"And what else do you see?"

"All kinds of colours."

"What kind?"

"Light ones and darker ones too."

"Aha. And what else?"

"Nothing else for the moment… Yes! I can see the vice."

"What?"

"The vice. I was always afraid that it would crush Biborka's soul."

"Fantastic!" cried the Shrink. "Now roll the film forward. Until you no longer see Mama's head. OK?"

"OK."

"Where are you now?"

"In Biborka's ear."

"Right. But where in the flat?"

"In the living room."

"Who else is there?"

"Everyone."

"Very good. What's happening?"

"They're having a fight for a change."

"They're quarrelling."

"Out of control."

"Very good. What exactly is happening? What is Mama doing, what is Papapa doing and what is Biborka doing?"

"Mama is sobbing, Papapa is shouting at her, *'You aren't the only one in the world!'* Mama is yelling that *'We'll be fine with Biborka'* and that *'Biborka wants you to leave too. Ask her, if you don't believe me.'* Meanwhile, she is laughing and crying, then she staggers out and slams the door."

"What about Papapa?"

"Papapa? Well, he froze, so to speak. He is shaking in a controlled way, if that has a peak."

"There is, Doctor. Definitely."

"Meanwhile, he is scrutinising Biborka. He asks her, *'Do you want me to leave too?'"*

"And she?"

"She snaps firmly, *'Yes. That's what I'd like too.'* I tell you, my dear Shrink, I was totally stupefied. She was implacability incarnate. She was so cruel, that it was painful, even for me. I looked away from Papapa's hurt look."

"What about the vice?"

"The vice? That's a good question, my dear Shrink. I was sure it would be there, but it had melted into thin air. Disappeared without a trace."

The Shrink cried heatedly,

"Where are you now, Doctor?"

"The vice."

"No. You."

"Still in your right ear," I replied in amazement.

"Take it that I shook your hand."

"Thanks. I appreciate it." And it did indeed feel good. "What I don't know, my dear Shrink, is what did I do to deserve it."

"Put it down to my excitement. The key must be here."

"You should know, my dear Shrink. I felt it too."

The Shrink put her hands together and raised them to her mouth. The images flitted here and there, the thoughts galloped in all directions.

"Doctor. We can agree, right, that Biborka is basically a kind-hearted creature?"

"We can."

"Still, she was released when she committed this vicious thing. Isn't that true?"

"It seems so."

"That was when her anxiety disappeared."

"That's right."

"That was when she could throw off the vice."

"Presumably."

"But what then was this vice, Doctor?"

"Perhaps Mama's head," I said pensively.

"But she adores Mama."

"Only her neck and shoulders are too small to bear it."

"Other children adore their mother or their father, and they aren't full of tics."

"That's true."

"Wait, Doctor." The Shrink grabbed her head. "What else could the vice be than what Biborka said at that time. By saying it, she was released from it."

The Shrink jumped up and down from joy.

"Doctor, that's the key. We found it. We found it."

I listened uncomprehending.

"Listen here, Doctor. If Biborka really would have wanted Papapa to move out, it would not have pressed on her mind that once she would have to face the question, would she want Papapa to leave? She had to comply with Mama's wishes. *'You wouldn't mind if we would be alone the two of us, would you? You can't stand this constant quarrelling either, can you? You want him to leave too, don't you?'* Except that she loved Papapa and still loves him, but she couldn't admit it to Mama or to herself. She was in hellish turmoil over the conflict between what Mama wanted from her and what she felt deep in her heart. And she was released from this conflict and acute pain when she chose openly and finally."

"Between Mama and Papapa."

"That's right. Between *her mother and her father.* Between her two *blood parents.* As a small child, she had to make such a heavy and painful choice which more fortunate people don't have to make in all their lives."

"But she could have lost Papapa. She could have leaped from the frying pan into the fire."

"Well, yes, Doctor. It is one of the strangest things in life that even the worst certainty is better than a painful uncertainty. Have you ever been in love? Pardon me for asking such a thing."

"My dear Shrink, you can't ask me anything that could insult me," I said sincerely.

"All right. Then we're on the right road going in the right direction." The Shrink laughed. She went on. "True love is one of the wonders of the world. It can melt together two completely different worlds. We can experience two lives and two miracles in one body. And yet, how many of my patients have said, just don't let me fall in love. For up to then he's been his own master. But should he fall for someone, every moment of his life becomes unpredictable."

"Hm. If that's true, he's crazy to be in love."

"But I tell you, it's worth it." The Shrink smiled. "Aren't you hungry?"

Oh, Danny. How this wonderful woman could play with my little flea soul! Of course, I was hungry, but I had no mind at all to dine on her.

"I ask you," added the Shrink, "so as not to leave you in uncertainty. In a quarter of an hour they're coming for you, Doctor. And they're bringing Toffee."

"Oh thanks," I replied, disappointed.

"I would offer myself, but you wouldn't accept it anyway."

"That's true," I replied, and at that moment my disappointment disappeared. "Thank you, my dear Shrink."

"You're welcome. I thank you. I hope we can continue."

"If you don't mind, there's one other thing that puzzles me about Biborka."

"That's why I've left you fifteen minutes more," laughed the Doctor. "So? Do you want to ask, how can you know…?"

"Exactly. How can you know that the tics won't return? After all, nothing has essentially changed save that tiny detail that Biborka said what she said, let go from her soul what she let go of. But she's no different, and Mama and Papapa aren't any different either."

"Well, you know, dear Doctor, that the strangest thing in this human life is that the world becomes an entirely different world if you look at it with different eyes and a different spirit. Biborka gave to Mama what was hers, she told Papapa to his face that he should leave. Thereby she redeemed herself, she took Mama's head off her shoulders, and, as incredible as it may sound, at the age of nine she started to construct her own world view. At the age of nine, she began to live her own life. From now on, she will decide whom she loves, and whom she doesn't. And so long as Papapa is a good father to her, she will love him, independent of whether Papapa is a good breadwinner or not."

"Mama...?"

"As for Mama, Biborka had backed her up to then in this endless family war, *"Who is right?"*. That is how Papapa became a shiftless, crotchety pedant. But by Biborka's taking Papapa back into her heart, Mama's conviction that her marriage was completely bankrupt was weakened, in fact, it was shaken. She could notice his good qualities again."

"And Papapa? What do you think of him, my dear Shrink?"

"What about you, Doctor?"

"Isn't he a boring, pedantic fellow?"

"What do you think, Doctor?"

"I don't think so. I think that everything turned around because of him."

"How so?"

"Because I thought he would slam the door on Biborka. After all, you can't imagine greater cruelty and ingratitude than what Biborka did. If he had slammed the door, Biborka would have pulled on to herself the vice and she would have suffered from it from then on. From another soul worm."

"You see, Doctor, that is what the greatest treasure of human life is capable of: love. It is an even greater treasure than romantic love. Romantic love wants to take over. Romantic love is selfish. But love is not. Love is understanding. Patient. It bows its head."

"Bows its head?"

"Does it not?"

"There's no more stubborn man in the world than Papapa! He holds on to his truth as a dog to its bone."

"Don't you?"

"Yes, perhaps."

"What about me? Of course, Doctor. It's our plain duty. Love is humble, but it does not surrender, and it mainly doesn't self-sacrifice. It never makes one poorer, but richer. We accept the other person without losing ourselves. It really is the greatest treasure in the world. I only wish there was a bit more of it."

If you could have seen, Danny, how the Shrink became transfigured, while she said this in one breath. I was enveloped in it too. I took flight. I was boundlessly happy.

At this moment, the realisation struck me like a divine touch, you human beings are incredibly lucky. It's true, as many human beings, as many worlds, as many people, as many truths, and you must cram all these truths into one world, into one life. It's true that you have as many psychological ailments as there are pebbles on a beach, and you kill each other so it takes some kind of flea to stand it. But you have something through which you can enter easily into another's world, into another's mind. You can herd together all the independent minds of the world.

Love.

I recognised Red Fur's bark.

"My dear Shrink. Shall we see each other again?"

"Doctor. That's exactly what I wanted to ask you."

"Take it that I gave you a hug."

"My dear Shrink, I wanted to say the same thing."

The Shrink reached into the cabinet and took out something.

"Take it with you, Doctor. I will ask Abo's family to put it out so that you can see it when you go that way."

It was Biborka smiling at me.

Under the picture, written in clear pearly letters, *"Who is it that Dr. Flea healed?"*

***

So, did you make up your mind, Danny? Will you drop by and have a look at the picture?

Twelfth Tale
WITCHES' RING[7]

My dear good friend, Danny, imagine, I was an inch away from going quite mad. Although the Master warned me ahead of time, knowledge is not always pleasant. It can entail unwanted side-effects. Is it certain that I will sink? Of course, I retorted immediately: Sure. I say to him, *"I don't wish to die an ignoramus."* He replies, *"You know. You're always the one who decides."*

What about you, Danny? How do you choose? Are you sure you wish to hear it?

As you wish. You know.

You are the one who chooses.

Of course, who knows whether this will be my last tale? I'm just saying.

***

The truth is, my dear friend, I was thinking more and more about death. In the past tense. After all, that is why I

---

7   In this chapter I drew from the master of martial arts, József Fazekas' brilliant book, KiÚTvesztő [Exit from the Labyrinth] (private publication, Budapest, 2012)

encountered the Master. When I sank, thanks to him, he said, death makes life beautiful.

But at that time, I hadn't sunk. I hadn't gone through my initiation yet.

I was thinking, that you are still as young, Danny, as the dawn. Though if I were as old as you, I would have kicked the bucket a long time ago.

Of course, everyone has a different length of time allotted to them, the one shorter, another longer.

We fleas have at most three or four years.

When I learned this, I thought that's the way it should be. After all, you shouldn't sponge off others; you shouldn't suck others' blood. If you could build, create, like the good Lord, if you were useful to the world, you would deserve even a hundred years. From the depth of my heart, I tell you, my dear friend, that is the way it should be. After all, God made you in his image, and not in mine. It would be strange if God looked like a flea; not even I could want that.

Only I just felt that there is a little snag here.

Why was the whale given the lifespan of a human being? What about the tortoise? And the parrot? Not to mention the wretched clam. Does it do such great things in its life?

And don't I get a bit of an encore for my good services? At least a few months.

If I were God, that's what I would do. Wouldn't that be the most logical? The useless ones should perish soon; the useful should live long lives. That is how the world could be ordered the most easily. Don't you think?

So, that was what I was philosophising about.

I caught myself, my dear friend, as we were wandering about with my favourite moggy. I was paying attention to people whom I had shooed out of my mind until then. There is no way to embellish it, the blood of an old dog, an old man is a little bit smelly, that of a young one is decidedly fragrant. That is why I used to avoid anyone whose hair was grey, or knees were bent, as was his back, and his skin was desiccated. But now I was seeking just those.

***

It so happened that one lovely morning we were lolling about lazily with my favourite moggy, when we heard someone coming straight at us. There was no need to be alarmed, as we were residing in our main summer residence, the terminus of the Foreign Trade Park, in the pleasantly cool hideout of the humming engine-room.

Nonetheless, curiosity is a great master.

My tabby leaped up on a thick pipe, and lying low, we peered through the small window of the engine-room.

An ancient old man had just reached the fence. His hair was like a turtle-dove's feather. His back was like a cajoling cat's. His knees were bent, his skin was wrinkled, he held a long stick that reached his shoulders. He leaned on it, as he shuffled on.

I said to my favourite moggy, "Go rub up against his leg."

He didn't need much asking. He leaped from the pipe to the windowsill, then onto the soft grass. He slipped easily between the fence grate, and purring loudly, he pressed against the old man's beat-up brogues and long trouser leg.

There is no wild man who could resist this flattery.

I mumbled thanks to my tabby and I leaped.

I reckoned that we would go, struggle a few steps in that direction, then we'd turn back. I couldn't read him – as that wasn't what he was thinking about – whether he lived alone, or with others, whether anyone was expecting him, and was he living in one of those high rises or some old one-story family home? The man seemed so frail, that I genuinely believed that he would not be able to take the walk. I was even more surprised that we just went and ambled along, or to be more exact, we inched along toward the top of the hill. We climbed upward tenaciously, as if we didn't want to stop until we reached the lookout towering above us.

As if the lookout could run away.

After a short while, the old man began to huff and puff. But not even that made him stop. As if he were looking for trouble. It occurred to me that perhaps this would be his last trip. He was going to say farewell. He seemed to be readying himself for a good death. In the embrace of his beloved mountain and forest.

To be honest, I wouldn't have minded if that happened.

Rather than spending endless days, slow boring weeks with him, until death finally deigned to knock on his door.

I sat in his ear almost cheerfully, with the pleasant excitement of expectation, and I observed quietly.

Before we reached the lookout, he went left and shuffled into the dense wood. A huge number of mushrooms spread before our eyes. It had rained for days – with more or less interruptions – indeed, for weeks, though the sun also shone for a longer or shorter time. That was all that the mushroom folk needed. Even those that had been looking for years for the opportune moment to poke their heads through the earth.

The ancient old man surveyed them respectfully, and walked around them. Insofar as I could read his mind, what captivated him was that there had not been a trace of them before, and in a few days, there would no longer be any sign of them. Whoever wants to see them, must be at the right place at the right time.

Our ancient old man stopped for a long time before a single creature with a cap. He didn't touch it, but only gazed at it, smiling. I have to say, that even to my tiny flea eyes it was beautiful. Most mushrooms had flop-eared caps, but this one was astoundingly perfect. Only the greatest painters could show the magic of its yellow-green colouring. Its slender and straight trunk was topped by a floppy white collar; at its base an encircling volva.

I tried to figure out what my conveyance was so happy about. Perhaps the undoubtedly fascinating sight? Or something else? When I could catch his thoughts beyond what we saw, it was a spine-chilling name; what's more, it was the magical creature's name:

Death cap.

I gasped.

Death?

What could this heavenly being kill?

Incautious insects? Snails? Lizards?

We climbed on without an answer.

It struck me that our man moved very purposefully, even though the gigantic leafy trees and the dense tangled bushes often diverted us from our path. Nonetheless, at every opportunity we turned back to our original direction. We were fairly high up when the wood thinned out, and even more troops of mushrooms hidden in the trees and bushes appeared in view. They displayed the most astounding and variegated colours from snow-white to pitch-black.

Suddenly, the Master stopped as if he'd come into port.

I followed his look curiously.

***

Well, my dear friend, you won't believe it.

It was a witches' ring[8].

A genuine witches' ring.

Have you ever heard of a witches' ring?

Imagine an enormous ring, on a soft forest floor, in the humid shade of trees and bushes. It was astoundingly beautiful, astoundingly smooth and regular. From the centre to the edge it was five to six substantial flea jumps. It wasn't witches that were lined up in the ring, but beautiful mushrooms with caps, tight together on each other's heels. They were panting almost on each other's necks. But not for the world would they step out from there. Everybody was part of the ring, with proper dignity.

The Master watched transfigured, then we stepped into the magic circle.

He fished out of his pocket a rustling plastic bag. With great difficulty he laid it down in the middle of the witches'

8.   Untranslatable in this context. In Hungarian it is literally, 'witches' ring or circle', in English, this natural phenomenon is called 'fairy ring.'

ring and sat down on it with the help of his stick. He arranged his legs in the lotus position.

He shut his eyes and I no longer saw anything.

That is, of the outside world.

***

I was convinced that death was coming. My heart beat wildly. I tried to breathe as quietly as possible, so he wouldn't notice me and get the idea of taking me with him.

I shuddered at the mere thought.

I noticed that the Master was breathing differently now. He breathed in slowly and deeply. At first, he took the breath into his stomach and then into his lungs, finally – I know this seems impossible – seemingly into his head. In addition, he kept it inside for a good long time, then slowly let it out.

I thought that his body would instinctively know how to receive the Reaper. This seemed like a good sign, so I didn't have to watch him nor learn from him. He'll come for us, he'll take us, and that's it.

We just must wait patiently.

We sat and waited.

Suddenly, I had a strange feeling.

Like the kind you get at the last moment before falling asleep.

Until then the images of the day rolled before our eyes. Our liveliest experiences, the images of our successes, failures rushed by.

We are the protagonists in every scene.

The moment before falling asleep, however, presto, we disappear before our very eyes, we vanish before our attention. You could say, our egos disappear. The who is looking and the one whom we are looking at. Swirling, shiny colours fill our souls that grow quiet. It is as if we were in heaven.

Well, that is exactly what I felt, my dear friend, sitting in the Master.

Only now I did not go to sleep. I wasn't even sleepy. I listened, totally alert.

"Good heavens, where am I?" slipped out of my mouth.

The answer came immediately.

"Inside the witches' ring."

***

"Pardon me," I muttered. "I am Jimmy Jumper. A flea. I'm sitting in your ear."

He wasn't even surprised. I had the unpleasant impression that he had been conversing with fleas all his life.

Was it possible that I wasn't the only talking flea in the world?

I got depressed.

We said nothing for a while.

He imagined a flea who was sitting in his left ear – that was exactly where I was sitting – and he smiled. I had thick armour, my legs were muscular and hairy as they were in real life, but my head was more reminiscent of an impish kid. True, I've never seen my own head.

"I see what you are thinking," I observed. "Doesn't it bother you?"

"Why, what am I thinking about?"

"Me."

"Right. It doesn't bother me."

After a short pause, he added,

"When I was small, my mother often said, '*Live, as if God were always watching you*'".

I was awed.

What a mother!

I said to him in awe,

"What a mother!"

"Unfortunately, not a word of it is true." He smiled again. Not arrogantly, but rather with a quiet serenity. "My mother beat me until blood started flowing from my head. She was irritable. Poor thing, she didn't notice that she should stop."

"That's terrible," I muttered, aghast.

"Actually, it isn't terrible. I can thank my mother for many things. She and my father humiliated me so much that I had to start from the ground up. I had to stand up from the floor. I was the biggest liar in the world, the laziest in the world, the worst rascal in the world."

He took a breath, then continued.

"So as an adolescent I took a course in martial arts, so they couldn't hammer me anymore. True, it no longer depended on them that I realised with time that it was easier to defeat others. It is much more difficult to master oneself. But if one succeeds..."

"Won't die?" I asked hopefully.

"God forbid! Death is the coronation of life. The consummation of life."

I couldn't decide whether he was being serious or ironical.

I looked at him.

He was serious.

"You know what?" I suddenly got angry. "If someone crushes me with his claws, I would feel totally different. It wouldn't be the consummation of my life but a travesty."

"That's entirely different." He waved his hand. "That's an ugly violent death. I'm talking about a beautiful peaceful death. A peaceful death can embellish our lives by constantly following us. How can something that cannot be lost have value? Violent death never wanders about. It smites."

I thought about that.

Then I asked him,

"Now you are waiting for a peaceful death?"

"Who is?"

"Well, you."

"Why would I do that?"

"Because it is so lovely. For it is the coronation of life. The consummation. Heaven."

"It'll come on its own. From time immemorial it has come for everyone."

"Well, that's it!" A sudden chill came over me. Then something set me thinking.

"And what happens when a violent death precedes a beautiful death? Let's say war breaks out and you're hit with a bullet or a bomb? Or a robber appears? That would throw over everything, no? Then there's no crown, no consummation, no heaven. Phut! There goes our whole life."

The Master said nothing for a long time.

At first, I thought I had got him; he didn't know what to say. But then I noticed he was feverishly trying to find the end of the thread, where to grab it. Finally, he said,

"Believe it or not, little Jimmy Jumper, our fate is decided in our head."

***

Have you ever heard such a stupid thing, Danny? Of course, I didn't believe him. How could I have believed him? If, say, he stuck an unripe dogberry in his ear, and I wouldn't be able to move. If he'd leave it for a week, as sure as death I would suffocate. So then is my fate up to him or to me? Does it take place in his head or in mine?

Or I'll say more. Let's say that while we are conversing peacefully, mad men suddenly get the urge to start a war or explode a bomb. Then who is responsible for our fate? For our death? Them or us? It's absurd, isn't it?

I told the Master.

"That's absurd."

"That's nonsense."

"It's nonsense only to those who can't sense it." He smiled. "You said you can read my mind."

"If I wish to."

"So, wish it now."

He shut his eyes.

"We are sinking," he said in a floating voice, as if we were really sinking already.

"To hell?"

"You choose."

I didn't want him to think that I was trying to pick a fight with him, so I didn't reply. Whereas if he took me with him, where was my decision in this? Isn't that right?

So, I just paid attention.

The witches' ring appeared before us in its complete splendour: the proud, scaly white mushrooms, panting on each other's necks, treading on each other's heels.

Then we sank into the soft, moist soil, although we didn't move the size of a flea. Starting from us, thin, white threads radiated out, creating an ever-thicker net. As they reached the ring, the threads thickened so that they formed round mushroom bodies, then they rose out of the earth, they grew elongated, grew caps, thus shaping the dazzling mushroom troop of the witches' ring.

"The essence of life is hidden," said the Master in a celestial voice. "We see only the surface. The essence lies deeper. What you see here is the work of the mushrooms' threads. What you see in life is the work of soul threads. Question?"

"Are these poisonous mushrooms? Death caps?"

I could have guessed that he would not like my question. The Master had expected more from his disciple, but since we sat in the witches' ring, I couldn't get the thought out of my mind that we could even perish here. All right. That didn't interest him, but it interested me very much. The Master abandoned his heavenly voice and virtually barked at me.

"That is not essential now; it isn't important. We choose our own questions too. With our bad questions we can know more about appearance, with our good questions, the essence."

"What should I have asked, Master?" I muttered shamefacedly.

"I can't know that. Everybody chooses for himself. I know only what I would have asked."

"What would you have asked, Master?"

"Who moves the mushroom threads? And: who moves the soul threads? No?"

"Well, yes." I let it pass. "And who moves them?"

***

The truth is, my dear friend, that to me this was not really open to question. I could say, that "officially," that is, not even owing to my special position, I could not think otherwise than that Providence moves everything. Although in terms of Darwin's evolution, I, Jimmy Jumper, could hardly have been born. Neither from the battle between the weak and strong, from selection, nor as a consequence of a series of blind accidents. I was convinced that, at least divine intervention would be necessary. So, the existence of God and the role he plays could not be questioned, so far as I was concerned. But the existence of Christ's love could not be questioned either, for, as a result of my successful service, I didn't feel the tingling in my jumping legs or my armour, but somewhere in the deepest recesses of my soul.

That is why I was surprised when the Master answered.

"This too is a question of choice."

"But I don't believe that," I retorted.

For his part, he was surprised. Obviously, he wasn't used to having his disciples oppose him so discourteously.

"Aren't I right?"

"No."

"All right. Then let's back up a little."

Again, we saw the witches' ring in our mind's eye.

"What's this?" he asked.

"Witches' ring."

"Why do you think so?"

"Because the Master told me." I bowed. "Obviously he didn't make it up. Otherwise, he wouldn't be a Master."

"That's true." The Master nodded contentedly. "This natural phenomenon is called witches' ring in these parts. But the same phenomenon is called fairy circle or fairy ring a few hundred and a few thousand kilometres away. Folk wisdom takes hundreds and thousands of years to mature. Should we take one choice as more apt than the other? Or should we respect both? Regardless of which one we choose."

"Proper respect? Master! I think the truth cannot be a question of respect. If we studied it further, it would turn out very soon and very easily which name is the right one. Which one is the more established. That is the one we must accept. Don't you think?"

"I don't know."

"The Master doesn't know?" I was amazed.

"The Master knows that everything fits into life and it isn't always necessary to choose. We can choose not to choose."

"Master, this can't be true either! If everything fits into life, then its opposite can too, and that's absurd."

"That's nonsense."

"It's nonsense only to those who can't sense it."

"That's not true," I replied loftily. And I dare confess to you, dear Danny, that at those moments I imagined myself the Master and the Master my disciple. "On this basis, we could choose Satan for our God and God as our Satan."

"Bravo, Jimmy Jumper! You said it right! *We could choose.* And at one time, people of knowledge knew this well. The essence of life is the eternal movement of opposites. And the inscrutability that derives from this. What is scrutable and can be known forever doesn't move and doesn't make anything move. It is without interest and boring. It stands still. It ceases to be. It dies. There is no God without Satan, and no Satan without God. But you can choose between them. In your own life you can choose between them."

He took a deep breath and continued.

"People of knowledge indicated the outline of words as consonants. What do you think, what do these letters mean: STN?"

***

My dear good friend, Danny. I was thunderstruck. Since my mere existence forbade any belief in pure accident, I was unable to write this up to coincidence. Folk of knowledge themselves choose the vowels they wish to fill the frame. If he so wished, STN could become iSTeN[9]. But if they prefer, they could choose SaTaN. Of course, they did not imagine them as identical, but not even similar, only two main elements – that motivate and shape each other – of the same being.

9   Untranslatable here. Isten = God.

I became so excited that, filled with deep respect and humility, I asked the Master: let us sink further into the depths.

And while I could read his thoughts, he was ready for this. At that moment an unpleasant, intrusive boy's voice struck our ears.

"Grandad, what the hell are you doing here?"

A young boy of about fifteen years had planted himself outside the ring, and stared at us. We stared back at him. He cut an odd figure in his black-and-yellow helmet, and knee and elbow protector. His black jersey was soaked through, and his face was streaming with perspiration. We immediately realised that he was riding a mountain bike. Clearly, he wanted to relieve himself, and that was why he had left the trail.

"I'm thinking," answered the Master.

"About what?" the fellow asked.

"This." The Master signalled with his eyebrows.

The cyclist saw the ring, the regular troops of mushrooms, then shrugged.

"What's there to think about? There was a lot of rain."

"Other mushrooms don't grow like this."

He spoke as slowly and draggily as he walked.

"There are the kind that grow like this and others that don't." The boy shrugged. "What's so special about this? These mushrooms grow like this. Others are solitary, or grow in patches or groups. Some grow on the soil, others on logs and stumps. Or on the trunks of trees. We're not all the same either."

"I see that you have seen mushrooms before." The Master smiled.

"Well, of course, I've seen them. There are as many of them as there is sin. But I would be crazy to touch them. I don't wish to croak."

Now he looked at the mushrooms, then at the Master.

"Do you want to die here?" His eyes flashed suddenly. "Are these poisonous mushrooms?"

The Master didn't reply.

My heart skipped a beat.

He really was preparing for something!

Isn't that why they call this the witches' ring in these parts, because they are dangerous poisonous mushrooms? A human being sits in the circle, and after a while he slowly, quietly departs this life?

The death cap flashed into my mind. A collar adorned these mushrooms too, but they were fatter, and their trunks were club-shaped, even though it didn't encircle it like volva.

Fact was that the frightful darkness of "death by poison" did not appear in the mind and spirit of the Master.

"Is it poisonous or not?" urged our fellow.

"I ask you, does it matter?" The old man's words staggered forth. "It doesn't change anything essentially."

"I think, Grandad, that it does change things, very much so."

"Maybe you're not correct."

They faced each other off.

The fellow leaned over, pulled out a well-developed individual from the enormous ring and stepped into the witches' ring with it. He pushed his prey into our faces.

"If it's all the same to you whether it's poisonous or not, then take a bite."

He grinned maliciously.

"Where are your mates?" asked the Master.

I acknowledge with joy – thank heaven! – he didn't lose his presence of mind. Withal I reckoned that I might have to step in.

***

See, how strange life can be, my dear friend. There's no denying it, it crossed my mind that this bumptious fellow would make this old man eat the poisonous – should I not say murderous – mushroom, I would surely not have to wait long for the result. Finally, I could have a look at death. I could find out, how you can imagine: the soul departs the body. Or rather it is sucked, vacuumed out of us. That is, out of our body. After all, why should it leave of its own free will?

Only the Master meant more to me than the secret of death. Not less than the secret of life! Saying farewell is different when a human being's backpack is full. He is kidding himself if he thinks that things can continue.

I had no idea how I could get involved – I, a tiny nothing little creature – but I was sure that I wouldn't look on without doing anything.

Fortunately, our fellow looked like he was going to go back down.

He looked at the Master suspiciously.

"How do you know I'm not alone?"

"You are never alone."

"Truly not. But I assure you that they're expecting me. They're glad they can take a little rest…" He grinned.

Then again, he pushed into our faces the large scaly cap.

"Are you going to eat it or not?"

I saw for the first time the tattoos on his arm. Would you believe it, out of the light and dark spots the head of Satan took shape.

"Summon your friends. Then I'll eat it. The whole thing," the Master promised.

"You're not playing with a full deck," said the fellow in amazement. "You really have gone off your rocker."

And he looked at us so suspiciously as if we had really gone bonkers. As if we had eaten mad mushrooms.

"Let that be my concern," shrugged the Master.

"Are you going to eat it willingly?"

"Not on command."

"Then these can't be poisonous," the fellow said while looking into the Master's eyes.

"Maybe it's poisonous, maybe it isn't."

The other visibly had not the slightest idea what to think.

"What do you want from my friends?" he asked finally.

"Tell them a story."

"Farewell story?"

"Story of initiation."

"Initiation?"

"Yes."

"All right. So be it, Grandad! But you wished it."

"Yes, I did."

"OK. We'll be here right away. Until then take care of your food!" he said, pressing the splendid mushroom into his hand.

He stormed out.

***

"Shouldn't we blow too?" I asked.

"No, we shouldn't."

"I don't like the look of this fellow," I warned him. "He has a tattoo of Satan on his arm."

"He's just seeking his place in the world. When I was that age, I put a big nail through my left hand."

I couldn't catch my breath.

"Good God! What for?"

"For the same reason. Then I outgrew it."

We said nothing for a while.

"Violent death never wanders about. It smites," I commented.

"I understand." The Master smiled. "But don't forget, you always choose. Our fate is decided in our own heads."

"I'll believe it when I see it," I cried. So irritably that I surprised even myself. Perhaps, for I knew and was ashamed, if I couldn't hide in my secret hideaway, I was going to take to my heels to escape this Satanist kid.

***

Our fellow clomped out the bushes, with his troop. Seven chaps, as in the stories.

Like the seven dwarves, or seven thieves.

They lay their bikes down.

Involuntarily they stopped in their tracks at the sight of the ring; they were amazed at the uncommon sight.

They were birds of a feather, more or less. They all had protective gear and their leg, arm and neck were bulging with muscles.

"All right, Grandad, we're here." Our fellow waved. "The show can begin."

"Yes, it can begin," the Master roared. "Come here, lads." He waved them to come. "Step inside the witches' circle."

He looked at them with a serene and friendly smile. We looked at each of them, eye to eye. A few of them cut an uncomprehending face, another a suspicious one. Some were more curious, but others were rather bored. One's face reflected anxiety and alarm. Others – for example, our boyo – was seized with a kind of greedy excitement. And, finally, there was one mountain biker who smiled amiably back at us and knees held high, cautiously stepped into the witches' ring. So, wearing his complete protective gear.

The others followed without a word.

The Master raised a beautiful mushroom high above his head, like a priest raising the Eucharist before the altar.

"Would you like me to solemnly take this special phenomenon of the world to myself on the occasion of my hundredth birthday?"

"You're a hundred years old? That's fantastic!"

"I wouldn't like to live that long. My father's father is only seventy, but he already has a lot of ailments."

"Do you want to bite into it?"

"Do you want to eat it?"

"Isn't it a poisonous mushroom?"

"It looks like it."

"Come on. Poisonous mushrooms are red."

"The death cap isn't red. I've seen death caps. This is exactly like that."

"Death caps have collars and volva."

"This one has a collar, and a volva."

"This isn't a volva."

"It isn't only mushrooms with volvas that are poisonous."

"I don't think this is a poisonous mushroom; it's a magic mushroom. A psilocybin mushroom, you won't die if you eat it, you'll just go crazy."

"I once saw on the TV Indians eating it and they hallucinated, like what you get from marijuana."

"They weren't Indians, but Africans."

"It's all the same."

"Didn't Grandad promise to tell us an initiation story?"

"Yes, that's what he promised. And he'll eat the mushroom. The whole thing."

"Well, then?"

"Come on, tell us your story, Grandad."

"Speak."

"Get going, Grandad."

"Let's go, Grandad."

"I wouldn't like it," protested weakly the one that had smiled amiably at us.

There was silence for a moment.

Impassively, the Master raised the natural phenomenon high and asked, "Do you wish to take solemnly this special phenomenon to yourselves on the occasion of my birthday?"

My throat tightened. "This one isn't crazy, he's insane." I was seized with terror.

"Take it to myself?" asked the frightened lad.

357

"Bite it?" asked the suspicious one, aghast.

"Eat it?" asked the uncomprehending one.

"You eat it first, Grandad!"

"All right. First you, Grandad. Then we'll see."

"I'd gladly try it." The slightly bored one stepped closer.

"I wouldn't like to," the smiling one protested weakly.

"Shut up!" barked our fellow.

The Master raised his index finger.

"Everybody chooses for himself. Look into my eyes and decide: do you wish to trust or suspect? To believe or be afraid?"

"We'd like to trust."

"We'd like to believe."

"But we're not familiar with this mushroom, Grandad."

"And we don't know you either."

"Are you jerking us around?"

"Come on. What could happen? It's a great adventure."

"I believe, but I'm afraid," muttered the one who was slightly fearful.

The Master smiled enigmatically.

"All right," he blared. "But are you willing to enter into an initiation game?"

***

Oh, Danny. I am ashamed to confess that I didn't have any more trust than the children. Fear stirred inside me too. Indeed, if he really wanted to make them eat magic mushrooms, I was getting ready to say something to him that would discourage him and somehow rescue the boys. Perhaps it is true, that everything is possible in life, and you really do decide if you wish to become the slave of cigarettes or booze, or you wish to take drugs or eat magic mushrooms, then I am free to express firmly my conviction that everything that can enslave us takes away our greatest and most important treasure: our freedom.

Think about it, my dear friend. We eat the psilocybin mushroom and what happens? It dominates our consciousness. It decides for us. It dictates. Is that a good feeling? Well, why shouldn't it be? We feel a great sense of relief. Perhaps a light joy. For even the freest life has weight. Even the freest decision entails responsibility. Obviously, it is a good feeling to be relieved from this burden. All right, but for how long?

For so long, as the reign of the magic mushroom lasts.

And afterward?
Will you be better off?
How will you be?
How could you be?
It will undermine your dignity.
It will corrode it.
And crush it.
Your soul will bend.
You'll hoof it for another magic mushroom.
To throw off even greater burdens.
To free yourself from even weightier decisions.
And you'll hoof it for another magic mushroom.

Fortunately, the lads were all up for the initiation game. It's another story if it's a game. Then the initiation can come, the dance can come. For they had to dance. After they threw off the protective gear, they had to surround the Master, and take each other by the hand. Then they had to whirl to the right and to the left to the Master's hoarse singing and enthusiastic clapping.

Mushroom
Mushroom
Mushroom thread
It connects us, this mushroom thread.
Spirit
Spirit
Spirit thread
It connects us, this spirit thread.

Is that all it is, this game? When the Master suddenly shouted one after the other, "Break it up! Break it up! Break it up!" the lads had to let go of their neighbour's hand and they could run wherever they pleased within the witches' circle. At the third cry they had to stop still where they were.

The Master announced loudly, enunciating each word: the one who stopped the furthest from the others would be the victor.

The dance began.

Oh, Danny, I was sorry that I was such a tiny, nothing little creature! I would have fallen in with the circle; I would have held their hands too and flown apart when they had to.

The lads whirled round, along the mushroom thread to the left, on the spirit thread to the right when the Master asked me,

"What do you think, Jimmy Jumper, who's going to be the victor?"

"I've no idea," I replied. "Since none of them know where the others are going to run, I think it can't be foretold."

"Watch our fellow," replied the Master, and in quick succession he shouted, "Break it up!"

I watched our lad.

Everybody else – I could say completely instinctively – ran as fast as they could away from the others, radiating outwards almost to the mushroom ring.

Except for our lad.

He ran straight to the Master.

He grinned gleefully that he had won. He was the furthest from the others.

Holding his mushroom in one hand, his stick in the other, the Master pointed in front of himself.

"Kneel down!"

After hesitating briefly, our lad kneeled.

"In the sight of God, I announce with joy," recited the Master, "that you are the glorious victor of our first initiation game. We congratulate you from the depths of our hearts, accept our appreciation."

He tapped our lad on the shoulder three times with the stick.

The others applauded his theatrical movements warmly. Our lad was transfigured as if he had been enchanted.

"Then let the second initiation game begin," blared the Master. Sitting in the centre of the witches' ring, he shouted out the rules,

"Stand in a circle again, but with your back to me, and don't hold each other's hands. Close your eyes and I will say…

Snake venom
crow silk
good fairy
or wicked witch?

Just stand and wait," continued the Master. "Though, when I shout, '*Choose!*', everybody has to choose at once: do you wish to be a good fairy or a wicked witch? If it is good fairy, then raise both your arms, if it's a wicked witch you want, squat down. But be careful! We can't know ahead of time, which one is the right choice, only afterwards. Those will win who are part of the smaller group. If there are fewer fairies, then it will be the fairies; if the witches are a smaller group, then it will be witches. You will have three chances. And who will be the victor of victors? The one who has the most victories after the third try. Is that clear?"

"It's clear."

"Then start!"

The Master began muttering in a guttural voice, like a shaman,

Snake venom
crow silk
good fairy
or wicked witch?

He said it once, twice, three times. The lads stood with their backs to him, with eyes closed, and they obviously racked their brains feverishly on how to win.

"All right, Jimmy Jumper, now what do you think, who's going to win?"

The thought was stirring in me that it will be our lad again; after all, he had won the first game. He seemed to be the sharpest one of them all. Still, I couldn't say anything other than what I thought:

"If you asked me how many would rather be good fairies than witches, I might be able to answer. But I had no idea who would think what the others might be thinking."

"Then watch our lad."

After the second muttering, he shouted,

"Choose!"

Every last one of them squatted.

I was so flabbergasted, I couldn't even breathe.

"Good heavens! This is what the youngsters of today are like? Everybody wants to be a wicked witch? Nobody wants to be a good fairy?"

"Not at all, Jimmy Jumper. Everybody wants to win. And they all thought that since the others would choose to be good fairies, they had to choose to be wicked witches. All right, but now watch our lad."

The lads stood there waiting. They were most likely measuring, reasoning, counting silently.

Really, Danny, if you were playing with them, and you wanted to win, how would you have chosen?

"Choose!" shouted the Master.

And they all squatted again.

I couldn't say a word.

The Master was all hyped up.

"Don't worry, Jimmy Jumper. The essence of life is constantly playing hide-and-seek with us. No way are there so many young witches. They're only trying to outfox each other. But how? Actually, it's quite logical. *'If the majority want to be witches, I can win by choosing to be a good fairy. But since the others are reasoning the same way, I must choose to be a witch.'"*

"Attention, the last round is next," shouted the Master and again began muttering in a guttural voice,

Snake venom
crow silk
good fairy
or wicked witch?

"Choose!" echoed the forest.

Do you know what happened, my dear friend?

Well, of course.

I felt that the Master could explain whatever he wished about the lads' mind or their logic, I no longer believed him. All right, I understand that the essence of life is deeply hidden from us mortals. But it says something, that every lad, each and every one again chose to be a witch, hoping to win by choosing to be a witch. Of course, there was logic in the Master's hastening to reassure me, but the hard fact was that three times seven, twenty-one choices to be a wicked witch, the complete absence of good fairies was terribly alarming and depressing.

The Master seemed to look into my soul.

"Listen, Jimmy Jumper. It is so difficult to penetrate your tiny flea brain, for there is one single thing in which you are not very human: it is not important for you to conquer others. These lads still wanted to win, and that is what led to their decision. On the third try, they still all wanted to win, and this decided their choice. On the third try, they reasoned that they could not foresee what decision the others would make; for that reason, they would have to forge their own path. That is, they had to choose to be good fairies. But as the time to choose approached, it occurred to them that the others were surely thinking the same thing; that was why they could win only if they chose to be witches after all."

"Will it be like this till the end of time?" I asked bitterly.

"Oh no! The lads don't feel good inside their skin. They're going to ask if we could play yet another round."

Believe it or not, my dear friend, that was exactly what happened. The Master raised the mushroom high and the stick too, and announced the result.

"All right, lads, there are no victors in this round. All of you always joined the majority."

The lad who smiled back at us broke the gloomy silence.

"Can't we play another round? Does this really have to be the last one?"

The others immediately joined in.

"I'd like that too."

"Me too."

"Me too."

"All right, if you want it so bad, so be it," replied the Master and happily acknowledged the cheers. *"And now, pay attention to our lad!"* he whispered to me.

Snake venom
crow silk
good fairy
or wicked witch?

"Choose!" echoed the forest.

Every lad raised his hand, and they all radiated joy.

Except for our lad.

He quickly squatted. Then he looked around satisfied, then stood up, straightened up, and didn't even forget to beat his chest.

"I won," he announced.

"You've won," agreed the Master. Then he added, "You won, but you aren't the victor. They are." He pointed at the others.

Our lad stared with wide open eyes.

"How?" he asked angrily.

"Because they could rise above themselves. Above their own desire. This last time they weren't interested in winning or not. They desired what their hearts dictated. Except for you. You were still looking for how to triumph over the others. And you found the way. You won, but you aren't the victor."

"I say that I am."

"You choose." The Master shrugged.

"Of course, I do. I choose the mushroom."

"The mushroom?"

"The mushroom."

"You know."

"I know."

The Master handed it to him.

Our lad grabbed it and, as if it were a dagger, he stabbed the air.

"And now you will eat it. As you promised," he shouted wildly.

Before he reached the Master's face, fast as lightning, the latter grabbed his wrist.

He hissed in pain.

The mushroom fell out of his enfeebled hand.

It was as if he had been caught in a vice.

"Help!" he whimpered.

The others stood there without stirring. Coldly they looked on at the iron-fisted old man's infernal strength and their mate writhing helplessly.

"Can't we play another round, but really the last one?" The one who smiled back at us spoke up.

The Master let go of his victim.

It was as if a great stone had fallen from his heart.

Yes, from the Master's heart.

He nodded to the smiling one.

"You choose." He turned to our lad. "Would you like another round?"

That one massaged his wrist. He looked at the Master, then at the others.

He was struggling with himself.

"Let's play! Let's play!" the others shouted.

"You choose!" said the Master. Then he began to chant.

Spirit
spirit
spirit thread
it connects us, the spirit thread.

"So?" he asked and continued to chant.

Snake venom
crow silk
good fairy
or wicked witch?

The cyclists raised their hands high.

What about our lad?

Our lad straightened up with great difficulty. Then, as if he were wrestling with a great weight, he threw up both arms.

"You won." The Master smiled.

"I won." Our lad nodded.

The Master took the torn, tormented mushroom that had turned red here and there, and raised it before himself.

"Do you want it?"

The disciples didn't understand the question.

The Master bit into it.

The disciples jumped to him.

The Master stopped them with a raised hand.

"It is a blushing parasol mushroom," he announced. "It's an edible, delicious mushroom. It belongs to the family of agaric mushrooms."

The disciples heaved a great sigh of relief.

I too sighed in relief.

The Master took another bite from the mushroom, chewed it slowly, then swallowed.

"It's good roasted, fried, even in soups. It isn't poisonous even raw."

He smiled faintly.

"Happy birthday!" shouted the smiling one.

"Happy birthday!" shouted the others."

"Happy birthday!" our lad muttered, massaging his wrist.

"Thanks, lads. Go with God's grace."

They looked at him, uncomprehending.

They gathered their protective gear and put them on.

"Are you sure, we shouldn't stay, old man?"

"Sure."

"Shouldn't we take you home?"

"Leave me to myself," asked the Master.

The lads shrugged their shoulders.

"Well, then…" they said, and each grabbed his bicycle and started pushing it toward the bushes.

They looked back.

The Master was sitting, eyes closed, in the exact centre of the witches' ring. As before in the lotus position. But now his head leaned forward, his back hunched. His stick and the mushroom next to him.

The cyclists stared at him for a while, then first one then the others began to rummage through their leather bag, then their leather waistcoat. They took out their smartphone and turned toward the Master.

"Don't take photos," said the Master with eyes closed. "What the machine sees is the surface. The essence lies deep."

The cyclists nodded.

Silently they put away their phones.

In the next moment it was as if the earth had swallowed them.

***

Dark clouds were gathering in the Master's head. *"I'm not worthy. I'm not worthy."*

"What happened?" I asked anxiously.

"I'm not worthy."

A tiny very old woman appeared in his head, wearing a black dress and black kerchief.

"Auntie Mariska," he explained. "The grandmother of one of my disciples. She is sitting in the kitchen quietly by herself. Her husband died not long ago. She sees through the window a dark man entering the veranda and puttering about the flower pots, looking for the key. That is where the locals put it when they go away from home. He can't find it. He pushes down the door latch. It doesn't open. He's getting ready to push the door in with his shoulder. Thereupon Auntie Mariska goes to the window and begins to shout, *'Józsi, ring the alarm bell!'*"

The Master heaved a great sigh and added,

"This old woman had more horse sense than me. I'm not worthy of being called Master. I'm not worthy of being the Master of anyone. I deployed physical strength which my mind should have set in order. I wanted to teach, but I showed a bad example. I'm not worthy."

He collapsed into himself.

Then he lay down on the moist, black earth of the witches' circle.

He kept his eyes closed, so I couldn't see anything of the outside world.

"Master. I want to say something."

I had no idea what I wanted to say, but I sensed that I had to step in somehow. I had to stop him.

"Master!"

Feverishly, I racked my brains.

The truth was, my dear friend, that I was frightfully alarmed that he would cash it in. That he would let his spirit be taken. There was still an enormous empty space yawning inside me. I was tormented with so many doubts. There were so many things I would have liked to learn from him.

"Master."

Finally, he spoke.

"God can see my soul. He must have seen how proud I was in paralysing that kid. At the age of hundred!"

"Hundred!" I repeated, awed.

"But that incredible strength didn't come from the body, but from the recesses of the spirit and soul. How peculiar…"

"What's peculiar?"

"It's a long story."

"Tell me," I begged him.

"It won't fit."

"Me?" I asked in alarm.

"No, me."

We said nothing for a while.

I saw us heading for a shop late evening. The streets were almost deserted. Two lads clambered out of a dilapidated, red car, and headed straight for us. Or we were heading for them.

"Who are these two fellows?" I asked.

"What fellows?"

"One was husky and bald, the other taller and thinner, both were wearing tracksuits."

A faint smile flitted across the Master's face.

"Oh, yes, of course. I was just talking to one of my favourite disciples…"

"Grandad, give me your telephone."

It was the husky one. The other one was ready to jump, to attack.

"You know, Jimmy Jumper," the Master said dreamily. "At first, all I could think about was revenge. I trained hard to pay back everyone who had hurt me, who had beat me, harmed me, humiliated me. I didn't wish to kill them, but I just couldn't wrap my mind around the fact that I had to pay for my transgressions, while others got away with murder. Resolutely, I waited for the moment I was strong enough and clever enough to strike back at the world.

Fortunately, there was something that always held me back for years: fear. At home and at school they undermined my confidence so that I concluded that my time hadn't come yet; I wasn't strong enough or clever enough.

I was dissatisfied with myself; I was dissatisfied with the world.

I watched my fellows.

I noticed that it almost hurt me to see their joy and their successes. And I was incapable of sharing in their joy.

For the question always came up immediately: and *I? I? I?* Why wasn't I as fortunate as they?

My master noticed my diligence and determination, but he also saw my turmoil. *'Try to be grateful.'* He looked into my eyes. *'To you, Master?'* I asked, rather impudently. *'Of course not! To whomever it's due.'*

He said no more; indeed, he turned away, so I couldn't ask any further.

Who the devil should I be grateful to? And why should I be grateful? What did I get from life to be grateful for?

Since I felt a great deal of dissatisfaction, discord, even bitterness, I decided to try it. I would go to war against my mind.

In the first weeks, the task seemed insoluble. I felt, however, it was now or never. If it doesn't succeed, I will give up the struggle forever. I was born to be unhappy; I would croak unhappy.

I tried, I practised, perhaps some kind of gratitude will come over me. I tried to get out of myself, and imagine myself in others, place myself in their life situation. Then I had an idea: I would try to feel that the goods of others belonged to me, but without stealing from them.

I was the most surprised.

My idea turned out to be a good one.

After a while, after a long struggle, I began to feel something. I didn't really know, what it was, because it was difficult to describe; it was a new feeling for me. I virtually felt my blood begin to tingle. I was completely changed. Little by little my envy disappeared. I forgot to be envious of my fellow human beings, of the belongings of others. I forgot about my material cares. For gratitude took up all my attention. And because it turned out, if only at the last minute, some idea pulled me out of the fire.

I had to watch only one thing: not to step back into the old trap. I should not let go of gratitude even when more difficult, gloomier times came. They always come because that is their job. Their job is to present us with ever new trials and temptations. Are you there, Jimmy Jumper?"

"And how, Master!"

"I told you, don't call me master. I'm not worthy. Before those two fellows attacked me, I thought never in my life would I lay a finger on anyone with the intention of hurting them. Now too I tried to avoid it. In the same way as I had succeeded so many times. I didn't pay attention to the outside world; I just went my own way, at my own speed. I turned into myself. The only problem was that these fellows were determined to appropriate my telephone. Or to pick a fight with me and beat me senseless."

The Master frowned.

"Jimmy Jumper, what would you have done in my place?"

I said nothing.

"It occurred to me to give them my telephone. Here! Take it! If you want it so much… Once an Indian, a kid, asked an old Indian man: 'In your opinion, is life good or bad?' The old man replied, 'There are black wolves and white wolves. Envy, lying, evil are all black. Goodness, patience, love are all white.' 'Which wolf will win?' 'The one you feed.' For decades, I had been feeding the white wolf in myself. I thought that there isn't a telephone in the world that is worth feeding the black wolf for. It did occur to me, that I shouldn't feed my attackers either; they should not be able to rob with impunity, because it was worth it. You only had to waylay earthly mortals, and they hasten to hand over their little valuables. Nothing doing.

There was one more thing, Jimmy Jumper, which I couldn't bear to think of.

To allow myself to be beaten up.

For the news to go around that two rowdies from Pest beat a martial arts master to a pulp.

Nothing doing.

The taller one stood further behind, so he was less liable to expect my attack. I punched him in the nose so that the blood flowed. I didn't have to focus on the target, my hand was guided by the years of practise. The stocky one was all riled up at the sight of the blood on his mate. He leaped to the right and left, while bellowing, *capoeira* and tried to imitate the martial movement named. It wasn't a good show. Suddenly, he started for me, and at that moment all my practise and experience of long years, nay, decades came together in me. My whole body moved together. From the right, I kicked him in the ribs, at the height of his liver. I felt his ribs give way then the strength flew out of his body.

Then a fairly incredible thing happened.

Writhing on the floor, the stocky one whimpered,

'That was fantastic! How did you do it?'

I invited them to a beer.

They accepted gladly.

While I talked to them, I looked at their faces. I was shocked to realise how much I loved them.

How much I loved my white wolf.

How much I loved life.

And how painful it was that I had fouled it.

I vowed to never again lift even half a finger on anyone else.

I will learn more, I will practise more, I will learn to control myself.

I was certain that only I was responsible for the attack.

That that incident ended up in a brawl.

I must have done something wrong.

I must have fed my black wolf instead of my white one.

There, what a frail creature Mother Teresa was, and it never occurred to anyone to attack or rob her.

Everything is decided in our heads.

I'm not worthy."

***

Gloomy dark clouds crowded in on the Master. I could not see what the weather was like outside, for he still lay prone with eyes closed on the moist black soil.

I was getting very hungry.

But something whispered to me that it would not do to start feeding.

The Master was silent.

I sensed that I too should sit quietly and wait.

But I couldn't command my thoughts.

I imagined that we were waiting here in the dark, and Death appeared outside, holding an ungainly scythe, he bowed deeply and knocked courteously:

"Are you at home?"

I started to laugh.

My tears flowed.

"Oh, sorry," I whispered. "I forgot where I am."

The Master said nothing.

Blindingly bright white clouds appeared around the dark clouds. They advanced as slow as snails. As slow as snails, they dispersed the darkness.

"Thank you, Lord."

Those were his last words.

He didn't whisper them.

It erupted from him.

His heart beat slowed down. I didn't feel its inevitable pulsation, its strong beat.

I woke up to the realisation that death would be here in a moment.

At first, I was overcome with terror. I had to take to my heels and get away from here.

Then curiosity set in.

Then a deep sense of shame. He is lying here completely vulnerable, helpless, defenceless, and here I am peeking at him. I wanted to watch something which was not my business. It was his own private affair. It concerned him and no one else.

"Should I leave?" I asked. To tell the truth, more to myself, for I felt that he was more dead than alive. A living dead.

Well, my dear friend, Danny, you won't believe it!

From far, far away, somewhere among the boughs, as if from a heavenly source, the Master's voice broke in,

Spirit
Spirit
spirit thread
connecting all the spirit thread.

It connected me so, that I immediately understood it: The Master wanted me to stay with him at the last moment of his life. My tears began to flow. It was so moving. When the blindingly white clouds gently sniffed up the last dark patches, and his breathing stopped, his heart stopped beating, but I no longer felt any kind of fear or dread. I felt only joy. That I could be with him as he wished. That I could say farewell to him in the name of the world, and the white and black wolves.

He who goes like this, whom we let go of, the spirit thread does not let go of him.

I wandered for three days and three nights, until I found my way back to you, my dear friend. But in those three days he didn't leave me for a single minute; he didn't move out of my heart and mind for a single moment. And the Master is still with me.

I don't wish anything more from this world, dear Danny, than that it won't be worse for me either.

Take my hand, when I take my leave.